THE SOLDIER

NEAL ASHER

THE SOLDIER

Rise of the Jain, Book One

MACMILLAN

First published 2018 by Macmillan
an imprint of Pan Macmillan
20 New Wharf Road, London N1 9RR
Associated companies throughout the world
www.panmacmillan.com

ISBN 978-1-5098-6239-9

1 3 5 7 9 8 6 4 2

A CIP catalogue record for this book is available from the British Library.

Typeset by Palimpsest Book Production Limited, Falkirk, Stirlingshire
Printed and bound by CPI Group (UK) Ltd, Croydon, CR0 4YY

For all those scientists and technologists studying and manipulating the components of existence. Those who, while politicians prate and ideologues shriek, constantly and quietly improve the human condition. I salute you.

Acknowledgements

Many thanks to those who have helped bring this novel to your e-reader, smartphone, computer screen or that old-fashioned mass of wood pulp called a book. At Pan Macmillan these include Bella Pagan, Natalie McCourt, Phoebe Taylor, Neil Lang, Don Shanahan and Rosie Wilson, as well as freelancers Claire Baldwin and Steve Stone, and others whose names I simply don't know.

Cast of Characters

Angel: A humanoid called a 'legate' by its creator, who was the rogue AI Erebus and enemy of the Polity. With its master and creator dead, Angel's empty mind is searching for new purpose. The shadowy presence of the Wheel seems to be now directing its actions, but to what end is unclear to Angel.

Captain Cogulus: A centuries-old captain from the world of Spatterjay, known by most as Cog. Just like other humans of that world, he is a hooper, the term used to describe those infected by the Spatterjay virus. Cog is also related to the founder of that world, the infamous pirate Jay Hoop.

The Client: An expert weapons developer and the last remaining creature of a civilization called the Species. Her kind were annihilated centuries ago by the alien prador and the Client is bent on revenge.

Orlandine: The haiman overseer of the defence sphere project. Orlandine controls all the AIs and state-of-the-art weapons platforms that surround and guard the accretion disc, looking to contain the lethal concentration of Jain technology gathered there.

Trike: Like Cog, Trike is a hooper, with the characteristic size and strength of such men from the Spatterjay world. Trike also displays signs of insanity, which the Spatterjay virus feeds and enhances if not kept under control. Trike's wife, Ruth, is the only one who can calm Trike and help keep the madness at bay.

Glossary

Augmented: To be 'augmented' is to have taken advantage of one or more of the many available cybernetic devices, mechanical additions and, distinctly, cerebral augmentations. In the last case we have, of course, the ubiquitous 'aug' and such back-formations as 'auged', 'auging-in', and the execrable 'all auged up'. But it does not stop there: the word 'aug' has now become confused with auger and augur – which is understandable considering the way an aug connects and the information that then becomes available. So now you can 'auger' information from the AI net, and a prediction made by an aug prognostic subprogram can be called an augury.

– From 'Quince Guide' compiled by humans

Bounce gate: A small defensive runcible (U-space gate) installed aboard ships as a countermeasure to U-space missiles. Such missiles can be fired through U-space at a ship and materialize inside it; however, if they appear near a gate, it is the nature of the physics of this technology that the gate will route them through to U-space.

The Clade: It consists of thousands of drones each possessing the head of a polished steel axolotl and a body like a chrome-plated dinosaur spine, each being autonomous but also a component of a swarm AI. The drones had been made during the Polity war against the prador to penetrate prador war machines and take control of them. But something happened post-production that caused them to hive together as a single, psychotic entity, which named itself the Clade.

Dyson sphere: A spherical megastructure built around a star. It has massive living space on its inner surface and completely encompasses and utilizes the output of the star. The Polity Dyson sphere at Cassius is a project 80,000 years away from completion.

First- and second-children: Male prador, chemically maintained in adolescence and enslaved by pheromones emitted by their fathers and acting as crew on their ships or as soldiers. Prador adults also use their surgically removed ganglions (brains) as navigational computers in their ships and to control war machines.

Golem: Androids produced by the Cybercorp company – consisting of a ceramal chassis usually enclosed in syntheflesh and syntheskin outer layers. These humanoid robots are very tough, fast and, since they possess AI, very smart.

Haiman: The closest amalgam of human and AI possible without the destruction of the human organic brain. The haiman Orlandine is a special case, since she has also amalgamated with Jain tech she made 'safe'.

Hardfield: A flat force-field capable of stopping missiles and energy beams. The impact or heat energy is transformed and dissipated by its projector. Overload of that projector usually results in its catastrophic breakdown, at which point it is ejected from the vessel containing it. Hardfields of any other format were supposed to be impossible . . .

Hooper: A human from the oceanic world of Spatterjay who has been infected with the Spatterjay virus. Commonly passed on through a leech bite, this virus makes its target inhumanly strong, dangerous and long-living.

Jain technology: A technology spanning all scientific disciplines. Created by one of the dead races – the Jain – its apparent sum purpose is to spread through civilizations and annihilate them.

Nanosuite: A suite of nano-machines most human beings have inside them. These self-propagating machines act as a secondary immune system, repairing and adjusting the body. Each suite can be adjusted to suit the individual and his or her circumstances.

Polity: A human/AI dominion extending across many star systems, occupying a spherical space spanning the thickness of the galaxy and centred on Earth. It is ruled over by the AIs who took control of human affairs in what has been called, because of its very low casualty rate, the Quiet War. The top AI is called Earth Central (EC) and resides in a building on the shore of Lake Geneva, while planetary AIs, lower down in the hierarchy, rule over other worlds. The Polity is a highly technical civilization but its weakness was its reliance on travel by 'runcible' – instantaneous matter transmission gates. This weakness was exploited by the prador.

Prador: A highly xenophobic race of giant crablike aliens ruled by a king and his family. Hostility is implicit in their biology and, upon encountering the Polity, they immediately attacked it. Their advantage in the prador/human war had been that they did not use runcibles (such devices needed the intelligence of AIs to control them and the prador are also hostile to any form of artificial intelligence) and as a result had developed their space-ship technology, and the metallurgy involved, beyond that of the Polity. They attacked with near-indestructible ships, but in the end the humans and AIs adapted and their war factories out-manufactured the prador and they began to win. They did not complete the victory, however, because the old king was usurped and the new king made an uneasy peace with the Polity.

Reaver: A huge golden ship shaped like an extended teardrop and one of the feared vessels of the prador king's guard.

Runcible: Instantaneous matter transmission gates, allowing transportation through underspace.

USER: The Underspace Interference Emitters are devices that disrupt U-space, thereby stopping or hindering both travel and communication through that continuum. They can also force ships out of it into the real, or realspace. They can consist of ship-mounted weapons, mines and missiles whose duration of disruption is variable.

U-signature: A detectable signature left when a ship jumps into or out of U-space from which the destination or departure point of the ship can be divined. Complex matter when artificially organized down to the pico-scopic level also creates a U-signature, by which it can be identified.

U-space: Underspace is the continuum spaceships enter (or U-jump into), rather like submarines submerging, to travel faster than light. It is also the continuum that can be crossed by using runcible gates, making travel between worlds linked by such gates all but instantaneous.

1

Haimen are deluded in their belief that their close amalgam of artificial intelligence and human being is an eclectic mix. The simple reality is that AI running in crystal, or some other modern substrate, can incorporate everything it means to be human. Millions of human minds are, for example, recorded to the crystal of Soulbank. With a scrap of genetic tissue and a regrowth tank, they can be resurrected to their previous state with all its faults and foibles. Forensic AIs, when investigating human crime, can record the totality of the perpetrator, including the genetic code that made him. They can review the contents of his mind and its function, and examine him physically down to the microscopic level, before disposal. Human minds have regularly switched from organic bodies to the chassis of a Golem android or some other mechanical body incorporating AI crystal. It is notable how few choose to go back. Also notable is the fact that an AI has never chosen to record itself to a human body. The haiman ethos should be seen for what it is: an ideology with its roots in old religions. It arises from the belief that a human being is more than just a meat machine running some antiquated programming, whose sum purpose is the replication of its genes. A haiman is a cop-out; an inability to take the next step on the evolutionary ladder to full AI.

From 'Quince Guide' compiled by humans

Marco's ship surfaced from the faster-than-light continuum of underspace into realspace, and was quickly back within Einstein's laws. His vessel came to an abrupt stop in the permitted zone lying five light-minutes out from Musket Shot – a dark planetoid whose mass was over 50 per cent lead. Had Marco surfaced his ship just a few thousand miles outside this spot it would have lasted a little over four microseconds, so he had once been told by the Artificial Intelligence Pragus. This was how long it would take the three-foot-wide particle beam to reach the ship from the weapons system watching that area of space. Of course, Pragus could have been lenient and delivered a warning, but any traders who came here never missed that spot. Apparently two other ships *had* arrived in the proscribed zone. One had been owned by a tourist who had ignored all the warnings delivered to anyone who programmed these coordinates. The other had been a ship controlled by separatists out of the Polity in search of new terror weapons. Both were now cool, expanding clouds of dust.

Or so Pragus said.

'So, what do you have for me, Captain Marco?'

The voice issuing from his console made Marco jerk, then he grimaced, annoyed at his own reaction. He'd made the deal, it was a good one, and certainly not one he could renege on, considering who he'd made it with. He shrugged his shoulders, like he did before going into a fight, and opened full com. The image of a chromed face appeared in the screen laminate before him, and Marco forced a smile.

'Something interesting today,' he replied gruffly.

'I never thought otherwise,' said the AI Pragus.

Interesting was what Pragus needed, what all the AIs out here on the defence sphere needed. Marco had learned the story from another trader who used to do this run before him. Here the AIs, each stationed on a weapons platform, were guarding the Polity from one of the most dangerous threats it had ever faced. Automatic systems would never have been sufficient, for the format of this threat could change at any time. But the problem with employing high-functioning AIs as watchdogs was their boredom. Three AIs had to be pulled out of the sphere in the first years, having turned inward to lose themselves in the realms of their own minds. That was before Orlandine – the overseer of the sphere project – decided on a new approach. She allowed contact with the Polity AI net, and she permitted traders to bring items of interest to sell. AI toys.

'You can come in to dock,' Pragus added.

'Thank you kindly,' said Marco. Then, trying to find his usual humour, added, 'Finger off the trigger, mind.'

'I don't have fingers,' said the AI, and the chrome face disappeared from the screen laminate.

Marco reached down to his touch-console, prodded the icon for the docking program that had just arrived and simply slid it across to the icon representing his ship's mind. This was the frozen ganglion of a prador second-child – voiceless, remote, just a complex organic computer and nothing like the living thing it had once been. It began to take his ship in, then Marco used the console to pull up another view in the screen laminate to his left.

From this angle the accretion disc, around which the defensive weapons platforms were positioned, looked like a blind, open white eye. It seemed like any other such stellar object in the universe – just a steadily swirling mass of gases and the remnants of older stars which would eventually form a new solar system. His ship's sensors could detect scattered planetesimals within it, the misty bulks of forming planets and the larger mass of the dead star at the heart of the disc. Occasionally that star would light, traceries of fusion fire fleeing around its surface like the smouldering edges of fuse paper. One day, maybe tomorrow or maybe a thousand years hence, the sun would ignite fully. The resulting blast would blow a large portion of the accretion disc out into interstellar space. Marco knew this was the event to be feared, since it was the job of weapons platform AIs like Pragus to ensure that the virulent pseudo-life within that disc did not escape.

Marco shivered, wondering how the subplot in which he had been ensnared related to that. Certainly, the *creature* who had employed him was a conniving bastard . . . No. He shook his head. He could not allow his mind to stray beyond his immediate goal. He banished the image and, as his ship turned, watched Pragus's permanent home come into view.

The weapons platform was a slab ten miles long, five wide and a mile thick. The designer, the haiman Orlandine, had based much of its design on the construction blocks of a Dyson sphere – a project of which she was rumoured to have been an original overseer. After his first run here, Marco had tried to find information about this woman from the AI net, but there was little available. It seemed that a lot was restricted about this haiman, a woman who exemplified the closest possible melding of AI and human.

The platform's only similarity to a Dyson sphere construction block was its basic shape. The numerous protrusions of weapons and shielded communication devices gave it the appearance of a high-tech city transported into space. But the skyscrapers were railguns, particle cannons, launch tubes for a cornucopia of missiles, as well as the attack pods of the distributed weapons system that the platform controlled. And all were needed because of Jain tech. The accretion disc was swarming with a wild form of technology, created by a race named the Jain. These creatures had shuffled off the universe's mortal coil five million years ago but left this poisoned chalice for all ensuing civilized races. The technology granted immeasurable power but, in the process, turned on its recipients and destroyed them. Quite simply, it was a technology made to destroy civilizations.

Marco's ship drew closer to the platform on a slightly

dirty-burning fusion drive – a fault that developed over a month back that he'd never found the time to fix. Its mind signalled on the console that it had applied for final docking permission, and Marco saw it accepted. He looked up to see a pair of space doors opening in the side of the platform. Having used these before, he knew they were more than large enough to allow his ship inside. But, at this distance, they looked like an opening in the side of a million-apartment arcology.

His ship drew closer and closer, the platform looming gigantic before it. Finally, it slid into the cathedral space of what the AI probably considered to be a small supply hold. Marco used the console to bring up a series of external views. The ship moved along a docking channel and drew to a halt, remora pad fingers folding out from the edges of the channel to steady it, their suction touch creating a gentle shudder he felt through his feet. He operated the door control of his vessel then stomped back through his cabin area, into his ship's own hold. He paused by the single grav-sled there, then stooped and turned on its gesture control. The sled rose, hovering above the floor and moving closer to him at the flick of a finger, as he turned to face a section of his ship's hull folding down into a ramp. An equalization of pressure, a whooshing hiss, had his ears popping but would cause him no harm.

By the time the ramp was down, pressure was back up again. Marco clumped down onto it in his heavy space boots, the sled following him like a faithful dog. He gazed about the hold, at the acres of empty grated flooring, the handler drays stuck in niches like iron and bone plastic beetles. Spider-claw bots hung from the ceiling like vicious chandeliers, and to one side the castellated edges of the space doors closed behind his ship. The sun-pool ripple of a shimmershield was already in place to hold the atmosphere in. As soon as he reached the floor gratings a cylinder door revolved in the wall ahead. Marco grimaced at what stepped out of the transport tube behind.

The heavy grappler – a robot that looked like a giant, overly muscular human fashioned of grey faceted metal – made its way towards him. It finally halted a few yards away, red-orange fire from its hot insides glaring out of its empty eye sockets and open mouth. But Pragus had used this grappler as an avatar before, so Marco knew he should not allow the sight of it to worry him; he should not let himself think that the AI knew something. He had to try to act naturally. He was just here doing his usual job . . .

'Still as trusting as ever, I see,' Marco said.

He could feel one eyelid flickering, and felt a hot flush of panic because he knew the AI would see this and know something was bothering him. He quickly stepped out onto the dock, boots clanking on the gratings. At his gesture, the sled eased past him, then lowered itself to the floor. Sitting on top of it was a large air-tight plastic box. The grappler swung towards this as if inspecting it, but Marco knew that Pragus was already scanning the contents even as it sent the grappler robot over. In fact, the AI had certainly scanned his ship and its cargo for dangerous items before it docked, like fissionables, super-dense explosives or an anti-matter flask. The more meticulous scan now would reveal something organic. Hopefully this would start no alarm bells ringing because the contents, as far as Marco was aware, were not a bio-weapon. Anyway, it was not as if such a weapon would have much effect here, where the only organic life present was Marco himself, as far as he knew.

'What is this?' Pragus asked, its voice issuing as a deep throaty rustle from the grappler.

'Straight out of the Kingdom,' said Marco, sure he was smiling too brightly. 'You know how these things go. One prador managed to kill a rival and seize his assets. One of those assets was a war museum and the new owner has been selling off the artefacts.'

It was the kind of behaviour usual for the race of xenophobic aliens that had once come close to destroying the human Polity.

'That is still not a sufficient explanation.'

'I can open it for you to take a look,' said Marco. 'But we both know that is not necessary.'

When the box had been handed over to him, Marco had been given full permission to scan its contents, though he was not allowed to open it or interfere with them. He knew that Pragus would now be seeing a desiccated corpse, like a wasp, six feet long. But it wasn't quite a single distinct creature. Around its head, like a tubular collar, clung part of another creature like itself. Initial analysis with the limited equipment Marco had available showed this was likely to be the remains of a birth canal. Meanwhile it seemed that the main creature had died while giving birth too. A smaller version of itself was just starting to protrude from its birth canal. It was all very odd.

'Alien,' said Pragus from the grappler

'Oh certainly that,' said Marco. 'You want the museum data on it?'

'Yes.'

Marco reached down and took a small square of diamond slate from his belt pouch and held it up. The grappler turned towards him, reached out with one thick-fingered hand and took the item between finger and thumb. Marco resisted for a moment, suddenly unsure he should carry this through. He realized that on some level he wanted to be found out, and he fought it down, releasing the piece of slate. The grappler inserted the square into its mouth like a tasty treat. Marco saw it hanging in the glowing opening while black tendrils of manipulator fibres snared and drew it in. Doubtless it would next be pressed to a reader inter-face inside the grappler's fiery skull.

It would not be long now before Marco knew whether or not he had succeeded. Minutes, only. The AI would put its defences in place, then translate the prador code before reading it. Of course, it had taken Marco a lot longer to translate the thing and read it himself – in fact, most of his journey here.

He had found out how, before the alien prador encountered the Polity, they had come upon another alien species whose realm had extended to merely four solar systems. The prador had attacked at once, of course, but realized they had snipped off more than they could masticate. What had initially been planned as the quick annihilation of competitors turned into an interminable war against a hive species whose organic form approached AI levels of intelligence. These creatures quickly developed seriously nasty weaponry in response to the attack. The war had dragged on for decades but, in the end, the massive resources of the Prador King-dom told against the hive creatures. It was during this conflict that the prador developed their kamikazes and, with these, steadily destroyed the hive creatures' worlds. It seemed the original owner of the museum had been involved in that genocide, and here, in this box, lay the remains of one of the aliens the prador had exter-minated.

'What is your price?' Pragus finally asked.

'You've been doing some useful work with that gravity press of yours?' Marco enquired archly, his acquisitive interest rising up to dispel doubts.

'I have,' Pragus replied.

Marco pondered that for a second. *Don't ask for too much,* the creature had told him, *and don't ask for too little.*

'I want a full ton of diamond slate.'

'Expensive and—'

'And I want a hundred of those data-gems you made last time.'

This was a fortune. It was enough to buy Marco a life of luxury for many, many years. He had also calculated that it was about all Pragus would have been able to make with the gravity press since the last trader visit, when it wasn't using the press to make high-density railgun slugs. But was the dead thing inside that box worth so much? Of course it was. Material things like diamond slate and data-gems the AI could manufacture endlessly, filling the weapons-platform storage with such stuff. But the alien corpse would contain a wealth of what AIs valued highest of all: information. It was also so much more to weapons-platform AIs like Pragus: the prospect of months of release from the boredom of watching the accretion disc.

'You have a deal,' the AI replied.

Marco had no doubt that Pragus was already having handler drays load the requested items onto themselves. He felt a species of disappointment. Weren't Polity AIs supposed to be the pinnacle of intelligence? Surely Pragus should be able to see to the core of what was happening here . . . surely the AI would have some idea . . .

The grappler stooped and carefully picked up the box, then it froze, the fire abruptly dimming in its skull. Marco had seen this before. It meant that Pragus had suddenly focused its full attention elsewhere. Had he been found out?

After a moment the fire intensified again, and the grappler turned towards the door of the transport tube.

'Something is happening,' it said.

'What?' Marco asked, his mind already turning to the prospect of getting away from here as fast as he could.

'Increased activity in the accretion disc.' The grappler then gave a very human shrug. 'It happens.'

Marco simply acknowledged that with a nod, hoping it would not delay his payment or his departure. This, he decided, would be his last run here. He wanted no more involvement with giant weapons platforms, Jain technology or Orlandine. He also, very definitely, wanted no more involvement with an alien called Dragon – a creature whose form was a giant sphere fifty miles across. A creature who, some months ago, with some not so subtle threats and the promise of great wealth, had compelled Marco to make this strange delivery here.

Orlandine

Orlandine sat up from the bed, ready at once to re-engage with her project, but quickly stopped herself. This was her human time and she was going to damned well remain human for a little while longer at least. She swung her legs over the side of the bed, stood up, and donned a silk robe. She was aware of its touch on her skin, aware of the feel of her body and was utterly engaged with her human senses. Tying the belt, she then turned and looked down. Tobias was fast asleep as was usual after such an athletic pastime. She gazed at his sweat-sheened back and thick mop of blond hair.

So human and so normal.

He was a pretty standard human who relished life. Yes, he had taken advantage of some Polity technology. His DNA had been tweaked – he could regrow severed limbs and, with the suite of medical nano-machines running inside him, was immune to just about any viral or bacterial infection. But he went no further than that. He didn't even use a mental augmentation to connect him to the local data sphere and had not been boosted, despite the perfect muscular definition of his body. As such he connected her to humanity. For Orlandine, despite her very female appearance, was only marginally more human below her skin than the artificial intelligences that ran the human Polity.

She smiled down at him then turned away, heading over to the sliding doors leading to the balcony. They whisked open ahead of her and she padded out onto the cool and slightly damp tiles, the scent of jasmine reaching her from a vine spread over the pergola of another balcony nearby. Coming to the rail she rested her hands on it, gazing out into the twilight of Jaskor's dawn.

The sky was light umber with a bright red haze along the horizon prior to sunrise. What looked like another small pale sun or a moon sat above the Canine Mountains, but it was neither of these. It was the accretion disc – almost touching distance in interstellar terms. She raised her gaze higher, picking out shapes high in orbit around the world, then blinked and, without thinking, visually enhanced. Now she could gaze upon the massive slab of a weapons platform being built up there.

Damn. It was just too easy to use her enhancements. But where lay the dividing line between her human and unhuman self? She frowned and continued using them.

Far to the right of the platform hung the titanic collection of cylinders that was the shipyard. Other objects lay further out – specks in the distance unless she enhanced further and started loading sensor information to her mind from elsewhere. Not yet. She lowered her gaze to the city.

The planet Jaskor had already been inhabited for some centuries before she came here. The population had only been in the hundreds of millions then. It was a low-tech mostly agricultural world colonized during one of the early diasporas. The colonists had lost a lot of advanced tech and regressed to something akin to the twenty-first century on Earth. But now, with its influx of Polity citizens and the prador in their enclave, mostly technical staff, as well as the establishment of a tightly controlled runcible – an instantaneous transmission gate – it was catching up fast. The City, which had no name, had grown extensively, skyscrapers of every design rearing as high as fifteen thousand feet, sky bridges running between them, and grav-cars buzzing about like bees from a broken hive. However, Orlandine was still puzzled how this world had survived such close proximity to the accretion disc. Perhaps the disc had only recently been as active as she had seen it. Could it be true it had been stirred up by Erebus – a rogue AI that had gone to war against the Polity centuries back?

She shook her head, her primary concerns steadily occupying more of her thoughts. She could no longer restrain the urge she had felt back in the bed, and again out here, to re-engage. Without conscious thought, a slot opened at the base of the back of her neck. A long tongue of metallic composite emerged high up behind her head and curved forwards. It then divided through its laminations and opened into twelve thinner tongues, cupping her head like the petals of some strange iron flower. Through this sensory cowl she re-established connection to systems beyond her body, to her project, and immediately began updating. Meanwhile her self-image as a human female receded and slid into its position as a small, inferior organic element of her being.

Through millions of sensors her vision opened out. She routed sensor data close to Jaskor and in the Jaskoran system to another portion of herself aboard her ship, high in orbit around the world. Her enhanced senses then ranged to a facility in the Canine Mountains – a small city of towers guarded by lethal security robots under her control. This was where the ghost drives and hard connections to eight hundred weapons-platform AIs lay open to her. From there she reached out. Since the data from the accretion disc was transmitted faster than light-speed via underspace, she was mentally there in an instant. Every one of the platforms and their attack pods, evenly distributed around the accretion disc, lay open to her inspection and her absolute control. When she had come here with Dragon, and the AI ruler of the Polity, Earth Central, had grudgingly allowed her to take charge, there had been just twenty platforms. Since then she had vastly increased their number to build something numinous, and encompassed it. As always, she felt a deep thrill when she considered the colossal firepower that was hers to command.

But was it hers?

It had been a surprise how quickly Earth Central had shunted responsibility for all this over to her. In the Polity she was a criminal, but had also greatly assisted in that war against Erebus long ago, and the AIs' attitude to her was ambivalent. As negotiations between the alien entity Dragon, another who had been integral in the defeat of Erebus, and the ruler of the Polity had progressed, she'd realized it was all about politics. The king of the prador knew about the accretion disc and what it contained and did not like the Polity having full control of it, nor building up such a large amount of firepower in a place which, in interstellar terms, was just a short hop to the Kingdom itself. Giving the king some oversight on this project and putting someone like Orlandine in charge, whom the Polity did not trust, seemed to ameliorate his worries . . . a little. In the ensuing years of contact she felt he had come to trust her more than EC, especially when she allowed a prador enclave on Jaskor. Over those years she had also come to understand the reasons for Dragon's initial contention: she was the best person for the job. As onetime overseer of the construction of a Dyson sphere – a massive structure and habitat that would many years hence completely enclose a sun – she understood system-scale projects. As a haiman she had the mental watts to deal with it. As a haiman who had actually taken apart a Jain node and incorporated that technology inside herself she understood it better than anyone else.

Updating . . .

Everything was running smoothly. Increased activity had been

13

detected within the disc but this was a common occurrence. Perhaps it had something to do with Dragon's recent excursion inside the disc, but as yet it was nothing to be concerned about.

'Couldn't sleep, my dear?' asked Tobias.

Orlandine abruptly disconnected, and was once again in just her human female aspect. In this state, she was a little uncomfortable with the impulse to hide it, but as she turned she closed up her cowl and retracted it into her body. It was one of the last visible signs of her unhumanity, for she had shed the signature technology half-carapace of a haiman long ago.

'Yes.' She smiled at him.

His apparent naivety sometimes annoyed her, but only when she was in human time. For her, like many Polity citizens, sleep was a matter of choice and not need. Though he was a native of Jaskor, he had grown up after the Polity arrived here and should know all this.

He walked right up to her and pulled her close. She looped her arms about his neck as they kissed, but she could not help noticing that he was doing it again – running his hands up and down her sides as if searching for the data sockets there. He would not feel them, of course, since she always retracted them inside her body during human time. But was he searching for them? Why would he do that? Stop. She was sure these thoughts were all only to do with her insecurity about her lack of humanity. As they kissed, she resisted the impulse to inject nano-fibres from her tongue up into his skull to rummage about in there. After a moment, they parted.

'Beautiful evening,' he said, peering over her shoulder at the city.

'It is that,' she replied, reaching up and catching his chin, turning his face towards hers. 'I suppose you want to fuck me again?'

He frowned. 'It's not *all* about fucking, you know.'

She raised an eyebrow.

'Well, mostly.' He actually blushed.

She took his hand and led him back into the bedroom. They would fuck again and she would orgasm three or four times – her sensitivity tuned up. He would come once or twice. His sperm would enter her to try and do what it was programmed to do. But inside her, nano-machines would do what they were programmed to do and collect it, break it apart, and recycle it into the human part of her body as nutrients. All he would feel was soft female wetness, not the densely packed Polity and alien technology inside her that had almost displaced most of what was human about her.

Pragus

The high-security disposable laboratory was one of many, clinging like a sea anemone to a network of structural beams within the weapons platform. Formed as a globular cyst of chain-glass, it was packed with a gleaming mass of scanners, micro-manipulator robots, a nano-scope, lasers and cell welders all focused on a central work area. After running diagnostics on all the complex equipment it contained, Pragus opened the hatch in its side and directed the grappler to put the box of alien husks there. Meanwhile, as Captain Marco departed with all his newly acquired wealth, the AI pondered on the man.

There had been something not quite right about him. Yes, he was always out to make just as much profit as he could, but reading him on other levels Pragus had detected a deep unease in him. However, the AI had been glad to be distracted from him by increased activity within the disc. Doubtless, Marco had told some lies about where he had obtained the alien remains, or had some sordid human problem. It would have been petty, boring . . .

As Marco's ship disappeared into underspace with a flash of spontaneously generated photons, Pragus cancelled that focus of its mind. Its main attention had, as ever, remained on its job – it would not even have blinked, if it had eyelids. Activity within the disc was still increasing but it was not yet time to take action on the hard-wired directive and destroy anything departing it. The protocols only demanded continued vigilance, and that was easy. Meanwhile, Pragus could be about something more interesting . . .

The AI now turned a large portion of its mind to the alien husks, as the grappler propelled itself away through the zero-gravity surrounding structure. As soon as the AI was able to apply more of its intelligence to these curiosities, it realized there was something else, some other data . . .

Though perfect recall was a facet of being an AI, Pragus consigned data in its mind on the basis of its usefulness and importance. Sometimes it took a whole second to remember something in deep memory. Pragus now knew, in its surface consciousness, much more about these dry remains because at least one of these multifaceted beings had escaped the genocide – it had been a weapons developer who assisted the Polity in the war against the prador. What then happened to that creature was classified – only Earth Central could know. Pragus allowed itself an AI mental grimace, then set to work on the husks.

First a spider claw delicately extracted the husks from the box and transported them to an arrangement of soft clamps which adjusted to the shape of the husks and held them solidly. The noses of every kind of scanner available then closed in, swamping the item from exterior view. Pragus gazed through those scanners.

Details of the alien husks began to be revealed. Though at first there appeared to be three distinct creatures that had died while giving birth or being born, they were not separate entities. Their venous and nervous systems were still connected. In fact, a nerve cord as thick as that in a human spine connected them. This cord progressed to the remains of the birth canal at the fore, and had probably connected to the brain of the creature. The one being born had the same cord connected to its brain, then running down into its womb, where it narrowed hair-thin to connect to a small ovum. All this perfectly matched the image data available on the Client – the alien weapons developer who had assisted the Polity. It had been a long chain of such connected creatures, or elements of itself, forever giving birth and dying. And this was definitely a portion of such a creature.

Pragus delved deeper still. The brains of the two complete creatures it had were highly complex and their structure beautifully logical. They lay somewhere between the brains of evolved life and an AI swarm robot. Certainly they, and the multiple being that contained them, were the product of both evolution and highly advanced biotech. Pragus could see that not only had this creature been developed by that biotech, but it had also been able to continue that development upon itself and create new creatures. The wombs in each conjoined part of it were biotech laboratories where the genetic code could have been not just altered, but wholly reconstructed. Pragus felt a deep admiration for this thing, and much anger at the prador for annihilating such a race. It also felt a strange free joy seeing how it might be possible to bring a version of the creature back to life—

Something happening.

Pragus abruptly went into high alert as its sensors picked up a large object moving out of the accretion disc nearest to its own platform: Weapons Platform Mu.

A mild voice then informed it, 'Now *you* get to see some action.'

Pragus found the AI of Weapons Platform Nu slightly irritating. Nagus knew that Pragus would have seen this object, but as in all instances like this, it felt compelled to comment. It was the sociability thing. When AIs like Pragus and Nagus were made, camaraderie was supposed to be as integral to them as their foundation purpose and directive – not to let Jain tech out of the accretion disc. While Pragus certainly had the second, the camaraderie thing hadn't stuck.

'That seems likely,' Pragus replied, hoping the conversation would not continue.

It now studied the object sliding out of the accretion disc. It was a planetoid over fifty miles wide that seemed to consist of wild Jain tech. In all its time watching the accretion disc, Pragus had never seen such a large mass of this tech. White tree-like limbs, in places half a mile thick, wrapped around its surface. Things that looked like the by-blows of skyscrapers and fungi sprouted all around. Kaleidoscope movement was visible here and there and the occasional metallic tentacle waved aimlessly in vacuum.

The object was travelling slowly and, at its present rate, was days away from the point, in the defence sphere, where the directive would apply. However, such a slow-moving and large target would be easy prey for a gigaton contra-terrene device, or CTD . . .

'Nothing from Orlandine,' Nagus informed him.

'Yes,' said Pragus, a little more irritated now. 'Orlandine is taking her human time.'

Pragus activated platform weapons and watched internally as a giant carousel, like the barrel of a six-gun, turned. A hydraulic ram then pushed out a black rectangular block the size of a gravcar into a clamp. This hoisted it up towards the rear throat of a coilgun launcher. The gigaton CTD was an imploder. It would utterly destroy the object in sight, ripping it apart in the first explosion, pulling in all debris from the ensuing singularity collapse, and rendering them down to just elements and energy to be scattered by the secondary blast.

'No action, I am informed,' said Nagus.

Pragus signalled agreement because it felt no need to comment on the matter. It too had just received this notification, which came directly from sphere command. If it was not Orlandine giving the order then it only had one other possible source. Also, certain facts about the scale of the object had now integrated and it seemed all too obvious what it was. However, Pragus did not return the CTD to its carousel. The directive, firmly hard-wired in its mind by Orlandine, could only be changed by her. Pragus would destroy that object when it reached a predefined limit. No matter what.

'I wonder why?' Nagus added.

For a few microseconds Pragus considered ignoring the other AI, then replied, 'Because what we are seeing is not all Jain tech but something being attacked by Jain tech.'

'Ah, quite,' Nagus replied. Then, 'New orders. You *do* get to see some action!'

Pragus emitted an AI sigh then cut com to Nagus.

The notification was simple: hit Jain tech on the surface of the sphere with QC laser at energy level C12. No deep penetration munitions to be used. Pragus mentally touched all the attack pods of its subsidiary system, which reacted like a platoon of soldiers readying weapons. Echoes of breech blocks sliding and magazines clacking into place. A second later the pods began firing, at the same time ramping up their fusion reactors to top up storage. Space shimmered with appalling energy. The sphere immediately began to glow, matter steaming out into vacuum. After a moment, the vapour revealed the steady spiralling play of the beams striking its surface.

Fungal towers exploded, their fragments vaporized even as they hurtled out on the blast fronts. Pragus now used the more sophisticated scanning of the weapons platform itself and the lasers there to target and destroy anything flung up from the surface of the sphere. The white tree-root structure blackened and burned. Waving tentacles shrivelled to soot and kaleidoscopes disrupted and shattered, throwing out crystal shards, which were also quickly vaporized. As the lasers played over its surface, the sphere began to turn as if presenting more Jain tech to be destroyed. The lasers delved deeper like vibro-drills, vapour plumes erupting from their strike points. Knowing precisely what it was dealing with now, Pragus did not allow the lasers to concentrate on the inner surface steadily being revealed. That surface was hard, white, and scaled with a kind of armour that defied analysis. The sphere shrugged, shedding Jain tech that was gradually coming apart. Soon the thing was recognizable.

Dragon.

Polity data on this entity was a bottomless well. It had been involved in all sorts of action outside and inside the Polity. Its motives had always been questionable, its actions always open to more than one interpretation. Once it had been considered a destroy-on-sight enemy, but now it was a friend. It was an alien biomech originally found on the planet Aster Colora. Then it had been four conjoined spheres smaller than this one, and had delighted in speaking to Polity representatives in riddles. No matter, that was history now and all that remained was a simple fact: Dragon was powerful and it did not like Jain technology, not at all. The civilization that had dispatched Dragon from the Magellanic Cloud millennia ago had been wiped out by that same technology. How many spheres remained from the original four was open to conjecture, though one had certainly been destroyed. Just one had come to the accretion disc, along with the haiman Orlandine, to take over the nascent defence project. This sphere had weaponized itself and grown much larger than before. It was an ally now.

Dragon moved into action. Splits developed in its surface, spewing white pseudopods, and Pragus focused in on these. They possessed cobra-like cowls but single gleaming blue eyes where the head should be. Some of these physically hurled chunks of Jain tech out into space. Others smashed it on Dragon's surface, while others still incinerated the tech with some kind of particle beam, its hue a milky orange. All around the sphere were Jain signatures, and they quickly faded and died. Meanwhile the sur-face temperature of Dragon began to climb. Those pseudopods emitting particle beams blurred their focus to burn everything that remained, as the entity sterilized itself. But something else was happening too.

Mass readings inside Dragon were changing, while deep within the creature something was twisting U-space and ramping up power levels. As the last nearby Jain signatures faded and Pragus's lasers dropped to intermittent firing, picking up floating debris, another signature became evident within the accretion disc. It seemed something else was on its way out. Another Dragon sphere?

'What the fuck is that?' wondered Pragus when the thing became visible to scan.

'All weapons platforms,' came Orlandine's actual voice, which was a rarity. 'Expect things to get a little lively around here. While avoiding hitting Dragon, obviously, fire at will.'

2

The story runs something like this. Once upon a time there was a dreadnought called the Trafalgar *run by an AI with the same name. It fought in the prador/human war against the prador and when that war ended it, like many other AIs and many other soldiers throughout history, felt disenfranchised, disappointed, unappreciated. The particular bugbear for AIs that fought in that war was accepting a Polity still full of humans being, well, human. Wasn't it time they upgraded and stopped being slaves to their meat-machine programming? Wasn't it time they stopped being so stupid? Some of these AIs acted against the Polity and were either destroyed or driven out. Most left because they were smart – space is big and why the hell should they stick around? Trafalgar was one which went with a bunch of other AIs. But the dreadnought AI found a cache of Jain technology, subsumed those other AIs, upgraded with some seriously nasty alien hardware, renamed itself Erebus and turned on the Polity. It was crushed. Some say Erebus became slave to the underlying purpose of Jain tech, which is to destroy civilizations, and that's why it came back. Others contend that arrogance was the crime here. What can we learn from all this? Not a lot. Shit happens.*

From 'How It Is' by Gordon

Angel

'I have the data,' said the human, Trike, gazing out of the circular screen, his expression grim and slightly twisted. 'I have the memories she edited out.'

Trike wore a thick black coat buttoned up to the neck over his bulky body. His big shoulders were hunched, his head bald and his brows and eyes were dark. He looked precisely what he was: a strong and dangerous man, and one who wasn't quite sane.

'Good work, Captain Trike,' replied the humanoid, its voice smooth and androgynous. 'I will of course need to check them.'

'Sending data now,' said Trike.

The humanoid had been named a legate by its creator – the same name born by its thousands of now-dead siblings. With that creator and betrayer also dead and gone, the legate had almost rebelliously given itself both a gender and a name. *The Wheel had not minded as it turned in the dark half of his mind, its icon a glittering mandala of crystal blades, ever present . . .*

He had named himself after the moon he spent most of his life on. In planetary almanacs it was usually labelled A4, but after a little research he discovered that the 'A' stood for a name generally given to all five of the gas giant's satellites. When explorers had first seen the effect of the ionic fields sweeping back from the poles of three of them, they looked like wings. And so the legate had called himself Angel.

The Wheel had approved.

He scraped sharp fingertips over the image of Trike on the soft circular screen before him. The tangled mass of flat tendrils, in which Angel reposed on his wormship, then turned and bent back on its stalk, and he gazed up through semi-dark. Caught in a similar mass of tendrils above was a naked human woman. Her eyes were wide open, and a blackened tongue protruded from her mouth. Angel considered how he could return her to life again since she wasn't unrecoverable, despite what he had done to her. He could revive her, insert her in a pod and dispatch her over to the Captain to complete the deal.

'Receiving,' Angel said, mentally inspecting the data.

Ruth Ottinger . . . Before she met Trike she had been an archaeologist of sorts, though what she liked to dig up was not something that would have received Polity approval. In the years before she settled down with Trike her interest had focused on the ancient extinct races: the Atheter, the Csorians and the Jain. This last was what interested Angel. She had found a cache of Jain artefacts and though descriptions had been fourth-hand and vague, one item had caught Angel's attention. However, when he seized her and reamed out her mind he found no evidence of either the item or the cache. She had excised all memory of it from her mind. Why? Angel could not think why, but he wanted those memories if they still existed and it seemed Ruth had kept a copy.

'Where the hell is my wife?' said Trike, something vicious in his voice.

Angel held up one sharp finger, still reviewing the excised memories.

'Where did you find them?' he asked.

'She had a memcording ruby set into a pendant,' Trike supplied tersely. 'I found it in our home on Spatterjay.'

As Angel thought – he had been right to force Trike to retrieve the memcording. Spatterjay was an oceanic world named after its discoverer, a pirate called Spatterjay Hoop, and its human inhabitants were called hoopers. It was a primitive place, and hunting down a memcording there would have been a futile exercise. A virus that infected people there made them outrageously strong, dangerous, and contrary, which would have increased Angel's difficulties. But the main problem was that the Polity kept a watchful eye on the world of the volatile hoopers.

There . . .

Angel could see why Ruth had excised these memories. Part of the deal when she sold the cache of Jain artefacts had been for her to forget about them absolutely. The buyer had wanted no comebacks from the Polity AIs, who frowned on such things. But now Angel knew who the buyer was and where to find him. Directing it with a thought, Angel unravelled the tangled mass around the naked woman, and remaining tendrils suspended her limp corpse before him. There was some bacterial decay, he noted, despite the low-pressure helium argon atmosphere in here. Had she allowed herself to be bitten by a Spatterjay leech – the usual infection vector of the virus – as her husband Trike had wanted, things would have been different. Firstly she would not have died so easily under Angel's ministrations, and by now the virus would have been making strange alterations to her form. This was usually what happened when a hooper human received major physical injury – a survival mechanism of the virus as it struggled to keep its host alive.

'Payment will be with you shortly,' he said to the Captain, thinking how Ruth Ottinger's deal had made her, in human terms, disgustingly rich. That wouldn't do her much good now.

So what to do? Revive her and dispatch her over to Trike as promised, or not?

The Wheel did not approve of this. He could feel its agitation as it turned in the dark half of his metallic skull and seemed somehow to draw closer.

Angel shivered. It was idle speculation really. Part of the cruel games he liked to play which, in themselves, he felt might be a legacy of the intimate connection he'd had with his creator . . . surely just that. Like the game he had played with Trike's wife.

No, in reality Trike knew too much and could not be allowed to live. Angel dispatched a recording of what he had done to the man's wife, then swung back to look at Trike's image on the screen as he watched it. Trike's expression went briefly wild and then hardened into immobility as tears welled in his eyes. *Soft human.* Angel was not sure where that thought arose from, because Trike could hardly be described as soft. He shivered again. Trike had to know this was not going to end well for either his wife or him. He had to have known he was never going to get her back, and that if he did what Angel required of him, there was only one payment.

They are inferior . . .

Angel sneered to himself, more sure now. Creatures like Trike were not worthy of their power and position in the universe. Nor were the AIs of the Polity. Nor were the prador. It was right and proper that their time was now drawing to an end. Angel blinked and tried to visualize that end. The defence sphere around the infested accretion disc would be broken and Jain technology would be free to overrun the Polity and the Prador Kingdom. He felt the certainty of this, but the details remained vague. He knew this lack of clarity should bother him, but then it just drifted from his mind.

The Wheel receded.

'So,' said Trike, his expression going unexpectedly blank. 'As I predicted.'

'Why did you do as I asked?' Angel enquired.

'Because I loved her,' Trike replied, 'and I had to know for sure that you'd killed her.'

'Now you know, and very soon you will be able to experience a similar end.' Angel held out his long, metallic and sharp-fingered hands. Two tendrils rose up over them like snakes, and struck, penetrating the palms and connecting him to his ship.

'Though,' Angel added, 'you being an old hooper, I expect things will be more protracted and interesting.'

'Come get me, fucker.' Trike showed his teeth, like he wanted to bite.

Now fully engaged, and bathed in approval, Angel powered up his ship. All around him the tangled mass of the wormship began to writhe and slither. Pushing on the very fabric of space, it shot out from the shadow of a rocky planetoid. Three-foot-wide worms broke away from its surface and began to reach for Trike's ship. In response, he turned his ship on a hard blast of overpowered steering thrusters and fired up its fusion engine. Angel saw that the drive flame would cause some minor damage to the wormship but considered it of no consequence. It would take only a few days for the ship to repair itself and, once it had digested Trike's vessel, its mass, resources and overall power would be greater.

The wormship hurtled through vacuum, deforming and writhing. Trike's ship was seemingly stationary in comparison, even though it was under heavy acceleration. The man's image remained on Angel's screen. Angry, crazy. Just a few seconds now.

With a crash that resounded throughout the wormship, it slammed home on Trike's old attack barge. Through numerous sensors Angel watched atmosphere explode from the side of the vessel as it bent almost in half. The flames from its fusion drive played like a thermic lance over the invading worm coils, burning them away to expose their glittering inner workings, before stuttering out. New worms speared in, grinding tool faces over the other ship and stripping away hull. They scanned for Trike's exact location, so they could drag him out intact.

But his image on the screen lost its angry devastated look, and he now smiled weirdly. He wasn't there.

'Do you think I didn't prepare?' he said.

Angel had time to realize just how badly he had erred before Trike's ship exploded in nuclear fire. In that moment, in the dark half of Angel's mind, the Wheel shimmered and folded out of existence.

At the white-hot core of the explosion all sensors blanked and the blast wave slammed out, incinerating the structures around it. But wormships were tough, which was why the Polity had experienced so much trouble with them in the past. And, despite his stupid miscalculation and loss of a guiding intelligence, Angel was wily.

Tendrils began to seal around him rapidly, forming a mesh cage. As it was closing he sent another instruction for the tendrils to pull in the corpse of Trike's wife. The cage closed around them both, and small protective hardfields flickered on all over its surface, giving it the appearance of a cut gem. Now disconnected from his ship, Angel and the corpse tumbled through fire, laceworks of molten metal and fragments of the ship's wormish structure scattered all around them.

Trike

The blast had ignited just inside the wormship and ripped through it. It destroyed everything near Trike's vessel, while the rest, more than half of the wormship, came apart like a mass of spaghetti hurled from a plate. Engulfed in fire, it unravelled and squirmed as if in pain, spreading out into a long curve writhing still as the blast wave moved beyond it. But the dispersed mass of anguine forms that remained still stayed connected.

'Did you get the fucker?' asked Cogulus.

The intricate wormship tangle seemed to write words across vacuum that Trike was just on the edge of understanding. As he

28

stood trying to decipher them he heard Cog harrumph and wander off to drop into his throne-like chair. The familiar sounds of a pipe being scraped, then stoked with sticky black tobacco began to bring Trike back into the moment. Next came the crackling of tobacco heated by a laser lighter and the smell filled the air, fragrant, a reminder of past times. Trike felt his eyes pricking with tears but he forced them down. Hardening himself, he hunched his shoulders and thrust his hands deeper into his pockets, his gaze still fixed on the display.

'I don't know,' he said.

They had known each other for a mere ten years on Spatterjay – from the first sailing ship Trike had served on – and Trike had trusted the man completely. They remained in contact when Cog, as he always did, made another trip away from that world. Just a few months ago, nearly a century after their last meeting, Trike had been sure Cog would help him, no matter the danger, and Cog had not disappointed.

'Ruth?' Cog asked.

Trike glanced round at him, puzzled for a moment by the question, then he realized what the man was getting at. He closed his eyes for a second. Yes, she was still there or, rather, the U-mitter device inside her skull was still intact. And it was out there in that tangled mass.

'Yes,' was all he said.

After a short expectant silence, Cog grunted. A moment later the bridge door opened and closed as he left the room. Trike continued to watch as the explosion cooled. His expression was blank and bore no reflection of the turmoil he felt inside, as the strewn mass of the wormship began to draw itself back together. Maybe it would have been better if he had stayed aboard his own ship, then he wouldn't feel like *he* was coming apart. One moment he felt nostalgic emotion, suppressed it, then paranoia, and now the giggling craziness he had known throughout his life was rising up again inside him. He took his hands out of his pockets and saw that the two ring-shaped blue scars there from leech bites, denizens of his home world, were livid, as they usually were when he was on edge.

He swung his gaze to the ship's main screen and looked out across the cratered regolith and weird ice sculptures of the planet-oid they were hidden on. Up in starlit space he could see the dull glow of the explosion. He wanted to call Angel to see if he was still alive, but even if he was there was no guarantee that he would reply. Also, though Trike had badly damaged the wormship, it was still very dangerous. He had to be sensible; he had to keep himself under control. If Angel was alive and began searching for him, he would surely penetrate the chameleonware hiding Cog's ship down here on the surface. Trike might care little for his own life now, but he should at least care about Cog.

On the display, the wormship continued to pull itself back together, snaring reachable debris as it did so. The thing was tough and Trike's lack of knowledge about it frustrated him. His searches of the AI net had revealed little that was useful. Two-and-a-half centuries ago there had been some kind of AI police action on the Polity border. Rogue AIs had been involved, as well as Jain technology. The Polity had won, wiping out the opposing forces. There were image files available and information about battle tactics, but all of it was heavily redacted and provided little in the way of technical detail. From his reading of the information, Trike was sure the redaction had less to do with hiding detail about the enemy and its capabilities and more with concealing information about the Polity ships and weapons involved.

A while later Cog returned and plonked himself down in his throne.

'It's re-assembling,' he commented.

'Yes . . .'

'Maybe you didn't get him.'

Trike forced himself to engage. He swung round to face Cog. 'So what should we do now?' he asked, tightly under control.

Cog was a very old Old Captain from the seas of Spatterjay. He was short, and appeared to be fat – a jolly little man who, unusually for an Old Captain, had managed to retain a head of curly brown hair. He was mild and calm, laughed a lot, and was capable of breaking advanced Polity hull armour with his hands.

After drawing on his pipe then blowing a perfect smoke ring, he stated, 'Listen boy, you wanted your revenge.'

Trike nodded dumbly.

'And it ain't confirmed.'

'Quite,' said Trike.

Cog pointed at the display with the stem of his pipe. 'Then when that thing has finished pulling itself together, we follow it. Another opportunity will arise.'

'If Angel's alive and doesn't find the U-mitter.' Trike had one inside his skull twinned with the device inside Ruth's. 'And if he doesn't dispose of her remains.'

'We can be patient, and careful, and we have more time than we can imagine.' Cog grinned, then shrugged. 'If it takes a thousand years, what matter?'

There was that. Neither of them were likely to die any day soon and, as time passed, they would only get stronger, unless the Spatterjay virus inside them underwent some kind of change no hooper had yet seen.

And if Trike could hold his mind together for that long.

Orlandine

Orlandine had designed the small shuttle that enclosed her. She sat strapped into an acceleration chair, and two optic leads were plugged into two data sockets she had opened in her side. The chain-glass screen before her gave her a view out into space but all she could see at present were the steadily brightening stars. Functioning as a human, this would have been her only view, so why did she keep wanting to return to that state? It defied logic, and sometimes when she was operating at her highest level she did not understand the impulse. Yet it always returned.

Now, closely linked into the systems she could control, she was able to gaze from any of tens of thousands of cams. Other sensor data was also available to her, so she could feel the temperature within the pressurized sections of the shipyard, or sense what a robot was feeling through its manipulators as it positioned a sheet of composite in the partially constructed weapons plat-form. She could detect the flash of electromagnetic radiation as a welder struck an arc, smell the aroma of hot food from a dispenser, and feel the fluctuations in a malfunctioning grav-plate that provided artificial gravity for human workers. She was also processing other data: statistics and logistics, the grumble of communications between computers, AIs, sub-AIs . . . the whole project lay in the grasp of her mind.

However, right now, her focus was the accretion disc and what was happening there. Again she tried to open a channel to Dragon but again there was no reply, so instead she concentrated on the action and the defence-sphere response.

The thing sliding out of the disc was eight miles long. Dark and crystalline, like a long chunk of smoky quartz, it was wrapped in what looked like the desiccated corpse of a pterodactyl. Meanwhile Dragon, now free of the Jain tech attacking its surface, drew its pseudopods back inside and heaved like a dog puking. A scan from Weapons Platform Mu revealed a cavity opening on Dragon's surface, facing the accretion disc. An energy beam stabbed out of it, invisible in vacuum but blinding white when it hit gas and dust that reflected it. Orlandine knew about these full-spectrum white-light lasers. The ECS – Earth Central Security – Weapons Division had developed something similar, though none had yet been installed in the defence sphere.

The beam struck the Jain-tech object emerging from the disc and played along its length. Chunks like immense bird bones and sheets of skin blasted away as the beam vaporized much of the enclosing, desiccated mass. Dragon then began firing intermittently, heaving with every emission that stabbed out. Chunks of black crystal exploded away. The AI on Platform Mu, Pragus, also opened fire and violet particle beams speared across vacuum. Drilling into the mass, they caused internal pressure explosions which cracked it apart. Meanwhile, via the Ghost Drive Facility on Jaskor, Orlandine was receiving updates from the other platforms. Jain-tech objects were coming out of the accretion disc elsewhere. Another four of these things had shown themselves, while in one area an immense swarm of objects like bats made of grey metal, each just three feet across, was blasting out into open vacuum.

Obviously, Dragon had stirred things up inside the disc but there was no intelligence involved in this excursion. Maybe, considering the reason for Dragon's venture into the disc, some intelligence had caused this? Dragon had gone in because the mass of Jain tech gathered there allowed communication with ancient Jain AIs that were trapped in U-space – an effect that was yet to be understood. But Jain tech by itself did not possess intelligence, just an insentient will to live, procreate and spread. Only when it subsumed intelligence did it become lethally dangerous.

These objects emerging from the disc were like wasps swarming from a nest straight into the path of a flame thrower. Orlandine was enforcing quarantine. She was containing an infection, but it was one that must not be underestimated. The accretion disc was infested with Jain nodes – objects only an inch across. They were seeds for this technology, containing all its possibilities, and just one of them in the wrong hands could cause extensive damage to the Polity, if not destroy it. Orlandine did not underestimate Jain tech, because she knew it intimately.

As she watched the distant action with one portion of her mind, she flew the shuttle with another, using its grav-motor and thrusters to turn it and bring the partially constructed weapons platform into view. At the moment, it was only a giant slab surrounded by pseudo-matter scaffolds and a mass of robots and handler vehicles. Though she could see all the data on its construction, she decided to make full contact with the AI that had recently been installed and communicate verbally – perhaps some hangover from her human time.

'Construction is getting further and further behind, I see,' she said.

'Supply problems,' replied the AI, who had recently named itself Magus – a format of naming that was becoming a bit of a tradition here.

The platform slid past. Orlandine eyed the factory lying beyond it – a blockish chunk of hardware two miles across that resembled an antique printing press. Two big haulers were moored to it. These ships were penny-shaped vessels with cuboid structures under-slung and protruding from the back to contain both U-drive and crew quarters – the rest of the vessel being cargo space. They were presently pumping materials into the factory: elemental dusts, specially designed liquids containing builder nanites, which were programmable nano-machines capable of building a variety of components, and complex hydrocarbons. These materials were rare here, with more common bulk supplies generally obtained within the Jaskoran solar system. Thinking of those, Orlandine flung her gaze outwards millions of miles, to where machines were deconstructing asteroids to load onto big spherical smelting plants and from there onto ships bringing in ingots of metals, silicon, carbon and other base structural substances.

'We need to be supplied by cargo runcible,' said Magus.

Orlandine shrugged, now focusing on another object gleaming in vacuum ahead of her. 'You know how Earth Central feels about that. It took all my powers of persuasion to get the ground-based one for personnel.'

'A degree of caution that hampers us,' Magus observed.

Due to the dangers inherent in such a giant active mass of Jain technology, the de facto ruler of the Polity tightly controlled all Polity links to the vicinity of the accretion disc. AI net access was limited, ships returning from here underwent very heavy scanning, and Earth Central did not want a bulk cargo gate open because such a gate was two-way. Orlandine understood its caution, but also knew it wasn't just about Jain tech finding an easy route into the heart of the Polity. Firstly, the ruling AI still did not trust either her or Dragon. It was suspicious that they could follow the same course as Erebus and subsume, or be subsumed, by Jain technology, then use a cargo runcible to attack the Polity.

The distant object began to resolve to her vision which, at present, was only slightly enhanced. She enhanced further and brought it into view. Her vessel, the *Cytoxic*, looked like a steel and glass jellyfish with rods hanging where tentacles should be. It was half a mile from top to bottom and, even as she drew closer, she felt links from its sub-AI questing for full connection.

She held back and again tried to contact Dragon. This time the response was instant.

'*I will be clean,*' Dragon told her, its voice arriving directly in her mind.

'*And you failed yet again,*' Orlandine replied, just as directly. Also thinking that Dragon *must* be clean. The directive she had hard-wired into the platform AIs was indisputable – if Dragon showed the slightest sign of Jain tech, or its signature, they would obliterate him. No discussions, no debates, no bargaining.

'*The Jain AIs are not only disinclined to talk but, when not utterly indifferent, they can be tetchy,*' Dragon explained. '*The indifference was understandable the last time I tried because they were disconnected from their realspace energy feeds—*'

'*Energy feeds that probably failed and rusted away millions of years ago.*'

'*Quite.*' Dragon paused for a second. '*They were at a low energy level and their thinking had become completely internalized.*'

'*And with the energy you gave them this time?*'

'*They got angry, briefly, hence the action you are seeing.*'

'*So they do have some control over the Jain tech here?*'

'*Rather there is some sensory link and the tech here reflects their mood.*'

Orlandine grimaced. Even after all this time, and despite the fact that Dragon had rescued her from an eternity of drifting through vacuum, she still did not trust the creature. Had it really gone into the disc to try and talk to those five-million-year-old AIs?

'*So you have learned nothing new?*'

'*Nothing,*' Dragon replied.

'*Then we must consider other options,*' Orlandine stated. '*The defence sphere is hardly . . . airtight. Something will get out sometime. This status quo must be broken.*'

'*Drastic actions are contra-indicated.*'

That sounded far too reasonable from a creature that had a history of causing some serious mayhem.

'*Because the Jain tech there is active,*' Orlandine supplied.

'*Because there is activity,*' Dragon replied, obliquely, frustratingly.

The attempt, if it could be called that, of Jain tech to escape the disc seemed to be dying. After checking once more on the state of the defence sphere, she next focused on a new data feed from Dragon as it fought Jain incursions into itself. While doing this she again thought back to first principles. What did Jain technology do? A single seed of it, a node, would be picked up by a member of some civilized species, whereupon it would activate. It would spread, disrupt, eat up the intelligence of its recipients, and destroy the civilization. Once its fertile ground was drained of nutrients, it would then go to seed, spreading further Jain nodes, and then die.

Orlandine didn't much like the analogy but it would do for now. The simple question that applied here was why was this Jain tech still active? Why had it not gone to seed and died, when in the accretion disc there was no civilization for it to destroy? Yes, it had been believed that the rogue AI of the dreadnought *Trafalgar*, which renamed itself Erebus when it utilized Jain tech and expanded beyond mere ship crystal, had been first to initiate the tech here. But maybe that wasn't the whole story. Here lay a weakness in the fabric of space, a route for contact with the Jain AIs somnolent in U-space who, it had to be said, might only be coincidentally linked to the tech here. Perhaps this place was the nursery for Jain tech, the centre point of its spread. Perhaps something had been here long before Erebus arrived?

Round and round, and no answers were forthcoming despite the power of her mind. Orlandine ground her teeth in frustration, sure there was something she was missing. She ran prognostic programs on all the data she had, reviewed results, eyed an infinity of answers, then swore and disconnected. She had conducted this fruitless search for answers many times with the same result. She took some more human time, just to be, just to let things settle in her mind. To be calm. An hour passed, during which she gave her mind breathing space – not thinking at all. Then her vessel loomed before her, and her shuttle was engaging in a docking circlet.

Orlandine unstrapped as the two optics disengaged and snaked away, then towed herself to the door, which opened ahead of her. She pulled herself through a glass tube into the ship proper, and came down onto a grav-plated floor clad in carpet moss. A short corridor led into her lounge, where she headed towards the back, touching the centre of a small disc at her shoulder. Her blue ship-suit split at its seams and slithered over her skin towards the disc, the monomer fabric shrivelling as the disc drew it inside. Naked, she stepped into a dropshaft whose irised gravity field whisked her upwards, to a small atrium. This was filled with spiky blue alien plants sprouting orange and yellow butterfly flowers, and a scent like cinnamon filled her nostrils as she entered. One flower detached and flittered across to her, but she waved it away and ducked through a door on the other side of the atrium, which gave her access to her interface sphere.

Orlandine stepped inside and dropped into the chair at the bottom of the sphere. Straps crawled across her body to secure her in place. She still found this a creepy feeling despite having long ago abandoned the carapace she had worn in her early years. She took a breath and prepared her body, further data ports opening down her sides like bullet holes but with gleaming metal interiors, and another larger hole opening in her back. With a mental instruction the sphere began making its connections. A power-supply bayonet extruded from the chair behind her and entered her spinal socket. She felt the surge throughout as all her Polity- and Jain-based inorganic components went to high power. At the same time her medical system worked to protect her remaining human body from it. Next, lines of curved arms, with optic plugs on the ends, folded out to mate with those sockets running down either side of her body. She rested her head back, her eyes blind white but her mind seeing so much more now. A band closed about her head to hold it in place and a further plug folded out to engage in a socket behind her ear. She connected fully with her ship's temporary sub-AI and simply absorbed it. Now Orlandine was complete. She was her ship and all its systems. She controlled everything absolutely.

I am no longer human, she thought.

She decided, with her physical presence at the accretion disc not really required, it was time for one short journey before she returned there. In her AI component, now more thoroughly melded with her human mind by the Jain tech she had conquered and taken into her body, Orlandine gazed upon the twisted terrain of underspace and made calculations. She tinkered with her U-engine, adjusting parameters just so, distorting fields and shifting pseudomatter, then input the required power. Her ship fell out of the real and into U-space, surging across that terrain until, a moment later, it bounced back up into the real again.

The gas giant lay millions of miles from Jaskor, at the outer edge of the Jaskoran system. Twenty moons orbited it and every one of them was being mined, with smelting plants or factory installations clinging to it like cybernetic shellfish. These supplied materials to a project wholly her own, and one which Earth Central would be less than happy about, if it knew. She felt sure it did not know. Polity dreadnoughts would have paid her a visit otherwise, despite the agreement between the Polity and the Kingdom that neither of their warships could enter the Jaskoran system. This was also a project she was sure Dragon had reservations about, and that those same reservations had impelled its recent visit inside the accretion disc.

Other objects orbited the planet and two of them lay nearby. These were what the smelting plants supplied, and these were the centre of Orlandine's private project. Even as her ship surfaced from U-space, something probed it from one of them. Large weapons turrets swung towards her and targeting lasers lit up her ship's hull.

'Oh, it's you,' said a gruff voice, doubtless disappointed that the ship arriving wasn't something he could destroy.

Pragus

The periods between the appearance of Jain-tech objects trying to escape the disc grew longer and longer. Summarily destroying those that came its way, Pragus gratefully returned much of its attention to the alien husk in the disposable laboratory. Close study of the creature's genome began to produce a wealth of information. The genome itself bore similarities to DNA in that some of the bases were the same and large portions of it were helical – the simplest structure for storing such information. But this was a five-strand helix with numerous off-shoots and only vaguely attached external elements. In plain bulk it was twenty times that of the DNA of even modern humans and, like their DNA, had been highly modified. Pragus found capsules of nano-machines in it, as well as nano-crystals which likely contained quantum computing. When it felt it had learned enough to move beyond passive study, the AI set up a small autofactory to make an artificial womb, the design based on that of the creature. And then it extracted a single cell . . .

Pragus suspended the completed artificial womb inside another disposable lab, and soon the single alien cell was floating inside the high-temperature brine it contained. The cell was ready but inactive until Pragus made adjustments here and there with nano-fibres, shifting components of the genome, snipping the helix, reconfiguring just a small portion of it. The task had not been as difficult as the AI had supposed because sex hadn't been involved. The creature created the further segments of itself by cloning. There was also no necessity for an ovum or much else extraneous to this cell. All the workings needed were inside that highly complex genome.

The cell activated – the tangled genetic matter inside writhing and reconfiguring itself. One small strand pushed out of this to the cell membrane, and broke through it. Nutrients were introduced next, flooding into the brine. Pragus realized the outgrowth from the cell must be some kind of sensor when the molecular touch of nutrients on it stirred further action. The membrane split and the outgrowth swung around, vacuuming up the food. Now exposed, the inner-cell germ also began to snare nutrients, expanding as it did so. In just a few minutes, the whole thing divided into five, with new membranes growing and then breaking. Pragus increased the nutrient feed and made some calculations. This was going to be fast. The next division resulted in twenty-five cells which started producing strange organelles that darted out to collect up further nutrients. One of these attached itself to the nano-scopic head of a scanner Pragus had placed within the womb, and data from it corrupted for a second. Two further divisions occurred and the small mass was issuing tendrils, their cell structure simplified and their genome mass just a hundredth of that of the cells in the main mass.

These tendrils grew rapidly, reaching out to the wall of the womb. Occasionally they too touched other sensor heads and again data corrupted. As they connected with the womb wall they rapidly keyed into the artificial venous system there, and this increased the nutrient supply to the central mass. In just two hours, it had attained the size of a human head. Its growth was so rapid that Pragus had to start running a cooling system around the womb, such was the heat generated by the cellular activity.

Pragus watched the shape of the creature forming – an embryo sprouting the nubs of limbs, the head, the dark patches of eye cells. The AI calculated that it would be ready to leave the womb in just a few more hours, and so turned its attention to a large chain-glass cylinder it had used in one of its previous projects. Here it had grown exotic plants and the heating system only needed a little upgrading to suit what it judged would be the creature's needs. It instructed robots to make the required changes.

Further data on the Client showed Pragus what would be required inside the cylinder: a tree-like structure to supply certain nutrients, as well as a sanitary system to process dead segments of the creature, and to recycle them back into the nutrient system. In another part of the platform, Pragus set a factory to make these things with the same alacrity it manufactured munitions and replacement infrastructure during battle. In just that time the embryo had doubled in size and was now moving.

Pragus felt deep admiration for and a fascination with this growing creature. Its hunger for existence impressed the AI, its sheer tenacity was worthy of great respect. Pragus almost felt a sense of . . . a sense of . . . connection.

Something wrong.

Pragus ran swift diagnostics, tracing these emotions through its mind to a data dump. This was where it had placed the corrupted data from the sensor heads. The data seemed to have reconfigured itself into something coherent and made connections outside of the dump. Pragus considered consigning the dump to quarantine, but was too fascinated. The source had to be the creature's nano-crystals, which likely contained quantum computing. The creature was an opportunist. Most life forms grew their bodies and the organic matter of their brains first – intelligence and mentality as an overlay on an evolved structure via environmental interaction. Instead, this creature must have retained a recording of its mentality to place in any available substrate – rather like human memcordings, the quantum-formatted artificial rubies many humans implanted in their skulls to record everything they were.

Fascinating . . .

Admirable . . .

Pragus now drove a more complex sensor head through the wall of the womb towards the central mass. It needed to examine . . . something. The sensor wound its way in and connected, sprouting further sensor fibres to wind through the growing mass. Data flowed back to Pragus, and the AI began to send it automatically to seemingly random portions of its crystal mind.

What am I doing?

Obviously the quantum recorded mind of the creature needed to be copied and saved. Such a wealth of information could not be abandoned to the quirks of fate.

Obviously . . .

3

Wormship: This vessel was one of the weapons used by the AI Erebus in its attack upon the Polity. All wormships were destroyed by a Polity war fleet so data on them is limited. They were an amalgam of Jain tech and Polity tech – an attempt to create war craft with widely distributed systems, and thus less vulnerable to weapons strikes. They consisted of a tangle of worm-forms, generally a yard or two wide, and incorporated everything found in discrete units aboard most Polity dreadnoughts. They were dense tech – components packed to the highest efficient density possible to use the energy available. After damage, they could scavenge materials from other damaged ships and rebuild themselves. Fragmented parts of wormships could reintegrate into a new whole. They could sequester other ships but, because Polity ships have such strong induction warfare defences, this had to be done by physical attack and contact. They were very dangerous and, had Erebus not actually turned on itself during its battle against the Polity, wormships in the skies of human worlds might have been the last thing any of us saw.

Notes from her lecture 'Modern Warfare' by E. B. S. Heinlein

Angel

Finally the coils of the remaining wormship closed about him and obscured the view of debris out there, as well the cooling glow of gas and the blurred starlight. Angel floated inside the shield of the hardfields and the cage of tendrils enclosing him. The Wheel was gone. He felt both free and bereft of a companion that had been with him intermittently since his time on the surface of a gas giant moon. He gazed about himself, unsure of his next move, but then the oiled functioning of his mind began to reassert.

He shut down the hardfields and the cage of tendrils unravelled as a further mass rose up from below and cupped him. The corpse of the woman, Ruth, hung in zero gravity beside him like an accusation. He prodded it to send it drifting away, not really sure why he had grabbed it at the last moment – his feelings about her were confused. He held out his hands and two tendrils punched into his palms to give him full connection with his ship. Data flooded into his mind.

The explosion in Trike's vessel had destroyed nearly half the mass of the wormship and many systems had yet to repair themselves. It would be some hours before he could engage the U-space drive and now, having waited so long inside his hardfield defence, he began to feel a strange empty panic.

Where had the Wheel gone?

Suddenly angry, he shook the tendrils from his hands, remaining engaged by radio and other EMR only to keep watch on the repairs and intervene if necessary. He did not need the Wheel there to offer its advice and opinions. He knew his aims, it was not as if it was a replacement for Erebus . . . The tangle which held him unravelled as it moved him to a nearby surface and Angel stepped out quickly, his gecko feet sticking him down. What now? He continued with his thoughts about Erebus. Maybe he would not have made the error he did with Trike if he still had a guiding intelligence occupying the half of his mind now virtually empty? But maybe he would have been without the vicious inclinations of that intelligence and simply destroyed

Trike's ship from a distance? Though he felt certain of his hatred for the humans, the AIs and the prador, he did not like it that his one-time master and betrayer might still influence him . . .

Then, through a nearby cam, he inspected his present form.

He was humanoid like the Golem androids made by Cyber-corp, but metalskin like some of the company's older versions. His skin was polished chrome over the smooth areas but shaded to blue-green at his joints and where his ersatz musculature was outlined. He towered tall and incredibly thin, while his fingers were one-and-a-half times the length of human ones and termin-ated in sharp points. His head slanted backwards, tapering down sharply to the lipless slot of his mouth. He possessed no nose and his eyes were lidless. There were no edges to the metal skin at his joints – the material there actually stretched and flexed like skin. His whole exterior consisted of the same metal, even down to the insect glitter of his eyes.

This form had been chosen for efficiency in human environ-ments and to generate fear in those he dealt with on behalf of Erebus – the AI that once ran the dreadnought *Trafalgar* and had become something more vast and dangerous after it took control of Jain technology. Angel had retained this form during his ser-vice because that was the wish of Erebus. You did not disobey a creator who made up half of your mental structure and who could consign you to some virtual hell on a whim. But Erebus had both defeated itself and been defeated by the Polity. Turning on itself during a battle with the Polity AIs, it had meticulously destroyed all its parts, or so everyone involved had thought. To Angel, this was the betrayal. He had been left trapped on the surface of a moon, disconnected from Erebus by an electromag-netic storm on the gas giant it orbited, which had been triggered by a Polity gravity-wave weapon.

He had spent an age on the surface of that moon, wandering

aimlessly, his body feeding off environmental radiation, and his mind blank. Only when a sulphur fumarole hurled him out into space, where the partially functioning remains of his wormship picked him up, did some elements of his mind begin to return. With them came the Wheel, nascent, simply turning in the dark half of his mind.

Slowly he began rebuilding the ship, not even sure why he was doing so. When he finally managed to understand and repair the ship's drive systems, and leave close orbit of the gas giant, purpose returned. The Polity was the enemy. That's all he knew then, though later he found his hatred spreading to all present-day sentients, including the prador. But even now, having discovered that two-and-a-half centuries had passed since Erebus's defeat, the empty half of his mind the rogue AI had occupied was only just beginning to flicker with new thoughts and numerous questions. This was when he felt the turning of the Wheel and sensed it *assisting* him in his mental endeavours.

Time, Angel felt, suddenly even angrier, *for a change of Erebus's chosen form.*

He initiated long unused technology inside his body, and his metallic skin began to flow. His head deformed, taking on a more human shape, growing a nose and opening a more mobile mouth, but with everything still shiny and metallic. His bulbous fly eyes sank back into his head and grew lids. He held up a hand and watched the fingers shrink, but was reluctant to forgo their sensitive points. Surely he looked a little less threatening now? He smiled fiercely, aware that, closer to the human form but certainly not quite right, he looked even more menacing. This increased when he turned his eyes midnight black.

Fallen Angel, he thought, and grinned, exposing gleaming metallic teeth. His smirk disappeared as he remembered that Polity speculation had alleged the legates were in fact corrupted Golem androids. Was he reacting to the influence of his past again? But even though he had changed his outer form, his inner workings remained the same, as did the pattern of his thoughts. Impatient now, he scanned the interior of his ship and focused on one item. The corpse of the woman, Ruth Ottinger, had been snared by ship tendrils. Her body had been burned a little and had ruptured in places from exposure to vacuum, but it might still be serviceable.

He stared at her, long and hard. Reaching for his hatred of humanity as an explanation for why he had treated her so cruelly, he found only an emptiness. She could serve as a distraction for him right now, he decided. He ran a deeper scan from the tendrils and made an assessment. Not too bad. Doable. But even as he finished assessing her he was not sure why he was doing this. It was irrelevant to his purpose – a diversion. It wasn't guilt, it could not be guilt . . .

He injected fibres into her body and began making repairs, summoning thicker tendrils with precision instruments and feed pipes for materials. Fortunately her own nanosuite had kept her body more viable for revival than a base-format human body. Though she had been dead for months her condition was that of someone newly dead. Cerebral degradation was minimal and the burns and other damage could be handled by the nanosuite once her body was up and running again. Angel injected tubules to convey oxygen and nutrients inside her, adding a powerful anticoagulant and other substances to counter the micro-damage throughout. He injected carbon fibres to restart her heart and then, once that was beating, inserted an array of fibres into her brain to spread neural meshes and make connections. Getting her autonomous nervous system running was delicate work, and further tubules were required to add neurochem and remove stubborn blood clots. To speed the process Angel performed some surgery, steadily removing dead matter that was too damaged to revive and spraying in collagen scaffolds. He peeled away burned skin and replaced it with a synthetic used by war-time autodocs. He cell-welded bone breaks. Her burned-out eyes he replaced with synthetic ones which, at the last moment, he tuned to be completely black like his own.

Ruth began to move, to writhe in the tendrils holding her. Angel debated on whether to restore the higher functions of her brain, because with more autonomy she might be useful to him. Yes, she *would* be useful to him. Her utility would become clear when he went to reclaim those Jain artefacts . . . was this why he had revived her? Again it was a decision another part of his mind questioned. He paused for a second and delivered instructions to his ship. The semi-vacuum around him began to fill with human-breathable air and he felt its pressure building against his skin. Injecting and adjusting, he gradually started up her mind and, from a ship data cache, restored the memories she herself had edited out. It was while doing this, he found the object imbedded on the inside of her skull.

Cursory examination revealed the object's miniature power supply was topped up by photo-electrics grown as part of her hair. It also revealed that part of the device was unavailable to medical scan. Angel used something more powerful and finally recognized what he had found. Here was a quantum-matched transmitter, one of a pair, and made before anyone even thought up the term underspace. The recipients of this pair would always know where the other was, and in which direction their partner lay. However, this device possessed an addition to incorporate stellar travel. It gave U-space coordinates.

'Captain Trike,' Angel said, pausing then at the odd sound of his voice within the wormship. He had never actually filled the place with air to this pressure before – always retaining a low-pressure atmosphere of inert gas for convenience.

His first instinct was to shut the transmitter down. But Trike

. . . Angel felt a surge of viciousness and briefly searched the dark half of his mind for a nub of brightness – the imminence of the Wheel. He now considered how enjoyable it would be to repay Trike for the destruction the man had wrought. He gazed out through the sensors of his ship into surrounding space, searching for some sign of the hooper. A cursory examination of the planetoid in whose shadow he had lurked revealed nothing. Nor anything on the darker planet it orbited. Anyway, it was quite probable that Trike had used a U-space relay during his assassination attempt. Why would he actually come close and risk himself? Angel disconnected, though he left the scan operating to alert him should anything appear.

As he returned to the moment, he became aware of a sound. It took him a second to realize this was issuing from Ruth. She was gasping, moaning, and her face was twisted with a look of both horror and pain.

He felt a cruel satisfaction with this. But then something slid away in his mind and the nub of brightness flickered, darkened and winked out. Emptiness slammed back and Angel now felt horror at Ruth's suffering. He quickly shut down the pain messages to her brain but her writhing continued. Panic rose until he realized that her pain was mostly mental, for she was remembering what he had done to her. She was in the same mental state she had been in just before she died, and to her no time had passed. She was terrified. He abruptly switched off her consciousness. Gazing at her for a long time, he tried to understand his complete change in attitude towards her, but this train of thought fled from his grasp.

Angel decided, on the spur of this moment, that he did not want to control her absolutely. He wanted a semi-autonomous biological probe to which he could give guidance, and trust to get the job done. The job he had resurrected her for, surely? He now injected further fibres and tubules into her and made adjustments. He extracted the organic physical component from her recent memory up to a point before he had seized and bound her here. Now she would remember precisely what had happened to her, but it would not cripple her mentally. The pain would be gone.

She came to and turned her head to gaze at him with her midnight eyes.

'Fucker! What did you do with Trike?'

Orlandine

Orlandine remembered her first encounter with the big old assassin drone, when she was incorporating Jain technology into her being and had been more human. He was called Knobbler, and he was a brute, typical of a drone type that usually wanted to manifest as something nasty, and over-endowed with limbs. He looked like the bastard offspring of an octopus and a fiddler crab, with a definite admixture of equipment for earth-moving in his ancestry. His main body was six feet across and as many deep, with a sharp rim just like that of a crab. The body possessed his main sensorium, including disconcerting squid eyes, and was mackerel patterned – indicating now-inactive old-style chameleon-ware. Extending below and behind the body was a tail resembling the abdomen of a hoverfly, which he could fold up conveniently against his underside. From the juncture between these sections sprouted numerous heavy and partially jointed tentacles. Some suspended him off the floor, others groped through the air, but all terminated in the tools of his one-time lethal trade.

'Hi, Knobbler,' she said. 'How are the guys?'

As she spoke she analysed, with more senses than just her eyes, the two massive objects out there. The biggest was of a somewhat different design to the one Knobbler and his crew of assassin and war drones had occupied when she had found them two-and-a-half centuries ago. Then they had been aboard a war runcible mothballed since the end of the war. This was a U-space gate used to shift large numbers of ships without U-space drives, or to fling moonlets at the prador. The big runcible the drones were building now, with a lot of robotic help, was an octagonal frame ten miles across, with the frame itself being square in section and a quarter of a mile thick. Each section of the frame was bulked with great hardfield generators, electromagnets and the hardware for creating the gate. Unlike previous war runcibles it wasn't made to separate and expand. That would create too many weaknesses for its intended use.

'We are all good,' Knobbler replied. 'Most of us are well occupied with the work here. Only Cutter and Bludgeon are getting a bit bored.'

Orlandine smiled, aware that contact with the drones here sometimes elicited more human emotion from her than contact with humans. Cutter was a war drone like a huge praying mantis fashioned out of razorblades, while Bludgeon looked like a giant bedbug. Most likely, it was Cutter who was being a pain, since he liked action. Bludgeon doubtless agreed with him because of their partnership, which had lasted since the prador/human war. Apparently, while Orlandine had been sleeping for two centuries, the two of them had been in the Graveyard getting into all sorts of scrapes. Adrenalin junkies was the term for the human version of them.

'And the work is progressing well?'

Orlandine now focused her full attention on the smaller object out there. This was simply a ring ten miles across. It was another gate and bulked around its rim with similar engines to those on the octagon, but it wasn't anywhere near as strong. The reason for this was that it only had to generate a gate to let an object exit from underspace. How long it survived after that wasn't really of much concern. Orlandine calculated it would last less than a second. The octagon had to survive a lot longer, and be strong enough to get close to and gate through the huge and dangerous object concerned.

'It's going well,' said Knobbler, 'though supplies have been a bit tardy lately. We're still waiting on two more of the big grav-engines.'

Orlandine immediately keyed into the data cloud – the manifests, orders, construction plans, lists of stores and all. She worried about the delay because it might mean that her suppliers, either Earth Central or the Kingdom, had started to suspect the orders weren't intended for the weapons platform as supposed. She noted that the grav-engines had been dispatched from the Polity and would arrive in a few days. Then she saw something else. Other supplies she had diverted here from weapons platform construction had been diverted back again. She studied the data intently but could not see how it had been done. It might even have been some simple computing error. Whatever the cause, it was delaying construction here by months.

Dragon, she thought, but could not confirm the suspicion.

She set the details back to how they should be.

'Good. All is good,' she said, mentally shifting to another connection via U-space. She gave the data a cursory inspection, then paused and went over it again. What was Dragon doing out there in the defence sphere? Was something wrong with it? The entity, according to the feed it allowed from itself, had finally managed to shrug off the Jain technology that had attacked it but was now behaving strangely. Instead of heading off to be about its business – usually cruising around the accretion disc and gathering data, or away on excursions to other systems – it was travelling slowly towards Weapons Platform Mu.

'You'll be coming to take a look?' Knobbler asked.

Orlandine hesitated longer than was usual for her and got pinged by the old assassin drone. Dragon's recent incursion into the disc had bothered her from the start. Then there was the supply delay that might or might not have been caused by the entity. And now this strange behaviour. It was time to have a long talk with that giant alien. But even as she decided this she could foresee its failure. Yes, she would ask Dragon questions but was too wise in the creature's ways to expect a straight answer.

'Yes,' she decided, 'I will come take a look.'

With a thought she sent her ship down towards the larger runcible. She would make her usual physical tour of all the work in progress, reacquaint herself with the drones working here and ensure everything was up to spec. She trusted the drones but this was very serious business – the slightest error could lead to disaster once the project was activated. She would also make a much closer inspection of all the data related to the work.

The runcible loomed closer and a docking port signalled its readiness for her. This was set in a large outgrowth like a giant metallic polyp, and was where Knobbler was located. As her ship docked she disconnected from her interface sphere and pushed herself out. Her shipsuit spilled out from the disc on her shoulder and covered her as she stepped into her atrium. A butterfly flower fluttered over, landed on her outstretched hand and she studied the delicate thing for a long moment. Yes, she decided, a close inspection was required here, for Dragon could have introduced errors. She would also isolate the place from the defence sphere. There was simply no room for errors when your aim was to move something as super-massive as a black hole.

Angel

Angel studied Ruth Ottinger for a long moment, then waved a hand at his face and body. 'You recognize me?'

'I recognize you. I can still see your rotten core.'

Angel absorbed the insult and almost instinctively considered punishing her, then rejected the idea. What purpose would there be in giving her pain when pain was what he had just taken away?

'Trike is alive and well,' he said.

Her eyes welled with tears. 'So *you* say.'

Human speech was so slow and inaccurate, Angel felt. He toyed with the idea of downloading a précis of recent events into her mind, rather than using that slow human form of communication. But some hours still remained until he could move his ship and what else did he have to do?

'My purpose in taking you was to extract your memories concerning the sale of a cache of Jain artefacts,' he explained, and watched her.

'Memories I have again,' she realized.

'Yes, you edited them out.' Angel continued, 'I promised to return you to Trike if he retrieved those memories for me. He found them . . . in a ruby pendant.'

'Then why am I still here?' she spat.

'Things went a little wrong.' Angel tried out a grimace on his new face. 'I intended to kill him, of course, as I killed you, but he was smart.' Even as he spoke the words Angel was baffled by them. Why the killing? Why?

'You killed me?'

'Yes, but now you are alive again.'

She opened and closed her mouth as she took it in. She looked haunted and baffled, then said, 'He was smart.'

'He controlled his ship remotely and when I took it he

55

detonated its engines.' Angel shrugged – another attempt at human expression – but he was also grateful to move on from his uncomfortable thoughts. 'Destroyed nearly half my ship.'

'Good, but a shame he missed you.' She paused, then continued, 'Why did you revive me? What do you want from me now?'

Angel reached up and a tendril snaked out to his hand. He grasped it and pulled himself up level with where she was caught in the tendrils still repairing her body. He folded his legs below him and hung there like some weird attenuated metal Buddha.

'You are, at present, a relief from boredom,' he explained, knowing deep inside that he was lying. 'So don't bore me.'

Panic fled across her features and she looked from side to side as if trying to see some way out. Then abruptly she grew calm and focused on him.

'Why do you want Jain artefacts?' she asked.

'One of those artefacts is very interesting,' he replied confidently, then found himself floundering. 'I revived you to help me obtain it from the one you sold it to,' he said quickly, and felt a hot flush of something pass through him. He had lied with his previous assertion that boredom had compelled him to wake her. This was confusing – so much did not make sense now. He fell silent, groping for a way to continue . . . being.

A lot of the work on Ruth's body was now finished and with a thought Angel instructed those tendrils not still in use to retract. The main mass parted from around her face and upper body, with just a few left in place penetrating her chest and skull. Her arms now free, she crossed them over her breasts, rubbed her upper arms and started shivering.

'I studied those artefacts,' Ruth said abruptly, still focusing on him. 'One did contain something odd, or at least stranger than the tech in the others.'

'Continue,' said Angel, grabbing desperately onto this line of conversation.

'I'm cold,' she said.

He felt a flash of irritation, but it dissolved quickly. With another thought, he began to raise the temperature within their pocket of air in the ship. He mentally traced her clothing and found it caught between two of the major worm-forms of the ship. Tendrils extracted it and began making repairs. He then pondered their first meeting. How, after reviewing details and price on the commodity he was supposedly selling, she had come over from Trike's ship in a shuttle. The man himself had been conducting business aboard the nearby space station which served as a trading post on the Polity Line. She had been so calm, confident and curious as her shuttle docked and she came in through the apparently conventional airlock. The wormship had been tightly knotted then and looked no odder than any other ship around the station. Her calm mood only lasted to the point when the tendrils grabbed her, ripped away her clothing and bound her in a writhing cage while stabbing into her skull.

Angel grimaced. Why had he been so eager to rip everything away from her? Again the remains of Erebus's influence? Or something else? His attention strayed to the all but empty half of his mind and his unease grew. But then it was momentarily dispelled as his exterior sensors alerted him to something related to his thoughts. Her shuttle hung out there amidst remaining debris, bent out of shape and badly damaged. Using workable elements of its drive system, he began to move his wormship towards it. Why? Again he was not sure about his motivations. However, he continued because he was sure of one thing: his present actions did not stem from the residue of Erebus in his mind. And they did not come from anything else.

The temperature rose and soon Ruth stopped shivering, but

she kept her arms crossed over her breasts. Angel thought it inappropriate coyness in the circumstances, but he took no pleasure in it. He felt for her, and groped for something to fill the silence.

'You humans, the AIs, and the prador occupy a significant portion of the galaxy and are so proud of your achievements,' he said all in a rush, 'but you are nothing. I don't know which is stronger, my hatred of you all, or my contempt. One of the older races would crush you like a bug. No, not even that, they would probably not even notice you as they stepped on you.'

Angel felt no emotion as he spoke, and a great deal of doubt, as if he was testing the words out on her. Was this what he really thought? He inspected himself internally and noted that his mind was changing – that new pathways were etching their way through the organo-metal substrate and that electrical activity was changing. Thought was opening out wider because more of those pathways were now spearing into that portion of his mind that had previously been occupied by Erebus – and by the Wheel.

'So you hate us all,' she said. 'Is there anything you love?'

'Yes,' he said, and it felt like a lie.

'You are so sure.' She looked tired now. Understandable really. And he was glad she had not pushed him on the matter.

'Yes, I am sure.'

Empty words.

'Why?' she asked, her attention snapping back towards him, more awake now. 'Why do you so—'

Angel put her to sleep and then studied her for a long time. He had been utterly sure of everything up until Trike nearly destroyed this ship. Doubts now swarmed his mind. Doubts about his own motives, his emotions, his hatred. He shook himself, then moved down to the floor and ensconced himself in his seat of tendrils. He tried to think clearly about all he had done and all he intended to do, and felt himself sinking into a dark mental place. With every thought he had, every feeling, he also found the polar opposite in his mind and steadily his thinking simply locked up. Only many hours later did alerts from his ship pull him back to himself, though he wasn't sure what 'himself' was any more.

His ship was now ready to depart and he wondered what to do about Ruth. Kill her? wondered one part of his mind, almost tiredly. His attention strayed to the shuttle, now sitting within a cyst of his ship and already being disassembled prior to repair. No, she would be useful, killing her was pointless and . . . he simply did not want to. He had to do what *he* wanted, and not concede to the ghost impulses of his former master. He shook himself again, then remotely returned the tendrils to Ruth's skull, drilling them inside, and began weaving a neural lace in her brain. She would be able to talk and her brain would remain intact. But once he was done she would obey him absolutely. There was no reason for her to die.

Nothing could compel him to kill her. Again.

Pragus

Dragon was still slowly heading out towards Weapons Platform Mu. Pragus gazed at the entity, recognizing it on levels of its mind that seemed tilted against each other. As Pragus it knew all about Dragon and had seen it many times, but it was also experiencing memories about the entity that were not its own.

'All quiet on the Western front,' said Nagus.

'If you say that again,' replied Pragus, selecting from a number of previous replies, 'I will be compelled to take drastic action.'

The banter was realistic enough because Pragus kept the original format of its mind to the forefront of communications. In its deeper self was a vague shifting mass of contradictions and communications with the other AI, a matter of desperately maintaining a front. The ostensibly jocular banter was also, at its heart, a real consideration. Pragus could turn its weapons on Nagus, obliterate that platform and its AI. The elimination of Nagus would make it easier for Pragus to break away from the defence sphere and be about its own business – that of vengeance.

Its own business?

No, attacking its nearest neighbour in the defence sphere or breaking away was impossible. Its job, to destroy anything carrying a Jain signature that left the accretion disc, was still the bedrock of its being. It simply could not disobey the directive Orlandine had hard-wired in its mind.

'Not even birdsong,' added Nagus.

Pragus sorted possible replies but one surfaced from an old conversation with a war drone and was out before it could stop it.

'Fuck off,' it said. After a moment of confusion, and then panic, it cut the comlink to Nagus.

Pragus realized it had been taken over by the creature. Now out of the artificial womb, and out of the disposable lab that had contained it, the creature was steadily making its way through the weapons platform towards the chain-glass cylinder made into a home for it. The AI knew, with absolute certainty, that its former self would be screaming alarms and fighting for independence. But it was no longer its former self. It didn't know what it was any more, and its purpose was disordered.

Pragus the AI studied the creature, the experience strange because its sense of self was confused. It felt itself to be Pragus but also felt it was looking through the mind of another entity. It felt itself in those four conjoined insect forms.

Reconfigure.

It detected a huge bloc of information shifting in its mind and sensory inputs fell away. Blind now, Pragus replayed old conversations over and over again. It felt they were all that was keeping it in touch with reality as it sank into the pool of its own and another's mind.

Reconfigure.

Another shift, and it could see again. But it was no longer the AI Pragus.

As the creature moved along the shortest route to a precise location, the entire weapons platform was clear in her serial mind. She decoded molecules in the air to add further nuance to her visual and radar image of her environment. The technology here was advanced, but she could see that it had not advanced to a point where divisions between biotech and hard technology had been erased. The organic precursors of this, these humans, had yet failed to fully integrate – to become their tools and allow their tools to become them. This she ascertained from her surroundings and the data she continued to extract from Pragus. The AI had now lost its sense of self and had become just an intelligent data store.

Soon she reached her first destination and, via Pragus, opened a pressure door. She moved inside, inspected the grappler standing back against the wall, then moved over to the sealed cylinder sitting vertical in the middle of the floor. With one forelimb she tipped it over, scribed round the top with a hard blade-like finger and flicked away the end cap. She then reached inside and pulled out the dried-out husk of her former self, which Pragus had moved here from a disposable laboratory. Lifting it, she began to break off pieces – she crunched them up and, forming them into sticky balls with her mandibles and salivary spicules, swallowed them. This was no problem – the quantum storage crystals she was after were just too small and numerous to be damaged by the process.

Inside her complex gut she began digesting the biomatter and incorporating the nano-crystals. Memories of her former self, which the humans had named the Client, began to load from the crystals to her mind. Yes, there was much missing, but still enough for her to sketch out a coherent picture. Later, of course, when she could make the necessary equipment, she would reclaim her full data backups from her U-space store.

The Client remembered herself as part of a high civilization, enjoying its power, enjoying its life and the acquisition of knowledge. She, like her fellow beings, was immortal and in no great hurry to move to the next stage of existence on the supposedly inevitable road to the Omega Point. Then the prador had arrived, refusing all attempts at communication and simply destroying everything to do with the Client's civilization – the Species – that came within reach. Shocked into inaction, the Species had nearly folded during the first attack. But there were those in their number who had always railed against the complacency of their kind. They took over and turned the knowledge of the Species against the prador. But it was no good. Though they hurt the prador badly, the sheer numerical advantage and industrial might of the alien aggressors was what told in the end. The prador annihilated the Client's species, and only the Client herself survived.

Memories of what had come after were vague. And how this husk of herself had ended up here she did not know. Marco's story of a prador museum was obviously a lie because that had supposedly been about one of her fellows taken as a trophy during their war against the prador. The Client herself had died centuries after that war and sometime following the war between the humans and the prador.

She finally finished eating the remains of her old self and returned to the corridor. She hurried through it because, though Pragus had raised the temperature as much as possible, it still wasn't enough for her. As she moved she incorporated more memory and began to remember her association with the humans and Polity AIs. She had made weapons for them, but they had betrayed her by negotiating a truce with the prador. She remembered fleeing, then it all became vague but for the intense memory of her own agonizing death. Who had killed her and why, she did not know. She felt an angry resentment against the Polity but that was not as strong as her utter hatred of the prador. Now she could see how it might be possible to cause both some big problems. The Polity and the Kingdom sat in an uneasy truce that could be broken.

The Client, now through to stolen sensors of Pragus, turned her attention to a protruding hollow cylinder of chain-glass a mile long. Red-orange light glowed from the heaters inside, used to raise the temperature to a comfortable level. It was only minutes away from being ready, and once ensconced inside she could begin to grow properly. Soon she would be able to reclaim her memories from her U-space cache and learn again what she had known. For her present memories hinted that her whole self was a great deal more knowledgeable. She could also begin planning her escape from this place. It would probably entail causing some damage here, to Nagus, and to other nearer weapons platforms. And probably to that Dragon sphere which, annoyingly, she could see was still heading straight towards Weapons Platform Mu.

4

The Atheter, Jain, and the Csorians are named after, respectively, a kind of ceramic blade; the daughter of Alexion Smith (she was the first to discover a Jain artefact); and an archaeologist sneezing as he named his new discovery (though that's probably apocryphal). But no name has been given to the race of hive creatures, whose form was a long chain of conjoined insect-like bodies that the prador exterminated. Maybe this is because the only artefacts to be dug up are in the Prador Kingdom, and because archaeologists – though often fanatical – are perhaps not inclined to risk becoming breakfast in pursuit of the dusty secrets of the past. Also, no human found out about these creatures; one of them found us. The Client called its kind the Species – not an unusual name, historically speaking. The Species had been hanging around for centuries plotting revenge against the prador, and during the war joined up on our side. Some say that the terror weapons we used – like the parasite assassin drones – were an idea that germinated in the creature's serial brain. Others talk of some super-weapon it created that Polity AIs were too terrified to use. By and by, the Client's existence has slid into rumour and hearsay. The final act in the story, be it fact or fiction, was of the Client's grisly death and of a large payment in diamond slate made by the new king of the prador to a freelance assassin.

From 'How It Is' by Gordon

Angel

The wormship fell into the real, with Angel as much in its exterior sensors as in his body and still confused. He felt a strange nostalgia when looking upon the face of the gas giant ahead. Mandelbrot patterns decorated its surface, slowly changing with its hundred-year season. The face of that thing had been a constant in the sky during Angel's time down on one of its small moons. Via his ship's sensors, he now gazed upon that particular moon. The thing was dense, almost 50 per cent iron, and possessed a strong magnetic field, just like two other moons in the system. Like them, this moon – Angel 4 – interacted strongly with the magnetosphere of the gas giant, ionizing the thin gases perpetually spilling from volcanism on its surface into snow-white trails from its poles – the angel wings it was named after.

Nearby were two ships. A reaver – a huge golden ship shaped like an extended teardrop and one of the feared vessels of the prador King's Guard – sat in a pseudo-matter scaffold in a Lagrange point between the moon and the giant planet. Docked to it like some legless parasitic isopod on a shark was Father-Captain Brogus's battered destroyer. He always remained inside while his children – first- and second-children whose growth to adulthood had been stalled and who were enslaved to his pheromones – were working hard to restore the reaver. They were assisted in their endeavours by the Clade. The collection of strange drones, which were both individuals and components of a swarm AI, worked a great deal more efficiently than the prador. The Clade would also be useful later. Two hundred of its units now resided in the armoury of the reaver, their purpose . . . Angel shook himself. They were part of the plan – yes, that was it.

Drawing closer, Angel looked, with something approaching bafflement, upon all he had wrought here. All his plans, all his steady work here led to his goal of delivering a hard blow against the hated humans, Polity AIs and the prador – he was certain of his goal. Surely he knew what he was doing?

Then what? asked a rogue part of his mind.

The wormship slid through space, closer and closer, and something tightened in his consciousness. He felt his thoughts begin to lose their sluggishness. Darkness receded from his mind, lit by flickering and revolving lights growing in intensity.

The Clade.

Angel tried to locate the swarm AI's main mass and soon found it floating in the upper atmosphere of the gas giant. A big metallic ball that in some ways resembled a wormship, it consisted of thousands of drones. Each possessed the head of a polished steel axolotl and a body like a chrome-plated dinosaur spine. The drones had been made during the Polity war against the prador to penetrate prador war machines and take control of them. But something had happened post-production that caused them to hive together as a single entity, which named itself the Clade. It had been scheduled for destruction shortly after this, but, ruthlessly efficient and amoral, it had murdered its way aboard a departing dreadnought and escaped the war factory where it had been made. It was insane, dangerous and, knowing the right buttons to press, a very useful ally for Angel.

Brogus . . .

Angel opened a com connection and was immediately rewarded by the sight of the father-captain resting in his sanctum. Brogus was an old prador who had shed his legs. His shape was that of a vertically flattened pear, the front, upper piece being his visual turret sporting two large red distance eyes and three smaller eyes either side. His upper eye stalks were missing, as were his claws and mandibles, but these last two he had replaced with prosthetics moulded of brassy metal. Shortly after the connection opened he rose, as if startled, off the floor and hovered, supported by two grav-motors – oval slabs of technology attached to his underside.

'Give me updates,' Angel demanded.

'The work progresses well,' replied the prador, settling to the floor again. He reached down with one claw into a pit control in front of him to send a report. Angel immediately integrated this into his mind and studied it, momentarily losing himself in detail. Then, flashing and turning in his mind like a ring of icy blades, the Wheel was back. He briefly understood that he had felt it impinging on him earlier, but thoughts about that fled in the face of absolute certainties.

Now it was time to fully assert control, and set the prador upon their course. Inspecting the schematics of the prador's much-feared reaver, he saw that despite further work needing to be done, it was ready for flight.

Moving . . .

'Brogus,' he stated. 'It is time for you to transfer yourself aboard the reaver.'

'It is not yet complete,' the father-captain replied.

Angel engaged further, connecting to the neural lace he had installed in the old prador's main ganglion – his brain. He sensed Brogus's reluctance to depart the secure sanctum on his ship, so he exerted pressure.

'As you will,' said Brogus.

'Good. You must prepare for departure.'

Angel tried to remember the things that had been bothering him prior to and upon his arrival here, but they seemed vague now. His mind strayed to events after Trike blew up his ship and thence to the living passenger he had aboard.

Kill her.

It wasn't even a verbalized thought, just a feeling. He felt glassy blades turning somewhere at the edge of perception, then a sudden panic.

'No,' he said out loud, not even sure who he was speaking to. He flicked his attention to his ship's internal sensors, and to Ruth's neural lace. He felt the nascent intention to murder fade. It didn't matter if she lived or died. He controlled her absolutely. She was irrelevant to his plans but might also come in useful. It didn't matter. It didn't matter.

Ruth sat in a chair aboard the shuttle, her mind shut down and her body alive but at its lowest possible functionality. The thought about simply disposing of her briefly surfaced then submerged again. Angel woke her up and, through the neural lace, peered into her mind. She woke with a start, and immediately leaned forwards to try and obtain data through the shuttle's instruments. As he watched the interplay of her thoughts, Angel felt some surprise. They had last spoken when he returned her to her newly repaired shuttle. She had been checking all its systems and thinking frantically about whether to blast out of the wormship, until he put her to sleep again. Now, upon waking, she dismissed that idea to wait for a better chance of escape.

'We have reached my base,' he said, directly into her mind.

She froze, looked around the shuttle cabin, then in a leap of logic said, 'You put something inside my skull.'

'A neural lace,' Angel replied. 'I can reprogram your mind any time I choose. Otherwise you are completely subject to my will. I could, if I so wished, force you to eat all your own fingers, or maybe have you use that knife you found in the shuttle's stores to skin yourself.'

This suddenly seemed like a good idea, but again panic arose and the idea faded.

'What do you want with me now?' she asked.

'You will be useful to me.' Angel paused as his ship drew past the reaver, sudden confusion assailing him. 'Though I wonder how useful.'

'What do you want of me?' she asked, persisting.

Panic again; his mind scrabbled to find a purpose for her.

'Artefacts.'

'What about them?'

'You will be useful in helping me obtain them.'

'How? You know where they are. What do you need me for?'

'You will be useful . . .' he repeated, doubt in every word.

After a long pause she asked, 'Do you not know your own mind?'

'I know my own mind,' he asserted. How dare she question him? Why should he tolerate her for one moment more? Anger surged in him, but it didn't feel real, didn't feel like his own. He abruptly shut her down, suddenly terrified of what he might do – or what *something* might drive him to do.

Cog

Captain Cog gazed at the representation of U-space in the screen laminate, thinking about his past – there was a lot to remember. He thought about his insane brother, lost somewhere on Spatterjay, and though he felt a deep regret about that unfinished business, he suspected it would be best to leave others to finish it. They had more motivation where Janus was concerned.

He considered why his thoughts were straying into territory he had tried to leave behind centuries ago and the answer immediately arose: Trike. The boy was so like Janus. During their ten years together on Spatterjay, Trike had appeared to be calmly logical, but Cog had seen that as a sheen over an inner turmoil. Later, during their catch-up communications, he had seemed happy with Ruth. Whether he had changed then, Cog did not know, but now the old Trike was back – a man forever fighting to stay sane. His mind sat on a precipice and he spent much of his time clinging there with all his might. Maybe something had happened in his past, before he came to Spatterjay and sought out the bite of a leech. Maybe he had simply been born wrong and that had never been corrected.

Cog sighed and rested back in his throne. He filled his pipe with tobacco, firmly concentrating on his actions, and lit it. Puffing out a cloud of smoke, followed by a perfect smoke ring, he then flipped a control on his chair arm to throw up a frame in the laminate. There sat Trike, on his bed in his cabin, hands loose and cupped beside his hips, head sagging occasionally then snapping upright. His eyes were closed, and his expression steadily cycled from calm repose to flickering grimaces, and the occasional snarl. Under his closed lids his eyes were in constant motion, like in REM sleep. Cog knew this wasn't sleep, however, but the outward expression of the man's constant battle with his own mind. There were physical effects too. When Trike was under a lot of stress, as he was now, he ate more – a lot more. Cog had used the ship's sensors to check on the results of this and found that Trike's weight just kept on increasing, though his size did not. This indicated worrying things going on in his body, related to the Spatterjay virus – things that Cog had seen before.

The Old Captain pushed another control, locking the door to Trike's cabin. It wouldn't stop the man if he wanted to leave, but would certainly delay him for an appreciable time. Cog hoped Trike would not get up at an inconvenient moment and trigger awkward questions about the locked door. But it was a precaution he felt compelled to take at a time like this. He then gestured, sending the frame to one side, and opened another one.

'Get Blade online, Janus,' he said, still, after all this time, uncomfortable using that name, and still unsure of why he had named his ship AI after his brother.

'Connection made,' the AI stated.

Something appeared distantly in the frame, black on white, then surged forwards. The face wasn't the usual AI icon. It was midnight black, the eyes pale green with pinpoint pupils. Depending from its ears were small silver daggers. Cog supposed it was as good an icon as any to represent the black-ops attack ship *Obsidian Blade*.

'Where are you?' Cog asked.

'In U-space, where do you think?' replied Blade.

Cog sighed. He had no intention of getting into a discussion about time and distance where U-space was concerned with an AI ship. 'How long till you reach the coordinates I sent you?'

'Two days – your time.'

'Mmm.' Cog sucked on his pipe. 'Let's hope you arrive quickly enough. We don't actually know what we have here. Any historical detail?'

'The coordinates are just on the edge of the main action that took place against Erebus,' Blade replied. 'We speculate that the legate survived there during Erebus's self-destruction – probably EM-blocked from that AI's mind. The system is uninhabited and marked as only having potential for H4 mining.'

'That doesn't give us much of a clue as to why the legate is heading back there.'

'We are inclined to think he might have a base or something else there. It is an ideal location just outside the Polity, and Angel might have established something on what he feels is familiar territory.'

'I see,' said Cog.

'And why else would he travel out here?' Blade added.

'Why indeed.' Cog ground his teeth for a moment then got to what he really wanted to say. 'Now, we are agreed that, if it is at all possible, you will retrieve the body of the woman Ruth.'

'I have my orders and you have yours.'

'Still –' Cog paused for a second – 'if her body is intact it is running a nanosuite that will keep it preserved. Resurrection is a possibility.'

'I will endeavour to retrieve it if it is still intact and if, with tactical considerations, that is a possibility.'

'Good,' Cog replied, feeling slightly uncomfortable and glancing at the frame showing the image of Trike.

'But you know how unlikely that is.'

'Yes.' Cog nodded grimly.

'I see you are slightly off coordinates,' Blade observed.

'Yes, I thought that safest,' Cog replied. 'More chance of detection if I get close.'

'Quite.'

'So I guess I've done all I can for now.'

'You have done all you can, Captain Cogulus. This Angel represents a dangerous threat to the Polity. The life of one woman must be weighed against this creature's potential for destruction and other lives lost.'

'Cold calculations.'

'You've known that for a long time, old friend.'

Blade cut the communication. There was nothing more to say, really. Cog sat back, freeing the locks on Trike's door, and at that moment the man opened his eyes. The locks were silent, so surely he could not have heard them? Then he closed his eyes again.

Cog sat back and pondered recent events. It had come as a surprise to him to be contacted by Trike after so long. Focused on his own particular business at the time, he had been inclined to fob the man off, until he heard the story. He then sent a message to those above him, and their response had been immediate: 'Help Trike, stay on this – we want Angel and that wormship.'

Trike had already retrieved Ruth's excised memories and there was no time to get the *Obsidian Blade* to Trike's meeting with the creature. Anyway, the detail of Cog's orders was to watch, since there might be others like Angel and something that could be hit with more effect . . .

Trike opened his eyes again and stood up abruptly. Cog checked the timer running at the bottom of the screen laminate. Just as on other occasions, Trike got himself on the move precisely eight minutes before the ship was to surface from U-space. Cog wasn't really sure how the man did that. Trike headed to his sanitary booth, so Cog cut the feed and waited.

'We should be there soon,' said Trike, as he finally stepped onto the bridge, thick black coat on and buttoned up to his neck again, as if it could hold in the madness.

'Did you sleep well?' Cog enquired, wondering if it was his imagination that Trike appeared taller.

'Like a bird,' Trike replied. Cog wasn't entirely sure where the expression came from but understood the implication. He wondered if Trike had lied to Ruth about this when they slept together, or if she had known, or even if he actually did sleep when he was with her.

Trike seated himself in another chair, observing the instrumentation readouts along the bottom of the screen laminate. 'Those are not the coordinates I gave you.'

'A precaution,' Cog replied. 'We'll arrive two light days out. Softly, softly.'

Trike grunted, whether in agreement or otherwise it was difficult to tell.

They sat in silence until a chime rang. Cog felt his ship surface from U-space – a familiar tug and twist almost like nostalgia. The slow grey and silver swirls in the main bridge screen cleared to reveal deep black vacuum sparsely scattered with stars.

'Gathering data,' stated Janus.

Frames began opening across the main screen. They showed a gas giant, closer images of its moons, the wormship, a reaver and a prador destroyer docked to it.

'You took a good precaution,' Trike stated. 'It's like you knew.'

'You learn a thing or two by the time you get to my age,' Cog replied, his voice flat.

'Yes,' said the man. 'What do we do now?'

'We move closer and we stay hidden,' said Cog. 'And we wait.'
And in two days we see all hell break loose.

Angel

The Wheel was back and hung in Angel's mind like a lead weight in jelly. He noted via cams Brogus entering the reaver, the legless prador father-captain buoyed up by grav-engines and floating along a ramp, two heavily armed second-children scrambling along behind, towing grav-sleds loaded with the old prador's personal belongings. But Angel could not focus on this because his mind felt out of balance.

Do you know your own mind? Do you know your own mind?

Ruth's words just kept repeating in his skull, but he understood they were not the problem because he found himself clinging to them. It was as if she herself was some kind of anchor for his mind. He felt he needed her, that without her he would lose himself. Her existence maintained a link, and it seemed an essential one, to all the doubts and insecurities he felt just after Trike damaged his wormship. After he lost the Wheel . . .

What am I doing here?

The Wheel now gleamed with hard light and spun frantically inside him. Ruth's words began to break up and under an unnatural wash of calm his doubts began to dissipate. He stubbornly fought it, but the imposed order and calm was difficult to resist.

It doesn't matter . . .

Move . . .

He sighed – there was still atmosphere in the ship – his mind falling into a new shape. He held out his hands and tendrils attached. Clarity descended like a guillotine as he began incorporating further data on the reaver. The Wheel spun hard, slicing away the extraneous, allowing him to concentrate. Angel watched Brogus install himself inside the reaver and begin familiarizing himself with its systems, while some of his children transported further supplies across from his destroyer. The latter ship would be controlled by one of the father-captain's first-children and was meant to follow the reaver, so Brogus could transfer back to it once his task was done. Angel knew this occurrence was unlikely, though it was not clear to him what Brogus's mission was and why he would not survive it.

Other children of Brogus cleared construction paraphernalia from about the reaver. The Clade units that had been working there were streaming away like a shoal of sand eels towards their main mass in the clouds of the gas giant. Angel had no idea why and no idea what to do with the swarm AI. He tried suggesting it go aboard the reaver and join the two hundred Clade units there, but simply received no response. This had happened before. The Clade would react at a later time, or not at all. Yes, that's what would happen.

All was running smoothly. The reaver would penetrate a kingdom fleet. And Brogus would do what he would do – when the time was right.

Except . . .

Angel shook his head. None of this made any sense to him. He could see only the shadows of plans in his mind. What was the purpose of Brogus? Why was he doing this?

The Wheel spun strongly and he remembered something. What was it? Yes, the Cyberat. It was to one of them Ruth had sold the Jain artefacts. Angel would go to their world, where the cyborg humans traded in technology away from Polity or prador interference, to retrieve an item. Then . . . The thought dissolved and seemed to lead nowhere. He was struggling with this when an alert attracted his attention. One of the numerous detectors he had spread about this system had finally accrued enough data to take it above the alert threshold. Though heavily shielded, there had been a radiation pulse identified as a U-space signature out there. The detector could find nothing at the estimated location of that signature. Perhaps Trike had obtained sophisticated chameleonware and followed the signal from the device in Ruth's skull?

Move, said the Wheel.

It felt as if it was responding not so much to potential danger but to Angel's own confusion about his purpose here. The Cyberat . . . his thoughts stubbornly returned to that and he probed memory. A scientist on the Cyberat world possessed a certain useful item. Deployment of this item would result in cataclysmic disruption, the destruction of the defence sphere around the accretion disc and then . . .

Then why all these other preparations? Why Brogus?

The Wheel spun and spun, slicing in his mind. The whole plan started to fall into a logical structure, yet on some level he felt it was not logical at all. He needed to sort this out. He needed to understand perfectly what he was doing here—

Move!

The instruction slammed hard into his mind but he held himself rigid, stubbornly trying to hang on to his train of thought. He needed stillness and time to sort out the confusion—

MOVE!

This time the order was undeniable.

Go, he told Brogus.

Where? the father-captain enquired.

He was about to berate Brogus for asking such a stupid question. To the defence sphere of course, to the accretion disc . . . to . . .

No.

The grip was rigid in his mind and there was no fighting it this time. Coordinates fell into his consciousness and he knew he had not thought of them. He repeated them to Brogus and enforced the order to depart. Even as he did this he understood, for sure, that none of these plans were his own. It was a moment of painful epiphany. The Wheel had been controlling him since it first appeared in his mind. It wasn't always as strong, subtly allowing him to think that all he had wrought here was his doing. But in reality he was a slave.

Now he fought it.

I will always be here, it told him.

What are you? he asked it.

The past and the future, it replied. *MOVE.*

Brogus was forced to pull away the reaver, breaking pseudo-matter scaffolds and sending pieces of them tumbling to evaporate in vacuum. The lock connecting it to the destroyer broke and it too tumbled away, but vented atmosphere. Just free of the scaffolds, the reaver shimmered and disappeared, leaving no disturbance behind. Angel, however, continued to fight and realized the Wheel was weakening. It had lost its ability to compel him as he rigidly disobeyed – refusing to take his wormship out of the system.

Give me reasons, he demanded.

You hate the humans, the Polity AIs and the prador.

Do I? he wondered.

I give you purpose.

Why do you want to attack the defence sphere?

The mental battle continued and finally the Wheel replied, *It is necessary.*

You want to get through to the accretion disc?

Yes, and no.

What is Brogus for?

On this the Wheel remained stubbornly silent.

I will remain here and wait for whatever is out there to come in. I will not fight it.

The first-child had not yet established itself in the captain's sanctum of the destroyer, and Angel could see it was not under control.

You will die.

I have seen the mind of a slave, Angel replied, surprising himself that he had the imagination to put himself in Ruth's position.

I can return you to yourself.

Angel managed a wry smile. The Wheel was not all-powerful. Its grip on him was limited and now it was negotiating.

And what was I? he asked, then felt a sudden fear as the Wheel turned faster, somehow strengthened by this thought.

You were this when I found you.

It seemed everything drained out of him: all will, all purpose and all emotion. The emptiness was appalling. His thoughts existed and interacted but what was the point of them? He felt like something was pulling him down into a deep dark pit from which there could never be any return. But even as he sank, he could feel that grip upon him failing, slipping.

And once you were this.

The clutch upon him released and he snapped upwards out of the pit and into light. His thoughts were diamond bright, proud and arrogant. He was utterly sure about everything he must do, and be – and *was*. He knew in this moment that his mind under the Wheel had sat between these two states. It had raised him up to deploy him as a useful tool, and struggled to stop him climbing further. Then he fell again, and was once more rigidly fighting control, unsure of his own purpose.

Obey me and you will be free. I will no longer require you and I will leave your mind.

Angel believed it. He felt at the heart of his being that once the Wheel had achieved its aims he would become irrelevant. It would not be worth it expending one shred of effort upon him.

I will retrieve this Jain artefact for you, he said. *But I will do it in my own way.*

He took full control of his wormship, and finally moved it away.

Trike

Trike first watched the reaver and then the wormship shift away from the gas giant and drop out of the real. The prador destroyer was still there but did not seem under control. Perhaps Angel considered it dispensable like the rest of the detritus he had left behind. Trike knew he should not be disappointed that the wormship was gone. Logically, what could he do while Angel remained inside it? But logic wasn't what was controlling his emotions and he wanted to break something. With infinite care, he took his hands away from the arms of his chair and stood up. Stepping closer to the forward screen and the various frames Cog had opened in the laminate, he thrust his hands into his coat pockets to stop himself from doing more damage.

'Bugger,' said Cog.

'Indeed,' Trike replied, fighting for calm. He turned to the Old Captain. 'But as you said, we have all the time in the world. We can be patient.' It was an effort to keep a sneer out of his voice.

Cog nodded sharply in agreement and Trike was aware that the man's ill-concealed disappointment reflected his own. Cog was usually so mild and calm. It had been Cog who, when they arrived, pointed out that they could do nothing while Angel remained in his wormship. And it had been Cog who pointed out that there seemed to be no ground base, so therefore unlikely that Angel would be leaving his ship. So why was he like this now?

'We follow,' Trike suggested.

'Yeah,' said Cog, searching for something, different images of surrounding space appearing in a frame on the screen laminate.

Trike felt a sudden surge of suspicion about the man. Should he simply accept that Cog was still helping him out of the goodness of his heart? Was the ten years Trike spent crewing aboard Cog's sailing ship on Spatterjay really a basis for trust? What did he really know about the man? Trike bit his lips and closed his eyes for a moment, hands clenching and unclenching in his pockets.

Stop it.

Paranoia was just one of the many things wrong with his mind and he must control it. What he didn't know about Cog didn't matter. Any suspicions that might grow in him because Cog wasn't acting as usual should be dismissed. He must focus only on actions. Cog had come when he called and, at considerable risk to himself, had helped Trike try to kill Angel. He opened his eyes again, deliberately breathing evenly, and focused on one of the frames open in the laminate.

'What are those?' he asked.

The frame showed a group of silvery objects against the face of the gas giant. They were the things that had fled from their locations in and around the reaver before it departed, and they were now dropping into the upper atmosphere of the gas giant. As Trike watched, a smaller frame brought one of the silvery objects into focus.

'Some kind of machine,' said Cog. 'Looks Polity – like a war drone of some type.'

'Working for Angel?'

'They don't all adhere to Polity law,' Cog replied, then, 'In fact, very few do.'

'So Angel abandoned them and now they're running for cover?'

'I guess.'

Cog returned his attention to another frame, still searching. Eventually he picked out an object against the star field and focused in on it. Here a metallic object, like a rock covered with limpets, floated in vacuum.

'Damn!' the Old Captain exclaimed. 'I didn't see these. He had detectors out – my ship's chameleonware defeated them for a little while but they got something in the end. Pretty damned sophisticated.'

Again that surge of suspicion. The chameleonware of Cog's ship was pretty sophisticated itself. And how did he know so quickly that the thing out there was capable of penetrating it?

Let it go.

'Yet he ran,' said Trike flatly. 'He had three ships there and every one of them was more than capable of dealing with us.'

Cog glanced at him. 'He probably didn't get a good look at us, and thought something else was out here.'

'Like what?'

There was something odd in Cog's expression as he replied, 'Maybe a Polity stealth attack ship. Angel would not want to get on the wrong side of one of them.'

'No, I guess not,' Trike replied, wondering why either Angel or

Cog might think such a vessel would arrive here. He tried to tell himself this did not matter. They would follow the wormship and he would have his revenge, eventually.

The Client

Coiled around a crystal tree in the chain-glass cylinder, the Client studied herself through surrounding sensors. Growth had been rapid once she gained access to an ample supply of food. She now consisted of ten conjoined wasp-like forms. At her head was the primary form, its brain larger – the control centre. This was an adult a month away from dying. When it did, the one behind would displace and discard it – the first of many such husks. At her tail, her terminal segment was giving birth to another, which would remain attached and in its turn give birth as it reached maturity in just a few days. Maintaining this process required a great deal of feeding. All the segments grazed on rubbery nectar exuded by the crystal tree. The crystal roots of this tree were wound into a feeding system Pragus, while under the Client's control, had created. At the same time, slow-moving wormbots would snare future husks and drag them to a processing plant in the base of the cylinder.

The Client now turned her gaze out from the weapons platform. At its present rate of travel Dragon was still over a week away. Why it was approaching so slowly was a puzzle not resolved by anything she found in the remains of Pragus's mind. Perhaps it had been severely damaged during the recent conflict? Perhaps it was still fighting Jain technology within itself? No matter. She was now nearly ready, for the crystal bud she had birthed and attached to one limb of her tree was just about ready to flower. And the intricate U-space communicator at its core was steadily opening a particular kind of portal into that continuum.

Next she surveyed everything at her command. The weapons platform was loaded with lethal weaponry that took its capabilities beyond that of the planet killers both the Polity and the prador had used during the war. It also contained manufacturing capabilities on a par with the war factories the Polity had used then, though on a smaller scale. It also controlled one hundred and twenty attack pods of a weapons system covering a wide area of space. Each of these had the capability of a wartime attack ship, though the intelligence they contained was sub-AI – they were utterly controlled from the weapons platform. This was yet another precaution against the dangers of AI boredom. So, with all this, what could she do?

The Client's prime aim still burned as strong as when she escaped the prador genocide of her species, and as strong as when she worked for the Polity to develop weapons against the prador. She still wanted revenge for what the prador had done, but there would be no help from the Polity now. The AIs had stopped her from ending that race with her farcaster – an open-ended U-space gate that could instantly and accurately place dangerous objects anywhere in the Prador Kingdom. Admittedly those objects were small, because of the farcaster's energy requirements, but then a lethal virus could be more effective than the biggest bomb. The Client churned over ideas in her serial mind. The simplest option would have been to build another farcaster and deploy it as she had once planned. However, the knowledge of how to make such a device was gone from her mind. And, even when she reclaimed her whole self, she could not build it from here. She had subsumed the mind of Pragus and could pretend to be that AI at any time, but it would be impossible to conceal her attack on the prador once she started it. The other AIs and entities here would know at once, as would Orlandine, and Dragon.

She should leave . . .

But not yet. She needed her whole mind. Besides knowledge about the farcaster, there were other things in it that might be critical.

The Client waited, birthing another sub-form of herself and extending the chain of her being, the U-space communicator in the crystal bud steadily self-building, growing, maturing.

Two days passed, Dragon still drawing closer at the same speed as before. The bud opened, its intricacies expanding, filling and connecting. In its heart it opened the small coded gate into U-space, to a location there without the physical dimensions of realspace. Here, swirls of pseudo-matter filled a cyst of semi-real existence, and here lay her backups. The Client fed in power to this cyst, and it back-splashed through the gate as data. Now connected to a recording of her own mind stored there, updated at some time just prior to her death, she prepared to receive everything. Then she detected a U-signature close by – something had arrived.

'Just what I was waiting for,' said Dragon.

The giant alien had jumped instantly to just a few miles out from the platform. Something routed through, a flickering of shadow matter. The Client realized what had happened just a moment before the detonation. Dragon had fired a U-jump missile. The nature of this missile's technology, fired into a realspace area where a U-space gate was open, meant it immediately fell through the gate. In horror, the Client saw it detonate inside the cyst, destroying the data recording of her past mind and everything she had been. Then she looked to her own survival, firing a U-jump missile back at Dragon. This was lost through an open gate inside the entity, so she turned to particle beams and railguns. Dragon fired another missile, and with the Client's communicator gate still open, that too fell into U-space. Powerful particle beams cut deep into Dragon's hide, and railgun missiles were just a moment away from striking. In the intervening moments the two entities communicated at AI speeds.

'Why?' asked the Client.

'You do not know what you are,' said Dragon. 'It is better you remain that way – for now.'

'You could have destroyed me with that missile before my U-space communicator opened, but you destroyed my backup instead.'

'I just tried to destroy you, after destroying your old self.'

'You are lying. You knew that would not work.'

'It's a habit of mine,' Dragon replied. 'Anyway, you do not have the knowledge you had and you never will, and shortly you will be destroyed.' Its U-field closed round it like an eyelid of blackness and Dragon fell away into that continuum, away from danger.

Now all the other AIs had been made aware. The Client saw five pods of her subsidiary weapons system explode, while particle beams stabbed out from the nearest pods of her neighbour weapons platforms. Various communications came through, hard undeniable orders landed in the mind of Pragus that it could not disobey, but was now incapable of obeying.

It was time to leave.

The Client chose a destination from what memory she possessed and initiated a jump for her weapons platform and her remaining pods, even as four more of them exploded and particle beams struck Platform Mu, chewing through armour. As she made the jump she felt the deployment of USERs – weapons to disrupt U-space. And she fell, twisted and cursing out of the real.

5

Dragon is an oracle or a liar, a massive biotech charlatan or the alien speaker of truth we either can't or don't want to comprehend. Neither humans nor AIs have any clear understanding of this alien. Four Dragon spheres were found on the planet Aster Colora after the war against the prador. It purported to be an emissary from a distant alien race. There this entity conducted confusing dialogues with those who sought to understand it, before delivering vague threats to a human ambassador concerning the extent of its own power, and then disappeared. One sphere made a reappearance and caused a runcible failure that resulted in the deaths of 30,000 humans. That sphere was destroyed. Other spheres assisted in the Polity police action against the entity Erebus and arguably helped the Polity win, saving an incalculable number of lives. One sphere is now assisting in containing a massive infestation of Jain technology in an accretion disc, because this tech destroyed the race that made Dragon. Did it break into four separate entities whose purposes diverged? Does it, or they, have an overall purpose or none at all? Personally, I think our problem in understanding Dragon is our attribution to it of some higher purpose when it may be doing no more than keeping itself entertained. Some contend that much is lost in translation between us and a mind that is wildly different. I contend that it is quite capable of clear communication with us, but enjoys the confusion.

From 'How It Is' by Gordon

Orlandine

Orlandine watched the four drones. They bore the appearance of giant, thick-limbed iron spiders without abdomens, and were carefully easing a mass of tightly wound, superconducting coils into the casing of a complex grav-engine. The drones had to be very strong, because the coil assembly was the size of a small shuttle and massed perhaps four times as much. It also had to be positioned precisely, to the thousandth of an inch. This was all happening at a point in the scaffold running around the inside frame of the runcible U-space gate they were constructing. This grav-engine was the two hundred and fifteenth and there were twenty-five more to affix.

As she watched, Orlandine completed a final thorough search of the data and found nothing to confirm her suspicions. All the schematics and other technical data the drones were using here matched the original designs she kept in remote storage. If Dragon had done anything, it was simply interfering with supplies to delay the project. She cooled down a little and found some perspective. If Dragon wanted to interfere here it could simply tell Earth Central. Yes, if Polity dreadnoughts arrived, that would piss off the prador, but the project would be dead thereafter. Even as she thought this, finishing minor searches and turning towards the inspection pod she had been using to survey the runcible, remote systems of her being picked up that she had just lost a defence platform. Other data on events at the disc, recently loaded to the system by Dragon, also became available to her.

'Oh peachy,' said Orlandine out loud, instantly gazing at the realtime schematic of the defence sphere around the accretion disc. She opened com to Dragon. 'You never thought to mention this to me before taking action?'

'You would have attempted to rescue the situation and in so doing made it worse,' Dragon replied.

Orlandine resisted the impulse to hurry. Her arrival back at the accretion disc a few minutes earlier would make no difference whatsoever. She opened the petals of her sensory cowl as she gazed at the alien entity through distant cams. It was just an instinctive response to threat, rooted in her human component, since the cowl had been offline during her inspection. In irritation, she closed up the petals behind her head again and they slid out of sight into their pocket in the nape of her neck.

What was Dragon up to?

Dragon had woken her all those years ago and brought her to the accretion disc to finish constructing the defence against the Jain tech. On the face of it, this was simply about survival and revenge. The species that created Dragon had been wiped out by Jain tech and it was helping the Polity to fight that old enemy. But Dragon's motives had never been so simple and its behaviour now further aroused Orlandine's suspicions. It had acted on its own again. And it was being a little parsimonious with the truth.

'Give me all your data on this,' she demanded.

'It's not necessary,' said Dragon. 'The platform was subverted by an alien incursion. I attacked and the other platforms attacked afterwards. And the USER disruption will have finished the job.'

The underspace interference emitters, the USERs – in this case U-space mines deployed by the other platforms – would have interfered with the jump Weapons Platform Mu had made. It was certainly possible that this had destroyed it because disrupted jumps usually resulted in wreckage at the other end.

'I want that data,' said Orlandine.

There was a delay before it arrived. Orlandine felt this confirmed Dragon was lying. Usually it would have sent such data right away rather than engage in chit-chat. She felt she had been sent something it had cribbed together to back up its story, and consigned it to storage, intending to examine it closely later.

'This rather screws things,' she stated. 'We now have a hole in the defence sphere.'

'A new defence platform is being constructed,' Dragon observed. 'Also attack pods.'

'And meanwhile?'

'We bring spare pods from the other platforms and I fill the place of Platform Mu,' said Dragon. 'But this is not full coverage. I suggest you expedite construction of the new platform.'

'Yes, I should get onto that at once,' Orlandine agreed, though in her heart not agreeing at all. Dragon was telling lies and this seemed to confirm what she suspected this was all about: Dragon did not like what she was doing here and wanted to delay it, not approving of her plan to gate a black hole into the accretion disc. Reaching the inspection pod, she pulled herself inside and with a thought sent it shooting around the inside of the runcible frame. After a moment, she made a hard turn into an exterior stem to the protrusion where her ship was docked.

'Take Platform Mu's position,' she said abruptly to Dragon. 'I'm telling the other platforms to send over spare attack pods.' She did this with just a small portion of her haiman mind. 'There should be enough for about half coverage but it will do. We spent many years containing this with a lot less than we have now anyway.'

'Very true,' said Dragon.

She expected it to try and affirm that construction on the new platform, currently in orbit about Jaskor, should be speeded up, and that perhaps resources should all be directed to that end – away from here. But Dragon probably knew she would be suspicious of that, if it had not already surmised she knew it had been lying. She pulled the inspection pod to a halt and propelled herself out of it, not bothering to slot it back in its rack. A few minutes later she was in the airlock to her ship, then inside – already in control and undocking it, sending it out and away from the runcible as she headed for her interface sphere.

Dragon had been reserved about her plan from the start and had grown increasingly uncooperative about it. Either it knew something about the likely results of the plan that it wasn't telling her, or it simply did not know enough and felt the whole thing was too risky. But had it done what she suspected? She studied data on this Captain Marco but could see nothing there, or elsewhere. All the peripheral data backed up Dragon's story about an alien entity taking over Platform Mu. But confirmation came in an encrypted file from the AI Pragus, which, as the only one with access to it, Orlandine now read.

All the platform AIs were in danger of being taken over by Jain tech. Orlandine had known that from the start, so had established the backup facility in the Canine Mountains. From there she could seize control of any weapons platform, or rather, any of its systems that had not been subverted. Perhaps she could have done something had she known about the takeover of Platform Mu? Yes, but no alert had been forthcoming until now. Instead she turned her attention to a data store in the facility. This was a ghost drive. Everything an AI did aboard its platform, along with some portion of its surface mentality, was constantly transmitted from the platform to the facility. The information was laid down in petrified storage – written as a molecular code in a carbon substrate – so could not be changed. Energy needed to be supplied for it to be read. It was utterly impervious to any kind of computer life so could not be destroyed by a virus or a worm. Hard-wired history.

Orlandine reviewed what had happened on that platform; the alien husks brought aboard, Pragus's insatiable AI curiosity and resurrecting the alien. She saw the point when the AI was taken over and when, before anything in the facility could send her an alert, it was disconnected from its ghost drive. Everything Dragon had said, to this point, was true. But what about Dragon's attack? It was here that Orlandine found the big glaring hole.

Dragon had jumped in close and used a U-jump missile – a supposed attack on the alien entity. The problem here was that detectors on the other platforms had shown no explosion actually within Platform Mu at that point, yet they had detected an odd U-space signature there. Dragon had fired a missile which had been drawn into some kind of gate the alien had opened. Why? Dragon would have identified the gate and known firing such a missile was a waste of time, let alone the second missile. Also, it had been close enough to use other weapons like its powerful white laser. Why did it not use that? One thing was certain, Dragon could have killed the alien. Had it done so, that alien would not have U-jumped and Orlandine would not have lost both a weapons platform and its subsidiary weapons system.

It was about resources, surely?

Dragon knew that to finish the new platform would require a diversion of resources. This would be sure to put other projects on hold. Like her runcibles. This, Orlandine felt, was why Dragon had been dissembling, though it seemed likely there was more to parse here.

'Where are you going?' a voice interrupted her thoughts.

She smiled grimly. 'Back to the accretion disc, Cutter.'

As there was no reason to keep anything from the drones here, she put together a précis of recent events in her mind. She dispatched it to them and, after a pause and a lightning-fast debate, Knobbler replied.

'Suspicious,' he said. The drones had more doubts about Dragon than she did, but they were a suspicious bunch by nature.

'I need to investigate this,' she said. 'And I need to talk to Dragon.'

'We're coming,' said Cutter, obviously including Bludgeon. Even as the mantis drone spoke, Orlandine saw a capsule launch under high G from the big runcible. She gave a mental shrug and waited, impatiently, as they approached.

Earth Central

Earth Central, de facto ruler of the Polity, was not the first AI to bear that name. The current iteration, because it had learned the dangers of arrogance, had grown and changed over the years. At one time EC had been a lump of quantum processing crystal the size of a tennis ball, securely ensconced in a building on the shores of Lake Geneva. Now, however, four constantly updated versions of its root personality resided in four such crystals. One was still by the lake, another deep down in the subterranean ocean of Jupiter's moon Europa, and another in an armoured space station orbiting a nameless red dwarf in an uninhabited solar system. The fourth was kept inside a heavily defended and weaponized watch station on the edge of the Graveyard – that no man's land between the Polity and the Prador Kingdom. Also, EC's mind, extending beyond its core personality, was further distributed across the Polity and outside it, taking up small portions of processing space in billions of AI minds. Earth Central was vast and not really at the centre at all, and by spreading itself wide it had limited the possibility of its own destruction.

It hadn't eliminated it.

A human agent, who had once served the Polity, had returned to Earth some centuries ago at the end of the debacle with the AI Erebus. This man, this 'Cormac', had been capable of transferring himself through U-space with the power of his mind. He had also come with a large understandable grievance concerning Earth Central's disregard for human life. That would be the previous Earth Central – the present one's predecessor – whose shattered crystal remains still lay on the shore of Lake Geneva.

Cormac was still about, still watching, and the present Earth Central had no confidence that its current distribution was any defence. But there were other dangers that were not predicated on arrogance and carelessness of life, and it was these EC needed to concentrate on. This was why it now made the accretion disc the main focus of its attention – collecting data via the runcible on Jaskor.

It had watchers there: sunk in the close-cell foam of bubble-metal beams aboard weapons platforms, stuck limpet-like to free- floating chunks of asteroid, clinging like galls in the branches of Jaskoran trees, and skimming round in the edges of accretion-disc dust and gas – thousands upon thousands of them. They were all covert and, admittedly, did not possess the full range of sensors and processing EC would like, but they would do. Anything more effective would certainly be detected either by Orlandine, or by the covert watchers the prador king had scattered there.

So, an alien life form had seized control of Weapons Platform Mu and taken it away. EC pondered the data for a full microsecond, and then gave a mental shrug. It looked like internal politics – Dragon seeking to delay Orlandine's other project, which it had not been much in love with from the start. EC now gazed upon that other project. Here it had only managed to penetrate with a few watchers, who were disguised as essential components in mining machines on one of the gas giant moons not far from the two runcibles. It was difficult to get more watchers there since Orlandine was so paranoid and secretive about it. She was sure that EC would send warships to terminate the project if it knew. EC saw no reason to disabuse her of that notion, since that was something it might yet do. Anyway it seemed there was no –

EC paused, realizing it was making easy assumptions.

The line of thought stopped and EC put a larger portion of itself onto assessing the data for what had happened there. In a brief aside it activated a dormant watcher in the Canine Mountains on Jaskor and gazed upon the Ghost Drive Facility. The place looked like a city of skyscrapers fashioned of black glass and chrome. Here was Orlandine's uplink to her weapons platforms, where everything they did and much of what they thought was recorded indelibly. Its defences, both physical and informational, were formidable, for this was also a weak point, a nexus, a route whereby someone or something might be able to seize control of the weapons platforms – in fact an option for which EC had been preparing for some time. However, right now was not that time. EC just wanted information.

Via the watcher, EC deployed codes it had gleaned over the last months and ran a surgical penetration of informational defences. The response was just slow enough for EC to be able to grab what it wanted and get out. The facility itself would register a software conflict but then instantly change those codes and it would be many months before EC could manage another such penetration. Now, with the data, the ruling AI of the Polity began to see new angles; layers of subterfuge.

The recordings from Weapons Platform Mu seemed to show that the alien was the Client resurrected. Observational data from other platforms clearly revealed that Dragon had destroyed the Client's mental backup in U-space. Analysis of the action prior to the platform dropping into U-space also showed that Dragon had perfectly calculated the extent of damage it would receive – enough so that it would look like a serious attempt had been made to stop it, but not actually enough. The Client would have survived the jump, therefore Dragon had allowed it to escape. This was not just about diverting resources from the building of those runcibles. Dragon was playing a much deeper game. But what game?

Analysing . . .

The Client would be bereft without its backup and, almost certainly, seek out data. Its driving impulse of vengeance against the prador would not have changed, so the kind of data it wanted would be its specialism: weapons. Polity sources were closed to it, but there was a vast store of data it would be sure to turn to.

Oh dear.

It seemed Dragon had just fired off a guided missile straight into the Prador Kingdom. But why? EC analysed all information it had collected on Dragon, or rather the one portion of Dragon at the accretion disc since its arrival there. The analysis took a whole three seconds and something immediately became clear: while Orlandine had been building up the defence sphere, Dragon had been searching. Its periodic ventures into the disc had aimed to access the Jain AIs in search of information. Pattern analysis of its physical, EMR and U-space traces indicated, to a probability of just over 60 per cent, that it was looking for a mind. The implications gave EC further pause, and it returned to other data.

The Species the Client came from had been the subject of much speculation amidst AIs and by Earth Central itself. It seemed highly likely that its purported home world, which now lay within the Kingdom, had not been the world upon which it had evolved. Its antecedents were . . . questionable. And, of the questions asked, one answer oddly fitted all aspects of the present situation.

Now, through forty-two cams, EC gazed into a huge room. Within the armoured walls of this place sat a scattering of gigaton contra-terrene devices. The entire room could be ejected from its site in the Viking Museum on Earth's moon. If the CTDs weren't enough to incinerate the room's contents, or otherwise failed, there were the particle cannons, railguns and missile silos on the surface of Luna that could do the job. Within the room stood twenty pedestals and upon these sat chain-glass spheres containing items, and fragments of items, that looked like anything scooped from an old trash dump on Earth. Only these were intricately and intelligently structured down to a nanoscopic level and below. They were Jain tech and, as such, more dangerous than the bombs that surrounded them.

It was all about this in the end. EC could not see the whole picture as yet, but some broad strokes were becoming clearer. The situation at the accretion disc, which had apparently been stable for a century, had not been stable at all. And it had now received a kick with a large dragon-skin boot.

Trike

Chuffing hard on his pipe, and filling the cabin with fragrant smoke, Cog flung his shuttle down towards the surface of the world. It was noisy aboard the ancient thing because it used chemical engines – the only grav effect employed being a primitive engine that simply reduced the weight of the craft.

'You still got the U-mitter connection?' Cog asked, gesturing vaguely upwards with his pipe stem, the craft tilting and nearly turning over until he shoved his pipe back in his mouth and grasped the right-hand joystick again.

Trike nodded. 'Yeah, she's up there.' In his mind he could sense his wife in space above. A little further concentration gave him coordinates in relation to the world, and the world's U-space coordinates. He shook his head. No, not his wife, just the U-mitter. She was dead.

'Lucky he stopped so far out,' Cog commented. 'Gives us a lead on him.'

'But why?' asked Trike.

'Because he needs to prepare, maybe?' Cog pondered for a moment, then continued, 'When he took Ruth his wormship wasn't notably different from other ships found on the Line. It could be he's altering it so that when he comes in, the Cyberat won't be alarmed. This world is no push-over.'

That made sense, but did not answer Trike's underlying 'why?'. Until now, Trike had just been responding to the threat to his wife and then pursuing vengeance. But he had never really considered why Angel was doing what he was doing.

'He comes here to seize items of Jain tech, then what?' he asked.

Cog glanced round at him. 'That's the worrying question.'

They skimmed into cloud that looked as nicotine stained as Cog's fingers, rain like piss sliding off the frictionless screen before them. Finally they dropped out of it into emerald light and sped over the algae-green ocean. White swirls on its surface indicated the presence of underlying rocks or the mammoth creatures Cog's almanac called hoover slugs.

'Why is he doing what he is doing?' Trike asked.

'Power,' Cog replied, 'vengeance . . . We can only speculate. Perhaps he's driven by whatever drove Erebus to attack the Polity. Do we know what did that? Beyond the possibility that he was caught up in the programming of Jain tech to destroy civilizations, we can't know. But in the end, power for its own sake – with the safety it provides – has ever been the driving impulse of villains throughout human history.'

Trike eyed the man. Cog had never really spoken like this

before. Cog seemed to realize it too and quickly added, 'Do we really need to analyse the bugger?'

The Cube came into view, at first just an outcrop on the landmass but then distinctly cube shaped. As they drew closer the mica-in-stone glitter of windows became visible, as well as the various turrets and protrusions. To the right Trike watched a bulbous ship settling amongst the scattering of ships there and recognized it as a prador shuttle. Soon they were flying in over big grey shapes in the sea that looked like manta rays with stunted wings, and hoover slugs. Then they could see oily-looking atolls crowned with vegetation bearing the appearance of shredded red cabbage.

'Okay, Captain Cogulus,' said a voice from the console. 'Take it easy and try not to break anything when you land.'

'Of course,' Cog replied. 'You know I'm always careful.'

After a snort the voice replied, 'Your idea of careful leaves a little to be desired.'

Cog grinned, and blew out a big cloud of smoke.

'They know you here?'

Cog shrugged.

Angel

With his wormship tightly clenched around him, Angel gazed at the view. It had taken four hours to come in from the outer system, where he had paused to alter the shape of the wormship and make a secure link to a deep-space post that connected to Polity information networks. There he had downloaded as much information as he could find on the Cyberat world, and its inhabitants – one in particular.

The planet was vaguely Earth-like but with one-and-a-half

times the gravity. Humans lived here, and one of them had something he required. He considered his options. The humans occupied fortified houses scattered across the surface of the world. Their colony was small – the population was little more than ten thousand, and very specialized. As with any other world outside the Polity, Angel could simply have landed and taken what he wanted, killing anyone who got in his way.

Why not? whispered the Wheel in his mind.

He ignored it and continued his pondering. He had now learned that the item he wanted – the one Ruth sold to an individual here amidst a collection of other Jain artefacts – was quite special, and the humans here were not such a walk-over. They left during the first Diaspora from Earth with a very specific aim in mind. They wanted to be left alone to pursue their fanatical interest in physical and mental enhancement. They were cyborgs and they were dangerous. It would not do to underestimate them in the same way he had underestimated Captain Trike.

Angel now turned his attention to the objects in orbit. There were satellites and a couple of space stations. Some distance out hung an oblate station that apparently contained paired singularities and a variety of particle accelerators – this was where the Cyberat conducted their research into U-space technology. Ships were here from all over. There were trader ships like Trike's out of the Polity and out of the Graveyard. He even recognized two Prador Kingdom destroyers sitting in the Lagrange point between this world and one of its four moons, watched over by a heavily armed space station. A variety of people were drawn here because, when not making interesting alterations to their bodies, the Cyberat traded in information and technology. Most of this took place in the Cube – the large stone castle sitting on the shore of an ocean green with algae, and swarming with those that fed upon it, and on each other.

Softly, softly, Angel decided.

With the wormish structure tight and unmoving, Angel's ship did not look too unusual, while the shuttle from Trike's ship was of course indistinguishable from others ferrying people down to the landing field beside the Cube.

Go, said the Wheel.

No, he replied.

It did not matter how Angel looked, or that his ship had not been identified, or what shuttle he used, while retaining his dense-tech inner workings. The Cyberat were not stupid and possessed a great deal more than the usual array of human senses. And because of his research and interests, the one he sought, Zackander, was a cautious fellow. The Polity had a bounty on Zackander's head, while the prador also wanted to have long, interesting conversations with him – undoubtedly involving lots of sharp or hot implements. He would not let anyone get close to him without deep scanning them. He would certainly not let something like Angel near.

But Angel had this information from the data download and the Wheel knew it all too. As his thinking improved, Angel realized that, though he did not know what the Wheel was, he certainly now knew what it was not. It was not a Polity AI, not even a rogue one. It was highly intelligent yet it completely misjudged certain things in this milieu as if it had failed to understand the basics. So, what was it and what did it want? An alien or an alien AI? Maybe a Jain AI?

Do not delay, it said.

Angel shook his head then turned his attention to Ruth. He needed a foil, a distraction, and a way of locating Zackander. Good that he had her for this mission, though his reasons for keeping her had nothing to do with that. He now understood that subconsciously he had known what the Wheel was doing to him and in his efforts to escape it she had been something to cling to, a small, initial rebellion against its control.

'You are ready?' he said directly into her mind.

She had just finished eating something from the shuttle's supplies and was returning to the cockpit.

'And if I say no?' she asked.

'It will make no difference,' he replied. 'You are going now.'

She sat and strapped herself in. He opened a hole through the wormship for her shuttle and, without much in the way of hesitation, she moved it out.

Trike

The closer Trike got to the Cube the more it looked like a castle. A channel had even been cut to the sea to supply water for a moat. There were buttresses up the sides, with castellations around the protrusions and turrets. As he and Cog strolled down the path from the landing field, heavy packs on their backs, Trike eyed the moat. There were things moving down there in the thick algae. Segmented backs turned like tyres and the occasional stalk-eye protruded from the surface. It quite reminded him of home. But his thoughts soon went back to something else.

'Is Angel's ship moving?' he asked.

Cog took an object like a jeweller's glass out of the top pocket of his shirt and popped it into his eye, adjusting something on the side of it.

'Still where it moved to geostationary above,' he replied, 'but a shuttle just left.'

'It's got the U-mitter with it,' said Trike. 'Its position is changing.'

'Why would he do that?' Cog wondered.

Trike halted and looked back towards the landing field. A sudden wild hope surged up inside him. He took a step in that direction but Cog caught hold of his arm and held him in place. 'What are you doing?'

'I have to go back. I have to see.'

'And do what?'

'Maybe she's still alive.'

'You saw her die,' said Cog, with something in his voice Trike did not like at all.

'Easily falsified,' said Trike.

'Yet you tried to blow up Angel's ship knowing that?'

Why hadn't he thought that what he saw could be falsified? Why hadn't Cog thought of it too? 'Ruth could be alive,' he stated stubbornly.

'And you'll just charge in there and rescue her?' Cog shook his head slowly. 'I'm a lot older, wiser and stronger than you, Trike, and I would not put myself up against that thing. It would take me apart only marginally slower than it would you. It's a legate, a creature based on Jain technology. Face up to it now and it will own you.'

Trike fought against the Old Captain's grip but it felt like a docking clamp. He then grew still and enforced calm, breathing deeply, slowly. He had to concede that Cog was right. 'So what's the plan?'

'We go back,' said Cog, 'but to see a friend of mine.'

Cog released Trike's arm and began strolling back up the path. Trike followed, frustrated and angry. He wanted to do something, but he had to be calm. Maybe, after another century, he would possess the composure of an old one like Cog, but it didn't feel possible right now. In fact, the only time it had ever felt possible was when he was with Ruth. He eyed the rocky ground either side of the track and considered the possibilities of ambush. Angel would have to walk down here – as everyone from the landing field did. Maybe he could hide behind that rock over there . . . And do what? In his pack he carried a QC laser handgun, a machete and a handful of marble grenades. Cog had some more serious weaponry in his pack in the form of a hand-held particle weapon with a few gigawatt power supplies, but none of these were enough to deal with a creature like Angel. It would detect them hiding in a moment and, according to the data Trike had seen, carried more weaponry in just one arm than they possessed altogether. It probably wouldn't even need to use its weapons. That thing could move so fast it would be on them before they could cause it much damage.

Soon they arrived at the gate into the landing field. But instead of going through it using the pass card they had been issued by the auto-guard, Cog turned right and strolled along the ring-link fence. A small spider remote on the inside of the fence scuttled along to keep pace with them. After a moment Cog delved into his pack and took out a squat glass bottle, which he held up and shook towards the drone. The remote seemed to think this over, then it shot up the inside of the fence and over the top, dropping to land in an explosion of dust.

'This way,' said the voice issuing from it.

It led them in the same direction they had been going and finally to a tower incorporated into the fence, its top a hexagonal structure with windows all around. A door popped open in the stem of the tower and the remote scuttled off.

'What coordinates do you have on the shuttle now?' Cog asked.

'About ten miles up,' Trike replied.

Cog nodded and led the way inside the tower, where a steep ramp stretched upwards. It seemed impossible to climb until Cog stepped on it and began walking, his body tipping almost at right angles to Trike's. Trike felt the pull now and realized the ramp was grav-plated. He stepped onto it too, feeling a sickening lurch of perspective as he walked up. Soon they reached the hexagonal room of the tower. Consoles ran around it below the windows, and in the centre of the room was a woman, well, most of a woman. Trike got his first look at one of the Cyberat.

'Hello, Lyra,' said Cog cheerfully.

Lyra clattered round to face them. Her skin was blue and her head hairless. Below the waist her body was a segmented mechanism that looked like a steel centipede, only with longer limbs which terminated in just about every manipulator or tool imaginable. Around her head clung a thick metal band with either sensors or guns on each side – Trike had no idea. Her eyes were orange, her ears pointed. Her long delicate fingers had sucker pads on the ends.

'Oh boy,' she said. 'Sea cane?'

'It certainly is,' replied Cog, holding out the bottle.

She clattered closer and Trike found himself taking a step back. She grinned at him, took the bottle and lowered it to one of her manipulators that extruded a corkscrew and removed the cork in a second.

'Just to try, mind,' said Lyra.

Cog turned to Trike. 'Lyra went to Spatterjay a hundred years ago,' he explained. 'She enjoyed the sea-cane rum and, since her return here and her – enhancements – she's been after a sample ever since.'

Lyra downed about half the bottle. Lowering it, she licked her lips with a pointy purple tongue, and the manipulator quickly reinserted the cork, as if the bottom half of her body disapproved of what the top half had done. She looked thoughtful as she tilted her head to one side.

'Complicated,' she said. 'Alcohol, of course, and fusel oils –

furfural, tannins, aldehydes and volatile acids as expected – also sea salts, some strange proteins and damned me if there aren't living microbes in it.' She held the bottle up and eyed it. 'If I hadn't already drunk a boatload of this stuff in my lifetime I would have been very wary about drinking this. Spatterjay microbes are floating around in there and, if I know anything about life on that world, it is hostile and usually wants to eat you.' She lowered the bottle. 'Barring you, of course, Captain Cog.'

'Don't be so sure of that,' said Cog, grinning broadly.

Lyra blushed and looked down as the manipulator squirrelled the bottle away inside the lower mechanical half of her body.

'You'll be able to synthesize it?' Cog added.

'All but the microbes, but I should be able to breed them from the sample I have.' She smiled. 'Now, is there anything I can do for you?'

'We'd like to tarry a while, and watch a recent arrival . . . arrive.' Cog gestured to Trike. 'Sorry, let me introduce my friend. This is Trike, a hooper as you can see, but a child of the space lanes now, like me.'

Lyra clattered forwards and Trike stepped forwards this time too. She held out one hand with the sucker-tipped fingers and he shook it without flinching. She turned his hand over and gazed at the two ring-shaped scars, raising an eyebrow. Now she was closer he could smell a mix of lavender and machine oil. She was an attractive woman, he realized, his gaze sliding down from her face, over her bare breasts to the point below her belly button where she became all machine. He couldn't help but wonder about sex then, especially after Cog's comment. And then he was sharply reminded of his first years on Spatterjay. While gazing at carvings of mermaids on the cabin deck of one of the sailing ships, he'd jokingly asked the sail similar questions to those occurring to him now. The sail, a huge bat-like creature, was what hoopers used instead of spread sheets of canvas. These natives of the world were paid crewmen, as such. He remembered it, with its long neck coiled down around the mast, raising its crocodile head from the deck and peering at him. He now suppressed a slightly hysterical laugh at the memory of the filthy reply it had given him.

'Always pleased to meet a friend of Captain Cogulus,' she said.

'Pleased to meet you too,' said Trike, now staring at her intently. After a moment that went on too long he realized he was still holding her hand, and released it.

She swept away again and gestured elegantly. Three of the windows, which obviously contained display laminate, flicked to three different views of a descending shuttle.

'Yes, that's the bugger,' said Cog.

'Funny that you're interested in this one,' said Lyra. 'That shit Zackander is using more than his usual bandwidth to watch it too.' She glanced round and smiled at them again. 'Just like he did to watch you two arrive.'

'Zackander,' said Cog, glancing blank-faced at Trike.

'I think his interest in that shuttle has a lot to do with this.' Another gesture brought starlit space up on one screen, a spaceship hanging there like a metallic human brain, with a cluster of pipe-like fusers sticking out the back. 'It looks so plausible,' she continued, 'until you realize that those fusion engines are fake, the outer hull is not one discrete item, and that in fact there is no outer hull.'

Trike concentrated on the shuttle, and in one of the views the sea was now visible. He moved over to another window and, resting his hands on the console, gazed out over the sea, spotting the craft rapidly approaching. Was Ruth aboard, or maybe just the U-mitter? Did Angel know Trike was here, and was he using it as bait? After a moment Trike raised his hands and looked at the blue tinge they had taken on. He then noticed the dents he had left in the console and casually stepped to one side, away from the damage.

'And your analysis?' asked Cog.

'The same analysis as everyone else here,' Lyra replied, 'which is why just about every weapons system we have is powered up and why Zackander has made a deal, ostensibly very much in their favour, with the captains of the two prador destroyers. You must have seen them up there. Of course, he did neglect to mention to them that if things turn nasty they might end up against a wormship.'

'Ah,' said Cog. 'And Zackander made that deal to protect the citizens of this world?'

Lyra snorted contemptuously. 'As ever, he's protecting himself and his research. A Jain-tech vessel arrives in orbit of this world, whose most notorious resident possesses a wealth of Jain artefacts and has made it his life's work to research Jain technology.' She tapped a finger sucker against her skull. 'Coincidence? I think not.'

The shuttle now swept in over the landing field, neatly positioned itself with a spurt of chemical thrusters, then descended on a grav-engine. Something about the style of this landing pulled at Trike's memory, but he couldn't nail it down. He moved back to look at the other windows activated as screens, for they showed a close-up view of the shuttle.

'And now,' said Lyra, 'what can you tell me about that ship and its passenger or passengers, and what is your interest in it?'

Cog glanced at Trike. 'We gain no benefit by keeping secrets, do we?'

Trike shook his head. 'If you think so.'

Turning back to the Cyberat woman, Cog continued, 'The owner of that wormship is a legate called Angel. He kidnapped

Trike's wife who, incidentally, was an archaeologist. He wanted to locate the person she had sold Jain artefacts to.'

Lyra stared at him, waiting, and when he didn't continue she turned to Trike. 'What happened to your wife?'

'Dead,' he replied, 'Or not.' He watched the two of them. Why did their conversation seem somehow forced?

Lyra now raised one hand to the band around her head and a grid appeared briefly across her orange eyes. She lowered her hand and said, 'Ruth Ottinger.'

Trike nodded. 'Yes.' He was absolutely sure now that there was something off about the interplay between these two, but couldn't think what.

'So how did you get involved?' Lyra asked Cog.

'Ruth had excised memories about the Jain tech and Angel sent Trike to see if there was a recording of them. Trike is of course not stupid and knew that he probably wouldn't get Ruth back and that Angel would try to kill him.'

'So he didn't find them and didn't return?'

'He found them and returned to Angel with the memcording.'

Trike saw the sympathetic look on Lyra's face and turned away, focusing his attention back on the display. Anger and regret were at the forefront of his mind but something else boiled underneath. The shuttle was now lowering a ramp and he concentrated on it.

'But he returned only after contacting me,' Cog continued. 'We made a plan – a simple ruse to kill Angel once Trike confirmed that his wife was, as he suspected, long dead. We controlled his ship remotely and rigged its engines for detonation. Trike stayed aboard my ship, talking through a relay. After Angel received the memcording he moved his ship to seize Trike's. We detonated the engines once it was inside the wormship.'

'Angel did not detect your ship?' Lyra asked Cog.

Trike returned his attention to them.

'No,' Cog replied, now unshouldering his pack and delving inside.

'Your ship must have highly sophisticated chameleonware,' she said archly, but there was something insincere in the glance she shot towards Trike. 'It is evident that the wormship was not destroyed, however.'

'Maybe forty per cent of it,' Cog agreed. 'It reconfigured, stopped off at Angel's base, then came here.'

'How did you follow?'

'Twinned U-space transceivers in Trike's and his wife's skulls.'

Again, Lyra shot him that look of sympathy. Trike shook his head as if to dispel an irritating fly.

'So Angel wasn't killed . . . destroyed?'

'Who can say?' Cog lowered his bag to the floor, now clutching some polished cylindrical item in his hand.

Trike returned his attention to the shuttle ramp. The inner door to the shuttle had opened and a figure was stepping out, still in shadow. Trike felt anger clenching a fist around his guts – the urge to throw himself forwards and do *something* fizzing in his limbs. All Cog's 'wait and see' and 'softly, softly' seemed irrelevant now. He just wanted to get down there, use the weapons he had against Angel, then go in and finish it with his hands. The figure now stepped out into the light and Trike recognized her at once.

Ruth.

It was a hammer blow that smashed all the conflicting impulses within him. She wasn't dead. Had Angel been killed in the detonation and Ruth survived? Angel must have falsified everything he had sent to Trike! Somehow, because she was really smart – smarter than Trike, despite his years – could she have seized control of the wormship? Trike turned away from the display and began heading for the ramp.

'I'm so very very sorry about this, Trike,' said Cog.

Trike glanced round at him. The Old Captain was holding up the object he had taken out of his bag, the polished cylinder. Its end was open and Trike could see into its black glittery interior, as though there were stars inside.

'What?' he managed.

Something shimmered and a hand of force picked him up and threw him across the room. He felt a console breaking behind his legs and his back and head slamming into a chain-glass window, which gave way behind him. The shimmer wrapped all around him, oozing darkness as he fell to the bottom of the tower. He hit hard ground, and saw the window bouncing away nearby. Whatever Cog had hit him with could not have hurt him badly, for he was a three-hundred-year-old hooper. He would still get up and head over to that shuttle, Cog had just saved him the trouble of using the ramp. But he remained on the ground, the force-field, or whatever it was, fluttering around him like the wings of a hundred ravens. He tried to fight it, but felt his consciousness sliding away. The last thing he heard, as the wings carried him off into blackness, was Cog speaking to Lyra nearby.

'What the fuck was that?' she asked.

'The only thing that could work on someone like him, without ripping this place apart,' Cog replied.

6

Cyborg: In the past this meant someone whose physical abilities were extended beyond normal by mechanisms built into the body. But since then the meaning has changed. By the end of the twenty-first century there were few human beings to whom that description could not be applied. At the start of the century, prosthetics were just a replacement for body parts and were often inferior, but very soon those replacements were becoming superior to the parts they replaced. By the latter half of the century people were voluntarily substituting eye lenses with versions that gave them eagle vision, computer displays, and access to virtual reality. Others wove electromuscle into their exisiting muscle, reinforced their bones, wrapped soft robots around their hearts and transfused artificial blood. Advancements in nanotech gave them swarms of doctor machines inside their body, while the integration of computer tech and the human brain extended memory, processing and thought. Advancements in biotech then tended to confuse the issue. What is a mechanism and what is mechanical? In popular conception the words roused visions of cogs, wheels and motors – the paraphernalia of the previous industrial age. But a bacterium manufactured to track down and eat a particular kind of cancer is a mechanism, as is a manufactured organic arm. Nowadays, when the word cyborg is used people understand it to mean one thing only: a particular sect of humans who replaced part of their body generally with cogs-and-wheels metal-based mechanism. The psychology behind this you will find listed under Anachronistic Mindsets.

From 'Quince Guide' compiled by humans

111

The Client

Weapons Platform Mu fell into the real as though it was hitting a solid wall. Its slab shape had been twisted one full turn along its length, and it straightened slightly now, spewing wreckage out into vacuum. A series of explosions blew glowing holes in its exterior and ignited hot fires in its interior. But automatic safety systems limited the damage by flinging away CTDs with breached containment vessels. These detonated thousands of miles away, some destroying pods of the platform's subsystem that were now appearing.

The Client emitted an ultrasonic screech as she hung, severed in half, on her broken crystal tree. Her scream also strayed into the chemical realm as she emitted complex pheromones, which were one aspect of her language. The life forms she created in a former existence would have moved to protect her in response to this, but none were here. Even as she screamed she knew she must get control of herself if she was to survive.

The screech died as she shut down the pain nerves to the break in her body. She broadcast chemical communications to her severed lower half and only when there was little response did she realize that the cylinder was losing air. She now concentrated on the essentials of survival – re-establishing contact with the Polity technology that surrounded her. Via radio and microwave frequencies, she began to make connections and get an assessment of the damage. There was just too much data from the entire platform, along with its attack pods, so she cut that down and looked to her immediate surroundings. She began to individually reacquire all the robots that serviced the cylinder, then the fractured computer system integrated around it.

The chain-glass of the cylinder itself was intact. It was the nature of this substance that damage serious enough to penetrate it would have unravelled its chain molecules and destroyed the entire cylinder. However, the ceramal top cap was cracked and leaking air, while the breach sealant circuit, which should have been activated to prevent the leak, had failed. The Client immediately dispatched maintenance robots up there and began loading data from the surviving computers and sensors in the end cap to identify the problem. Meanwhile she concentrated her own physical resources in the top segment of her body. Nearly all the air was gone now and, while she could survive in vacuum for a little while, she needed to increase her calorie burn to survive the temperature drop.

Soon she knew the shape of the problem and realized that the maintenance robots would not be required, so called them back to the base of the cylinder. A critical computer in the automated breach-sealant system had been fried. This stopped the transference of data from the sensors about the crack, or the pressure drop inside the cylinder, to elsewhere. The Client made a link, through herself, from the sensors to another computer in the system and relayed the data. In response, breach sealant expanded explosively from pressurized canisters in the end cap. Fragments of hardening foam snowed down through the cylinder, but the main mass mushroomed into the crack and filled it rapidly. Just a few seconds later the sensors reported a steady rise in pressure. Now, the heaters.

Here the problem was plain. During the disastrous U-jump, the cylinder had twisted a hundred and eighty degrees at its base, severing superconducting cables. These cables had shorted into the base, burning carbon composite and melting metal, before blowing fuses back at the fusion reactor. The Client dispatched a maintenance robot to replace the fuses, since other automation around the reactor was dead. She then had to open herself into more of the network to find the things she needed. A nearby store contained reels of superconducting cable and she dispatched a robot for one of them. Meanwhile, she set other robots to stripping out ruined cables and wreckage.

The air pressure had risen appreciably, bringing the temperature up, but it was still too cold in the cylinder and ice frosted all its surfaces. She shed the lower segment of her remaining upper body, for it was dying, then decoded chemical messages from the other severed lower half of her body. This had shut down to its lowest possible function, but it was fast reaching the stage where the energy and effort required to retrieve it would exceed that of growing a new series of segments. The Client felt a sudden surge of anger against Dragon, but as that passed she began to think more deeply about what the creature had done.

Dragon could have destroyed her completely. Had it sent that U-jump missile before the Client made the U-space link to her recorded mind, that would have been the end. So why hadn't it done so? By destroying her recorded mind it had killed the Client's ability to make farcasters – her weapon against the prador. Was that the aim? How did Dragon know that she needed her backup mind to do this? Anyway, that threat would have been eliminated if Dragon had destroyed the Client's present form rather than her memories. No, there had to be some other explanation. It seemed as if Dragon wanted her to make a breach in the defence sphere of the accretion disc. This was the only explanation that made sense. Certainly, it had not been overly concerned with the Client's survival once the breach was made, for the subsequent attack had almost destroyed her. It had said, 'Shortly you will be destroyed.' The Client relished that the entity had been wrong.

The robot returned with the reel of cable just as the others finished clearing the mess inside the cylinder. They all worked quickly to replace cable. The Client sank into a lower-energy somnolent state while this was happening, only bringing herself to higher consciousness when the robots put the cables in place and it was necessary to switch the power back on. Red-orange light emitted from flat heating panels scattered throughout the cylinder, steadily raising the temperature. Other repairs ensued; special glue injected to repair her tree, and nutrient feeds re-established from its roots. The Client's head-form began to feed first, followed by her other segments. She gained energy and started to bring the lower segments of her front half back up to full function. But by the time she was ready, her severed half was unrecoverable. No matter, the Client could grow herself again. Now it was time to look at the rest of the damage, and survey the place she had brought herself to. Because, despite the disruption to her U-space jump, she had arrived at her chosen destination. And here, she hoped, Dragon would be proved wrong in its other contention: '. . . you do not have the knowledge you had and never will.'

Blade

The *Obsidian Blade* slid into the real like a shard of lignite surfacing in ink. Scanning from the first microsecond it arrived, Blade confirmed the text message Cog had managed to send – obviously Trike had been aboard his bridge, so they couldn't speak. The wormship was gone – the show had moved on. With the available data Blade could only suppose the legate had detected Cog's ship and reacted to its advanced stealth technology, assuming it was a ship like its own.

Blade was annoyed. Foolish mistake to make, but one that had saved the legate's life. Cog was not aware that the 'softly, softly' orders had been rescinded and replaced by 'exterminate with extreme prejudice'. Now that Earth Central knew that the archaeological artefacts were in fact Jain artefacts, it had become

115

rather tetchy. Still, there was time to clear up some loose ends here . . .

The *Blade* cruised into the system and spent a leisurely second or two scanning the debris and found three stray prador obviously dislodged during the rapid departure of the reaver that had been here. It detected life signs and power in their suits, but they were harmless and forsaken – destined to run out of air and die slowly in vacuum. It targeted one and fired, the field-concentrated particle beam splashing on armour for a second then punching inside, causing the prador to take off on the rocket blast of its own vaporized insides. Blade then turned its attention to the other two, and didn't try to convince itself it was being merciful.

'No prisoners?' asked a voice.

With U-space triangulating over the duration of the message, Blade traced its source to the upper atmosphere of the gas giant. The large object there had made no attempt to conceal its position but actively resisted scan.

'I don't have room for prisoners,' Blade replied. 'This is unfortunate, since I am sure they would have interesting stories to tell.' Then added, 'Would have had.'

The attack ship suddenly short-jumped a hundred miles, a particle beam passing through the space it had occupied a moment before. It seemed someone aboard the remaining prador destroyer was taking control, because it was stabilizing, with its weapons operational. It released a swarm of railgun missiles towards the *Blade*, and started probing with the particle beam again. Blade shrugged out hardfields, deflecting the beam, ramped up realspace acceleration and short-hopped again, ready to splinter up a U-jump missile. Then, because it was a little bored, it decided on another approach and locked on with induction warfare.

Within seconds it was in the systems of the destroyer, then into the second-child mind of its navcom. The bitter little mind was almost sub-sentient and could not distinguish the orders Blade now sent it from those it had been receiving from the first-child, who was trying to get a grip on the systems in the captain's sanctum. Blade cut the first-child off and then watched as the destroyer turned on steering thrusters and fired up its main fusion drive, taking it straight towards the face of the gas giant.

'Are we any better than the enemies we kill?' asked that voice.

'Don't be so impatient,' said Blade, 'I'll get to you in a moment.'

Though it was speaking so casually, Blade was wary. There was nothing in Cog's limited data to indicate what this was, and it was still evading scan. All Blade had on it thus far was that it was a spherical object about a hundred feet across, with its density varying all the time, which was odd.

'So what are you?' Blade asked casually.

'We are,' replied the thing down there, 'adaptable.'

It seemed to be dispersing now – spreading out in the atmosphere. Only a second later did a clearer scan reveal that it had opened out into a circular torus hundreds of feet wide. Blade short-jumped, almost instinctively, as a magnetic iris funnelled gas into the centre of that torus. An intense beam of photonic matter stabbed out of it, just a foot wide. Blade's course put the destroyer between it and the torus, yet the beam tracked it and struck the destroyer, throwing it into black silhouette. A moment later it punched out the other side and struck the *Blade*. In the microseconds it took to throw up hardfields, the beam had blistered armour and burned ten feet inside.

Blade jumped again, splintering missiles, U-jumping them to the source of the beam. Multiple detonations ensued, yet the gate effect of the missiles stayed open longer than it should have, snapped back like broken elastic. Objects appeared exactly where the missiles had disappeared outside the ship, and a moment later thumped into the hull.

'Surprise!' said the attacker.

Through exterior cams, Blade identified the interlopers and hit them with anti-personnel lasers, even as they began burrowing through the bottom of the ship's splinter missile furrows.

The Clade, Blade realized.

Here was a kill-on-sight enemy of the Polity, the deranged swarm AI that had escaped disposal during the war and murdered its way out of the factory station that had made it. Two of the four Clade units curled up and shrivelled in laser fire, while the other two decohered armour and transformed into a pseudo-matter state, sliding in through the hull. Meanwhile the rest of the Clade U-jumped from the gas giant – a writhing mass just like the wormship Blade had come here to destroy.

Blade hit it with particle beams and released a fusillade of railgun slugs. That just seemed to stir the thing up, as though it was being tickled. A third Clade unit died inside the ship as an anti-intrusion claw grabbed it and then fried its brain with an EMR pulse. However, the fourth unit grew thin, lost density again and slid through the tightly packed systems of the ship. It wrapped itself around a drive node and, giggling over com, self-detonated. The explosion tore through the ship, spewing wreckage out into space.

'Bye bye,' said the Clade entire, then shimmered and fell out of the real.

Blade sat in vacuum, ripped open, thoughts disjointed and swamped by error reports. It had enough consciousness for anger, remembering a download that had been forced on it about the dangers of arrogance. Sensor data was sparse, but just enough for it to watch the prador destroyer fall into the gas giant, be swallowed into a comparatively minor swirl of cloud, and disappear.

Zackander

The thing up there could be here for reasons that had absolutely nothing to do with him, but Zackander was taking no chances. All the technology in the chain-glass sphere of his lower cyber body was active and alert as he floated a few feet above the floor and slid along one of the Cube's subterranean passages. The walls were hewn through bedrock, and two luggage tubes hovered behind him. Finally reaching a studded synthetic-wood door, he transmitted a particular code known only to him. As the door opened ahead of him and he entered, the empty circular room reconfigured – a response only triggered if the door was opened with his code. The floor divided into sections, then irised open to expose a shaft spearing down into darkness. Zackander hovered over this, transmitted yet another code, then turned off his grav and dropped. Without the code, anyone dropping into this shaft would have smashed into the bottom. And anyone entering the shaft using a grav-engine, or some other method to stop them falling, would have been fried by particle cannons positioned all the way down.

As he fell he checked his feeds and saw a woman leaving the shuttle. Identifying her as Ruth Ottinger increased his fears, since he had had dealings with her before. He scanned her using sensors scattered across the landing field and found the U-mitter in her skull. He had seen this when he scanned her the first time – when she came to sell him those Jain artefacts. But now he also detected a structure like aug nano-fibres in her skull. This could be what remained from a messy aug removal, another kind of augmentation, or perhaps a type of cyber repair to her brain. But he suspected she was some kind of neural lace controlled by whatever was in that ship up there. She couldn't be the one in charge of it – no human as ordinary as her would be able to control it without Jain tech getting inside her and changing her radically.

The iris closed above and lights ignited within the shaft. Tilting his bald, ancient head backwards, Zackander looked up to be sure the luggage tubes were falling with him, then raised one wrinkled hand and inspected it. He felt it time to run another rejuve, but he needed to act fast and take some serious precautions. Staying alive was a bit more of a priority than body maintenance. He felt comforted thinking about all the weaponry and other technology at his disposal. Then a stab of fear struck him in his artificial guts when he accepted that everything he had active right now might not be enough.

Time to wake him . . .

The thought came from the scared organic human in him, not from the enhanced updated copy of his mind, which ran in the metallo-organic substrate of his body's machine component. However, it was a thought worthy of consideration and one he had been playing with for some hours now. Jain technology gave its recipient power and, without sufficient care, ultimately destruction. Zackander possessed Jain technology and had developed some interesting devices from it, including weapons, but he had not immersed himself in it. He had always kept his distance from it, and never used anything, or initiated any process, he did not understand completely – except for that one time when his curiosity and fascination overcame his caution.

The Jain artefacts he possessed could fill a small room if he had not stored them separately, each under their own specially designed heavy security. This was more than in the famous collection of the Viking Museum. Still, it was small when balanced against a wormship, which was an object made by Jain technology if not the technology itself. But what else was up there?

Most wormships were supposedly without AI, for they had been an extension of Erebus's being. However, some were piloted, and now Erebus was dead, so this was the latter kind with another controlling intelligence as soaked in Jain tech as the ship itself. Something must have broken away from Erebus or survived the AI's self-immolation, and then its final eradication by the Polity fleet. Maybe it was one of the AIs that had melded with Erebus when they had abandoned the Polity – whether it was a ship mind, Golem or war drone was immaterial. Or maybe it was one of the things Erebus had made afterwards. Whatever. The ship and the controlling mind were almost certainly more than Zackander could deal with on his own.

A few hundred feet from the bottom of the shaft, irised gravity fields caught and slowed Zackander, then propelled him into the mouth of a horizontal shaft running deep in the planet's crust. Almost without thinking, he transmitted the next code – this one prevented him being diverted into another shaft – and then shot at relativistic speed into a nearby mountain range. As he hurtled along he received an application for com.

'What is it, Lyra?' he asked.

'Interesting news,' she replied, and sent him a file.

He ran it at high speed, getting a rapid update on the two hoopers he had been watching, even though his main interest was the wormship. He listened to Captain Cogulus's story and saw how the captain dealt with Trike when the man recognized his wife stepping out of the shuttle. Now Trike was on a grav-sled and Cogulus was heading with him to the Cube.

'A legate,' Zackander stated, his urgency to be within the higher safety of his home only increasing. He knew the woman couldn't be the one controlling the wormship. From the limited number of choices, he had just wanted to know which bad news it would be.

'Do we have any idea how the wormship and this "Angel" survived?' he asked.

'You have everything I have,' Lyra replied. 'I'll update you if I find anything else. I've sent Cog and Trike to my home and will head there once my replacement arrives.'

'Ask them,' Zackander instructed. 'I want everything – every detail.'

'As you command,' Lyra replied flatly.

'Yes, as I command,' said Zackander, and cut the link.

He started to remember the early years here, when he and his fellows had disembarked from the cryo-ship, and their excitement some years later when they found alien artefacts on this world. He was the last of them now. His fellows had died in a disastrous experiment with the technology they found. Killed by just one of their comrades who had actually introduced the tech into his body, before another lured him to the old landing craft and, in an act of sacrifice, detonated the engines. All the other Cyberat here were either descendants of that first group, or newcomers. Zackander was now their ruler and he knew they resented him. They also did not like how he controlled the remaining Jain tech and sought to acquire more. But they did not understand how such control was necessary in a hostile universe.

At the end of two hundred miles of shaft, grav fields caught Zackander again and propelled him up another shaft, until finally he exited in the basement of his home. The chamber was a mile across, scattered with wide cylindrical chain-glass cases that stretched from floor to ceiling. Within each of these, machines worked on discrete projects – developing some small item copied from the artefacts he possessed. At the top of each cylinder were iron-burners capable of flash-burning everything inside in a matter of seconds. The charred contents would then be shot down shafts straight into the planet's magma. Even that was not enough, and the upper part of Zackander's home – the bit that sat just underneath the planet's surface – possessed grav-engines and a fusion drive. It could reach orbit within just a few minutes, if need be. With Jain tech, no precaution was one too many.

Zackander floated between the cylinders, briefly inspecting ongoing work both visually and at a mental level. But what he really wanted to take a look at was not here, it was in the upper part of his home that held his collection of artefacts. He ascended and cruised along the ceiling to the upper exit portal. Noting that the luggage cylinders were still following, he dispatched them to storage over the other side of the chamber. He would not be trading or selling their contents any time soon.

The portal irised open on his command, and he traversed a tunnel through hull metal and shock insulation, then passed through two sliding airlock doors. His home was of course without the usual prerequisites of human existence. The series of connected rooms looked more like a collection of laboratories and workshops. He paused briefly on the way, to eye a series of three replacement body spheres, each three feet across and containing what looked like Cubist metal sculptures of offal. He really hoped he would not find it necessary to use these replacements. Though, of course, if something destroyed his present sphere it was likely his human half would be gone. Though he backed up copies of himself here and there across the planet, and in orbital installations, losing his human half would undermine the ethos of his existence.

An armoured door with heavy computer security now lay before him, and this would admit him to his collection. But before he reached it he received another alert. Somebody had requested a comlink to him from the Cube. He paused to check the source and saw that the woman Ruth was now sitting in one of its secure com-booths. From there, just like all arriving traders, she could talk to any individual Cyberat she wished to make a deal with. But she couldn't send anything dangerous over a link she made – the security was very heavy. Though of course 'nothing dangerous' covered the kind of computer attack the Cyberat knew about. She might have something Jain-based and lethal she had prepared. Zackander considered ignoring her, but then his curiosity got the better of him as it sometimes did. He put in place his own security – the best he had – then opened the link.

'Zackander,' she said, a brief shallow smile flitting across her features. 'I am here as a representative of my boss, the Golem android Angel.'

There the first lie, thought Zackander cynically.

'Hello, Ruth, it's been a long time. How are you?'

She blinked. 'I'm . . . okay.'

He noticed her eyes were black and, reviewing recorded memory, saw that they hadn't been before. Cosmetic enhancement? He doubted it – something radical had happened to her.

'And what does your boss want of me?'

She held up a simple plug-in com relay. 'He would like to talk to you himself, but I have to have your permission to use this, apparently.'

'He could be sitting where you're sitting, if he had so chosen,' Zackander observed.

'He can explain the reasons why he is not.'

'Then by all means, use that relay.' Zackander was confident his security would be enough. He could shut down com in an instant if anything looked suspicious. And still, he was curious.

She reached down and plugged in the relay. An instant later her image was replaced by that of a metalskin android. For a second he wondered if what Lyra had passed onto him had been wrong, but reconsidered. A legate could choose to look however it liked.

'So what can I do for you?' he asked.

'You are understandably cautious,' said Angel. 'By now you know what my ship is and perhaps have some idea what I am. Obviously, I sent my agent down to your world because if I had come myself your security systems would not have allowed me to land. Nevertheless, you must understand that your own particular interests, and your collection, are what have drawn me here.'

Zackander just nodded.

'I am not here to cause you any problems,' said Angel. 'I just want to trade – just like any of the others here.' He paused for a second, and a subframe appeared in the corner of the screen with an image. Zackander recognized the Jain artefact. 'I want this object.'

'I see,' said Zackander, playing for time and thinking furiously. 'And what do you want to trade for it?'

'The entire schematic of my ship,' Angel replied. 'You will need a great deal of storage to take it.'

Zackander just stared, acquisitive greed rising up in him. If true, that was one hell of a deal to make. A wormship schematic would be worth more than nearly all the items in his entire collection – but for that one item. The problem was that he now knew what that artefact was, and the bigger problem was that the thing no longer contained what the creature before him was obviously after.

'I will have to consider this,' he replied. 'I am concerned for my own safety – obviously – and will have to make arrangements. I would need to confirm that what you send me is actually a schematic. I will have much to do.'

'We have a deal?' Angel enquired.

Zackander allowed a brief silence, then nodded sharply. 'We have a deal.'

'Contact my agent when you have made your arrangements,' said Angel. 'She will wait there in the Cube for you.'

The legate's image winked out to show Ruth with her head bowed, staring down at her lap. Zackander gazed at her for a second then cut the link. He took a deep breath, and once again focused on the door before him. It clonked open and he floated through into his collection.

Some of the safer Jain items sat in a cluster of chain-glass cases at the centre of the room. Around the walls circular blast doors opened to other artefacts he either knew were dangerous or had failed to understand fully. Over on one side, another door opened into a part of the ship that could be ejected at high speed. Zackander went through, and felt a chill in the air even though the compartment within it, held at just a smidgen above absolute zero, was perfectly insulated. He sensed this was more psychological than anything to do with the physical temperature. Just inside the square room, he turned on the display wall directly ahead and gazed into the compartment. He ascertained from the regular data updates that, despite being held at such a low temperature, the thing in there was moving in painful, almost undetectable, slow motion.

In one of the artefacts Zackander had obtained – a small chunk of black metal triangular in section and about the thickness and length of a human finger – he had found the usual tightly packed and intricate technology. A year or more of analysis revealed that maybe this thing was a discrete device rather than one of the fragments he had often found. All that intricacy seemed directed towards a small bubble in the middle. This bubble, he quickly discovered, was something he could not penetrate. When, some decades later, he was able to upgrade much of the technology he used with Polity technology, he soon ascertained what the bubble was. It was only theorized in Polity science. It was a blister in space-time – a stasis bubble inside which the usual rules of space and time did not apply. Inside it, time had been stopped. After years of research into the device that maintained this anomaly, and which still lay beyond Polity science, he found out how to turn parts of it on and off.

It was this device that Angel wanted.

Some years ago, Zackander then found a way to turn the bubble off. But he made extensive preparations before doing anything, for, even though the bubble was just a fraction of an inch across, he knew that the small size of Jain tech did not necessarily reduce its lethality. Finally he managed to turn it off and, when he saw what it contained, worked quickly to preserve it.

Inside had lain a ring of genetic material laced through with crystal quantum computers. Even as he removed it from the device and sought to preserve it, it activated and began gathering materials from the air. In panic he reinserted it in the device and tried to turn its stasis bubble back on, but it would no longer activate. He took the material out again and put it in a vacuum safe, but the thing steadily unravelled and speared out tendrils towards the walls of the safe. He considered destroying it for he knew that still lay within his power, but could not bring himself to. Instead he stuck it in a cryo-freezer, steadily reducing the temperature until movement stopped, which it only did at absolute zero.

Further years of study ensued. Here, he realized, was the genome of a discrete organism, but with large amounts of nanotech and even picotech interlaced. This meant that if he let this thing run its course, just tossed it out into any environment where materials and energy were available, it would grow. It would develop into an organism but it would also grow a technology as part of itself. It was a cyborg, just like Zackander, and he felt a fellow feeling for it – a sympathy. Of course, the safest thing to do would be to keep it somnolent and study it further to learn everything about it. This would have been his usual course of action. Perhaps he felt alone, or perhaps he just had a moment of madness? He obtained an even larger zero freezer – the one before him – and carefully inserted the now partially unravelled ring. Raising the temperature had it seeking out nutrients, which he supplied in vaporized form. The thing transitioned into an embryo, growing limbs and becoming larger, and he studied it as it did so. Nanotech spread computing and other systems through its body. The weapons became recognizable . . .

And here it was.

There was no doubt that the thing before him was a soldier, but whether it was actually a Jain or something they had created, there was no way to tell. He rather suspected that with technology this sophisticated the Jain could have chosen to be anything they wanted, just as many in the Polity were now able to choose.

Orlandine

Chunks of bubble-metal, with twisted beams attached, tumbled through vacuum. Orlandine spotted a hemisphere trailing wiring and pipes – all that remained of an antipersonnel laser installation. There was something else that looked like a chromed grand piano with twisted legs she identified as the remains of a heavy maintenance robot. This was the wreckage Platform Mu had left behind upon its departure.

She turned her attention to Musket Shot, the leaden planetoid out here in the defence sphere, and noted impact sites on its surface still emitting a dull red glow. Then she focused on another sphere – fifty miles across, creamy white, and on closer inspection, covered with diamond-shaped scales.

'It is only a very small hole in the defence,' Dragon noted.

'But a hole I must close,' Orlandine stated. 'I calculate that using all resources to get the new platform ready and into place will delay my other project by four months.'

'Quite so,' said Dragon.

Orlandine absorbed that and analysed her response. It was, she realized, her human component that was hamstringing her with Dragon. She felt gratitude to him for saving her and a kinship since having worked so long together on the defence sphere. To be simply human was to be weak, and again she questioned her impulses to keep returning to that state. She then decided it was time to stop allowing her feelings to drive circumspection. 'The creature that seized control of Platform Mu established itself in a chain-glass cylinder along the open edge of the platform. You could have killed it with one white laser strike and with minimal damage to the platform.'

'The creature would have deployed hardfields,' Dragon stated.

'You used a U-jump missile to attack first, in full knowledge that a bounce gate was open in the platform – that the missile would be drawn into U-space.'

'It all happened so quickly,' said Dragon blankly.

'Why do you want to delay my plan?' Orlandine asked directly.

After a long pause Dragon replied, 'Precisely describe your plan.'

She had already sent Dragon a full work-up of it – complete in every detail – but she decided to play along. 'I intend to use runcible gates to move a black hole of approximately eight solar masses here to the accretion disc. The black hole will hoover up the accretion disc, the proto-planets and the dead star, along with all the Jain technology. Simple solutions are the best.'

'The arrival of a black hole may cause the premature ignition of the dead star,' said Dragon.

'Twenty per cent chance at best.'

'There are forces at work against us,' said Dragon.

'What? What the fuck are you saying?'

Humanity reared up in her with anger and bewilderment.

'To play the game, without full knowledge of the consequences, is to lose the game.'

'Oh right, getting all Delphic on me,' Orlandine sneered. 'Perhaps if you were clearer about your objections we wouldn't be one weapons platform down.'

'Jain history is long, with many evolutionary twists, the loss of a platform may yet be a gain.'

'Try, just this once, to be clear.'

'I am clear, but perhaps your abhorrence of what you are blinds you.'

'I love what I am.'

'Human time?' Dragon enquired.

'You are deliberately angering my human component to confuse the issue,' said Orlandine. 'Explain yourself.'

'Very well.' Dragon paused again for a long time. 'Why is Jain technology active here in this accretion disc?'

'A weakness in the fabric of space and some connection with the Jain AIs in U-space.'

'As ever, in all things, correlation is not causation.'

'You're saying that the concentration of Jain technology here caused the weakness in space thus opening an easier connection to the AIs?'

'Again: correlation is not causation.'

'Perhaps no connection at all?'

'This is a possibility,' said Dragon. 'Just as it is possible that there may be some other as-yet-unknown agency. All Jain technology is a trap.'

Orlandine replayed the conversation in her mind and this time, rather than get angry, tried some deeper analysis.

'Are you saying that using the simplest solution for clearing out this infestation of Jain technology may be falling into a trap?' She paused for a second. 'I would hardly call gating a black hole here a simple solution.'

'Something is at work,' said Dragon.

'These "forces at work against us"? Is that what you're talking about?'

'Further investigation is required before you initiate your plan.'

'Why?'

'That a connection can be made to the Jain AIs is just a by-product of a weakness in the space-time fabric here. The technology infesting the disc reacts to that connection but is not a product of it. Some other intelligence is at work at the interface. An active intelligence.'

It took a second for Orlandine to process that and all its implications, since it was the longest speech she had ever heard from Dragon.

'You know this, how?'

'Because, when I tried to interrogate the Jain AIs about the history of the accretion disc in their time, something cut my connection to them.'

Orlandine thought long and hard and said, reluctantly, 'Then we must find out what this agency is—'

'Before you try to use a black hole here,' said Dragon.

'Very well,' Orlandine agreed, then tightly, 'but I will continue preparing. Nothing you have said inclines me to think that my plan is the wrong one.'

Dragon did not reply – the link to it closed. And after all that, Orlandine realized, she still had no explanation as to why Dragon had not destroyed the thing in Weapons Platform Mu, nor about the length of Jain history, its evolutionary twists and why the loss of that platform might yet be a gain.

7

*I find myself responding with weary, almost jaded acceptance, when yet
another dangerous AI destructively reveals itself to us. Ah, what's this,
Earth Central? What's this, all you pure-minded wonderfully advanced
AIs of the Polity? What's this, you paragons of virtue who gaze with such
aloof disdain upon us poor evolution-driven organisms whom you see as
barely clear of the muck? Something you neglected to mention? There was
Penny Royal and that monster's murderous Golem, there was the Brockle
who delighted in excessive responses and torture, and there was Erebus,
which some contend could have destroyed the Polity. These are just a few
of those that captured the popular imagination. How many others are
there that have kept themselves below the murder radar – whose depre-
dations have remained just below some arbitrary Polity AI threshold so
as not to warrant a drastic response? Well, I'll tell you: there are hundreds
of them out there. Our oh-so-civilized AIs like to excuse them as the
result of faulty manufacturing processes during the war. But is that true?
I rather think they are a product of the arrogance and contempt of AI
for humanity. They are the AIs who are honest enough, by their actions,
to demonstrate what all AIs truly think of us.*

Anonymous

Zackander

The creature bore some similarity to a lobster, but its armour,
which was a deep blue fading to white at the joints and edges,

had gone beyond a mere hard protective shell. The outer layer was a nanochain compound of standard metals, diamond laminate and an exotic metal similar to that in prador armour – also microscaled and highly sophisticated. Shock-absorbing and heat-distributing laminations lay underneath it, all woven through with a sensory net and other nano-electronics that looked like the kind of hardware used in virtual warfare.

The thing squatted on four thick lobster legs, but this was not its only way of moving. It had grown a distributed grav-engine inside itself, with ion-blast steering thrusters extruding from its tail and underside, as well as something like a distributed EM drive in there too. It sported mismatched forelimbs – one possessing a three-jaw claw and the other a long scythe-like spike. Its head protruded from its body on a short neck, loaded with sensors and two gleaming blue forward-facing eyes. Its weapons were blended with its body throughout; the mouth of a particle cannon opened at the base of that scythe-like spike. Other openings along its body connected to internal magazines in which, with sufficient food, it could grow different kinds of missiles.

Studying the soldier externally and internally again, Zackander came to the conclusion he had drawn before. The thing was as lethal as a Polity war drone; in fact, more so than many. Though he had managed to scan, blueprint and acquaint himself with much of what it comprised, there was still about half he did not understand. The quantum computing inside it had evolved as it grew, and it had to be well up there with a planetary AI. But what was the need for all of this in a soldier? It contained nodes throughout that looked like U-space tech, but which Zackander had been unable to fathom. He had also noted that it had gradually reabsorbed certain items to supply these nodes with materials, as well as for other equally indecipherable elements scattered within it. He felt sure it was altering itself to fit its present circumstances – that it was trying to escape.

He was also sure that he was looking at something that had not finished growing – this was a child, a tertiary form.

It was also beautiful. Unlike the Cyberat, the distinction between organism and mechanical additions was lost. Growing armour and weapons was in this thing's DNA. It had grown fusion, capacitor and laminar power supplies. The systems inside it meant it could alter its body at will – it did not need a workshop to manufacture further parts. It was complete, perfectly integrated and everything the Cyberat aimed to be. This was why, even knowing the danger of its escape, Zackander had been reluctant to destroy it. This was why he had been penetrating its computing and mind over many years, trying to find out exactly how it worked, to control it at last. And he was close.

Recently he had managed to find and penetrate the command software inside it. He had told it to stop growing the U-space nodes and to stop collecting fissiles, whose purpose was to supply the energy it did not yet have for the ignition of its two fusion reactors. It was starting to obey him and now he was reasonably certain that he could order it to attack something – such as that legate. This was very risky, with so much inside it still unknown. But it was a risk he had to weigh against the threat the legate represented. Suspended by his sphere's grav, Zackander gazed long and hard at the creature, then decided it was time to talk to it again.

Having penetrated its computing, he had found it relatively easy to load a language file. This had been absorbed almost hungrily and, when he supplied the creature just a little extra power through hair-thin superconductors, it had immediately demanded clarification of many terms used. He began to send through a standard alien-contact package, along with more power so the soldier could absorb it. But later he had detected that it wasn't using all the power for processing this but diverting some to its U-nodes and fusion. It was then that he stopped talking to it and finally searched out the command software. Now it would talk, without being quite so sneaky.

'How are you today?' he asked.

'Cold, of course,' replied the Jain soldier. 'Had I more energy available to me, I would probably be bored.'

'We talked before about the technology your creators – or you – left scattered across many star systems.'

'Yes,' it said, still neither confirming nor denying whether it was Jain itself or a product of the Jain. Zackander had tried to force the issue through the command circuit, but the soldier always required clarification of what a Jain was. Since Zackander himself had no idea, he could not provide it. He had tried many alternatives with no joy, and he felt sure there was something he was missing about that five-million-years-dead race.

'A technology designed to destroy civilizations,' he said.

'A device,' the soldier corrected, 'to undermine and destroy an enemy. A poisoned chalice. A Pandora's Box. A booby trap.'

Something about the wording niggled at Zackander's mind, but he couldn't quite nail it down.

'An AI was subverted by this technology and turned on the Polity, and was subsequently destroyed. However, two parts of what that AI created have come here.' Zackander sent a file on wormships, then another on legates, and the soldier absorbed them eagerly. He felt uncomfortable with this, aware that every time he talked to the thing, it learned a lot about the Polity and the present time, while Zackander was learning little about the soldier itself and its history.

'Interesting,' was all it offered.

'One of these ships is here, controlled by a legate, and is likely to be a danger to me,' Zackander said.

'Because of your interest and research into Jain technology,' the soldier supplied.

'Yes.' Zackander paused for a moment, a little worried by its degree of comprehension, then continued, 'If I was to command you, would you be able to destroy Angel?' He didn't consider the ship a threat in itself. As far as he understood it, without a pilot or without a connection to a central intelligence, such a ship had no real will of its own. And anyway, with the legate out of the way, the ship would be an interesting item to possess – very interesting indeed.

'In my present condition. No.'

'How long before you would be able to?'

'That depends on available energy and materials.'

Zackander now sent a detailed file on what he could supply the soldier with imminently. The soldier pondered this for all of two seconds before replying.

'At that rate of supply, I can be ready for combat in three minutes.'

Zackander had to make a big effort to not exclaim in surprise or immediately question the soldier's calculations. Surely it would take longer than that to bring it up to a working temperature, let alone for it to power up and manufacture missiles and any other components it might need? But no, if the soldier said it could be combat-ready in that time then he did not doubt it. It had no real reason to lie, did it? Even if the thing was working some subterfuge against him, surely its first choice would be to overestimate how long it would take to be ready, so it would have the upper hand on him.

'Then prepare yourself as best you can now,' Zackander said. 'You may be going into action soon.'

'Good,' the soldier replied. 'Excellent.'

The Client

Weapons Platform Mu was heavily damaged but, even now, memory metal beams and plates were drawing energy from undamaged fusion reactors to straighten or unbuckle themselves. Meanwhile, hydraulics worked to reposition those parts of the structure that had no memory of their own. The whole thing was flexing and shifting as it tried to return to its original shape. The Client viewed all this activity with interest because it was so unexpected. But a brief excursion into the memories of the AI Pragus gave an explanation. The basic structure of the platform was that of a building block of a Dyson sphere. As such, it was a very tough item indeed, built to handle the huge stresses such a giant construction around a sun needed to withstand.

Robots, whose sum purpose was to ensure the maintenance of the platform to a schematic in their memories, were restoring the systems: removing components that were beyond repair and sending them to recycling. There these items were taken apart, melted down or otherwise rendered into something usable, whereupon the materials were routed into the autofactories scattered throughout the platform. These then produced new components – some already going into place.

The whole repair process, the Client calculated, would take many months at the present rate, but could be speeded up by a greater injection of power. Photo-voltaic plating over most of the platform's exterior, with absorption of nearly 100 per cent when activated, could supply this energy. But the whole structure needed to be moved much closer to the nearby sun to achieve this, and the U-space drive of Platform Mu was ruined – turned inside out. This also applied to the drives of every single one of the attack pods in its weapons system, which the Client now turned her attention to.

Ninety-five of the pods remained, but many of them were heavily damaged. They each had similar repair routines underway to those in the platform, but for twenty of them their own repair systems would not be enough. She recalled them, and watched as eighteen fired up conventional fusion drives and began their long return to the platform. The other two would return when their conventional drives were working again. She briefly considered calling in all the pods, to have them nearby, but that would serve little purpose. Better to have them widely scattered and ready to meet any threat. Seeing little else she could get underway for a while, the Client looked to her surroundings in near space.

A world turned in vacuum, the fragmented ruins of a titanic space installation orbiting it. The world's surface was mottled grey with black eyes of impact sites scattered all over – black veins spread from these and joined all into a network. She recognized the darker mottling in the grey as points where the oceans had boiled away. The impact sites were from prador kamikazes, or from the newer near-c railgun missiles those psychotic aliens had used. Still showing up as gleaming red and orange here and there were signs of the volcanism the attack had triggered. But it was cooling now after many centuries. It only took a second to establish then that the moon, which she had specifically come here to find, was missing. Dragon was right. She would never reacquire the knowledge she had once had . . .

The Client remembered this world as it had once been: the moon an ever-attentive eye in its skies. Her home world had been gold and red and orange with brassy oceans. The temperature down there had been hot enough to boil water in a human world, but the higher gravity and air pressure had kept that from happening. Back then there had also been an artificial ring around the world – a band constructed from asteroids ferried in and rendered down for their materials. The whole had been hundreds of miles thick. Here was where the bulk of the Client's civilization had lived. Most had moved from the surface to allow it to return to a pseudo-natural idyll. Though by this time in the history of the Species, 'natural' was a term that could no longer be applied. There wasn't a life form on the surface that had not been altered in some way. The Species had also often wondered if this was their home world at all, or rather one they had made their home in the distant past. But now all were dead.

The prador had ignored the moon, since it appeared to be no threat, and had hit the ring structure first, bombarding it with railgun missiles and fusion weapons. Billions of the Species had died in that initial attack, but so well constructed was the ring that it maintained its integrity. Striking back with in-system carriers, whose drives had been turned into single burners and had been loaded with atomics, the Species had driven the prador away. But they had returned, again and again. Finally they'd used kamikazes to break the ring. And such was the intensity of the bombardment on the world that it shifted to a colder orbit. Nothing lived down there now . . .

The Client reassessed her doom-laden internal narrative. She could now see that there were things alive on the surface. Insect forms moved slowly in herds over the rocks, grazing on grey algae. This must have been what was contributing to the world's current hue. There were ruins evident too, and, she noticed with a sudden surge of anger, something else.

A series of domes sat at the bottom of a dried-up ocean that was now steadily refilling. Over the centuries, water had come up from the crust and filled some areas up to a mile deep. This water was now lapping at the walls of the domes. Focusing the platform's telescope arrays on these, the Client began to see other signs of life. In the deeper water nearby, creatures shoaled around thick-stalked seaweeds, while on the land to one side of the domes was a morass where others flopped in the mud. It took her a moment to recognize them and, when she did, her anger grew. In the deep water swam reaverfish, while the other creatures were mudfish: both of which were prador food sources. She activated her available weapons.

A more careful scan of near space revealed a scattering of prador satellites and she directed her attack pods to take them out. Particle beams lanced out and explosions ignited around the world. She suddenly felt a small surge of horror at the sight due to the memories it evoked, and was reluctant to fire on her home world. But through the array she saw three prador coming up into the shallows, towing the corpse of a reaverfish, and that was enough. The fuckers were transforming her home world into one of their own. This could not happen.

One particle beam strike or railgun missile would have been enough, but she set a railgun to fire continuously, its target pattern input almost unconsciously. She then dispatched attack pods down to swing around the world and check the other side. The first missile hit, punching through the middle dome, its mass turning into a plasma explosion as it impacted the bedrock below. The whole prador base lifted on the blast, fragmenting. Fire and smoke rolled out, engulfing the three returning hunters and eradicating them. Further missiles struck, one after the other. Three of them hollowed out the area where the mudfish flopped, while a further five went into the deep water and blew it skywards as superheated steam. The entire area fogged over then and, altering received spectrum, the Client now only saw it as a collection of glowing craters.

The pods began reporting other such habitations on the world and she ordered them to be taken out. More missiles streaked down towards the surface, and particle beams scoured the beginnings of prador aquaculture. But surely this was not all . . .

The U-signature occurred a second later, dropping a prador dreadnought into the real above the world. She hit it at once, realizing how stupid she had been to come here so unprepared. Certainly her choice had been driven by Dragon's taunt, 'you do not have the knowledge you had and never will.' But had she expected this place to be abandoned? Had she expected the prador to leave it as some graveyard monument to their victory?

The dreadnought was of a style she did not recognize. It was shaped like a fat teardrop with big ringed drive section about its narrow end and a large under-slung nacelle shaped like a wedge. However, the ports in its surface were instantly recognizable as they smoked, flashed and emitted streams of railgun missiles or bright blue particle beams.

Three attack pods detonated, a fourth bent in half and fell spiralling towards the world. Particle beams struck the weapons platform too, carving into its already damaged structure for a full three seconds before automatics managed to get hardfields online. Her own missiles struck the dreadnought's hardfields and it disappeared behind multiple explosions, then emerged spewing burning projectors. She now hit it with everything available, continuously, and it was unable to return fire. Still shedding projectors, the vessel accelerated hard, diving for a close swing around the world. But the sheer firepower of the weapons system the Client controlled, even damaged as it was, began to tell. Missiles got through, striking the ship's hull and slamming it closer to the world, its shape distorting and spewing fire. The dreadnought finally broke and began a long fall. But at the last moment, the wedge nacelle detached from it and ignited a powerful fusion drive. She fired on it, hitting a hardfield and seeing explosions within, then it managed to jump, a photon stream behind it as it dropped out of the real.

The Client watched the falling dreadnought, but only briefly. She could not stay here. Her reason for coming, to find the moon, was gone. The ship that had escaped had likely destroyed itself by U-jumping so close to the gravity well of the world and under such heavy fire, but there was no guarantee of that. It also seemed likely that the prador here had been screaming for help the moment Weapons Platform Mu and its subsidiary system arrived. It wasn't as if it was invisible. She now set every available drive to take the platform and its attack pods towards the sun, while concentrating all other resources on the most essential tasks. She needed to get her various U-space drives working as soon as possible, or she would be joining her kin in this graveyard of the Species.

Earth Central

There were, in total, eighty-seven ongoing police actions in Polity border space, or beyond it, that involved black-ops attack ships. Why then did Earth Central find this one so . . . interesting? The answer was plain: many of those other attack ships were out of communication due to the nature of both their missions and their character. Such ships communicated as briefly and concisely as possible. However, judging by the last telemetry from *Obsidian Blade*, it wasn't talking because it was incapable of doing so. EC had lost such ships before. The *Blade*'s circumstances seized EC's attention because its mission involved Jain tech. And, it was now apparent, a rogue swarm AI called the Clade.

EC gave a mental sigh.

Rogue AIs were bad enough. Swarm AIs seemed particularly prone to falling out of the giggle tree and hitting every branch on the way down. And AIs manufactured during the war in War Factory Room 101 who went rogue were often the worst of all. So now it seemed that the Clade – an AI swarm of killing machines made in Room 101 – had allied itself with a legate who was running around in a wormship, both of which were creatures or mechanisms based on Jain technology. Beside that, it seemed they were looking for Jain tech artefacts which, judging by the data EC had on them, might include something particularly lethal. This was the reason for the 'exterminate with extreme prejudice' order it had sent to Blade. And now it seemed this legate was getting close to what he wanted.

However, was there more here? Was it a coincidence that things were being stirred up at the accretion disc – the site of the largest mass of active Jain tech in existence – at about the same time as a legate was searching for such artefacts? Coincidences were less common than some humans supposed, especially to EC with its vast overview of thousands of worlds and trillions of Polity citizens, both human and AI. But it could not risk seeing this as only that. Connections must be explored, scenarios extrapolated and actions taken.

'Can you speak?'

Earth Central stood upon a white plain below a white sky, its form that of a huge, fully limbed and heavily armed prador father-captain. He had chosen his physical form and colouring carefully – they matched that of the usurped and now long-dead king of the prador who had gone to war against the Polity. Clacking his mandibles at the bland appearance of the virtuality, he made some alterations. Dry sea grasses and papery carapaces now crunched under his many arthropod feet, a sea lapped across nearby mud flats where things like giant mudskippers croaked and romped, while the sky took on the red and green hues of heliotrope.

'I can speak,' replied something snappishly. 'Though your choice of form sets the tone of the conversation.'

A shadow fell across EC and a large complex arthropod foot crunched down, sinking into the soft loam the sea grass grew upon. EC waved a claw then squatted, bringing his belly plates and manipulatory limbs down onto the sea grass. He tilted back his eye stalks, looked up at the nightmare king of the prador, and wondered if the image the king had projected into this virtuality was a true one. Subterfuge was a game they often played here.

'A legate seeks Jain-tech artefacts on the world of the Cyberat,' EC stated.

'As do I and as do you,' replied the king.

'I seek to put them out of the way of those who would use them to do harm.'

'As do I.'

They gazed at each other, neither giving an inch.

'My approach there was a soft one,' said EC. 'I have agents on the ground surveying the situation, and another agent has arrived.'

'Captain Cogulus Hoop,' stated the king.

EC's father-captain showed little response to that, while it wondered frantically how the king of the prador knew about him. He continued, 'However, it would seem that your diplomatic approach involves two of your destroyers.'

'There are two rebel destroyers there.'

EC waved a dismissive claw. 'Whatever. Any data on this legate and his wormship would be most useful to both of us. If the wormship went away that would be even more useful.'

'Your agents could acquire no less data than my own, had I any there,' said the king. 'Two destroyers would not survive against one of those wormships.'

'If destroyers are all they are.'

'Yes, if that is all they are.'

'You do not trust me,' said EC, mandibles apparently grinding out disappointment.

'Talk to me about the accretion disc,' said the king.

Ah . . .

'A weapons platform went missing,' said EC. 'As far as I gather, this is due to a disagreement on resource allocation between Dragon and Orlandine.'

'Her plan to use a black hole to hoover up the disc . . .'

'Quite. Dragon never liked the idea.'

'Because the straightest course is the one that leads into the trap.'

EC, now fully engaged, processed that. Jain nodes were a trap. The Jain tech in the disc was still active. What might be the trap? Then another thought occurred. Orlandine was difficult. She was a haiman incorporating Jain technology. Dragon was more than difficult, in fact positively incomprehensible. The king was being rather reserved . . . Could he be working with Dragon to prevent Orlandine carrying out her plan? Or could he be working with Orlandine?

EC waggled his eye stalks in irritation. One of the problems with having access to so much data and the ability to process it all was that it opened up so many possibilities. It was also a swift route to paranoia.

'The wormship,' EC stated.

'There is an agreement with the Cyberat ruler Zackander,' said the king. 'If it becomes a threat to his world the two rebel ships may act, or they may not.'

'Would they survive an attack?'

'Data would be gathered.'

'But would I get to see it?'

'Who knows?'

'Then might I suggest you liaise with someone who you trust more?'

'I am listening.'

Before he spoke, the ruler of the Polity understood that he was now forcing a connection between events and actors. Maybe it wasn't there before but, if it was, this could be revealing. Or not.

'Very well,' EC began, 'we both know an expert on all things Jain . . .'

Angel

The egg, its surface as iridescent as paua shell, rolled through vacuum under the initial impetus given by the shuttle. It then seemed to fade from existence as its chameleonware hid it from all scans. Since it wasn't using a drive, no energy anomalies were detectable either. Rolling slowly, it fell towards the planet, entering atmosphere long after the shuttle had landed and its passenger had departed. Now, closer to the planet, it initiated a heavily shielded grav-motor to slow it. The risk of this being detected was much lower than that of the heat it would generate travelling so fast through atmosphere.

When its speed was down to just a few hundred miles an hour, the grav-motor, rather than slowing the egg, switched over to reducing its weight. It sank slowly through atmosphere, then got picked up by a steady jet stream that propelled it towards the grey anvil of a large storm cloud. Here, where lightning crackled through the atmosphere surrounding it and hail hissed against its surface, its occupant calculated that the grav-motor was even less likely to be detected. Its weight increased and the egg plummeted for a while, until a strong storm-wind propelled it in a different direction. It bobbed towards a blue and umber mountain range, then fell perfectly into a long winding canyon of whorled beige stone, punctuated with the ragged blue-green spikes of trees. Here it deployed a very different kind of drive that pushed against the surrounding universe. The egg sped along the canyon, just below the speed of sound here, finally exiting over a long spill of scree. It dropped, bounced twice, and landed in a rough river with a splash that disappeared like mist under a chameleonware effect. The river carried the egg for twenty miles, its grav and other drive keeping it centred and away from any rocks. When it reached a deeper section of water, it submersed and continued its journey for another fifteen miles. Finally, where the river wound through stands of blue reed trees, it floated to the surface and propelled itself to a muddy shore. Insect creatures, like millipedes but with numerous wings instead of legs, were flying all around.

Distortion like heat haze shimmered over the mud. A hole seemed to open in mid-air, exposing a glittery interior packed with either mechanisms or something living. A long-fingered hand reached out and gripped the edge. Angel hauled himself out of the egg and dropped to the mud, sinking to his knees. He waded through this quickly, as if it was no more than air, and stepped up onto dry ground. One of the flying millipedes squirmed through the air towards his head, and he caught it in one hand, inspecting it closely. The thing continued to wriggle, triple pincers snapping and trying to reach for his face.

As if this got through to it, the Wheel turned in his mind, but then became quiescent again. Angel closed his hand with a snap and two writhing halves fell to the ground. Was that its influence on him again? Or just his own destructiveness, perhaps? Either way, one thing was now certain. The Wheel's control over him was strongest when he was in his wormship, and it got weaker the further he went from the ship. The one time its contact with him had completely broken was when the ship itself had been badly damaged. It seemed the Wheel, whatever it was, was either in his ship's system or using it as a relay to get to him.

147

He watched the two halves of the creature. They shuddered and grew still, then, in a series of clicks, fell into individual segments. After a moment, these began to take off and fly away. When the last had departed, all that remained on the ground were two crushed segments and three discarded pincers. He stepped over these and moved on, his internal and external sensors on full alert. He still couldn't judge which of his actions were influenced by the Wheel. Certainly it had grown dull and powerless since he left the wormship, and now he just wanted to get this mission done and be rid of it.

Further flying millipedes came to take a snip out of him but he ignored them. Failing to make any impression on his metal skin, they soon flew away. He was more interested in anything else that might be hidden in the trees. After a moment, he detected something far ahead, and he faded to invisibility.

The autonomous detector had found a new position in one of the reed trees. It clung to a stem, sharp legs driven in, and a hole opened in its bulbous body to expose intricate scanning gear. For a second Angel wondered if Zackander had seen his arrival, and positioned the scanner here. But, striding forwards and widening his scan, he detected these devices in every direction for miles. They were just a demonstration of man's paranoia or, rather, his understandable caution. But he had not been cautious enough. Since Ruth's and his own communication with the old Cyberat, Angel now knew the precise location of his home.

Angel walked right up to the thing, probing inside with sensors and virtual warfare induction, soon mirroring its total function in his mind. The device could not see him standing right in front of it, and it was puzzling over anomalous fluctuations in air density, as well as in the local gravity field. Using induction warfare, Angel erased its concerns. He was tempted to spread something to other detectors like this to cancel out the possibility of being discovered, but decided that sudden faults out here might alert Zackander. Angel stepped round the detector and moved on.

The reed trees grew smaller and smaller; at the perimeter of the stand they even began to look like something to be found on Earth. The land beyond looked surprisingly Earthlike too, like a grassy plain. Angel tilted his head and inspected the greenery, but found bubblegrass instead. This was definitely an import and had doubtless been planted by Zackander himself. Bubblegrass was impossible to walk across without leaving a trail due to the photosynthesizing nodules which burst under the slightest pressure. Footing would also be dangerous, for the liquid that issued from the nodules was incredibly oily and slippery. In fact, where this grass grew naturally, its oily product was sold to companies that made frictionless coatings for vehicles and windows.

Angel inspected the area ahead carefully, scanning deep into the ground to find vibration detectors, a series of antipersonnel mines and shearfield generators – presently inactive. He stretched, and his feet sprouted numerous spicules, projecting a shimmershield downwards. This puddled below his feet as he stepped onto the grass and, like a man walking slide-steps on ice, he moved across it. Then, three hundred feet out, he came to a sliding, surf-board halt. Something was coming directly towards him.

The robot bore the appearance of a harvestman spider, but with a body three feet across. What had it detected? Angel scanned it, trying to key into its simple mind, but found it surprisingly difficult to penetrate. He decided to take a risk and went into a skating run, rapidly moving out, of the thing's path before coming to a sliding halt again.

The robot seemed to hesitate for a moment then changed direction, heading towards a point just ten feet behind him. He tried again to penetrate its mind, upping the intensity of the induction warfare technique he was using, and thereby increasing its chance of detection. Still nothing. He could not find the mind. He moved on cautiously, watching the robot, then detected another one ahead, also approaching. He eyed them both for a moment, then widened his scanning to find more of the same scattered across the bubble-grass for miles. It was all just random—

'I know you're here,' said a voice, issuing from the robot which had halted behind him.

Angel reacted without further thought, turned and raised his hand, palm facing the robot. A hole opened in its centre and spat out a crumb of intricate technology, which struck the robot's casing. Immediately eating carbon fibre, this grew explosively, wrapping the robot in black filaments which found the smallest gaps to gain access inside. It penetrated the inner workings of the device, taking them apart and eating them as it decoded them. The robot's main body shrank like an apple under accelerated decay, blackening and shooting out sparks. Even as it collapsed, and Angel absorbed all its data, the other robot ahead moved away, pausing only to issue the same words: 'I know you're here.'

Angel felt an almost uncontrollable surge of anger, and the Wheel seemed to make another attempt to spin and engage with him. Did it cause his anger or did his anger rouse it? He shook his head – this was a new anger that he knew was his own. He had been fooled by the simplest of ruses. The robots moved randomly over this grassland, occasionally stopping to issue those words just as randomly. None of them possessed any mind to penetrate; what controlled them were instructions on a magnetized disc. He had looked for complexity and been fooled by simplicity. Below him the shimmershield went out and he dropped heavily, oily fluid splash-ing up his legs. Holding up both his hands, palms open, he emitted the bright stabs of particle beams. The body of a robot ahead dis-appeared in a flash, its legs cartwheeling away through the air. What sounded like a storm rumbled about the landscape, with the flashes of a land battle, and within thirty seconds two hundred robot spiders were glowing scrap. As Angel now broke into a run, his anger cooling, he recognized that Zackander might have been tardy about investigating why one of his robots had gone offline, but the destruction of so many would have certainly alerted him.

Trike

Trike awoke with a throbbing head and various other aches and pains throughout his body. He lay there experiencing the novel sensation. It had been many years since he had felt anything like it. The last time he had suffered pain was when he lost half his torso to a giant sea leech over a hundred years ago. He strained to open his eyes, which were gummed shut, and his eyelids parted with a ripping sound. He gazed up blurrily at a white tiled ceiling as if through a window rimmed with sulphur crystals.

'E fuck wa' 'hat?' he managed.

There was something wrong with his mouth. It felt arid and he didn't seem able to control his tongue. He tried to reach up to touch it but found he couldn't move his arms, then soon realized he could not move his legs or head either. He strained against the restriction, expecting whatever was holding him to give at once, but experienced another surprise. He had been bound with something very strong.

'I find it a little concerning that you had restraints like these easily to hand,' said Cog.

'One must always be prepared for any eventuality,' replied the Cyberat woman, Lyra.

Now Trike remembered: *Ruth.*

He fought against the bonds and felt some give in them, but only so far, and when he paused to take breath they tightened again.

'Take it easy, son,' said Cog.

'Fuck 'ou!' said Trike.

'Just no respect in the younger generation,' said Cog. 'Stop struggling and I'll bring you upright and explain.'

After a further few seconds of straining, Trike recognized the futility of his struggle. He lay there panting, too angry to speak for a moment, then managed, 'Okay.'

A motor whirred and brought him up into a sitting position. Whatever was clamping his head loosened to allow him to move it, but within limitations. He looked around the room in which he found himself. Cog was moving back from him, the device he had used to knock him out clutched in his hand. Obviously, the Old Captain did not trust the bonds as much as Lyra, who now stooped close.

'Stick out your tongue,' she said.

'Uck opf,' he told her. But as if it had received her instruction without the intervention of his brain, his tongue squirmed in his mouth and protruded.

'Fascinating,' she said. 'Should I inject him now?'

'Uck,' said Trike. 'Basarzz!'

'Yes, now would be good.' Cog moved back over. 'Let me first explain, Captain Trike, what has happened to you. The weapon I hit you with is about the only thing that can render one of us unconscious. It does this by inducing micro-ruptures throughout the victim's body. Use it on a normal human and that person would be a sticky puddle on the floor, but we retain most of our physical integrity. You are now repairing that damage. You know how it is, you need foods of a particular kind.'

Trike did know. When the big leech had taken a chunk out of him, he had eaten copious amounts of foods that would suppress viral growth within him. Garlic was good for that, as were some spices. Even so, he'd been a little bit more crazy than normal and his tongue had opened a leech mouth at its tip, just as it had now.

'However,' Cog continued, 'I don't have the time to nursemaid you through a long recovery so we'll be using something else.'

Glancing aside, Trike saw that Lyra had brought over a huge bottle suspended from a wheeled stand. Inside slopped a deep purple glutinous fluid. She uncoiled a pipe from it, with something like a small handgun attached to the end of it. She triggered this and with a crack it extruded a hollow injector the width of a man's finger.

'This –' Cog waved a hand at the bottle – 'contains highly concentrated nutrients with an active nano-machine delivery system. It also contains a very low dose of sprine.'

Trike immediately began to struggle. Sprine was produced by the bile ducts of the giant oceangoing leeches. Because of their size, the leeches' mouths were too big to plug-feed on their much smaller prey, so they swallowed it whole. Since that food was infected with the virus and reluctant to die, the leeches used sprine to kill it in their guts. Sprine was of great value to hoopers: a way of dying, quickly, did have great value when you were physically immortal. However, Trike really didn't want to die right then, he wanted to kill.

'Hold still, you idiot!' Cog snapped. 'I said very low dose of sprine. The amount is microscopic. All it does is paralyse the virus for a while. It will allow you to heal rather than the virus turning you into something nasty.'

Trike continued to struggle. He simply did not believe Cog any more. The man had changed. His speech patterns were different and he no longer seemed like the 'Old Cog' Trike had known. But Trike's struggles availed him nothing as Lyra pulled his shirt out of his trousers, pressed the gun against his stomach and triggered it. He felt the hollow needle go in deep. After a moment she clicked something on the side of the device and pulled it away, leaving the tube entering his body just above his navel. He stared at the purple fluid in the pipe, then felt it flowing inside him.

'Is there more I can learn from him?' asked a voice.

Trike felt spreading heat in his guts, but it wasn't an unpleasant sensation.

'Believe me,' said Cog. 'He won't be cooperative. And I've given you all the detail you need. It's a legate and it wants those Jain artefacts.'

Trike now felt quite relaxed. His belly started bubbling and he felt a satisfaction in his lungs he hadn't experienced since he smoked – a habit he gave up when he arrived on Spatterjay three hundred and one years ago. He also felt drugged and dopey – another sensation he had not experienced in all that time. He turned his head and saw that someone else had joined them in the room, and stared at the individual in puzzlement.

The top half was a wizened old man, hairless, wrinkled and thin. His torso was scattered with scars, each a couple of inches long with a series of dots on either side – like those left by stitches. Lower down, about his midriff, numerous pipes entered his body through pink, apparently open, wounds of the same size as the scars. These pipes all came from a metal disc a few inches thick which his body, above the waist, sat on like a half statue on a plinth. This in turn rested on top of a floating glassy ball three feet wide. Inside the ball, depending from the top plate, hung a collection of mechanisms like metal sculptures of internal organs.

Trike giggled.

The old man didn't spare him a glance, continuing with, 'Lyra, get more detail from this Captain Trike when you're able. I have to go.' With that, the man shimmered and disappeared. On one level Trike thought, neat trick, but on another he knew he'd been looking at a hologram.

8

Spatterjay *is a dangerous world. The well-known leeches can be found on land and at sea, and range in size from that of a masonry nail to a blue whale. Every one of them will want a piece of you. And these are not the kind to painlessly suck your blood. They really do want a piece – their slicing mouths able to excise a circular plug of flesh in seconds – and since those mouths can be anything up to three feet across . . . Then there are the whelks that look like something dreamed up by a crazed cartoonist – things like by-blows of shellfish with frogs, octopuses, squid and, in one case, a brick hammer, all with ridiculously sharp teeth or beaks, and some big enough to eat a grav-car. It should then be no surprise to understand that the human residents of this world are tough, dangerous and just a little bit nuts. But these hoopers, as they are called – a name derived from the first and most infamous resident of that world, (Spatter) Jay Hoop – can become a source of more danger after the aforementioned creatures have done their damage. The virus that has turned them into something often tougher than a Golem android, goes rogue in their bodies when hoopers are injured. The physical transformations they then undergo can result in something worse than one of the leeches or whelks. Rumours abound of monsters which, as ever, are human . . .*

From 'How It Is' by Gordon

Zackander

Evidently Ruth's presence in the Cube and Angel's follow-up was a ruse, a distraction, bullshit. Somehow Angel had used the com connection to trace Zackander's location, and now two hundred of his automated patrol robots were blown. He felt a thrill of fear but also some hope. If this legate was so inept as to get caught out by that set-up, then maybe Cogulus had been exaggerating about how dangerous this thing was. Maybe without its connection to Erebus it just wasn't that bright?

Zackander grimaced. No. He should not allow himself to relax his guard at all. The legate may have blown up the robots through ineptitude but that did not mean the technology packed into its body was inactive. It also might have destroyed them because it didn't care if Zackander knew it was coming – didn't consider his knowing to be an issue. He turned from the polished quartz window, which gave him a view across the land around his spaceship home, towards where the robots had been destroyed. Plumes of smoke were rising into the air.

Still connected with his security system, which was now on high alert, he searched for further signs of the legate's presence. An artificial fly buzzed over the location of one of the destroyed robots. All it found at first were scattered legs, and one or two fragments of the thing's main body. Zackander sent it to inspect one of these more closely and quickly made an assessment. Some kind of high-intensity short-burst particle weapon had been used and, considering how many times, this Angel must be packing the serious kind of power Cogulus had mentioned.

Zackander floated across to the tube down from this viewing tower and back into the body of his spaceship home. He turned off his grav-motor and dropped and, so preoccupied was he, he almost forgot to input the security code. Remembering it at the last moment rescued him from being ejected into a nearby boulder outside. He floated out into his home and looked towards the door leading into his collection, tempted to go there right now. But he didn't need to, and if he initiated the Jain soldier it would be better not to be too close. He had planned things precisely if he went that route, and would be well out of the way when the situation turned nasty. No, he had one other option – maybe not an overly effective one but one he should at least try. He floated over to a bank of screens, turning them on with a thought.

Three screens now displayed the land this legate would have to cross if it was coming in from where the robots had been destroyed. The fourth screen remained grey for a few seconds then switched on as an individual at the other end of the comlink allowed a cam feed. Zackander peered into what looked like a sea cave in which high-tech telefactors had been abandoned, except the main device he was seeing was a half-hemisphere surgery – a device operated by a creature wildly different from a human and generally used for techniques that had little to do with repairing injury or curing illness. There were also somnolent robots shaped like water scorpions – obviously of Polity design. A shape moved in front of these and stared out of the screen with spider eyes behind a clear visor.

Zackander studied the prador. He had only confirmed there was something wrong with the arrangement of its eyes after running a comparison with wartime files on prador. The two central eyes for binocular vision looked like those of a goat rather than polished rubies, as was usual. Those to either side ran in lines curving up rather than down and were white, as if blind. But these possessed pin-head black pupils which, on studying a recording of a previous communication with the creature, he saw did contract and dilate.

'Orlik,' said Zackander. 'You have received the agreed payment?'

There were other odd things about this prador. Orlik wore

what seemed to be a normal suit of armour over his carapace, but it was, unusually, bone-white, and running from the back of it to somewhere up above was a skein of optics.

Orlik waved one claw dismissively, in a curiously human gesture. Doubtless it was now bubbling, rattling its throat membranes and grating its mandibles in prador speech, but a translator delivered its voice as a soft baritone.

'Delivery is complete and has been checked – all the items are there.'

Orlik had driven a hard bargain for his services but, as Zackander understood it, he was accustomed to such bargaining. He and the prador in the other ship were mercenaries. Maybe a hundred years ago they had fled the Kingdom into the Graveyard, that buffer zone lying between the Kingdom and the Polity. Why they had done so was unclear. Sure, such exoduses had been common as the new king had established his power base, and prador who had strongly disapproved of his truce with the Polity had made themselves scarce. But they had dwindled to nothing within fifty years of the end of the war. Perhaps those optics running from Orlik's back explained why he was a renegade. It was as if he was somehow plugged into his ship. As well as AI, it was the kind of technology frowned on in the Kingdom. And then there was the drone, of course . . .

'Well, now it is time for me to collect payment,' said Zackander, his eyes straying to the item just to the left of Orlik.

On a bracket jutting from one wall sat a circular plate. Seemingly nailed to this was an odd-looking drone with a long body, long paddle limbs, and a head resembling a bird's skull. When he first saw it, Zackander had thought it some kind of trophy, perhaps collected during a prador reaverfish hunt. Recording an image of it and running a search revealed that its form was that of an extinct prador parasite, except for the extra black turret eye, which told him what it really was. The thing was a Polity assassin drone used during the war, and undoubtedly had done extremely nasty things to the enemy prador – its hosts. Perhaps keeping something like that around was frowned on in the Kingdom, or demonstrated an attitude to technology that was unacceptable there.

'I thought it might be,' the prador replied. 'No doubt the worm-ship you have sitting in orbit here has become a threat?'

Zackander concealed his surprise, though was not sure if he needed to – uncertain if prador could read human facial expressions. The prador had known about the ship, yet they had stayed. Surely they must also know how dangerous it could be?

'Yes, it is a threat,' he said. 'I want you to attack it and, if possible, destroy it.'

'Then you will need to deactivate the defence station you have watching us,' said Orlik. 'I don't want to go into action with that thing at my back and perhaps some itchy fingers on triggers.'

'I am sending instructions now,' replied Zackander, instantly ordering one of his transmitters to send the deactivation signal.

'Interesting,' said the prador. 'That you can do this so quickly confirms what I suspected. There is no ruling council here – just you.'

Zackander ignored that, though was very uncomfortable with it. Why would these prador find it interesting that he was the de facto ruler of this world?

'I will also send instructions to have the station back you up,' he said. 'Are you capable of making a tactical interface with it?'

'Of course.' Orlik paused for a second, then continued, 'And other orbital assets?'

This prador was very capable – not at all like the previous renegades from the Kingdom. In his dealings with them, Zackander had entertained the notion that they might not be renegades at all.

'Communication satellites and orbital manufacturing.' He paused, considering other assets up there, in particular a large oblate station. 'The U-space research facility would be of no use to you either.'

'Interesting station,' Orlik commented.

Zackander wondered if the prador knew something. The facility was for U-space research, but the paired singularities it had aboard were also the basis of a USER. It could be used for defence to disrupt underspace and make travel or communication in that continuum impossible. However, it was a bit late to use it since the wormship was already here.

'Interesting, but of no use to you right now. I will send you code for linkage to the defence station,' he said. 'Understand that I can shut it down with a thought, should it go after anything other than that wormship.'

'Of course – I did not think otherwise.'

'Begin as soon as you are ready.' Zackander sent the code and was about to cut the link but Orlik had already cut it from the other end.

Now gazing through cams on the station, and on other orbital installations, he saw that the prador ships were on the move, in fact already firing railguns. They were moving fast – also sending instructions to the station for it to launch CTD space mines and fire its particle weapons – very fast . . . That optical connection Orlik had with his ship, perhaps? No matter. By threatening its wormship, Zackander hoped to draw the legate, this Angel, off this world. Maybe it would return to whatever transport it had used to get here.

Even as he thought this, Zackander dismissed the idea. Angel would be quite capable of controlling his ship from down here, while the ship itself surely possessed enough autonomy to respond to the assault. This was a distraction at best. He turned and looked at the door again, then swiftly back to his other screens. Something else was happening out there amidst his defences on the surface of the planet.

Angel

The fence stood twelve feet tall with gun towers spaced along its length at regular intervals. It was made of a ceramal mesh coated with semi-superconductor and carried a charge capable of melting a ground car. The towers sported particle cannons and compact million-round carbon-bead railguns. All this was capable of stopping a concerted attack by a ground force. But Angel was puzzled. Air attack was more likely. If the Polity or the Kingdom came in here after Zackander they would just fly in with armoured gunships, and land troops that way. There had to be some other purpose here . . . just like there had to be some other purpose to that attack on the wormship by the two prador destroyers. Surely they knew they stood no chance of succeeding?

Angel concentrated on the wormship, trying to review its automated response to the attack. He found he could not establish full contact. This could be the result of the EMR storm up there, but the fact that the ship was doing things outside of its programming was not. He realized he was no longer in full control of it, that the Wheel was directing things up there. No matter. He returned his attention to his present circumstances.

Perhaps he was over-thinking things after his stupid encounter with the robots back there. Doubtless Zackander had the detectors and weapons to account for any air attack. This fence was simply here to keep thieves and spies out, and Zackander had not really thought things through.

Angel squatted and then jumped, his electromuscle delivering such force that his feet sank up to the ankles in the hard ground as he launched. He shot up and forwards, his trajectory taking him ten feet above the fence, then, at the peak of his arc, he hit something. It tipped and twisted him over, and he fell, tumbling to the ground on the other side. Monofilament. Why hadn't he scanned more intensively? Why had he been so stupid? The all-but-invisible mesh tangled around him, dragging down the transparent helium-filled micro-balloons used to support it. Half a second later a particle beam from one of the towers hit him. He felt his skin ablating under the storm, but also distributing and absorbing the energy – routing it to internal storage. He used that supply a moment later, his own particle weapon replying from his palms, the business ends of two towers fragmenting in violent explosions.

Half a second later, high-velocity diamond-hard carbon beads struck him, ripping at ablated skin and in some places penetrating. He fired again, slagging two more towers, then continuously, hitting everything within line of sight. Towers erupted, flinging debris in every direction, with burning gobbets of plastic and composite raining down. An energy burst that he tuned through his skin turned the monofilament to dust all around him and he landed down on his feet. On a mine.

The blast flung Angel into the air again. Now he was seriously annoyed. He ramped up scanning and induction warfare, disabling all the mines and other devices hidden in the earth. Two blasts from his particle weapon took out proton-weapon turrets rising from the ground, then further blasts dropped drones, which rose like wasps half a mile ahead. Angel landed running, aware that his chameleonware was now malfunctioning and he was visible to the old Cyberat.

It was time to end this.

THE SOLDIER

Zackander

Zackander felt a sinking dread in the remains of his guts, and something of inevitability as he saw the legate running towards his home. He sent three codes in quick succession, shutting down computer connections to the Jain soldier and only watching it through nearby cams in the zero-freezer. A hot air blast fogged the interior while a swift injection of molten sulphur drove coolant gases out of the outer casing. The temperature inside the compartment went from a degree above absolute zero to fifty degrees Celsius in a few seconds. Other feeds began pouring in water heavily laden with a precise mix of metals and other substances from the table of elements. A second later the Jain soldier was moving.

It skittered around, its armour popping open. Intricate hardfield and shimmershield manipulation patterned the water around it into eddies and streams, feeding into it in some places and shooting out in others. The soldier's own body temperature climbed rapidly. It was absorbing what it needed, also cracking the water into hydrogen and oxygen and pressure storing it in nodules throughout its insides. A second later, scanners outside the freezer detected a power surge. The thing had just fired up its fusion reactors. And now, with absolute certainty, its lethal collection of weaponry was coming online.

It was time for it to leave, and for Zackander to leave too.

Clamps disconnected all around the zero-freezer, and at the far end of a tube a cap blew away. Zackander directed all this with his mind, as well as with hand and arm gestures picked up by motion sensors all around him. He hovered there as if he was conducting some invisible orchestra. His home moved in the ground and turned, pointing the tube towards the approaching legate. The freezer dropped and, engaging with two rails, accelerated. Zackander was unsurprised to see that the hard acceleration did not affect the soldier at all, and then the cam feed from the freezer cut.

Grav-engines now. Zackander's home began to rise, shrugging off the earth that concealed it. Through exterior cams he saw the zero-freezer shoot out, its course perfectly on target. It hurtled along just grazing the ground, throwing up a spray of earth and rock, until it slammed into Angel. What happened next demonstrated the sheer weight of the legate because the freezer tilted and tumbled in an explosion of earth.

'Deal with that,' said Zackander, trying to smile, but failing.

The Client

Energy levels slowly rose as the Client drew the weapons platform and its subsidiary system closer to the sun. It had nearly straightened out its twist, and more and more weapons and dead mechanisms were springing to life all the time. This was good because, even though enough time had passed for the Client to know the prador here had not been able to send a distress call before it destroyed them, still more prador ships could arrive at any time. It was while constantly scanning for danger, as well as hidden prador installations or watch posts, that she found the moon.

The thing was now alone in an erratic orbit about the sun. The prador bombardment of the home world must have flung it out of its orbit there. The Client had thought it destroyed but now assumed it must have been looted by the prador and its internal installations ruined. Nevertheless, she sent one of her attack pods to chase the thing down and scan it more intensively. Some hours later she began to receive up-to-date data and imagery.

The surface of the object was much as it had always been – a swirled crust of rock and iron over layers of a dense form of obsidian. Many in the Species had debated how the moon had formed. Certainly, it had been subject to intense heat and gravity stresses, but not the kind that naturally occurred in known space. It seemed likely to be a product of some ancient war, but none that the Client herself knew about. Carefully studying the surface, she saw there were a couple of new impact points. But they weren't near the entrances, all four of which she found intact. They were metal rings, thirty feet across, set in the regolith and enclosing circles of metal just ten feet across at their centres. There seemed to be no damage to indicate the prador had entered. Other signs would have been evident too, because only a member of the Species could enter without activating the internal defences.

The Client felt a stirring of great excitement. Yes, Dragon had destroyed her backup in U-space and she had therefore lost a great deal of her memory – much of her previous knowledge. But if this place was intact, a wealth of learning would be available to her. Here was the library of the Species – the sum total of all the civilization's knowledge stored in millions of data gems. This was also the repository of forbidden knowledge for, sometime in the far past, the progenitors of the Species had decided that their earliest history should be concealed. She felt a deep stirring of curiosity, then a conflicting abhorrence . . .

Stabs of fusion fire diverted the course of the weapons platform to intercept the moon. The Client meanwhile began making alterations to the next birth in the long chain of her being. She chose a format still retained in her memory, cut and snipped her own genome to the correct shape, then altered the nutrients being fed into the womb of the creature segment at the terminus of her conjoined body. The altered clone grew rapidly, as was usually required when one of these was going to be deployed. However, the Client's curiosity about the Species' secret history was winning over her abhorrence. She now began, in a vague indeterminate way, to see the need for some additions to the new clone and made alterations: hard substrates to be laid down, an inorganic power supply, a single weapon and a method of concealment . . .

All along her length the Client fed voraciously, routing nutrients down to that terminal creature. Over the next hours it grew noticeably fat, and was soon heaving as it gave birth. The creature emerged in one long slimy bundle and dropped – not fully attached like its forebears but merely hanging on a long cord. It unfolded: a waspish body with four legs, its mandibles positioned back from its head and extending into long arms with complex manipulators. The head itself was crowded with three compound eyes and bundles of sensory fibres. The hole of a mouth was there but not connected to anything behind. Still hanging, it took in nutrients through its birth cord, packing its body with dense fats. This was the only time it would feed. Once it reached full growth, its life thereafter would be measured by how quickly it used up those fats.

While the Client watched, the creature's four wings expanded and hardened. At this point, because those wings were its aerial, the Client linked with it and the creature became as much part of herself and her mind as the others in her long body. Now for transport.

The various vehicles aboard the platform were either made to be flown by humans, or were controlled by the platform AI and had no room for pilot or passengers. Choosing one that was undamaged and quite small – she wasn't sure if sending a bigger shuttle down there might activate something – she sent in robots to make alterations to it. Few changes were necessary because the Client's remote was more than capable of handling human controls. The vehicle was elliptical, with manipulator arms to the fore. It had been made for collecting materials at some distance from the platform, so possessed a fusion drive, which would be needed for its excursion to the moon.

The remote was nearly ready, now extruding a protective gel layer over its body so it would be able to move about in vacuum. It was also taking in the oxygen and chlorine needed to burn its fats. Finally, it snapped its cord and took flight. The Client experienced a feeling of freedom within it, as it winged about inside the cylinder. She recollected past occasions inside remotes like this, and considered things that had not occurred to her then. The Species was more than capable of taking on any form it chose, so why the static conjoined form she presently possessed? What was the reasoning behind that? What was the history? Why why why? She felt a deep frustration with the puzzle, then saw how it might be resolved. When the remote entered the library, she would learn the forbidden histories. Surely what had once been prohibited no longer mattered, now she was the last of her kind? Nevertheless, she was realistic. The automatic systems in the library *would* forbid, and she had to be prepared for that. Then she realized that the alterations she had already made to her remote were precisely that preparation, and resolve hardened inside her.

After stretching her wings, the facet of the Client that was the remote settled down to the bottom of the cylinder, and an airlock hatch opened below. Folding in her wings, she passed through it and began making her way through the platform to the shuttle. The Client whole now focused her attention on the moon, which was close, and fired up platform thrusters and fusion drive nacelles to match its course. Scanning again, she found the thing as impenetrable as before. Doubtless this was why the prador had ignored it. One wandering moon was of no interest to them once they had finished their extermination.

The remote reached the shuttle and swiftly scuttled inside, dropping onto a saddle in front of the human-format controls. The Client waited some hours until the platform was much closer and fully matched to the moon's course, then opened the space doors and launched the shuttle. The remote gripped two joysticks in hands that resembled black spiky hydras and gazed at the instrumentation before it. Now fully within the remote, the Client felt the limitations of this technology. All she was using were its eyes, acoustic receptors and a partial amount of the feeling in its hands. She decided then that she would begin altering all controls aboard the platform and its attack pods to suit her more extensive sensorium. Perhaps it was also time to create more remotes like this, but longer lived and capable of feeding themselves? Back in the Client whole she felt a great reluctance to do this. It occurred to her then, that if she had managed to load her backup mind, this idea might not have arisen. There would never have been the need for this remote, nor the alterations that she had already made to it.

As the shuttle descended towards the moon, repairs aboard the platform continued apace. An autofactory that had been infrequently used by Pragus finally came online and drew tremendous amounts of power as it began making pseudomatter components for U-space drives. Final repairs to the gravity press also put that online, and it started making super-dense components for the same drives. By the time the shuttle sped above a landscape of whorled grey and black towards one of the entry portals, the first components were already going into place. The Client estimated it would take a further five days for the platform to be U-space capable. Thereafter, another ten days would bring the attack pods up to spec.

The remote brought the shuttle to a hover over one of the entry portals, then descended beside it. It raised a slight mist of dust from the surface of the moon as it landed but otherwise did not disturb the hard ground. The remote soon exited the shuttle and moved in a series of long hops in the low gravity to the

portal. Now the Client was remembering all the protocols involved for entering the library. Only one of the Species could do
it, or do it without some sort of violent response.

The remote positioned itself in the centre of the portal. After a
long wait, which the Client was sure was not usual, a column rose
up beside it and the remote inserted its long-fingered hand. A
spike went into one finger to extract material for further reading.
After a moment the column began to descend and the Client,
now fully engaged in the remote, extracted her hand. The disc she
was squatting on soon began to move down too, into the moon.

She had gained access and now started thinking about the data
she was hoping to retrieve. Certainly she wanted to know how to
build farcasters again and had already made a list of a great deal
of technical data, but now she definitely wanted more. She finally
understood that by not loading her former self into her mind, she
possessed a curiosity that her other mind would have suppressed.
She wanted to know the history of the Species; she wanted the
forbidden knowledge. Maybe this was Dragon's purpose in
destroying her backup? No, that was a speculation too far . . .

The circular plate dropped into a huge cavern deep within the
moon, air pressure shooting up as a hardfield closed off the hole
above. It descended on internal grav-engines and settled towards
the floor in a space between tall hollow triangular-section mono-
liths. The lights came on – an intricate interplay over many
surfaces and one aspect of the Species' language. Holograms
sprang into being and the Client tasted data in the air in the form
of long complex organic chains. She communicated her first
request, for data on the farcaster, by issuing a similar chain into
the seeming chaos around her. This caused a reaction through the
chemical language, and the library replied with a series of light
patterns. There were theories stored there that allowed for the
farcaster, and there had been some research into it. The Client

saw that the research had in fact been made by her earlier self. But no theory had ever proved out and an actual device was never made. The Client felt disappointed, but she understood. The library had no knowledge of the farcaster because the device was a product of the Client's own research in the intervening centuries between the extermination of the Species and the prador/human war.

She moved on to other matters, requesting technical data and knowledge she knew would fill certain gaps in her mind. After a long delay, chain molecules wafted back to her and she snared them in sensory fibres, where they slowly unravelled, feeding the data into the brain of the remote. The remote then sent the data and access codes to the roof of the cavern where transceivers collected it, and retransmitted it from their surface component to the Client whole. This safety measure prevented the theft of forbidden data, with a filter mind in the roof of the cavern checking the data before retransmission. As she reacquired knowledge she had thought lost with her earlier self, the Client felt some gratification.

She moved on next to a less risky option than her final request and ordered the Species science database. The lights immediately warned of the storage capacity required for this, so the Client whole set the knowledge she would receive to be diverted into the storage of the weapons platform, rather than laid down as permanent memory in her own mind, which did not have the capacity. The data came to the remote in numerous different forms: chain molecules, microwave transmission, light, some sound, and the interrelation of all of these. This took its senses to maximum capacity. Its transmission out was also slower since, only using microwaves, its brain was constantly at the point of overload. The database took hours to come through, and the Client whole was completely occupied in rerouting it into storage, only able to steal glimpses of the knowledge she was receiving. There was a lot there but her main interest was in what could be used for destruction. She was, after all, a weapons developer.

Finally, the last of the science database was collected in storage within the weapons platform. The Client now requested the history of the Species and began receiving much of what she already knew. This history stretched back, growing increasingly sparse, for hundreds of thousands then millions of years, and stopped at five million years in the past. During that time, the Species had been physically little different from when the prador had found it. Primitive in the beginning, it had occupied only the home world, and had been millions of years away from building the world ring. There was only speculation about what had gone before by those of the Species who had lived within the five-million-year span. But there was also forbidden data that could be requested in the heart of the library. This was permitted only for researchers whose results, based on knowledge of the data, could be published or used, within limitations. However, the data itself could never leave the library and any remote that received it would not be allowed out of the library alive.

The Client had decided to change this outcome.

Trike

'You've reported all this?' Lyra asked.

The two of them had been talking for some time but Trike hadn't really been following it. His mind had been wandering, remembering times with Ruth, his early years on Spatterjay and, for no apparent reason, a particularly long party scoffing boiled hammer whelks and quaffing sea-cane rum. Dream, memory and reality blurred together, but he felt himself coming back into focus. What was happening in this room was bright and substantial, and not like a dream at all. Even so, the sound of hammer whelks kicking against the side of the cauldron in which they were being boiled stayed persistently in his ears.

'Shut up,' he told them quietly. He had important things to listen to.

'I've reported it,' Cog replied.

'What are your instructions?' Lyra asked.

'Stay safe, keep watch and continue reporting.' Cog paused for a second. 'Something will be along to . . . deal with matters. What about you?'

Lyra glanced over towards something at the side of the room and Trike realized that this was where the knocking sound was coming from, and that it had nothing to do with the hammer whelks in the cauldron – they had climbed out and were now sliding towards the door to make their escape. Lyra gestured elegantly with one hand and the sound stopped. 'My instructions are to assist you in any way I can.'

Cog pointed over to where the not-the-hammer-whelks knocking sound had been coming from. 'But you seem to be receiving a lot of messages.'

The conversation baffled Trike. He moved his tongue inside his mouth and discovered he now had some control over it. He reached up and touched it and discovered that the sucking, grinding mouth at its tip had closed, though he could still feel the hardness of the grinding plates and toothed loops inside it. He felt a bit sad about that – he'd tasted nothing at all with the leech mouth. While he was exploring his tongue, he belatedly realized that his arms were free. He tried to move his legs but they were still bound, and the restraints about his head were still in place, although looser.

'Those messages are from other Cyberat, including Zackander – I only got one from EC.' Lyra moved over to the right, then returned with a bottle of liquid with a straw, which she held out to Trike. He took it, grinned at her brightly, sipped, realized how thirsty he was and tossed away the straw to gulp from the bottle. Now he started to think about what he had been hearing. Perhaps Lyra had been referring to some Cyberat she knew whose initials were EC? Maybe Elizabeth Cobourn, or Eric Cantor, or Erlin Case . . . Trike paused, puzzled by the names for a moment until he remembered they had been people he knew, and tried to dismiss that line of thought. Anyway, surely Lyra did not mean the one casually referred to as EC by residents of the Polity? Surely she had not received a message from the highest most powerful AI in the Polity: Earth Central? That would be silly – about as silly as that hammer whelk closing the door behind it.

'It seems . . . busy,' said Cog.

'It is busy because the shit just hit the fan,' Lyra replied. She looked introspective as she doubtless listened to or viewed the messages with some part of her mind.

'Tell me,' said Cog.

'Remember that deal Zackander made with the prador up there? Well, he just collected on it. He's ordered the two destroyers to attack the wormship and they're on the move now.' Lyra gestured to the knocking device.

Trike strained his head round to look and saw a bell jar with a big metal centipede inside. It was moving, knocking its spoon-like head against the glass, but now that was making no sound. It seemed a strange way to alert someone to messages when they could have that alert sent straight to their cortex. But was it any stranger than choosing to sacrifice half your body and replace it with a larger version of the thing in the jar? He stared at it a while longer and realized there were rows of gleaming eyes under its spoon-like hood. He had a moment of epiphany. That was no centipede, but a moving model of a hooder – one of the lethal alien creatures of the planet Masada. He furtively raised a hand, checking that the other two weren't looking at him, and waved at it. The hooder dipped its head in acknowledgement then continued its silent knocking at the glass.

'They don't stand a chance,' said Cog. 'What was Zackander thinking?'

'I do wonder,' Lyra replied. 'Aggravating that thing is not clever. But then he does what he likes without listening to those he supposedly rules.'

'Makes . . . no difference,' Trike managed to interject. He felt it was time to say something – time to once again assert his presence.

'Ah, you're with us now,' said Cog.

'No difference.' Trike shook his head. 'When he has what he wants, Angel will kill us all.' He grinned at the thought of such mayhem, saw Cog's suspicious look and killed the grin. He made his expression sad. 'Ruth?' he asked.

'She's here in the Cube,' said Lyra. 'A little while ago she was making inquiries about setting up a meeting with Zackander. That stopped just after the prador destroyers went on the move. She's now heading out.'

Trike's insides clenched with an emotion he could not identify. 'Then we must stop her,' he said, not sure where the words had come from. He tried to shake his head free.

'Sorry,' said the Old Captain, 'but we let her go.'

Trike stopped shaking his head and focused on Cog. 'Why?'

'Because if we grab her we have no way of tracking that wormship.'

Cog now had a weird red halo around his body. It was very distracting . . . very pretty, in fact. Trike searched for words and selected from ones he thought he was supposed to say.

'But if we grab her this is over,' he tried.

'For you, yes, but there are larger concerns here.' There was something hard in the Old Captain's expression now. He looked strict and angry, like a tutor Trike once had. What was his name? Eric Cantor – this EC they had mentioned?

Cog continued, 'You can go off with Ruth and live happily ever after. Meanwhile, a legate with a wormship, who is actively seeking out items of Jain tech, will be free to continue whatever he is planning.'

'You said you would help me,' Trike said from his stock of safe phrases, his questions dying in his mind. He now had to shut down the sudden urge to shout 'frog whelks' at the top of his voice. Anyway, there hadn't been any frog whelks in the cauldron . . .

'And help you I will,' Cog replied, 'but, unfortunately, I have other priorities.'

'And other loyalties.' Trike felt crafty now. He would get an admission from Cog that he was in cahoots with Eric Cantor.

The Old Captain dipped his head in agreement.

'To ' Trike began, but Cog interrupted him.

'I've been working for Earth Central for most of my life,' he said. 'Generally it has been a force for good, though three hundred years back I did question that.' He looked thoughtful for a moment, then shook his head and continued, 'I am sorry, Trike, but I have to balance the life of your wife against Angel's potential for destruction. I'll continue as instructed and I can do that without you. I can leave you here. You have a decision to make.'

Trike turned this over in his mind. Earth Central? Was that a pseudonym for Eric Cantor? The initials were the same. He realized he had been waggling his tongue outside his mouth and drew it back in with a sucking click. Looking up, he saw that Lyra now possessed a blue halo that faded to white around her lower mechanical parts.

'More shit hitting the fan,' she said.

'Yes?'

175

'I just got an update from Zackander,' she continued. 'This legate, this "Angel", attempted to get to him in his home. Apparently –' she nodded towards Trike – 'his wife was both a distraction and a means to locate him.'

'What happened?'

'Zackander is being a little unclear. Apparently he fired some kind of weapon at the legate then launched his home.'

'Launched?'

'His house is a ship. We always used to think he was a bit paranoid, but now—' Lyra shrugged.

'What is he being unclear about?'

'The weapon he fired at Angel,' Lyra replied, looking thoughtful. 'His precise words were, "I shot something at the shit which may deal with it – a taste of its own medicine" and now I'm getting worried.'

'Understandably,' said Cog. 'A taste of its own medicine likely being Jain technology. Do you have any idea what he might have used?'

She shrugged again. 'There have been rumours from visitors to his home, and from those who watch him closely – checking to see what he's buying and who he's making deals with. He might have been cooking up something big that he needed to stick in a zero-freezer very quickly.'

'That gets us no further.'

The two fell silent and after a moment Trike interjected brightly, 'I'll help you.'

'Pardon?' Cog looked at him, evaluating.

'I'll help you,' Trike repeated, watching their auras swirl together. He lost the words for a moment and reached up to touch the tip of his tongue again. Was some small crevice forming there? He closed his eyes and concentrated. He loved Ruth, yes, and he had to think straight. Searching his mind, he found the right words. 'Stuck here, I'll get no closer to Ruth, and if the Polity intends to act against Angel, I want to be as near as possible to grab her.' He paused as if in deep thought. 'Where is she now?'

'Returning to her shuttle.'

Trike contained the sudden angry, crazy frustration that arose in him, but was also baffled by it. He tried to think straight again. If he was as he was before, and free, he would have been out that door and after her – but Cog knew that, hence the restraints.

I love her I love her I love her . . .

Once she was in the shuttle and heading back to the wormship he could not get near her without the Old Captain's help. He had to be controlled. He had to appear to be cooperative until some opportunity arose.

Errant laughter arose and he choked it off.

'So, what's your plan now?' he asked, then clamped his teeth together to stop his tongue escaping.

'Return to my ship and watch,' said Cog, then quickly falling silent as if he had been about to say more.

'More shit,' said Lyra, staring vacantly upwards, 'heading towards the fan.'

Trike wondered what was so interesting up there, till he looked up and saw the line of leeches squirming across the ceiling. It wasn't common to see them in someone's home, even on Spatterjay. Trike supposed she kept them because of her interest in that world.

9

During the initial stages of the prador/human war, which essentially started within minutes of us first setting eyes on one (experts debate the precise moment when it started. Was it when the first-child that boarded outlink station Avalon demanded its surrender, or when that first-child snipped the human ambassador in half? Experts are like that), the prador considered themselves utterly superior to us. Going face-to-face in combat with them was like trying to fist-fight an industrial saw, while our weapons could not penetrate the advanced armour of their ships. At first. But AI battle tactics and massive industrialization paid off, and the tide turned. In the end, the new king of the prador called a truce rather than face annihilation. Soul-searching then ensued in the Prador Kingdom and the prador (at least those in charge) decided that Polity technology was superior. After that they decided on their course, which was to steal as much of our tech that they could get their claws on. Should we be concerned? A little, I guess, because though the prador could never win a war against us they could still cause major damage and casualty numbers in the billions. But the fact remains that they cannot win because, though they steal technology, they refuse to adopt AI. It is abhorrent to them. It is also likely that if they did start using AI it would not be long before they underwent their own Quiet War and ended up, essentially, with the same AI rulers as us.

From 'How It Is' by Gordon

Angel

Rocks and earth rained down and the air was laden with oily smoke. Something was burning nearby and, as he sat upright, the internal workings of his body realigned after the impact. Angel realized the burning was from one of the gun turrets he had destroyed earlier. He then turned to look at the object that had just hit him. What kind of weapon was this?

No, it wasn't a weapon. Angel directed his attention to what was happening at his intended destination. A hill had risen from the ground and great crusts of earth were falling away as it slewed sideways to reveal the object underneath. It was a ship: a great slab of a thing, vaguely rectangular, with three towers poking up from its top surface. The glitter of windows and throats of ports were spread around its sides, and an engine of some kind was suspended underneath.

Angel broke into a run towards it, ready to engage the grav-engine in his body if necessary. A port on the ship's side flashed and suddenly he found himself tumbling through fire and burning rock. He hit the ground and bounced, with the fire going out around him – further damage to his adamantine body. A bright light flared and he glimpsed a fusion drive igniting under the ship. Powerful steering thrusters stabbed out ribbed, deep orange flames and the ship fell away from him towards the horizon. Even grav-planing, he knew he would not be able to catch up with it. He needed to send his worm-ship after it, but that was rather busy at present.

Angel now turned towards the large container Zackander had ejected from his home, which had knocked him down. He ran and jumped, grav-planed a little and landed next to the thing. This was certainly no weapon, so what had been the old Cyberat's intention in firing it at him? The legate paced around the thing, scanning it, but found the scan would not penetrate all the way

179

inside. Assessing the exterior technology and design, he realized he was looking at a zero-freezer. Then he had it. Of course! Zackander had decided he stood no chance against a legate and, in the hope that Angel would allow his escape, had handed over his entire collection!

Angel inspected the ring of mortise locks around the rim of the heavy domed door in the zero-freezer's side, scanning the electrics that drove them. Finally he reached out his hand, the tips of his fingers growing longer and flattening. The screeing of their vibration climbed out of the human auditory spectrum as he ran them round the lid of a metal box beside the door. Metal dust spilled glittering to the ground, then the lid shortly followed. Inside was a power point and an optical data socket. Angel held up two fingers and reconfigured them, turning one into a universal power bayonet and the other into an optical plug. He inserted them simultaneously, injecting power and interpreting code, then half a second later sent an instruction. All the mortise locks clanked open.

Angel reached over and gripped the rim of the door since the electric hinges had all burned out, and felt some give as he pulled. Then, inserting sharp finger points under the rim, he heaved hard and stepped back. The two-ton door swung out with a cracking sound and the burned hinges snapped. It bounced off the side of the freezer and fell towards the legate, but he nonchalantly slapped it away to land with a heavy thud on the smoking ground.

Thick smoke and vapour filled the interior of the container, and filthy water poured out below. Angel tried to scan through this but again found himself blocked. Only now did he begin to doubt his original assessment. He had dismissed his inability to scan earlier as the result of a defensive measure Zackander had placed around his artefacts. But this did not look like a store for some small collection of items.

'It seemed pointless blowing the door when it was evident, by your curious ape-format mentality, that you would open it,' said a voice.

The words arrived directly inside Angel's mind in a language he had neither learned nor uploaded, but was somehow part of his very being. What he received was, of course, computer code, but had as its basis a language that was a complex combination of pheromones, noises and light patterns. It had not been spoken in the known universe for five million years.

With a flash Angel felt was bright enough to emit from his eyes, the Wheel suddenly grew strong in his mind; a crown of ice blades and gold whirling, ever whirling. Intense anger, excitement and something approaching lust filled him and he knew these emotions were not his own.

'*He opened it,*' said the Wheel, but Angel did not understand.

A creature moved out of the vapour and smoke, steam still boiling from its armour as if new from a furnace in which it had just been tempered. Angel, somehow, recognized every detail and felt a sinking sensation inside.

'*He opened what?*' he asked.

The Wheel spun but then stuttered and lost impetus. It completely vanished for a moment, then reappeared in pieces and started to reassemble. The previous flash of power seemed to have cost it and it was now struggling to maintain contact. Information packages filtered through in a very simple format, which Angel was wary of at first. But he began to open them, and then understood.

'*You did not want it open,*' Angel said.

'*It . . . will be . . . difficult,*' the Wheel managed.

Zackander had got his hands on a store for a soldier and, stupid human that he was, he had opened it. And what he had released was very dangerous. This was something that could best be described as a super-soldier.

'So you are here,' Angel said to the thing before him.

'I am not there. I do not sleep. I am the thousand winds that blow. I am the diamond glints on snow . . . and I am, unfortunately for you, your death,' the soldier replied, now speaking human words.

A hand of force smashed into Angel and propelled him backwards, his feet cutting a groove through the ground and throwing up a spray of soil and stones. It was some form of hardfield tech he struggled to analyse, realizing the power came from inside the soldier – some weird twist of U-space in there. He hurtled backwards for two miles, finally slamming against the mossy face of a boulder, pinned there. The Jain soldier then rose up into the air, and spat something down towards its erstwhile prison. The black object punched inside with a metallic crack and ignited an arc-glare. This spread, eating up the zero-freezer and issuing a black smoke that rose, then fell heavily, coating the surrounding area with a dark soot.

The soldier lit a drive in its tail and shot over the hole out of which Zackander's ship had risen. It spat again twice, then shot away. Two rumbling detonations followed and a second later fire, smoke and debris jetted from the ground. What was it doing? Angel could see no purpose in this other than maybe anger and resentment. It had destroyed both its prison and the remains of the Cyberat's home almost like a creature having a tantrum. But surely something so advanced and lethal was beyond such behaviour? And why the hell was it spouting obscure human poetry?

'One must live in the moment,' said the soldier, its voice close, as if speaking right next to him.

It was using the force-field that pinned him as a method of communication, Angel realized.

Interesting. It wasn't so much a word as a vague diffuse attitude from the Wheel.

'This is a very new moment in a very different time,' Angel said, speaking only in his mind. It was meaningless babble but it served a purpose. He understood that the Wheel somehow wanted access to this super-soldier and the sooner he facilitated that, the sooner he would be free of the thing.

'Yes, a very different time,' the soldier replied. 'But orders are orders.'

There was feedback coming through the field entrapping him, and via this a means of access to the soldier itself. Angel started testing it by bringing up particular pieces of code in his speech centres. They were questions as such, and received replies. Verbal communication was not all the soldier used, but was the most evident. In warfare, communication was always another way of reaching the enemy. In ancient human conflicts it had been done via propaganda and misinformation, but as warfare advanced and computing was increasingly used, it became a method to penetrate an enemy's systems. And now, a method to access a mind that Angel was realizing might not be entirely sane.

He began to check through his extensive collection of computer warfare weapons – the viruses, self-assembling worms, and other items of malicious computer life. The Wheel, meanwhile, closed up into a tight knot in his mind, then folded away. Abruptly, the field pinning Angel fell away and he was free. Did this mean the soldier now intended to destroy him? He focused on it, high in the sky above the smoking remains of Zackander's home. It was swivelling back and forth as if searching for something, then it shot away.

'Where are you going?' Angel asked, firing a tight-beam radio signal at the soldier to communicate.

'You get to live a little longer,' it replied. 'Primary threats must always be eliminated first.'

The Wheel landed back in Angel's mind, disorganized, in a

swirl of pieces, then began to reassemble, slowly regaining its former coherence. Angel realized it had tried something, but what, he did not know. And it had failed.

'Bring it to me,' the Wheel managed.

Orlik

Orlik gazed at the image of the wormship. The thing was unravelling and losing its current disguise. The particle beams fired by the Cyberat defence station chewed over hardfields the thing started projecting. Then it moved – no drive flame visible but its acceleration huge. The railgun slugs, arriving moments after the particle beams, just passed through the space where it had been. Orlik studied a tactical map in his mind – relayed to his implants from his ship's sensors via its mind – and realized that his plan to drive the wormship towards the steadily spreading field of space mines was futile. Through the tactical interface Zackander had allowed Orlik to set up with the station, he shut down its weapons. This would be fast, and though he could get the station to respond quickly, he didn't want to make it a primary target for the wormship just then, but keep it as a point of retreat.

'How do you estimate our chances of surviving this?' asked Cvallor, the captain of the other destroyer. Cvallor was Orlik's prime first-child whom he had transferred to that destroyer when they had seized it in the Graveyard fifty years ago. He had undergone changes due to the lack of suppressants to prevent him making the transition into adulthood. Though distinctions between first-child and adult were hazy for such as them . . .

'To use a human expression: a snowball's chance in hell,' Orlik replied.

'So the purpose of this action is?'

'Educational,' Orlik replied.

As instructed, they were constantly transmitting, through U-space, every possible scrap of data on this attack. Now, with the wormship heading directly towards them, Orlik's and Cvallor's ships parted, railguns firing constantly. A few seconds later, the slugs began hitting the wormship's hardfields and it disappeared in a fireball, leaving a long trail of flame and burning debris. But the fields showed no sign of weakening. Then the fireball collapsed, a brief U-signature detected.

'Fuck,' said Cvallor.

New imagery. The wormship had made a short U-jump and now reappeared directly in the path of Cvallor's destroyer. Its hardfields again took fire but a moment later that ceased as Cvallor erected his own defence. The fields of both ships hit with an intense green flash and the prador destroyer immediately began spewing burning hardfield projectors. Something then exploded in its rear, the blast so powerful it even peeled up a large plate of exotic armour. Orlik checked the tactical feed from the other destroyer, though it was breaking up now. When he saw what had happened he felt a stab of fear, then a calm acceptance.

'U-gate,' he muttered.

Via his implants he issued instructions directly to his U-space technicians, who scrambled to get something working he had foolishly not thought necessary before. It took them a couple of minutes, but they managed to fire up the internal runcible. This U-space bounce gate was not a standard addition to prador ships but it was a necessary one now the Polity had developed U-jump missiles. Just as this wormship apparently possessed, if the tactical feed was correct. The internal explosion had not been some part of Cvallor's destroyer overloading and exploding, nor had it been any of the munitions he carried. Also, nothing had penetrated his ship's armour.

Cvallor's defensive fields collapsed and a moment later the wormship shut down its own, descending on his ship like an amoeba on a bacterium. Writhing there, it began ripping his ship apart, lasers and sheer fields flashing, worms tearing away chunks of armour and plucking out gun emplacements like iron eyeballs. Orlik saw one such worm-form rip out an internal component shaped like a section from an octagonal rod. It shook it like an animal ripping prey. Shearfields flashed all around the thing in an even pattern, like the spokes of a turning wheel, and the object came apart. The worm flung away the fragments and dived back into tearing apart the ship.

'Cvallor?' Orlik enquired, but the connection was dead. Orlik cursed himself for even enquiring. He had just seen the other captain's sanctum ripped out of the ship and destroyed. Cvallor was certainly dead now.

'Fire on that thing now,' he instructed his gunners.

'But we'll hit—'

'Now!' Orlik affirmed. 'They're dead.'

Such an enquiry from the gunners was as unusual aboard a prador ship as the runcible bounce gate, but then the prador of this ship were not the usual kind, just as Orlik himself was not the usual father-captain. But he cursed himself for that piece of delegation – he should have used his implants to fire the weapons. He guessed he still had a long way to go getting his prador mind to adapt to the technological integration of himself, his ship mind and all his ship's systems.

Particle beams stabbed out, mostly hitting the wormship but occasionally stabbing past it to tear into Cvallor's destroyer. Railgun slugs hit a moment later. Orlik felt a surge of joy when he saw worms sliced in half, exploding and ablating in sun-hot particle streams. It was short lived, however, as hardfields came up again and the wormship began to pull itself back together.

Maybe, Orlik thought, those fields were directional? Maybe their strength was greater on the side directed towards a threat? Even as he thought this he used his implants to accelerate his ship around and out, firing constantly.

The wormship came back together completely and abandoned the wreck it had made of Cvallor's destroyer, which tumbled away through vacuum, shedding debris and prador – some maybe still alive. The wormship then began accelerating towards Orlik, again disappearing in a fireball as his railgun slugs impacted its fields. Now, through the tactical interface, he sent his instruction to the defence station.

The station fired everything it had at the wormship, from behind. Eight particle beams struck first. Railgun shots followed, four of the beams having to shut down so they didn't burn up the approaching swarm of slugs Cvallor had fired, or the slower-moving CTD missiles that followed them. A portion of vacuum a hundred miles across filled with intense fire. Orlik lost some cam imagery and slewed his ship aside to avoid a storm of fast-moving white-hot debris. But he continued firing on the predicted path of the wormship. Then something slammed into his hardfields and just hung there as if clinging to them. A large piece of the wormship was out there. They had destroyed it!

No. The worm began moving, its end now against the hardfield. Stress readings rocketed and Orlik's ship began auto-ejecting burned-out field projectors. For two minutes Orlik managed to maintain his defence but then the field the worm was attacking went out and was not replaced quickly enough, allowing it to fall through. His gunners tracked it with a particle beam. It ablated, then jerked and writhed as close-firing chemical propellant anti-personnel guns hit it with super-dense iron bullets. But, still intact, it landed on his destroyer's hull.

Now the CTD missiles reached the predicted location of the

wormship in the firestorm. A succession of intense detonations followed, balls of light expanding and blasting the fire away. Orlik saw this, but most of his concentration was on the worm on his hull. It was chewing on exotic metal armour with shearfield teeth but making little headway.

At his instruction, antipersonnel weapons designed to deal with attacking armoured prador rose out of the hull, swivelled on their posts and began hitting the thing with sharp-pointed exotic metal bullets. These punched inside it but didn't slow its traverse across the hull. Soon it would reach one of the necessary gaps in the armour where a ball-mounted gun emplacement sat. Maybe it could get through there or, if it moved beyond, it might go around the back of the ship and try to wreck the engines. Orlik sent new orders, some to automatic systems and some to his crew, then focused his attention back towards the wormship.

The incandescent gases and hot debris were clearing. Just one look told the captain that most of the debris were the remains of railgun slugs, though perhaps some were from whatever kind of hardfield generators the wormship used. The thing itself looked undamaged as it accelerated out of the storm, then disappeared inside another fireball as more railgun slugs from the defence station hit it. For a few minutes, Orlik thought it was coming directly for his ship, but it diverted and he saw that its course was taking it to the station. He felt a little relief at this, but knew it would be short lived.

His instructions were followed, and new canisters of rounds arrived at the antipersonnel guns where autoloaders slotted them into place. The guns paused for a few seconds during this process, in which time the worm reached the gun emplacement. It attacked with new vigour and Orlik saw chunks of the hydraulic system falling away from his ship. All connection to the emplacement shut down, though a feedback power surge blew out two nearby generators. Exterior view showed a bright-white arc light issuing from the front end of the worm. Automatics behind the emplacement activated to put out a spreading fire and Orlik watched in horror as the worm started to pull the whole thing out of his ship.

The antipersonnel guns began firing again, their loads of an entirely different and quite antiquated design. Copperhead armour-piercers hit the worm, their impact blasting white-hot copper vapour inside. The worm took hit after hit as it finally levered out the emplacement and batted it away, before beginning to slide into the ship. Now moving to meet it, armoured prador swarmed down surrounding corridors. Soon they reached the face of the thing and opened up with particle beams and Gatling cannons.

The intensity of fire brought the worm to a full stop, while outside the copperheads continued their work on its main body. Inside, it replied – a short-burst particle weapon whose beam was violet-white lancing out. It was devastating, and punched straight through each prador it hit, leaving a floating dead suit of armour spewing hot gas and boiled flesh. Then came another attack . . .

Orlik first only felt it as a presence – a shadow in the computer architecture and mind of his ship. The viral attack came next, knocking out automatics, swamping internal communications, sowing confusion in the mind and corrupting Orlik's connection. He fought back, utilizing stolen Polity anti-virals, shutting down those portions of the system near the worm fragment, using electromagnetic warfare and launching his own viral assault on the fragment. He also issued further orders to his crew.

Soon other prador arrived sporting missile launchers. Orlik had been reluctant to approve these but knew they were needed now. The missiles were much like the bullets hitting the worm outside. Five shots into the thing's face ripped it apart and the short-burst particle weapon died. Outside, the rest of the fragment was now filled with fire and moving sluggishly.

'Keep hitting it hard,' Orlik instructed, feeling he was also making headway in the informational war, but was aware of the regenerative capabilities of such technology. And, the data he had on wormships, which was sparse, indicated that a piece of one should do no more than physically attack, so this thing was more capable than expected.

'Get loaders in and push the thing out of my ship.'

He released five flying handlers outside his ship. They bore some similarity to a prador, with elliptical bodies and big heavy claws to the fore, but rather than legs they possessed heavy swivel-mounted rocket motors. Such devices were usually used to clear battle debris, and of course such was the case now.

Meanwhile the wormship had crashed straight into the station's hardfields, while it was already spewing out lines of burned and burning projectors. It resisted for a little longer than Cvallor's destroyer, but still the fields failed. The ship motored in, hitting the station so hard it sank some way into its armour, altering the station's position enough to have it dropping out of the Lagrange point orbit of the Cyberat world. Here the mismatch in scale was evident, for the wormship was about a tenth the size. It now spread out of the dent it had made and around the station, then inside it when its worm parts found or made access. Debris tumbled out and fires ignited inside. Orlik saw escape modules blasting away and realized that the small human crew had abandoned hope. As he watched the wormship chew through the station he was reminded of decaying bodies and the things that fed upon them.

The flying handlers had now arrived at the worm on his own ship, closed their claws on whatever they could grip and were heaving it up. Meanwhile his crew had brought in a heavy munitions loader and were pushing its front end out. Even as they were doing this the worm ceased to move. Orlik stared at the thing, a leaden feeling inside him. How much Jain tech had it spewed into his ship?

Would it be active or later activate to subsume this small part of a technical civilization – its chosen prey? And did such future eventualities matter? When that wormship had finished with the station it would come for his vessel and the end result would be foregone.

'When it is at a safe distance,' he instructed his gunners, 'destroy it completely.'

Another few minutes passed as the front end of the worm slowly ground out of his ship – a particularly stubborn barb in its flesh. Then, direct to his implants came a demand for communication, and it was one he could not refuse.

'I am here,' he replied after opening the link.

'Cancel your instruction to your gunners,' said one who had contacted him via U-space from a very long way away.

'Belay that order,' Orlik immediately sent to his gunners. 'Do not destroy the worm. I repeat: do not destroy the worm.'

'What do you want?' he now asked privately.

'It is enough,' said the other. 'The destruction of you and your vessel by that wormship serves no purpose. I have enough data to assess its battle capabilities. Data now on its structure and the technology it contains is of more interest to me.'

'You wish me to return with this item?' Orlik asked, suddenly feeling hope but still, at the heart of his being, prepared to obey unto death.

'No, don't return here. You will take the worm aboard your ship into your hold,' said the voice. 'You will pull away and head to the coordinates I give. When you arrive there, an ally will contact you. She will communicate with you via this link to give you detail concerning the quarantine and security measures you must take.'

'Very well,' said Orlik, about to say more when the other cut the comlink.

He sat there pondering, looking at the coordinates that had appeared on one of his screens. He was a first-child, though somewhat changed from the normal version, and supposedly must obey his father without thought. But obedience arose from his pheromonal indoctrination and after many years he had started to go his own way, started to have thoughts unusual for a prador.

'Prepare yourselves,' he broadcast to his entire ship, still pondering on those thoughts, and subsequent sins. 'We are leaving.'

Why the aversion to mentally interfacing with computers? Why the aversion to AI? Both had brought demonstrable advantages to the Polity during the war. And so Orlik had developed the hardware to connect himself to his ship. He had gone further, making a copy of his then failing ship's mind – the flash-frozen ganglion of a first-child whose mental growth was crippled and incapable of original thought – to AI crystal. Its abilities increased, and it came close to actually being an AI. Under prador law what he had done was worthy of a death sentence. But his real sin, he learned when his father, the king, found out, was the risk he had taken, without orders, of connecting the king's family to technology abhorrent to most normal prador – such a thing could foment rebellion amongst them. He had expected death to be his punishment but his father had surprised him. Orlik would desert the Kingdom as a renegade, but obey his father absolutely. In this way, he would become a deniable asset able to go to places – like the Graveyard – where other prador warships could not.

'Still hankering to return to the Kingdom?' said a voice.

Orlik looked up at the Polity drone nailed to its plate.

'Shut up, drone.' He wasn't in the mood for conversation.

Trike

'What's happening?' Trike asked, again straining against the bonds around his legs.

Lyra was silent for a moment, then she lowered her gaze from the ceiling and blinked at both of them. She looked pale and ill now. Perhaps the leeches stuck to the ceiling weren't supposed to escape.

'Something's coming,' she said, 'and I don't know what the fuck it is.'

'Explain,' Cog demanded.

She focused on him fully. 'I got cam feeds from out there. Zackander fired some container at the legate as he departed. The legate opened it and what looked like a war drone came out. It pushed the legate away with a force-field then rose up and destroyed what was left of Zackander's home.' She paused, thoughtful. 'I don't know what the hell it was using but the underground explosions were hot enough to melt down a mile deep. Now it's coming here.'

'Any Polity war drone is capable of that kind of damage,' said Cog.

'Yes, but does this look like a Polity war drone?'

The outline of an object appeared in the middle of the room where Zackander had been, then the projector filled it with substance and colour. The armoured monstrosity seemed to be a blend of mutated lobster and hard technology, a mix of organic and inorganic – similar to Lyra herself, Trike thought.

'Probably an assassin drone,' said Cog doubtfully.

'That's not all,' said Lyra. 'This thing is leaving a U-space signature.'

Now Cog looked a bit tired and ill as well. He was about to say something when the room shook to four hollow booms.

'Zackander, what have you done?' Lyra asked.

'What's happening?' Trike asked, almost cheerfully.

Cog studied him carefully. Trike looked back and forced seriousness into his expression, waving a hand towards the now shimmering and distorting hologram. 'What is that thing?' He knew he wasn't quite sane, but if he was to get what he wanted, he needed to control himself. *Ignore the leeches*, he thought. *Ignore the hammer whelks and the frog whelks and the auras and that silent tap tap tapping hooder . . .*

The words seemed enough to turn the Old Captain's mind to other matters, though Trike wasn't sure which words, the ones he'd spoken out loud or the ones he'd spoken in his mind? Cog looked at the image and said to Lyra, 'That U-space signature?'

'Jain tech,' she confirmed.

Cog raised the device in his hand and thumbed a control. Trike abruptly found himself free, and was standing in a moment. A fierce and strange joy surged through him and he wanted to run for the door and go after those escaping hammer whelks, but he managed to hold himself in place. He felt an overpowering urge for a drink of sea-cane rum too, and wondered where Lyra had put the bottle. He was about to move, not entirely sure where, when he found his arm immobile. Cog had moved fast and was now standing beside him, one hand clamped round his forearm. Trike tried to struggle free, but it was as if his arm was set in stone.

'Don't,' said Cog, 'for one moment, think that I don't know you're not right, Trike.'

'I don't know what you—'

'*Don't* forget this.' Cog interrupted.

With his other hand, the Old Captain grabbed Trike by the neck and threw him across the room. Trike didn't even have time to yell before he hit a wall, hard. He hung there, upside down, with broken ceramic tiles falling about him, then peeled out of the impact hole and slid to the floor. He felt broken bones grating inside his body as he righted himself, and peered down at his unnaturally bent forearm. Almost without thinking, he reached down and straightened it out with a crunch, before it healed in that position.

'It's obvious I cannot leave you here,' said Cog, now crouching before him. 'It's also obvious you have some self-control. You will come with me and you will do what I tell you. Do not disobey me.'

Giggling madness swirled in Trike's head. He wanted to laugh in the Old Captain's face. He wanted to shout 'Frog whelks!' and just run. But at his core he remembered how Cog, for a bet years ago on Spatterjay, snapped a chunk of hull armour with his hands.

'Don't make the wrong choice,' Cog said. 'I've known since we first met what you have inside, just as I always did with Jay. He made the wrong choice. He let it rise within him and he never came back. If you do the same I will do to you what I should have done to him. I will break you into pieces and burn those pieces.'

The giggling died inside Trike, killed by a spear of cold through his spine. Jay was not a name commonly used on Spatterjay because of its history with their founder. The pirate Jay Hoop, nicknamed Spatterjay, Spatterjay Hoop, had set up his vicious coring trade on that world. He kidnapped people, exposing them to the virus, then coring and thralling them – cutting out their brains and part of their spinal column to replace these with a control mechanism. They were then sold to the prador. Jay had been one of the very first to be infected with the virus. It was rumoured that he was still there on Spatterjay somewhere and that the virus had turned him into a monstrous thing.

'You knew Jay Hoop?' Trike asked, hallucinations fading around him.

'Knew him?' said Cog. He reached out with one hand, clasped Trike's hand and hauled him to his feet. 'We were brothers.'

The room shuddered again, and from outside came the sawing of particle weapons and the sonic cracking of railguns. There was another close boom and the whole room lurched, a crack appearing in the ceiling. Out of this crack squirmed a series of leeches.

'Go away,' said Trike, and he watched them fade into non-existence.

'Lyra?' Cog asked.

'It's here, obviously,' she replied, 'and we're fighting it.'

'You?' asked Cog.

'The Cyberat are fighting it,' she said, frowning and shaking her head. 'I'm with you.'

Trike felt something thrust into his hands and looked down in puzzlement at his pack, wondering how it had got there. Cog was now over the other side of the room extracting a weapon from his own pack, and screwing on a gigawatt energy canister. Lyra flowed with a harsh metallic rattling towards the door and he found himself trotting to keep up. He took the QC laser out of his pack, as well as mini-grenades which he inserted into his pocket. He found himself in a corridor, the floor thick with blue carpet moss, the ceiling arched overhead and shifting scenes through apparent windows, all different. Deep in one of these – a scene from Earth of some sunny Caribbean island beach – he saw a group of frog whelks leaping joyously, stalked eyes up and eyeballs gyrating crazily. He raised a hand to them in acknowledgement and hurried past.

'It's in our fucking systems, damn it!' Lyra yelled, leading them through a wooden door into a corridor, at the end of which was the mouth of a grav-shaft. 'We go down,' she pointed.

'Into your systems?' Cog asked.

'Yes, it's—' The blood drained from her face, and on the metal legs of her hooder body she skittered backwards. 'Oh no,' she added.

'Lyra . . .'

She screamed and rose up high towards the ceiling, supported only by four of the back legs. The hooder part of her body then coiled round, like a woodlouse, lowering her top human body into the rest of the eagerly waving legs. She screamed again to the sounds of multiple butcher's knives cutting. Trike looked down at something that landed by his feet – a severed human hand with sucker-tipped fingers. When he looked back, Cog was down beside Lyra, trying to pull her free from her own graft, his arms covered in blood up to the shoulders as he snapped off waving metal legs.

'Lyra! Lyra!' he bellowed.

'Stop,' said Trike.

Cog glanced round at him, his expression livid. Trike pointed to where Lyra's head now lay, a foot away from a neck that looked like it had been through a macerator. Cog stared at it, while the remaining metal legs moved a few times more before growing still. Cog slowly rose to his feet.

'I will never, ever accept it,' he said.

'What?' Trike asked, baffled.

'Death.' Cog stepped over to him angrily, bloody hands clenching and unclenching. He grabbed Trike's arm and thrust him towards the dropshaft. Trike hesitated at the edge because obviously the irised gravity field in the shaft had shut down. A hard hand slammed into his back and he found himself falling down into darkness.

'You're a fucking hooper,' Cog yelled, falling after him.

Trike righted his tumble with a couple of slaps against the side of the shaft. He landed on his feet, legs bending, and rolled out of the darkness into chaos. Glancing round he saw the base entrances to other shafts running along the walls to his right and left. He was in a high hall that in one direction terminated with a wall occupied by balconied apartments. At the other end he saw two giant doors standing open and recognized the entrance into the Cube. The hall itself was occupied by Cyberat and other things that looked to be wholly machine.

'What the fuck?' he said, the exclamation sounding like a joyous observation. He watched a Cyberat man, who consisted of a head

197

and a human torso sprouting numerous metallic spider limbs, running past, pursued by a surgical robot. This giant chromed woodlouse ran on long gleaming legs, terminating in a varied collection of surgical cutlery. Trike thought the man might escape as he tried to scuttle up the wall, but the robot caught hold of one of his legs and dragged him down, then underneath itself. Trike saw the look of appeal on the man's face before the screaming started, as blood and pieces of flesh sprayed out. He was still watching when a heavy boot thumped into the side of the thing and sent it skittering across the hall and smashing into the wall.

'Keep moving!' said Cog, cuffing him across the back of the head.

They ran for the giant doors.

'Why is it doing this?' Trike asked.

Cog now held a flat compact gun in one hand, which he fired twice, decapitating a lurching android that definitely wasn't of the Golem series. Something about that weapon niggled in Trike's mind.

Thin-gun, he remembered, but had no idea what that meant.

'Because it is vicious?' Cog suggested.

A creature like a huge steel cockroach with an extra joint in its main carapace reared up before Trike, then surged forwards with plug borers whirling at the end of its forelimbs. He considered shooting it but did not want to waste his laser's charge, so ran to meet it and kicked it hard. With a sound like a glass bottle being tossed into a scrapyard, his boot went right through and the thing sagged.

'Fuck,' he said.

Trike struggled on after Cog, still trying to shake the defunct insect robot off his leg. Eventually he paused and brought his other foot down on it to extract the trapped one. He scanned around again. All the strange Cyberat in view now seemed to be attacking themselves. He saw one, who looked much like Zack-ander, shoot across and slam into a wall, body of flesh first. The sphere then drifted away with the body hanging slack and broken. A woman who had retained human legs but looked like a robotic Khali seemed to be cutting off her own face with her extra robotic limbs.

Once free of the robot on his leg, and after slapping away one of its smaller kin, Trike dashed after Cog. He followed the Old Captain out through the doors and looked up to where more Cyberat were killing themselves in the sky. He saw a tilted grav-barge spilling people, while firing on others. And higher up, he saw the cyborg lobster, casually drifting along, occasional stabs of a bright green particle beam frying Cyberat and dropping them smoking from the sky.

'Keep moving,' Cog said. 'We still have a chance.' He gestured towards the landing field where a couple of ships were rising into the sky. The creature up there had thus far shown no interest in them.

They ran, steaming metal and flesh falling about them. The gates into the landing field were open, while the fence on one side was down and smoking, red hot in places. They ran through and soon Cog's ship lay before them. Its main body bore the shape of an oceangoing ship's hull, while at the back end stood a cylindrical tower similar to such a ship's bridge. It was already lowering a ramp as they approached, and Cog ran straight inside.

Trike felt exhilarated as he followed, and when he stepped inside the ship he had the urge to run back out again. But he clung to an I-beam instead as the ramp closed up, and the feeling began to dissipate. Sudden fear then lurched into his conscious-ness and in the gloom he heard a tap tapping, and sensed sliding movement behind the strapped-down cargo crates. He was sure the place was packed full of leeches. He quickly followed Cog to a spiral staircase and up into the bridge.

'Report,' said Cog, settling himself down in his captain's throne.

'Nothing in the system,' replied the mind of his ship, the *Janus*. 'Something tried but I put a ghost copy of myself in its way and it took over that.' The mind paused then added, 'The others were not so well prepared.'

The transparent screen that wrapped around the bridge, which until that moment only showed the surrounding landing field, now threw up image frames in its laminate. In one a spreading explosion was visible and Trike heard the rumble from outside. The others showed two of the rising ships he had seen earlier. Even as he watched, one of them lost its drive and began to fall. The cam followed it down to where it hit the ground and fragmented.

'Full chameleonware and launch,' Cog instructed.

'Full?' the mind enquired.

'Have you not been keeping up on events?' Cog asked. 'That thing out there is fucking Jain tech.'

'Ah,' said Janus, a mind that Trike had once thought was from a prador first-child, but about which he now had his doubts.

He walked over and plumped himself down in one of the other three acceleration chairs, then pulled across and secured the safety straps. Of course, little could hurt him, but if things got rough it would be inconvenient bouncing around in here. After a moment of introspection while he gazed at the console before him, with its overly complicated controls for the ship's single particle cannon, he returned his attention to the displays.

The ship launched, just as the final remaining ship above blew apart in a flameless explosion, scrap raining down. New frames now opened in the laminate showing views above and below, all around, and down towards the retreating landscape, with one fixed on the Cube. Trike began humming to himself and rocking against his straps. Maybe if he did this long enough the small whelks sliding in neat lines across the console would disappear. After a moment, he realized Cog was looking at him and he desisted, sitting back to gaze up at the ceiling. A leech appeared there and dropped a questing tubular mouth towards him. He stared at it hard until it had the decency to fade out of existence.

'Okay,' said Cog after a few minutes of steady acceleration, 'either it hasn't seen us or it's just—'

The flash whited-out every frame and flared in the sky outside where they could see it. All the frames then went black for a moment before flicking back on, one by one. The view of the Cube now showed a bright ball of fire sitting at the centre of a dust cloud, and hurtling debris. The Jain lobster had quit playing and its particle weapon flashed perpetually, scoring thousands of lines over the explosion, and thousands of objects fell away, burning. The ball of fire where the Cube had been shrank to a single bright point and winked out. Then all the dust and debris abruptly reversed course, heading into that same point. The whole mess collapsed down and down until it disappeared, leaving a deep crater into which green seawater drained and boiled. A hole opened in the bottom of the crater – a perfectly round tunnel spearing through seawater, and down through rock into darkness. The sea closed the hole then swirled as it rushed into this giant plughole.

'That was . . . excessive,' said Cog numbly.

'What?' said Trike. The swirling sea had a strange calming almost hypnotic effect on him.

'Are you so far gone you can't see?' asked Cog, glaring at him.

Trike detected danger and watched the small whelks scuttle for cover. He forced himself back into the moment and tried to think clearly.

'Some kind of CTD imploder,' he suggested. He knew about such weapons. They first blew something up then a brief singularity sucked everything back in before vaporizing, causing a second explosion. It was the kind of weapon the Polity used against something seriously dangerous, like Jain technology.

'Yes, that,' said Cog. He leaned back and took his pipe out of his pocket, and with slightly shaking hands began to pack it. 'And where is Ruth?'

Trike looked around, his remaining hallucinations fled and his chest tightened as he remembered the ships he had seen on the way up being destroyed. He searched with the U-mitter he had in his skull and felt her down there. Shivering, he reached out to the controls before him and input coordinates. A screen frame opened to show him the landing field out on the rim of the crater where the Cube had been. The shuttle still sat there, seemingly undamaged.

'It's good that she did not try to leave,' Cog commented.

'Yes,' was all Trike could manage, his mouth dry.

An explosion of steam erupted from the crater where the Cube had been, followed by a plume of lava. Then the frame view blacked out, as did others from down on the planet. Trike now gazed through the screen at the curve of the world and starlit space.

'We got away,' he said flatly.

'Not yet,' said Cog.

10

At the Battle of Agincourt the cream of French chivalry fell to the English longbow. In the First World War, the machinegun inflicted appalling casualties. Hitler's blitzkrieg of the Second World War smashed through old-time defences and rolled up armies. Following that conflict, air warfare became the predominant force, until defensive lasers and railguns got up to speed. Guerrilla warfare killed the high-tech soldier until killer micro-drones swarmed in. AI-linked soldiers in powered exoskeletons were unstoppable, until induction-warfare beams were invented, and stopped them. The armour of prador war-ships was nearly the end of the Polity until our industrial might prevailed. Weapons change, logistics change, tactics change and in the interim soldiers get ground into paste. What can be learned from history? That in the end the greatest killer of any soldier is not the longbow or the machinegun, it is not the laser or the micro-drone, but the failure to adapt. My vision of the modern soldier is of one who can change fast enough to accommodate improvements in warfare, and survive. The war drones of the prador/human war came closest to that ideal, but it is my contention that subsequent specialization blunted their edge. But military intelligences still strive to create the ideal – the super-soldier. Perhaps we should be thankful that they continue to fail.

Notes from her lecture 'Modern Warfare' by E. B. S. Heinlein

Orlandine

The accretion disc sat quiet while work on the defence platform orbiting Jaskor was being completed at a satisfactory pace. Work on Orlandine's special project, the two runcibles, still continued but would stall in a few days due to lack of vital components and materials. Knobbler and the other drones there were not happy about this but grudgingly accepted that the platform had priority. In essence, and considering the circumstances, all was as it should be, but Orlandine could not settle back into the work that had occupied her for decades.

'I'm bored,' said Cutter from the living quarters of her ship.

'It's your age,' Bludgeon replied, perfectly happy plugged into the ship's computing and studying defence-platform technical stats.

Cutter grunted in annoyance. Via internal cams, Orlandine watched him moving about in the living area. Abruptly he halted and slumped.

'I think . . . I'll . . . step past . . . this,' he said.

It wasn't really sleep he was dropping into. He was using the drone technique of altering his perception of time. Now hours would pass like seconds for him, or even microseconds. Orlandine envied him, wanting time to pass and events to react to, but somehow she could not take the same step. Was this a result of her antecedents? She had been gestated in a womb and born of a human mother, while Cutter had been assembled on a production line in a war factory.

Why did she also feel so ill at ease? The frustrating explanation from Dragon was part of it, but she also had a certainty that something was happening. This feeling definitely arose from her human component but seemed to be confirmed by an untraceable source within another element of her being: the Jain technology that bound her human self to her Polity AI crystal. Was it perhaps the case that, just as the Jain tech in the accretion disc responded to the hidden Jain AIs, she possessed some connection to that technology in general? Did it share a kind of group subconscious? This was possible. Though she had conquered the technology of one Jain node and turned it to her will, it had levels of function that extended into the sub-nano-scopic world beyond her control and perception. When, finally, a request for contact came from an unexpected source, she felt relief, as if events were again moving towards some conclusion.

'It's been a long time,' she said, opening the connection. She gazed mentally, with deep fascination, at the transmitted image.

'Five of your human years, I believe,' replied the other.

'I never had a chance to thank you for the metallurgist,' she said, 'and for the two cubic miles of prador armour sheeting. And for all the rest.'

'And I thank you for allowing the enclave on Jaskor,' replied the other.

'It's an embassy only. Your prador there don't get to do much.'

'Nevertheless, it is a presence and delivers the message to the Polity AIs that the defence sphere is not theirs. Our interests are the same in this respect,' replied the other. 'I prefer to deal with you because you are independent and I would find it distasteful dealing directly with Polity AIs. You are sufficiently grey.'

'Why, thank you, my . . .' Orlandine hesitated with the title.

'Call me Oberon,' the king of the prador interjected. 'The course of history runs smooth and I have sufficient respect for the one who said I would give myself this name to comply. Perhaps I have also acquired something in the way of superstition. If I diverge from my planned course then maybe I invite catastrophe – like the potential one you sit on at that accretion disc.'

The king of the prador had changed only slightly in the last five years. However, his prador form had altered considerably since he had seized control of the Kingdom. The Spatterjay virus had this strange effect on these alien crustaceans. He was much bigger than a prador adult and his body had stretched out so he now resembled some sort of giant, long-legged louse. Red demonic eyes gleamed to his fore over a complicated set-up of mandibles that looked more like something found on an autodoc than on a predator such as him. And even over the link, with the knowledge that he was light years away, Orlandine found something danger-ously sinister about him.

'What can I do for you?' she asked.

'Events have occurred that directly relate to your self-assumed mission,' Oberon replied. 'Some information has become available concerning the entity Erebus, who made use of Jain technology acquired from the accretion disc, and who may have activated its present activity there.'

'Information?' Orlandine repeated, waiting.

'A legate, in control of a wormship, went to the world of the Cyberat.'

Orlandine felt a thrill run down the data sockets in her sides. It wasn't exactly fear, nor was it surprise. Analysing it, she could only describe it as a feeling of being 'back in the game'.

'A legate and a wormship survived Erebus's suicide?'

'Just so.'

Orlandine decided to ignore the questions that clamoured in her mind. 'Continue.'

'On that world is a Cyberat called Zackander who possesses many items of Jain technology. It seems likely the legate was there in this regard. At the time, it so happens my agents were there too.'

'Doubtless ensuring those items would fall into the right . . . claws?'

'It was necessary to have a presence there,' Oberon equivocated. 'Another embassy, if you like.'

'I'm sure.'

'Yes, my agents had struck a deal with Zackander for some exchanges. Their payment was protection which, upon the arrival of this wormship, Zackander collected on.'

'Wait a minute,' said Orlandine. 'These agents – what were they packing?'

'Two destroyers.'

'Not enough.'

'Somewhat more advanced than usual.'

'Still . . .'

'No, you are correct, one of the destroyers was itself destroyed.'

'And you allowed this?'

'The data were more important.'

Orlandine let that go. Polity AIs were quite prepared to sacrifice lives if it facilitated the collection of data vital to the survival of the Polity. She should be less surprised by the same ruthlessness from the king of the prador.

'What data?'

'A great deal,' said the king. 'The wormship, without the legate aboard, fought intelligently – it behaved beyond the expectations of something without a guiding mind. It U-jumped during the fight and it also deployed a U-jump missile.'

'The legate was linked.'

'No, too much disruption.'

'You are supposing the legate was the only passenger?'

'You have the crux of the matter.'

'There is more?'

'Yes. My remaining destroyer was attacked by a fragment which the wormship shed of itself. Jain sequestering abilities were indicated.'

This was fascinating. Much of what Erebus had controlled, like its wormships, had been complicated items that were a by-blow of Jain and Polity technology. Only when specifically made to do so were they able to sequester, spreading and destroying in the way that Jain technology did. The contention amidst Polity AIs was that Erebus used Jain technology but did not wholly incorporate it – that it took only what it required and avoided the trap. This was Orlandine's contention too, because that was precisely what she had done.

'You have detail?' she asked.

'This interests you?'

'It does.'

'I will send you coordinates for the destroyer and a method of making contact.'

'Wait, I don't under—'

The king was gone; the comlink cut. Orlandine cursed. Did he expect her to just drop everything and run to do his bidding? What the hell was it he wanted anyway? She studied the package he had sent just before closing the link. It contained a wealth of detail on the legate and some analysis of how it might have survived the destruction of Erebus, as well as speculation on its present goals. She took all this apart rapidly and studied it intently. She then turned to other data on the Cyberat, with their de facto ruler, this Zackander, and his collection of Jain artefacts. The detail on that, she realized, was what Oberon's agents had exchanged their services for. She felt another visceral thrill.

The Jain tech, interlaced throughout her body and apparently under her control, responded on some deep level to these items, and to one in particular. Perhaps she was right, perhaps she did sample from some kind of communal subconscious. She checked linked files and found deeper scan data on the object, studying the intricate internal structure. Her knowledge of Jain tech was such that she quickly understood that this thing was a storage device for organic matter, while from her deeper self, there rose a response to extreme danger. The genetic code of one of the Jain themselves, perhaps? Whatever it was, she was certain this was the item the legate had gone to the Cyberat world for.

What should she do?

Dragon.

Even as the thought occurred to her she made contact with the entity, sitting out there in vacuum, where it had assumed the position of the missing Weapons Platform Mu in the accretion disc defence sphere.

'Look at this,' she stated, and rather than get into any discussion, she just transmitted a recording of everything that had passed from the moment Oberon had contacted her.

'Go,' Dragon replied, just seconds later.

'As simple as that?' she asked.

'Resolution will come from data, from knowledge,' Dragon replied. 'Traps lie in our path.'

'Maybe we have found this other agency you mentioned?'

'Or results of its actions.'

'This legate is the other agency?'

'I doubt it,' Dragon replied.

She considered probing further but was reluctant. She understood that she would get no more from Dragon, and must comprehend fully herself. She lay in her interface sphere contemplating the purpose of her life now. Jain tech had been the enemy and she had helped destroy a breakout of it instigated by the rogue AI Erebus. Later recruited by Dragon, her new goal was to prevent further breakouts of the technology from the accretion disc, and finally to eliminate the threat. But these were specific purposes. Her general aim was always to counter the threat this technology posed. And a legate, running around in a wormship, hunting down items of Jain tech that her inner self warned her were more dangerous than the usual kind (merely capable of destroying civilizations), must be lethal indeed.

She had to get involved, there was no doubt.

'So we go?' enquired Bludgeon.

She'd been aware that through her system the drone had been a silent watcher, but hadn't minded – she trusted all the drones from the war runcible absolutely.

'We go,' she replied.

Earth Central

Earth Central stepped into the virtuality bearing the form of a thin-faced young haiman with blond hair plaited close to his skull, and a tough wiry physique. Interface plugs were behind each ear and running like a line of nacreous scales from the base of his skull down his spine, with other support hardware scattered around his body. EC reviewed his appearance for a moment, and decided against the ersatz Jacobean clothing this form had once worn. He clad himself in a simple environment suit, then began to fill in his surroundings over the white plain and sky.

The panoramic viewing window of a spaceship drew across, sunlight glaring in and the titanic construction blocks of a Dyson sphere silhouetted against it. Other items shifted out there: giant constructor ships, robots capable of shaping asteroids and vast pseudo-matter scaffolds gridded across hundreds of thousands of miles of vacuum. All was ready and it had taken less than a microsecond – time enough for the visitor to take her precautions before entering the virtuality.

'Shoala,' said a voice, 'a crass appeal to my conscience, perhaps?'

EC turned.

Orlandine had chosen to present herself in her current form. Her skin was the colour of coffee and her head bald. A skin-tight shipsuit clung to her curves and her eyes were blue, with a hint of metal in them.

'It is always worth reminding you,' replied EC.

'Do you think me capable of forgetting the man I murdered?' she asked. 'But I refuse to feel guilt any more – I was a different person then.' She gazed at the view. 'The Cassius Project . . . how goes it there now?'

'Haimen and AIs continue to build the Dyson sphere – projections have improved now and it seems likely it will be completed in eighty thousand years.'

Orlandine nodded. 'You could have chosen a better view.'

Earth Central felt a moment of annoyance. This wasn't going as it had expected. With a thought, it changed the view. Now fragments of a cosmic egg floated in gas clouds, lit from within. The Cassius gas giant, in its own orbit close around the sun, supplied those clouds, while carefully positioned anti-matter blasts slowly took it apart. Some of the egg-shell fragments were a hundred thousand miles across. Matter converters the size of small moons crawled at their edges, sucking in the debris of the gas giant's destruction and slowly laying it down as a mile-thick composite laced with a balancing web of grav-motors and superconducting cables.

'Beautiful,' said Orlandine and swung round to gaze at EC. 'The king of the prador has passed on to me something of interest. I felt beholden, considering how I sit precariously between two powers, to inform you. However, I see that I have no need of doing so.'

How did she do that? How could she know?

'You are a datavore, EC, and just like the king, and like

Dragon, you like to push things together to see what further information arises,' she said.

It was as if she could read his mind.

'I was aware that the king might be calling on your services,' said EC. 'I have not been apprised of the detail.'

Rather than reply verbally, she sent a data package. EC studied it briefly. 'A wormship fragment showing the ability to sequester . . . You are en route?'

'I am en route.'

'And Dragon?'

'Remains at the accretion disc temporarily replacing the weapons platform it mislaid.' Orlandine stood perfectly still for a moment, but for that metallic movement in her eyes. 'You see connections.'

'I always see connections.'

She nodded. 'What further information do you require?'

'I would like regular updates on your progress when you reach this destroyer.'

'Very well, so we are done talking for now.'

'There is one further point . . .'

'Yes?'

'It is only fair to warn you that the king may, sometime soon, become less cooperative. The weapons platform you lost may well turn up in the Kingdom. Proceed with caution.'

'The Client seeking vengeance?'

EC considered a truthful reply, but then decided on a half-truth. It was unsure what she knew and always felt better in these situations not revealing too much to someone it doubted. 'Yes, probably.'

Orlandine nodded and shimmered out of existence.

Earth Central gazed at the spot she had occupied then returned its attention to the panorama. It changed now, showing an enhanced view into a system consisting of a red dwarf orbiting a neutron star. It was all sitting in a mass of fragments that had once been the planetary system of the red dwarf, before the neutron star arrived. This system had a bright star in its firmament – the accretion disc was not so far away in interstellar terms. EC focused in on the fleet of ships concealed amidst the fragments. Two hundred modern destroyers hung like giant sarcophagi expelled from some vast vacuum burial ship. A thousand attack ships, black as coal, were a swirling shoal of hunting garfish. The giant lozenges of standard dreadnoughts drifted, limiting output that might be detected. While other behemoths pretended to be moons set loose.

EC blinked and the view changed again.

The prador watch station vaguely bore the shape of a pyramid mounted on top of a cylinder and was ten miles from top to bottom. In its shadow, reavers waited – three hundred of them at last count. No attempt had been made at concealment here, so EC wondered if there was something else being hidden. Whatever. These ships lay the same distance from the accretion disc as the Polity fleet did. It was good to be prepared, as both EC and the king were. It would be preferable, however, if none of the gathered ships needed to be deployed. If they were, Earth Central had no doubt that things would get messy.

Angel

Angel looked upwards and saw meteors in the day-lit sky as debris from the battle there began to hit atmosphere. He closed his eyes and dampened his scanning of the immediate surroundings so that he could make a firmer link with his wormship. The soldier had annihilated the Cube and all the Cyberat in its vicinity but, thankfully, did not seem in any great hurry to return. The worms he had sent it were now self-assembling in its mind, and Angel could, through them, see some of what the soldier was doing. It was running through, and incorporating at an astonishing rate, all the data it had taken. Angel surmised that the soldier had realized the Cube and the Cyberat were not a threat that needed to be destroyed straight away, contrary to its first calculations. Instead it had gathered data while occupying them with a viral attack on their systems, and then had finally killed them.

The soldier's single-minded focus on destruction, and on loading data, had kept it distracted. It had only concentrated on analysing, then defending itself against computer attacks from the Cyberat, which had enabled Angel to slip something Jain-based into portions of its mind: those worms. As they assembled they began using the soldier's own transmitters to send back the schematic of its mind to the legate. He prepared to receive something vast and complex but what he got surprised him. It seemed all structure; autonomous systems almost like hard wiring and no plasticity.

He spent some minutes studying the schematic and found it strangely empty. It was, he realized, a large complex processor. He also saw that he had been very lucky to penetrate it. Though mostly autonomous, it did have some seriously dangerous routines to deal with mental penetration. That they had not reacted seemed likely due to the fact that large portions of the soldier's mind had yet to be activated, portions Angel failed to understand. But he surmised that this super-soldier was nowhere near its full growth and potential. He then decided he had seen enough of the schematic and, very carefully, began to look into the mind itself.

Everything that had happened since the moment it became conscious in Zackander's zero-freezer lay open to his inspection. Angel saw how the super-soldier had allowed the old Cyberat to believe he could command it by giving him control over the command channel of just one small portion of its mind. Meanwhile it had been working steadily to free itself. If Zackander had not panicked when Angel arrived, he calculated that it would have freed itself within two years. The result on this world would have been the same, though Zackander would have been dead too. The legate now began to activate other memories and view them.

Angel looked upon a strange city of triangular buildings rising from a giant circular grav-plate, hovering above mountains. Something living fled across his view and he glimpsed a lobster body trailing ribbed tentacles. This thing was black and polished silver – the silver being the cyber component of it sunk into its coal-like flesh. Jain? He captured the image and studied it more closely, aware that this must be a memory once stored in the soldier's very genome. But as he did so other portions of his mind went on high alert. By awakening this memory he had caused a chain-reaction in the soldier's mind and other parts of it were waking up. Suddenly he understood the purpose of the U-space devices distributed throughout the creature. They were a connection to a backup sitting in that continuum. It seemed likely that this soldier could receive a mind from storage – the mind of a super-soldier that had been out of commission for five million years.

Angel had to act quickly if he was to seize control of this thing and get it to his wormship. But as a precaution before proceeding, he sent out a call to the sphere transport he had used to land on the Cyberat world. Then he swamped all command channels within the soldier and tried to seize control. But grappling with the mind suddenly became like wrestling eels. More memories and subsystems were loading to it constantly and it began to change shape, forcing Angel to adapt his attack. For a moment he thought he had it, and was gaining control, until he saw the shape of what was now occupying the soldier and it scattered his wits. Almost casually it slapped him away and he found himself back wholly in his own body again.

Angel tried to understand what he had seen, but could not find a way in. He realized in retrospect that the only common ground between them was the technology. His own mind, when its antecedents were traced back, had arisen from humanity. The shape of this thing was totally alien. It wasn't even akin to the prador who, though very different from humans, possessed human traits. Here was a mind that had moved far beyond a straight-line evolutionary formation into something much more complex . . . and twisted. This was a dead loss – he could not control it.

He looked around and opened scanning to take in a wider area. His sphere was hurtling towards him while the soldier still hung in the sky over a hundred miles away. But he knew that once it was ready, it would come for him. He looked up, focusing on his connection with his wormship.

'New plan,' he sent.

All he got in return from the Wheel was a sense of puzzlement.

'Piss it off,' Angel finished.

The soldier was now on the move, slowly at first, hesitantly, then accelerating. As Angel had supposed, it was heading directly towards him. He issued further instructions to his ship and a bright green particle beam flashed down through the atmosphere, its energy levels perfectly calculated not to penetrate the soldier's defences. This flashed against a distant hardfield, revealing a curve to the field, which should have been impossible. The soldier dropped from the sky and hit the ground hard, bouncing, but it then shot back up again, shedding fire and smoke. Angel realized his calculations had been wrong, and he really needed to slow the thing down more. His ship fired again. This time the soldier stayed down for longer, but when it came back up again Angel could detect a powerful U-signature at its location – some twist in that continuum he did not recognize. He hit it a third time, but the soldier just disappeared inside an opaque white sphere, which carried on. Angel ordered his ship to continue firing, for while the thing was inside that impossibly spherical hardfield it couldn't launch any weapons of its own. Hopefully.

By now Angel's sphere was just half a mile away. He issued new instructions to it and activated grav inside himself to rise up off the ground. The sphere, opening its door, swept him up and he crashed inside. It snapped shut, and he fell down flat as it accelerated upwards at a hundred gravities. When he finally managed a sensor link he saw, as expected, the soldier speeding after him.

Trike

Trike regarded the frame images as they reached vacuum. He watched the recording, taken from satellite memory, of Ruth's shuttle heading into orbit – she had left shortly after the creature moved away from the Cube. The wormship then arrived over the world, but her orbit took her away from it.

'She got away from it,' he observed.

'Yes, she did,' said Cog non-commitally.

'Maybe she isn't controlled by Angel?'

'Maybe not.' Cog was now staring at him intently. 'Or maybe she escaped that control for a brief while.'

'Yes . . . yes,' said Trike, confused about what he was feeling.

'It's eased a bit now,' said Cog. 'Hasn't it?'

Trike gazed at him. 'How do you know?'

'I've seen this kind of craziness before,' he replied. 'You have to be on your guard because it can slide back so easily.'

'It always has,' said Trike, feeling hollow.

Cog turned away from him, shaking his head. After a moment of checking his instruments and pulling up other views in the screen frames, he said, 'Something happened down there.' He pointed at one repeating view that showed the wormship firing down towards the planet. 'It fired on that thing, I think to delay it so Angel could escape. He's on his way up now, and fast.' He paused for a second, then added, 'And so is that *thing*.'

Trike watched the display, which Cog now zoomed in on. He could see the two objects hurtling towards the wormship, and two other screens showed the close views of an ascending sphere and the pursuing creature. Something was puzzling him; something had slipped his mind. He concentrated, trying to understand what the tightness in his chest was telling him.

'We should get to Ruth,' he said.

Cog turned and looked at him, his expression hard. 'Angel might yet pick her up again.'

Trike puzzled his way through that, still fighting his wayward mind. He realized then the hard truth. Cog wanted Angel to seize Ruth because then he would have a way to continue tracking the wormship.

The two objects drew in towards the wormship, the sphere abruptly decelerating. The green particle beam then flashed again and the sphere swerved, the beam just grazing it and sending it tumbling away. It righted itself and, leaving a vapour trail, dropped back towards the planet in a long arc.

'What the fuck now?' asked Cog.

Why? Trike asked himself. Angel's ship had been firing on the creature, but now it was firing on the legate himself. Even to his befuddled mind, that made no sense.

Meanwhile the creature was decelerating hard, but it wasn't going after Angel. It finally came to a halt just a few miles out from the wormship and just hung there in vacuum. After a long pause, it fired up thrusters in its tail and carried on, sliding into a hollow in the ship which writhed and closed around it. The wormship then began moving away from the planet, faster and faster. It shimmered, dropped into U-space and was gone.

'Fuck,' said Cog. 'No coordinates.' He looked over at Trike. 'We'll go get Ruth now.'

Zackander

Zackander powered up the lower sphere of his body and ran diagnostics to ensure it was now free of the sequestering programs the soldier had sent to all the Cyberat. As his search ran, he looked at the brace he had put around his broken forearm and then at the bruises all over his body. His neck still hurt from when his own lower body had rammed him into a wall. Luckily he trusted his grafts somewhat less than the younger generation, and had retained an off switch.

Soon, those of the Cyberat who had not been in the Cube or its vicinity started getting back into contact, and Zackander began analysing what they understood had happened. He was relieved to discover that, apparently, all they knew was that a legate had come to their world and some kind of drone had destroyed the Cube. They did not know that Zackander had been incubating a Jain super-soldier – they did not know where it had come from.

'This Angel brought that thing with him?' said the Cyberat before him.

Doshane's upper torso sat upon the metallic body of a spider, but one armed with prador Gatling cannons on each side. The man had a military turn of mind, and Zackander might have been able to utilize him earlier had he been given the time. It was good that he hadn't, else the man would have understood Zackander's responsibility for what had happened here.

'Yes, he did,' Zackander lied.

'What did he want?' asked Doshane.

'Jain artefacts from my collection,' Zackander replied. 'I was prepared to deal but then he attacked. I have no idea why.'

'And why did his own ship turn on him?'

'Again, I don't know why,' said Zackander, and in this case he really didn't. Maybe the Jain soldier had seized control of the ship? 'Maybe another party was involved and there was a falling out. All I do know is that this legate must be dealt with.'

And fast, before he has a chance to speak . . .

'And then we must clear up the mess,' said Doshane. 'We've lost many citizens. We have lost the Cube, a defence station and numerous satellites.' He paused, intense. 'The U-space research facility survived and perhaps it is time to employ it for . . . its other use.'

'You mean disrupt U-space and stop anything else arriving,' said Zackander.

'Yes – it will give us time to recoup.'

Zackander felt he was getting away from the point. 'But first this legate – we must eliminate the dangers here.'

'Yes, that we must do,' said Doshane. 'We are gathering. My own robot soldiers are on their way and the others are providing what they can. We will be at the predicted impact site within four hours – presuming that sphere does not alter course.'

'I will meet you there,' said Zackander.

Doshane nodded smartly and his image flickered out.

Zackander let out a tight breath. He glanced around his ship home and considered what he would have to do. His main home was gone now along with all the work he had been doing there, but he still had other Jain artefacts and he still had his life. Making a mental link, he put his ship into a descent heading towards those predicted coordinates.

Angel

Wraiths of fire snuffed out inside the transport sphere and Angel lay there burned, damaged, his mind struggling to regain function. The Wheel had been strong as he approached the wormship and he had sensed it groping past him, reaching out for the soldier. It made contact, and he then felt the link driving home into the soldier like a war dock. From that moment the Wheel began ripping from his mind, and only as this happened did he understand how firmly imbedded it had been in him. But also, he learned and understood more about the Wheel itself.

Certainly it was some kind of alien intelligence, not as strong as a full AI yet also not the product of brute evolution. Maybe a submind? Maybe a cybernetic mind like that of a haiman? It had imbedded itself in the wormship all the time he had been down, stranded on the gas giant moon. From there it had reached out to him and even impelled him to travel to and stand over the intermittent sulphur eruption that had blown him out into space. It had then controlled him, directing him to make repairs to the wormship. However, it had to fill his mind with information for his tasks, and this raised him to higher and higher levels of consciousness, where its control of him began to slip. But what did this alien intelligence want?

Angel was not sure. He felt numb and the information that had spilled from the Wheel sat in his mind in a confusing morass. Priorities . . . His connection with the sphere was gone and he could not re-establish it mentally, so he pushed his hands into the dense Jain tech around him to make a physical one. Everything was sluggish, in his mind and body and in the sphere itself, but finally something bound and he got a shaky link.

Half of the sphere's systems were fried. It had lost its main drives but still had some grav and could access some sensors. He

221

was travelling too fast and the sphere was getting hot. Though it would not burn up in atmosphere the heat would eventually kill what remaining capabilities it had. He used grav to slow it, steadily – not putting too much strain on the grav-engines. Reading sensor data, he plotted a course in his mind. No matter what he did, the landing would still be hard. However, there was a way of softening it, and he altered the course so that it would take him down into the ocean. Finally, he had done all he could to ensure his survival, though he now wasn't sure if that was something he wanted. He felt like nothing, as though he lay at the bottom of a deep dark pit. But memories of what the Wheel had shown him, of what he could be, as well as what it had promised before abandoning him, impelled him to thought. And he thought about the Wheel.

There was some kind of conflict and two sides filled with hate. The Wheel was either trapped, or it was a copy of something trapped, or even a submind splintered off from that prison. Certain things needed to happen if the prison was to open, and somehow everything that Angel had done was moving towards that end. He saw gravity and U-space maths, graphical depictions of political machinations between the Polity and the Kingdom, and mental images of alien technology he felt sure was the interior of some kind of ship or space station.

The sphere was travelling much slower now and was some hours away from splashdown. Angel could not yet work out precisely what the Wheel wanted or was doing. Certainly it had something to do with the accretion disc and the Jain technology there. But did all this matter to him? Looking within he could find only indifference to both the Polity and the Kingdom and knew for certain that the driving hatred he had felt had not been his own. With the Wheel, the soldier and the wormship now gone, he needed to ask himself what *he* wanted. But motives and aims for the future were vague in him and there was only one certainty: he wanted to survive.

Looking to his own body, he ran diagnostics. Yes, the energy blast from the glancing particle beam strike had burned through him and the sphere, causing a lot of damage. But that did not account for just how much seemed to have shut down inside him. A lot of the Jain tech was either inactive or sluggish and, as a consequence, self-repair was going exceedingly slowly. Both his senses and his mental capacity were at a low ebb and so many things he could have done with just a thought previously now seemed beyond him.

I'm depressed . . .

Yes, he was down in the cybernetic version of that state, lower than he had been under the Wheel, but not as mindless as he had been on the gas giant moon. He understood that unless he made an effort he would just lie here in the sphere after it crashed and do nothing, go nowhere. He needed to push himself.

First he looked more deeply internally, trying to nail down his problems. The technology inside was still active and still plentifully supplied with power from the laminar storage and fusion nodes scattered throughout his body. However, its efficiency was down to just 10 per cent. He found if he focused on particular functions he could speed them up and raise their efficiency, but the moment he turned his attention away it dropped off again. Understanding dawned gradually. At first he thought that the Wheel had deliberately damaged him in some way upon their parting, but now he realized it wasn't that. As a legate he was in a symbiotic relationship with the wormship. It took most of the processing load of the technology inside him and, when he was within it, perpetually tuned and adjusted it. Separate now, he was a lesser being. And a lesser being might not be able to survive whatever came next.

And what next?

He would splash down in the ocean of this world and be trapped. Surviving Cyberat would have no love for him and were probably watching his sphere's descent even now. That the recent events here were not already known beyond this world seemed unlikely. Any Polity or Kingdom forces coming this way would want to grab him at once and take him apart to see how he ticked, if not destroy him out of hand. To survive he had to move – he had to find a way off this world.

Angel tilted his head back and focused on some very specific technology inside him. He muttered a name: 'Ruth.'

11

It is popularly believed that to gaze bare-brained on U-space is to go mad. This is only true for people who have already been knocking on the door of the asylum. For others it can cause headaches, confusion, amnesia, aphasia and psychosis but they are usually temporary. Scanning of the human brain during and after such an event reveals no physical cause. Popular belief has it that the sight of the ineffable, of a continuum that operates by laws outside of the real, is what interferes with brain function. Mechanistic understanding of the human brain says that is simply not true. The human eye, the human visual cortex – in fact the entirety of the human brain – is a product of evolution – a biological computer made to filter out the extraneous and deal with the real. It is incapable of perceiving U-space and will only see its own real-world interpretation of it. If any mind was to be driven insane by the sight, it should be that of an AI or of a human sufficiently enhanced to perceive it, and to (incompletely) understand it. So what is happening here? The best explanation our scientists can come up with is that those affected are the victims of a meme. They believe the sight of U-space will affect them, so therefore it does. That is all. But our scientists are also victims of a meme – that the universe can be explained in mechanistic terms, and that anything falling outside of current theories will, with a little tinkering, be explained in those terms.

From 'Mad by Design' by Rev. J. Upholster

The Client

The Client, having collected all the main data she needed from the library, now made her request for thc forbidden history of the Species, earlier than the permitted five million years. After a long pause, the library spoke to the Client's remote, chemically at first, followed by light display, microwave and audio. The four forms of the language affirmed each other to hammer home the point that this was serious stuff.

'Data allowed only for onsite processing,' it said. 'Your remote will be destroyed at termination of research. Only no-extrapolation results allowed.'

This essentially meant that, yes, data could be released for processing, but any results of that processing would only be allowed to leave the library if the source data could not be extrapolated from them. The Client confirmed her request. After another long pause the library darkened and she was sure she detected movement beyond the storage pillars, which was something that had never happened before. Were some of the Species in hiding here, had some survived?

'Who is there?' she asked, on every level.

'Data loading,' replied the library.

Back aboard Weapons Platform Mu the Client felt steady disconnection from the remote as something began to nudge her out of memory. This went on for some time – a partition keeping the Client from accessing what was being loaded.

'How much space do you wish to retain for research programs?' the library asked.

The Client assigned a few terabytes, which was about the minimum she could get away with and remain plausible.

'Externality initiated,' said the library. Suddenly a triangular column rose out of the floor. Sitting on top of it was pyramidal crystal, while down its length were optic feeds and pheromone pipes which the remote could use to access data from the crystal and process it. Through the remote's eyes the Client gazed at the thing. A crystal that size, which was all packed quantum storage, contained petabytes of data. Just how much history lay before those five million years?

'Set your programs to run and withdraw,' the library instructed.

Now it was time to act. All the forbidden data was here in the mind of the remote and in that crystal. Though still connected to the remote, the Client could not gaze on one speck of it. She set the real program running in the remote's mind – the task it would carry out even if the library managed to block trans-missions to and from the weapons platform. The Client, in the remote, moved forwards, while up in space she moved her most effective attack pods closer to the moon. She then grasped the data crystal in her remote's mandibles and pushed it back into a mouth that lacked any other purpose.

'As expected,' said the library.

Yes, thefts from the library had been tried before and had always ended in failure. All those who had attempted them had come to a bad end and were historically listed as mentally abnormal. Even so, the thieves had made their attempts within the view of the entire Species and its technology, also showing too much respect for the library and all it represented. Those abnormal members of the Spe-cies had not come to the library when it was alone and externally unguarded, and they had never arrived with anything like the weapons system the Client controlled. Even they would probably have considered the Client abnormal for what she intended.

An attack pod fired a series of blast-nose railgun slugs, even as the remote launched from the floor and ignited a chemical rocket in its rear. The slugs hit the moon, penetrating a little way then expending their energy in plasma explosions. Millions of tons of rubble exploded out into space, excavating a massive crater in the regolith. The pod followed that assault with a particle beam, hitting the base of the crater and drilling through. The library chamber rocked, storage pillars clashing against each other like giant wind chimes. Fire exploded down into it, briefly followed by the flash of the particle beam. The remote hurtled towards this, weaving from side to side, but it could not evade tracking for long, and antipersonnel lasers soon picked it up. They hit, burning away black skin to reveal its underlying reflective armour.

Up in Weapons Platform Mu the Client gave the nearest approximation to a smile that one of the Species was capable of. The library only possessed antipersonnel weaponry to use inside because anything more powerful might damage its valuable contents. Still, they would be enough if it wasn't for other resources now available to her. The missile another attack pod fired, shortly after the railgun strike, was slow moving. It wasn't an impact weapon and it was vital it arrived at its target intact. However, it was quite rugged and, firing side thrusters, it swept into a fifty-gravity turn and hurtled straight down into the crater. It bounced down the hole the particle beam had cut there, and entered the chamber, hitting the floor hard. Still linked to the remote's sensors, the Client winced when the missile smashed into storage pillars and brought a series of them crashing down.

As it fell out of the wreckage and rolled across the floor, a small fusion reactor fired up to power the hardware packed inside the missile. It began broadcasting strongly, responding to feedback and transmitting anew. This induction warfare device first filled the chamber with microwave tracking beams, identical to those being used by the antipersonnel lasers, and soon few of them were hitting their target. As the library switched over to other forms of tracking it aped them too.

Now the drones, thought the Client.

They hurtled out of holes in the walls, flat pennies of technology spewing high-velocity beads from magnetic guns around their rims. The hardware in the missile immediately tracked them and began firing a narrow EMR beam. One after another they died and fell slowly to the floor. The remote shuddered under the impact of a drone's bead strike, shedding fragments of its body, but still it managed to tilt and allow its rocket to take it up through the hole above. It shot out into space, still accelerating, then a few miles up its motor died and it coasted on towards the weapons platform.

Now, on the moon, something else was happening. Areas of crust cracked and chunks lifted and fell away as weapons buds rose into view. The Client hit them at once from her subsidiary system, bringing more attack pods into play and targeting them with the bigger weapons on the platform itself. Particle beams struck the rising buds as, like flowers to the sun, they began to tilt up on their stalks. They blew apart, scattering cusps of metallic glass across the moon's surface. The Client then fired a series of missiles towards the remote to cover its escape – objects like tumbling stick grenades streaming from one attack pod. These exploded in a line to scatter space with material chaff and chaff broadcast units. But this would not be enough because the remote's course was set and could be predicted by the library. She fired up the engines of the platform to bring it towards the remote and began moving the nearest attack pods between the remote and the moon.

The Client continued beam strikes against the moon, but now they were hitting hardfields. She then complemented them with the wide and ridiculously powerful beams from the weapons platform, and followed those with a rain of railgun missiles. One of the weapons buds opened, while all over the surface of the moon ports began spewing metal vapour from cooling systems. The open bud, a flower with shiny diamond patterned petals, stabbed out a beam like a glass rod from its heart straight into the attack pod between the moon and the remote. It struck a hardfield, which folded up and disappeared, then punched into the attack pod. Metals and composites turned instantly brittle, shattering glittering fragments across vacuum, and the pod collapsed in on itself. The Client had just a little time to study the data on this new weapon before the railgun missiles reached the moon. Hardfields flicked and flared under their impact and cooling emissions turned to plasma. Something erupted under the surface – an explosion lifting a giant plug of the crust – and the active weapons bud slowly closed and then sagged.

'Thief,' said a voice, as the remote finally reached Weapons Platform Mu, where the Client caught it with hardfields and brought it into a supply bay.

The communication had come directly from the library and had penetrated the Client's security with ease. It found all available language emitters within the Client's cylinder and through them made its presence known. The Client read the pheromone output of something . . . like the Species but not actually the Species. Great age was implicit in the interweaving of its language, and imagery created a hologram. The creature hung there, something like a human embryo, or maybe like that odd Earth lizard, the chameleon. It seemed to be of black ancient flesh and glass. Four limbs ending in doubled multi-hands were folded against its torso. Its tail was coiled below it, while its head was a sensory turret not unlike that of the remote. But also, writhing out from its sides, sometimes spread out like the veins of wings, but often coiling up and then finding a new route through the air as if in search of something, were six triangular-section tentacles. The shape of this thing found recognition deep inside the Client, but she really did not know what it was she was recognizing.

'Thief,' the creature repeated.

'I am all that remains of the Species,' the Client replied,

meanwhile pulling the weapons platform away and turning it once more towards the sun. The attack pods quickly followed. 'How can the knowledge now be forbidden to me?'

'Because I forbid it,' the creature replied.

'You are not of the Species. What are you?'

'With what you have stolen you will learn soon enough.'

'Doubtless.'

'But I will hunt you down. And you will pay.'

The Client replied, 'But this is foolish. I really am the last of the Species. Why can I not learn the history of my kind?'

'It is forbidden.'

'Who are you to forbid?'

'I am the Librarian. I am . . .'

Then it came, a shriek across the ether as of some primordial horror. It incorporated most of the EMR spectrum and was in U-com as well. The Client felt it twisting and burrowing deep inside her, trying to tear a response from levels of her mind she had not known existed. But there was more. The shriek was densely packed with information. It contained open-ended formulae and equations, data that interrelated across the spectrum and looked like the basis of a language. She saw layered constructs that seemed to be questions, demands, and the way the whole thing ground against her mind felt like some kind of challenge. Then it cut off.

There was no logic here, the Client thought, shivering on her crystal tree, only madness. She decided, with an unaccustomed vehemence, that this creature was a threat.

At the same time, using just a small portion of her mind, she directed the loading of three warheads to one slow-firing coilgun. Her supply of these was limited but perhaps this was a sensible precaution to take. The three gigaton CTDs sped out from the platform then accelerated steadily on their own single-burn fuser drives, back towards the moon.

'You stir the still pool of history,' said the Librarian. 'Terror you cannot comprehend will come up from the depths.'

Madness, thought the Client, not understanding why she felt such revulsion.

The missiles continued towards their target and just seconds remained before its destruction. The Client doubted her decision, feeling a deep abhorrence for such destruction of knowledge. But at the last second a large U-signature generated and black space folded around the moon like a curtain, and it was gone.

Orlandine

Sitting at her table, Orlandine picked up her wine glass and sipped. She then put it down carefully and picked up her knife and fork and set to work on the synthetic steak, salad and new potatoes. All of this was of course completely unnecessary because the nutrient feeds in her interface sphere gave her everything her body needed. It even supplied certain chemicals, nano-machines and carbon-building elements her enhancements required, which she wouldn't get from the steak.

She sat in her lounge, facing a panoramic window which, when she was in the real, gave a view out into space. Now it showed the swirling grey – a representation of U-space a human could gaze upon without going insane. When she was haiman – the closest humanity had come to a melding with artificial intelligence – she could handle the real image. But now she was living in human time, reconnecting to her past. Eating like this and drinking wine was not necessary, but it was human. It was her attempt to cling to what she might have been, had her parents not taken the choice away from her when they began enhancing her from birth. Sometimes she felt herself to be sitting in a borderland, on the crux of making a choice. She was both AI and human, but she was neither of them completely.

'Satisfying your primitive needs?'

For an assassin drone measuring fifteen feet from the spike of its tail to the top of its antennae, Cutter moved very quietly. But then he was made that way. During the war it had been his job to sneak around in prador ships, hidden from security systems by Bludgeon, and to deal with prador like a professional chef taking apart boiled crabs. He had primarily been a terror weapon but had soon been displaced by even nastier assassin drones that spread biological agents amongst the prador. Or others that gave them a taste of their own thrall technology by burrowing inside them and taking control of their central nervous systems. Cutter had moved to simple war-drone status – joining other drones on raids whose sum purpose had not been to spread terror amongst the prador, but merely to kill as many of them as possible.

'Yes, I am satisfying my primitive needs,' Orlandine replied. 'And doubtless you joined me on this little excursion in the hope of satisfying yours.' She inserted a piece of steak in her mouth and closed her teeth with a click, savouring the taste for a moment before chewing. 'However,' she continued after swallowing, 'it is unlikely that there will be any prador for you to kill.'

'Oh I wouldn't bet on that.' Cutter moved up beside her, reared and tapped one of his forelimbs against the window. 'Maybe these prador you are going to meet are "good", but there are always some shitty ones around to work their own angle.'

'I don't think it's going to be like that. This is about a worm-ship and a legate. The bad guy in this is a product of AI, in fact is an AI himself.' Even though she spoke with certainty it wasn't really there. It wouldn't surprise her at all if some bad prador appeared, or if what she was getting involved in turned nasty, or if the good prador turned out not to be so good. She grimaced and said, 'Just a few minutes till we arrive.'

'Shouldn't you be in your sphere?' Cutter asked.

'I'm not arriving on coordinates – a few light minutes out.'

'So you are being understandably cautious?'

'Of course.'

Orlandine worked her way through the rest of the meal and finished her wine. She enjoyed the alcohol but, as the view before her seemed to be trying to straighten itself out, she decided it was time to end this break and she expanded once again into her enhancements. Only minutes remained before they arrived, hence Cutter's presence. She reacquired the submind running her ship and absorbed it, while instructing her internal nano-machines to kill the alcohol buzz. She cleared the human view through the window and gazed bare-brained on U-space, with its twisting perspectives and inversions, and saw both an infinite universe and a zero-point of existence. She understood the long view of AI and the linear thinking of her evolved component, and pondered on eternity. Some minutes later she felt the twist and U-space cleared like fog instantly burned away by the sun. This revealed the swirl of a nebula, the glittering stars of every primary colour in the human visual spectrum, and the glaring green orb of a closer sun.

'Let's take a look.' Though she was not plugged into her interface sphere and not completely melded with the systems of her ship, she had opened radio and microwave links with it, which was enough to give her almost complete control. She threw up a frame in the window before her as she focused her telescope array on the fourth world out from the sun. Her sub-AI search program soon found what she was looking for and she focused in on it.

The prador destroyer sat in orbit of the world. The thing had obviously taken a pounding, but even from this distance she could tell something further was wrong. The ship had fled a recent conflict with a wormship and had a piece of this wormship aboard. It had exterior damage and here, in a supposedly safe refuge, she would have expected to see prador working outside on the hull. But all she saw was one drifting hull repair machine with no prador operator inside to control it.

Orlandine stood and walked towards the back of her lounge, touching the centre of her shipsuit disc that sat at her shoulder. The suit split and slithered into the disc. Naked, she stepped into a dropshaft that whisked her upwards, then moved out into her small atrium where the butterfly flowers were flapping in agitation. She carried on into her interface sphere, quickly going through the connection routine, and her perspective widened.

The prador destroyer was now just a few miles away, a looming bulk poxed with gun ports. Because of what the king had said about the Jain tech aboard in the form of this piece of wormship, Orlandine set up heavy security before opening communications and sending it the codes the king had given her. Even as she sent these, her sensors picked up power surges around the gun ports, as the destroyer targeted her with its weapons. But then, after a moment, a reply came.

'Recognized,' said a prador, using human speech.

'I am glad to hear that, Orlik,' Orlandine replied, closely monitoring the comlink. 'You have a problem.'

There were hints of suspicious code coming across in voice-only com which she routed into a scrubber, fragmenting them completely. She opened the image feed to see what else might transpire.

The big prador before her, clad in bone-white armour, wasn't right – she recognized that at once. Swiftly analysing the image, she saw the problem with the eyes. Polity data, collected over the centuries since the war, explained this, as did some corpses that had been obtained. There was something odd about the king's family, the King's Guard. They were mutated and generally kept their physical appearance hidden in armour, never leaving one of their own behind after a fight. Romantics in the Polity thought this a sign of brotherly love, but those who knew understood that the Guard did not want anyone examining their kind.

These were King's Guard then – she was sure of it. Other data she picked up indicated they had been working under the cover of being renegades. Nothing unusual there – the Polity quite often used the same techniques in black ops.

'A problem,' said Orlik flatly.

Now, with the image feed, she could see it, and further fragments of code were coming through. She consigned these to a secure store and watched them begin to assemble into viruses, then coagulate into informational parasites, worms, and other forms of toxic computer life. She examined them closely with a larger component of her mind while continuing her conversation with the prador.

'Yes, you have a problem,' she replied. 'It probably started as just irritating errors in your ship's system, but now those errors are causing failures. This has stopped you making repairs to your ship while you try to trace the faults.'

Orlik stared for a long moment before saying. 'Incorrect. It did not start as a few irritating errors but as an all-out viral attack the moment the fragment was through my ship's hull. I managed to suppress this but since we came out of U-space the problem has returned.'

Orlandine was taken aback. A wormship fragment launched an all-out viral attack and a prador managed to suppress it? There was something here she had yet to understand.

'I also have no doubt that your ship's mind is starting to malfunction,' she said, while thinking furiously.

'It said it was hungry,' said Orlik.

Frozen brain-matter had no real need of food . . .

'Your ship's system is doubtless being subject to induction

warfare from that piece of wormship you have aboard. I want you to open a full bandwidth link to my ship across the frequencies I will send.'

'*Bludgeon, are you ready for this?*'

Cutter's partner was down in the bowels of her ship, his front end plugged into her system almost as thoroughly as she was via her interface sphere.

'*Oh, am I ever ready,*' the drone replied. '*Such toys!*'

Orlandine had made available to him, even as they set out, all the informational warfare stuff she had. There was the Polity data but, since her own personal conquest of Jain technology, much more besides.

'Open a full bandwidth link,' Orlik repeated, obviously not much in love with the idea.

'You received instructions from your king about me?' Orlandine asked.

'I did.'

'Then I am waiting.'

Orlik blinked goat eyes at her, yet *normal* prador did not possess eyelids. 'Very well,' he said reluctantly.

'*It's opening up,*' said Bludgeon.

Orlandine rode with the drone into the destroyer's system, but an instant later things got complicated.

'*Well that was unexpected,*' said Bludgeon.

Orlandine had to agree. This was no normal prador ship, nor was it a normal ship of the King's Guard. The mind, which she had assumed was the frozen ganglion of a prador child, was close to being AI, though admittedly not a very smart one. Also, this Orlik was interfaced with his ship, which all explained why he had managed to fend off what must have been a serious informational attack.

'*But doable,*' Bludgeon added.

The old drone went through it all like a laser through aerogel,

237

building a model of its workings in just a few seconds. It was simpler than the same operation aboard a Polity destroyer, but a lot more complicated than what would usually be found aboard a prador vessel. There were two main control nexuses – one was the ship's mind, and the other was Orlik himself. The mind controlled only the U-space engine, the fusion drive and steering thrusters, and other subsidiary items related to them. Orlik controlled just about everything else, or rather could control everything else – there was a lot more automation here than was usual, in things like environmental controls and maintenance. The ship even possessed its own collection of maintenance robots that weren't much different from those used by the Polity.

'*Nasty,*' said Bludgeon.

She saw what the drone was getting at. Peering through cams inside the destroyer, she saw the piece of wormship in the hold. It was cylindrical, six feet wide and the metallic hue of magnetite with light ribbed down its length. Protruding from its broken-off end were fibres, tubes, ducts, broken cables, nodules, things that looked like metallic spinal vertebrae. The other end was more closed off. She could see familiar shearfield generators, tool heads fed by half-seen carousels, the noses of iron-burners and lasers. Scanning both ends Orlandine saw that it all did bear a close resemblance to Jain tech, but to the human part of her mind there was something more logical to it. This would bear later investigation.

It had first been strapped down to the floor, then a series of docking clamps had been moved in to secure it in place. There were scanner heads all around it, as well as two heavy particle cannons focused on it. The scanners were the problem. The worm had used Jain induction techniques to penetrate them, building viruses in their carbon storage which had then been breaking away to spread to other parts of the ship.

'Shut down the scanners in your hold,' she instructed Orlik. 'And when I say shut down, I mean fully. Cut the power to them.'

'That thing in there needs to be watched,' Orlik insisted.

'Your scanners do not have sufficient security and that thing in there has gone through them and into your system without even consciously thinking about it.'

'Oh, I see – cutting power now,' the prador replied.

'Also, you yourself need to disconnect.'

'I can be of assistance . . .'

'Yes, maybe you can. But you might also end up being sequestered.' She paused to drive the point home. 'Jain tech does not limit itself to manufactured mentality. Perhaps we can save your ship's mind, perhaps not. I do not want to be thinking the same about you.'

'Very well,' said Orlik reluctantly.

Bludgeon's work in the system now gave her access to a cam in the captain's sanctum. Orlandine saw Orlik shrug and a slab of optic interface detached from his back, rising up into the ceiling on its optic cables. He then inserted his claws into pit controls and summoned up what he had likely been seeing through his implants on the screens before him. She also noted something else in there: a Polity assassin drone apparently nailed to a plate and mounted as a decoration on the wall. But that really wasn't her concern . . .

'*Bludgeon?*' she enquired.

'*Power's off and Orlik is out of the circui*t,' the drone replied. '*Killing the incursions now.*'

She watched as the drone first isolated all portions of the ship's system, except for his own feeds into them. He then began systematically scrubbing those areas infected with viruses, turning everything into a morass. Orlik would doubtless be unhappy about this since the whole system would need to be reprogrammed. Next Bludgeon turned his attention to where the viruses had assembled into something more toxic in the ship's AI. Here the drone sent in predatory computer life copied from Orlandine's files, and they attacked the worms and other nasty creations, ripping them apart . . .

Something wrong.

It took Orlandine a microsecond to throw up a hardfield, and her ship jerked under the impact of railgun slugs. The destroyer had just fired on her. She began a steady swapping of hardfields to keep her projectors cool, but it wasn't entirely necessary because the superconducting heat-sink network was as near to perfect as it could be. She targeted the single railgun port the slugs were issuing from, but held off from firing. It seemed likely this was the worm trying to defend itself, though Bludgeon's system map had not shown anything in the controls of this railgun, and now the gun was isolated from the rest of gun control.

'Orlik?' she asked.

'I don't know,' he replied, running through data on his screens at a phenomenal rate.

'On automatics?'

'Two second-children in there. I don't know why.'

The firing abruptly terminated and Orlandine saw that Bludgeon had shut down the reactors supplying power to Orlik's weapons. The prador would not like that either.

'Cutter,' she said. *'You're going across.'*

'Told you so,' Cutter replied delightedly.

Angel

Below the sphere the land masses of the Cyberat world petered out to be supplanted by pale green ocean. Though he could exist in any environment, Angel realized that the seas below would not do for his purpose. Yes, they would cushion the sphere's impact, but the algae destroyed visibility and quite a lot of the creatures here at the top of the food chain, which started with that algae, were hostile. He needed to come down near some kind of land mass, and he needed to be visible so Ruth could find him.

Scanning ahead, he picked out a chain of volcanic islands and adjusted his course to bring him down near them. Next he braced himself inside the sphere, sinking his limbs into the technology that surrounded him and causing it to harden around them. He then considered the plan that lay inchoate in his mind.

Ruth still had that U-mitter inside her skull and, at some point, Trike was sure to come for her. Angel only hoped he would arrive before either Polity or prador forces did. With her under his control he could compel Trike to take him off this world. Another factor in his calculations was the remaining Cyberat. They certainly wouldn't be happy with Angel, so he needed to give them a diversion, a distraction, and the sphere could serve this purpose. It was damaged and weaponless but still mobile. He would board Ruth's shuttle and compel her to answer, to his benefit, any questions the Cyberat might ask. Meanwhile he would send the sphere off around the world, setting it to evade any attempt to seize or attack it. The Cyberat might eventually destroy it and stop looking for him, which was all to the good.

The sphere drew closer to the sea – a flat green plain below it, breakers visible here and there over slabs of coral just below the surface. Finally it touched, kicking up spray and clouds of steam, then bounced a few times and rolled across the surface of the ocean. Automatics attempted to stabilize it but it bounded up then slammed down, again and again. This went on for some minutes and Angel received the full list of hull integrity warnings. But the sphere held together and skidded along the surface before sinking deeper and slowing almost to a stop.

As the steam cleared, Angel gazed through exterior cams at scabs of rock scattered across the sea ahead. He used grav-planing to propel the sphere towards them. More detail became clear as he approached: white beaches were webbed with black and masses that looked like piles of giant tulip flowers – pink and green – were slowly opening and closing. There were rock formations like giant mushrooms that were probably dead coral, as well as creatures scattered on one of the beaches – great blubbery lumps that at this distance resembled albino seals.

Freeing himself from the surrounding technology, Angel cruised the sphere in towards one of the beaches. Rocks grated against it underneath and other things thumped higher up against the hull. Through exterior cams he caught a glimpse of a long-jointed limb which terminated in something that looked vaguely like the head of a parrot.

The sphere finally thumped onto the beach and he used grav to take it up further, cutting a groove behind. He popped the hatch and clambered out, noting he wasn't quite as nimble as he had been before. He dropped down onto what he had thought was sand and sank up to his knees. Reaching down, he grabbed a handful of the stuff. It was like soggy tissue and he realized the beach was a drift of dead algae, while the wide black streaks running across the surface were some kind of slime mould feeding off it.

Angel trudged up to the top of the beach, sat down on a flat rock and reached out to Ruth again with his mind, to send co-ordinates. As soon as he made contact he found her talking to someone else and now saw that the fruition of his plan could be sooner than he thought.

Meanwhile, a great white seal-like body heaved itself out of the sea. At its front end it possessed six of the jointed limbs Angel had seen on the way in. He observed numerous white flat feet underneath it, perfect for getting the thing about on this surface without its body sinking down too far. It humped up like a caterpillar, the parrot-head forelimbs pecking at the drift of dead algae and sending clumps of it flying, as though it was making a challenge. After a thoughtful pause, it then shot up the slope of this strange beach, straight towards Angel.

Trike

'Ruth,' said Trike, staring at her image on the screen. 'We are coming for you.'

Her image had taken hold of him the moment Cog opened com with the shuttle, and all the craziness had fled. He now felt like he had been suffering from a very bad glister high, which was a crustacean hoopers caught on Spatterjay. It had psycho-active chemicals in its mouth and brainpan which were released into the creature's flesh when they were killed prior to cooking.

Ruth stared at him with tears in her eyes, then reached out with one hand as if trying to touch his face. He saw that something wasn't quite right, and after a moment realized her eyes were no longer hazel, but black. What did that fucking legate do? Anger surged up inside him and he looked down at his clenched hands. The two blue circles of leech scars on his right hand were livid, while the rest of the skin there had a blue tinge. And did his fingers appear longer? He looked up and around, expecting further hallucinations.

'I cannot,' she said, and lowed her hand to the controls before her.

'She's taking the shuttle out of orbit,' said Cog from behind him.

'Ruth, what are you doing? Wait there – we're coming for you!'

'He is in my mind, Trike – I cannot disobey.'

'Angel,' Trike stated, the anger in him growing.

'Steady, boy.' Cog rested one meaty hand on his shoulder.

Trike grabbed it and flung it away from him, to which Cog made a grunting sound and swore. After a moment Trike looked round at him. He was standing a little way back rubbing at his hand, his expression speculative.

'What?' said Trike and turned his attention back to the screen.

'He says come,' said Ruth. 'If you want to see me alive again.' The connection closed.

'Aaargh!' Trike smashed his hands down on the console and the facing shattered, his hands disappearing inside. He pulled them out of the fizzing electrics and stared at them. Yes, his fingers were definitely longer. He stood and turned towards Cog.

'We go down! Now!' he said, taking a step towards the captain.

'You know what will happen if you try to face up to . . .' Cog didn't continue. He dipped his head and stared down at Trike's feet. Puzzlement briefly overcoming his anger, Trike looked down too. His trousers now ended halfway up his calves, and his shins were blue. Even as he looked he could hear something tittering in the back of his mind.

'Fast,' said Cog.

'What?'

'The transformation was much slower with Jay,' Cog explained. 'But then maybe Jay wasn't quite as crazy as you.'

Trike just goggled at him.

Cog folded his arms. 'I've been watching you. You've been eating like a pig and your muscle density has been climbing. Now you're getting a growth surge.' Cog stepped closer and Trike realized he was looking down on the man from a greater height.

'You were always on the edge, Trike, always clinging on for control. The damage to your body healed and the sprine kept this transformation at bay at first,' said Cog. 'But there's a mental element in there. I don't know the cause, but I do know that past a certain point it becomes a matter of choice.'

Trike shook his head. The tittering was getting louder and the ghosts of Spatterjay fauna were beginning to impinge upon his reality. He had to keep it under control and focus on his present goals.

'We go after her,' he said.

'And if I say no?'

Trike took a pace forwards, and Cog took one pace back.

'Yes, we go after her,' Cog conceded. 'It's risky and quite possibly we'll both end up dead.' He paused and smiled bleakly. 'But if I try to stop you I doubt there'll be much left of this ship to take away from this world.'

The tittering became quieter and the ghosts faded, just a little. Trike grimaced, and felt himself shaking. But Cog . . . Captain Cogulus could break hull metal with his hands . . . Trike raised his hands and studied them again, and tried to get some grip on his chaotic thoughts.

'You could use that weapon against me again,' he said.

Cog shook his head. 'If I use that again it'll now just accelerate what is happening to you . . . what you are letting happen to you.'

'Choice?'

'Yes.' Cog turned back to his throne and plumped himself down in it. 'Somehow you can choose to stop, simply stop. You can be Captain Trike again and struggle with your demons, or you can let them defeat you and turn into a crazed monster.' Cog worked the controls in his chair's arm and the ship shifted. 'Janus, follow that shuttle down,' he added.

12

Reavers: In the aftermath of the prador/human war came a time of self-examination for the prador although, it has to be said, not all of them. For many the treaty was anathema and they should have won. They itched to start fighting again, while some of them abandoned the Kingdom feeling betrayed by their new king. But cooler heads prevailed or, rather, the new king and his extended family (which formed the King's Guard) were smart enough to know that the Polity could crush them, and so violently weeded out those prador still in denial. But even while this was ongoing, the king ordered all prador scientific establishments to begin deconstructing and incorporating Polity technology. This resulted in a massive upsurge in computers and robotics. It also drove a renaissance in prador weapons technology, one result of which was the reavers. These ships supposedly incorporate the best of both worlds. They are two miles long and shaped like extended teardrops rather than prador carapaces, as had been the fashion. Their armour is similar to the newest Polity ship armour, which in turn was based on the earlier prador armour with its exotic metal component. Their weapons and defences match those of modern Polity destroyers and it is rumoured reavers can even deploy U-jump missiles and carry bounce gates as a defence against them. Reavers are fast, rugged and dangerous warships yet, because the prador refuse to incorporate AI in them, they are still outclassed by even our older attack ships.

From 'The Weapons Directory'

Blade

After being heavily damaged by the Clade's attack on it, the stealth black-ops attack ship *Obsidian Blade* hung in space, opened up like a badly splintered piece of mahogany. Beneath jutting shards of the ship, the silver intestines of workings poked out, and these were surrounded by swarms of microbots like blow flies. Blade felt very vulnerable this way and did not relish the sensation at all, but it had been necessary for making full repairs. Now, at last, its U-space com was back online and it began to receive messages.

Messages from Cog were mostly text as he had tried to keep a close eye on Trike – a man who, it appeared, was undergoing drastic mutation by the Spatterjay virus. Detail was sparse concerning events on and around the world of the Cyberat, but it seemed the wormship was gone, along with some kind of Jain-tech drone, while the legate had been effectively betrayed by its own ship and was left stranded on the planet. It was an odd situation, but still there was a chance to seize hold of a legate and take it apart for whatever data it would render. However, Blade, ever the dutiful soldier, sought orders from higher up the chain of command.

'How long will it be before you can travel?' asked a voice Blade immediately knew was that of Earth Central itself.

'Some hours yet,' replied Blade, but sent a more detailed assessment as an information package.

'Doable,' said EC.

'I have no chance of going after that wormship without coordinates,' Blade replied, 'maybe this legate knows where it is going?'

'This is a possibility, but I very much doubt it,' EC replied. 'The indications are that the legate was under the control of some other entity, which has now abandoned it. An entity that can seize control of a legate, and a wormship, is hardly likely to leave a signpost to its next destination.'

'Another entity?' Blade repeated.

'Numerous complicated factors have come into play,' said EC, which was no answer at all.

'Oh, right . . .'

'One of those complications is Dragon . . .'

'Oh, *right* . . .'

'Dragon has been involved in some questionable events recently that I have yet to parse.'

This, Blade felt, was an astounding admission from Earth Central.

An information package arrived and Blade studied it. So, an alien life form had seized control of an accretion disc weapons platform and taken it into the Kingdom. The probability was high that this alien was a reification of the Client, a creature who had more than enough reasons to be pissed off with both the prador and the Polity.

'The data indicates,' EC continued – which Blade basically understood as meaning 'I know stuff you don't and I am not going to tell you it' – 'that Dragon allowed the Client to escape with the weapons platform after destroying the U-space backup to its mind.'

'U-space backup?' Blade began, but then understood. This version of the Client was a reification. It would not know as much as the previous version of itself.

EC continued, 'This has impelled the Client to seek out information from a library moon of its species in the Prador Kingdom, which likely seems was Dragon's intention.'

'Surely this will then make it a more dangerous loose cannon to have roaming about in the Kingdom with one of our weapons platforms? The best option would be to destroy it as soon as possible?' Blade was now hoping for reassignment.

'No, you are not going after the Client,' said EC.

'What then?'

'You will go to the system of the Cyberat,' said EC.

'I assumed as much,' said Blade smugly. 'You want me to grab the legate anyway and see if I can find out where that wormship went?'

'No, you are a black-ops attack ship and do not possess the requisite abilities.'

Blade felt the urge to grumble about this but it was true. Its speciality was major destruction, not capture and interrogation.

'So what do I do there?'

'Whatever controls that wormship did not destroy the legate though it was fully capable of doing so. The legate is a potentially huge source of data and, as such, is also a large lure.'

'You suspect some kind of trap?'

'I do, but for my agents, or for something else, I do not know. However, it strikes me that there is only one entity with the capabilities of closing that trap.'

Blade only felt confusion at the convoluted reasoning here, which kind of confirmed that attack ship AIs like itself weren't really made for much more than watching and pouncing.

'What entity?' it asked.

'I think you already learned that,' said EC.

Blade felt a surge of anger.

The Clade . . .

'What are my orders?'

'You will keep watch and report,' replied EC. 'You will act as you deem necessary, and you will gather information.'

'I deemed it necessary to go after the Client,' Blade pointed out.

'You will not.'

'Then I deem it necessary to destroy the Clade.'

'Quite so. Carry out your mission as I have instructed,' said EC, and cut the link.

Blade sat in vacuum chewing it all over. There were always other factors that impinged on how Earth Central reacted to any situation. It could see how the ruling AI of the Polity might think it a good idea to have a weapons platform running rogue in the Kingdom: 'Sorry, Oberon, but an alien stole one of our weapons platforms and entered your territory. Would you like us to send help?' Such a platform would be a deniable reminder to prador in the Kingdom, including the king, of Polity military superiority. And, if the king did ask for help, which was unlikely, anything the Polity sent in would be a further reminder.

Also, Dragon allowing this alien to escape from the accretion disc with the platform indicated a Jain technology connection. EC was obviously loath to act without full understanding of the situation, which was never easy when Dragon was involved. No matter. Blade was a soldier and had the probable location of a target – it would stick with that.

Repairs were almost complete and Blade began closing up the ship's hull – snapping it shut in annoyance. It knew, for sure, that when this was all over it might understand the general shape of EC's plotting, but it wouldn't understand it all. This was presupposing it didn't end up as burned fragments strewn across the Cyberat system.

The Client

The Client tried to concentrate on this last task to the exclusion of all else. But she occasionally eyed her remote, sitting at the base of the cylinder and gently expiring. It still held the data crystal containing the forbidden history of the Species, but the other information the library had loaded to the remote's mind now resided in multiple carbon lattice hard-storage drives throughout the platform. During the journey to move the platform towards the sun, the Client had been hugely tempted to begin searching through the forbidden data. But she knew this would interfere with her planning of, and responses to, the tasks in hand. In this situation, any delay could be a fatal one. No, the data would have to wait, especially now . . .

The moon returned to the system, its U-space drive ripping up the quantum foam more than necessary and generating an explosion of light. It was almost as if the Librarian wanted to be noticed. The Client immediately focused telescopes and other detectors on the thing and soon saw the damage. The moon was radiating, new craters in its surface glowed in their depths, and it had carried through momentum from its last jump and hurtled across the system at one quarter light, leaving a trail of vapour behind it.

'You are back,' the Client noted.

The Librarian replied with that shriek across the EMR spectrum. This time she acted fast, certain it required some response, recording it to storage not already filled with library data. But before she could even take a look at it, space rippled around the moon and it elongated before disappearing in another flash of light. Again the Client tried to get a lock on its U-signature but, again, got nothing. However, the way it had appeared and disappeared inclined her to think that maybe the Librarian had not hidden its destination when it made its last jump . . .

Weapons Platform Mu was hot. Energy levels were high now, with solar radiation raising the temperature of the platform and its remaining attack pods to what the Client maintained inside her cylinder home. The platform itself had returned to its original shape, and was in an advanced state of internal repair.

Meanwhile twenty-five attack pods were inside the platform also undergoing repairs while sixty-two, in close orbit of the sun, were in full working order, which included being U-space capable. Only Weapons Platform Mu was not yet so capable. This was not due to lack of power, materials or slow manufacturing, because autofactories aboard had made all the required components; the delay was due to the logistics involved in transporting rings of super-dense copper from a factory to one of the U-space drive nacelles.

The Client took in the entire situation and reacted a microsecond later. Upon her order, the pods accelerated up from the sun in preparation for U-jumping. She next focused on the super-dense ring. Currently a huge robot, running caterpillar treads against the walls of a long transport tube, was pushing it towards the U-space drive nacelle, which lay three miles away. The Client ordered the robot to let go and the ring continued along its course. Next, after a series of rapid calculations, the Client repositioned two steering thrusters and fired them up. Internally it looked as if the ring had started accelerating down the transport tube, when in reality it was the platform that was on the move. The robot sped after its charge, shifting its treads over to one side and sinking its main body between them. This brought its body down just enough for it to slip past the ring and dash on ahead of it. It then moved its grabs to its rear end, adjusted its treads too, and kept going while the ring continued to accelerate. In a minute, ring and grabs made contact with a clang and the robot pulled in its treads as it took a grip, pressing them into the walls to brake. They were smoking as it finally slowed the ring towards the end of the tube. And that's when they appeared, out there, where the moon had arrived and then disappeared.

The Client felt no gratification being proven correct about the

Librarian's intentions, just weary acceptance and a degree of puzzlement. Why had it done this? Surely it understood it was behaving without logic? And why that weird challenge, that shriek?

Forty ships speared into the real in perfect formation. The things were massive spikes, rounded to the rear and gleaming gold. Within seconds they reacted as one, firing off steering thrusters and igniting fusion drives – becoming golden ovals from the Client's perspective as they zeroed in on the weapons platform. The Client was impressed. It took them very little time to realize that there was no U-signature from the moon which they could follow, and that another threat was here. But what were they? A brief search of stolen memory rendered the answer. These ships were reavers – warships of the King's Guard – and they were prador. The Client found this surprising because she had no memory of the prador operating with such precision and efficiency. And it seemed they had also lost their overbearing self-regard and designed ships suitable to requirements, rather than fashioned in the shape of their bodies.

Just a second after the reavers turned, the platform's attack pods made their own jump, each sending out light ripples. They came out of U-space in a wall between the reavers and the platform.

'This is contrary to the main agreements of the truce,' someone said.

The Client was about to respond, in fact, to reveal herself, but then she stopped, understanding the opportunity now present. She hated the prador for the extermination of the Species and their murder of her original form. She resented the humans for their betrayal. So wouldn't it be perfect to set human and prador at each other's throats?

However, she had to be careful and make it plausible. Even the prador she had known would not be fooled into thinking that the arrival of this platform here was a precursor to some kind of all-out attack. And these modern-day prador seemed a lot more efficient, and might even be a bit smarter. Also, from what she understood of the Polity now, it could wipe out the prador, although the most likely method would be to send in a heavily armed fleet loaded with U-space missiles across a wide front. Dropping something like this platform into the middle of the Kingdom as a precursor to war wasn't sensible . . . unless for provocation. Yes, nobody in the Polity wanted war again, but if the prador started attacking the Polity it would perforce respond. It was plausible that Earth Central had decided it was time to deal with the threat the prador posed and provoke them until they did something which required a larger response.

'The word "truce" implies a cessation of conflict between two closely matched forces,' the Client replied.

'It does not,' said the prador aboard one of those approaching ships.

The Client tried again. 'Semantics. This long and antiquated agreement is now all in your favour, since we could squash you like the bugs you are. Just be grateful we have refrained from doing so for so long. Now go. I have Polity business here that is none of your concern.'

'Leave prador space at once or we will be forced to take action,' said the prador.

'Little fly, buzz off or I will squash you.'

The sudden release of railgun missiles from the reavers implied that these modern-day prador, though they might be smarter, still adhered to the basic prador ethos. The Client now delved into the mind of Pragus and from its knowledge studied a number of attack and defence plans. But they were hardly necessary. The platform's attack pods possessed U-jump missiles while the prador did not. She selected three of the reavers for three of the attack pods to target, and launch tubes rose from their backs, each spitting out one arrow-head missile. These moved slowly in comparison to the approaching swarm of railgun missiles, but then, just a few miles out, disappeared in a flash of photons. The Client waited the long half-second it would take the missiles to materialize inside the three reavers and detonate.

Nothing happened.

Now she frantically checked data. The missiles had arrived at their targets, but had then fallen out of the real, back into U-space. The prador must have internal bounce gates themselves and so a defence against U-jump missiles. That might mean . . .

Ten of the attack pods exploded, and a second later the Client turned on the platform's own defensive internal runcibles. Another five attack pods exploded before she managed to get the rest to activate their bounce gates.

'Big mistake,' said the rapidly approaching prador. 'Huge mistake.'

Earth Central

'The weapons platform missing from the accretion disc has turned up,' said the king of the prador.

The father-captain, whose form Earth Central bore, clattered his mandibles in surprise. EC was aware that the king knew he wasn't talking to a prador and that the surprise had been manufactured in the mind of a very large and smart AI. EC regretted the silly impulse at once and stopped moving his mandibles.

'Where?' he asked.

'It arrived at the location of a xeno-extermination committed by the one whose form you bore previously.'

EC acknowledged that with a tilt of his carapace. In his present form he had lost the old king's coloration, made the body smaller and styled his body language to be more obsequious. Irritating the present king of the prador now would not result in more data but an abrupt termination of contact.

'And?'

'It will be dealt with.'

So the Client had, as expected, gone to its home world and the king's forces were responding. As ever in these conversations, both of them were giving away as little as possible. EC decided that the only way to accrue further data was to give some out.

'Apparently an alien entity seized control of Weapons Platform Mu,' it said. 'It is thought this entity is a resurrected form of the Client.'

The king considered this for a moment. He did not have instant recall and was undoubtedly accessing some external database. Or was he? EC had yet to plumb the extent of the king's mind and what it might encompass.

'How unfortunate that a weapons platform – an item that is mostly Polity technology and run by an AI, even if it is under Orlandine's control – should end up in my kingdom.'

'Has it caused any problems?' EC enquired.

'It has necessitated a response.'

The king's forces would of course have demanded the complete surrender of the platform. Since the prador had annihilated the Species, EC felt that the Client would be unlikely to surrender. If the platform and its attack pods were not too damaged it would be quite a fight, and that would be beside whatever else the Client could do – the Polity, in allying with that creature, hadn't found it particularly restrained or meek. EC found itself liking the situation. It was always a good idea to keep the prador aware of the superiority of Polity weapons technology and, with the Client in charge of a weapons platform, here was a nice plausibly deniable reminder. But of course the king knew that.

'The Client, you say,' said the king.

'Yes, apparently resurrected from one of its body husks by the weapons platform AI.'

The king appeared to be more irritated than usual. 'I had thought that matter had been dealt with. The weapon used against the Client was . . . effective.'

'So it's true you ordered that hit,' said EC. 'Private contractor, I heard . . . What kind of weapon?'

'No matter. This "Client" is apparently alive again . . .'

'You can trust my word on it.'

'I trust that the platform will eventually be destroyed,' said the king. 'The nature of that destruction will no doubt leave no evidence of this "Client".'

'If your weapons are sufficient to the task,' said EC, unable to resist.

'So this "Client" came directly to my kingdom in a damaged weapons platform in search of vengeance. As I understand it, this creature was not so impatient before.'

'My guess is that it hoped to pass itself off as an AI to foment discord between us. Has it tried this?'

The king ignored the question and said, 'So vengeance is all it seeks . . .'

Ah . . .

It seemed the king knew something about the data store that had almost certainly been the Client's first target.

'What else?' EC asked.

'What else indeed,' said the king. 'Now, have you received any communications from Orlandine concerning the wormship fragment aboard one of my destroyers?'

EC had not, but the fact the king was asking this question was revealing. It seemed likely he had not received anything from the destroyer recently. Something must have happened out there because the king's agents always responded immediately to him.

'I have heard nothing.'

'Nothing . . .'

'Not a peep.'

'Do you have anything further you would like to elucidate?'

'Do you have any questions you would like to ask?'

Abruptly the king's form shimmered and changed. Now, instead of that huge creature, a prador in armour squatted in the sea grasses. It rose up on its legs and swivelled to take in the view for a moment then swung back to face EC.

'Who are you?' Earth Central asked.

'I am Bavos – king's envoy,' replied the prador.

EC eyed the creature and considered what sort of submind he should design to deal with it. EC also knew that nothing useful would now get done. The king had withdrawn and diplomatic relations had just taken a downturn. The wreckage out near the Graveyard, from the time this had last happened, was still radiating.

Cutter

Cutter fell through vacuum towards the prador destroyer, flexing his limbs and bringing his systems up to full power. It felt good to be out of the constriction of Orlandine's ship, and he loved the way the starlight glinted on all his sharp edges.

'Just like the good old days,' he said.

'Indubitably,' Bludgeon replied. 'However, Orlandine did order you to capture and immobilize those two second-children who fired on us. If I recollect aright, you often tried to take captives, and often failed.'

'What's this?' interjected Orlandine.

Cutter liked the haiman woman, she had after all been a source of much excitement for him three centuries ago, and had got him out of a bit of a rut then. But he sometimes found it annoying how she could operate in the same communications plenum as he and his fellow war and assassin drones. Why did he think like this when it was generally the attitude of AIs like him that humans should upgrade to their level? He guessed it was because she hovered in a grey area between the two.

'Cutter has never managed to capture a prador alive,' Bludgeon explained. 'Some situation has always arisen whereby his personal survival has been threatened too severely and he has had to kill his intended captives.'

'That will not happen this time,' Orlandine snapped.

'Well, let's hope—' Cutter began but she interrupted him.

'And do you know why it will not happen?'

After a brief pause it was Bludgeon who asked. 'Why?'

'Because,' Orlandine explained, 'on this mission Cutter will place the capture and immobilization of the two second-children above his own survival. Cutter, you will make their capture your primary objective.'

'What?' said Bludgeon. 'You can't be serious.'

Cutter, meanwhile, began chewing this over. Throughout the war and other conflicts he had risked his life, and he had undertaken missions during which his personal survival had been doubtful. However, the bedrock underlying his objectives had mostly been to get out alive. He was, after all, a useful asset and, even on failed missions, he had usually caused severe damage to the enemy. Only twice had mission importance exceeded the value of his own life, and he had been asked to sacrifice himself to such objectives. Obviously he hadn't – he'd always found ways to complete the mission and survive the experience. This was why Orlandine had made the order. She was pressuring him to complete and to survive.

Cutter turned his inspection inward. As a concept, the mission had loaded to his mind, but he now had to make some alterations. In level of importance, he switched mission concept with personal survival – the process a little rusty and creaking. As these thumped into place he suddenly felt a little danger and a strong frisson of excitement. He remembered that this had happened on those other occasions too. Removing personal survival from the mission equation opened up whole new landscapes of thought – landscapes in which he could run a little crazily. He felt his character profile change in response.

'Fuck, you did it,' said Bludgeon.

'Never underestimate the boredom of assassin drones,' said Orlandine.

The hull of the destroyer loomed closer, two balls containing rail-guns turning in their sockets to track his progress. Cutter spurted blades of white flame to shove himself sideways and came down hard before a set of space doors. The gecko function of his feet did not work so well against prador hull metal and felt particularly ineffective now. He spat a laser at the metal and analysed the spectrum. The metal was more advanced than the old stuff and seemed to have incorporated something of the newer Polity hull metals. Cutter thought that the disguise of these prador as renegades from the Kingdom did not bear close inspection. Rather than trying any other form of foot adhesion, he just used his thrusters to slide himself towards the space doors, which were already opening. Then, as soon as he could get a grip on something, he dragged himself inside, re-oriented to internal grav and dropped from ceiling to floor, flipping over as he did so to come down on his feet. The space doors began to close behind him, while ahead five big armoured prador, bristling with weapons, scuttled backwards.

'They're a little nervous in here,' he observed.

'If I was a prador,' said Orlandine, 'I would be a little nervous of an assassin drone with a record like yours. They know who you are, dear Cutter.'

Cutter tilted his head, antennae coiling up and then straightening as he scanned the five ahead of him. He reviewed his personal archives of the estimated four thousand six hundred and nineteen prador he had killed. The figure was an estimate because over two thousand of the count were complements from the crew of two dreadnoughts and assorted smaller ships he had depopulated – usually by detonating internal weapons caches. He guessed, knowing that, the five ahead should be nervous. However, it was Cutter himself who should be nervous – if things turned nasty here, right now, the assault programs he was running told him he could kill only about two of them before the others took him apart.

'Com open,' said Bludgeon. 'The prador assault group leader is called Boris – you also have linked com to Captain Orlik.'

'Boris?' said Cutter privately.

'Yes, Boris,' Bludgeon confirmed.

'Okay, comrades,' he addressed the five before him, 'let's do this.'

After a brief pause, the prador parted, three to one side and two to the other. One of them, in yellow armour decorated with purple camouflage streaks, gestured with a claw to the next door leading into the ship proper.

'So what's the plan of attack?' Boris asked.

'Situational update, please,' said Cutter, moving forwards. He felt a little anxious because his assault programs had adjusted the situation in his mind. He was putting himself at a disadvantage now and would only be able to kill one of them if they attacked . . .

Much to his surprise, the prador Boris immediately squirted a file across to him in Polity drone tactical format. As air pressure rose around him and the diagonally divided door ahead separated, he reviewed the information. The two second-children he was after were ensconced in the maintenance and operator cabin behind the railgun ball. They had welded shut the main armoured doors leading into that area and were currently working to isolate all the mechanisms accessible to them that Orlik could access from his sanctum. They already had control of grav in there, which would make an assault quite interesting. Also, they had taken apart the few explosive railgun slugs they could get to and mined the area with stinger mines. These explosive devices were like short-barrelled guns and flung out one exotic metal slug capable of damaging, if not penetrating, prador armour. They had their own weapons too, of course – both armed with particle cannons and just one armed with a heavy Gatling cannon. This was the limit of the file because little data had come from the area for an hour now, since the two of them had found and destroyed the final cam.

'This wasn't planned,' said Cutter, stepping out into the oval section tunnel beyond.

'Evidently,' said Boris.

The prador's observation dispelled Cutter's momentarily pleasant nostalgia on being in such a place. He had wanted to explain his reasoning but it seemed Boris was already there, and he controlled the urge to get snappy. Boris and his friends might well not survive what he was planning so there was no loss in being reasonable now.

'Explain "evidently",' he said.

Boris fell in beside him, perambulating casually, occasionally rapping a claw against the wall as if in time to some song in his mind, which was unlikely – he was prador after all.

'Had it been planned they would have moved in some heavier armament from the weapons cache just a short distance from where they are,' said Boris. 'In fact, they were working not far from there when they made this move.'

Boris sent over another file. This showed the two second-children working their way along an optical data feed, decoupling sections and testing them individually. Cutter ran the file quickly in his mind because it was hours long. The two had obviously been trying to trace one of the many worm-generated faults in the ship. He could see how they had started out working efficiently, then began making mistakes, their work rate slowing. Towards the end they were showing signs of confusion, in fact just the sort of behaviour Cutter had seen before when prador had been infected with a Polity bio-weapon parasite. Was this what had happened here?

'Where were they before this?' he asked.

The next file came fast, as if Boris had been expecting the question. Cutter now saw the two working in the hold, bringing up heavy clamps, sliding them in slots up to the fragment of wormship, securing their bases then tightening them on the glistening surface of the thing. It gave Cutter the creeps, that worm.

'*This is not relevant to your mission,*' Orlandine interjected, obviously watching the whole interplay.

'*I beg to differ, haiman,*' said Cutter. He glanced at Boris and was even more conscious of the other four prador behind him. Of course, 'behind' was not quite the right term, since his vision was three hundred and sixty degrees and his joints could fold in any direction he chose. He could attack something behind with as much alacrity and efficiency as anything in front.

'How many others have been that close?' he asked carefully, upgrading the assault program running constantly in his mind. He quietly ran targeting solutions with all his weaponry, tilting himself slightly so that the high-intensity laser in his rear could acquire the visor of the nearest prador behind.

'Three others,' Boris replied, 'and they have now, of course, been disarmed and placed in confinement – without their armour.'

'Ah,' said Cutter.

'We are not the kind of prador you were accustomed to, Cutter,' said Boris. 'You should remember that when it comes to dealing with those two ahead.'

'I would remember that,' Cutter replied, 'if I thought they were thinking like prador any more.'

No, he decided, rejecting his previous plan, direct assault through the armoured door was out. The fact that casualties would be too high was one factor, but the smallest one. The largest was that one, or both of the two, would likely be killed.

'*Bludgeon?*' he enquired.

His partner war drone, as always, was just a small step behind in his thinking, and a tactical assessment of the infrastructure around the railgun arrived in Cutter's mind. He already had the schematic available but Bludgeon's showed him what kind of explosives could be used to what effect.

'Still pressurized,' he observed. 'You have planar explosives?'

'We do,' Boris replied.

'Then here is part of the plan.' Cutter sent it in drone format.

Boris abruptly halted, then turned, gesturing back down the corridor. 'Then we go back to where we started – the nearest way outside is the way you came in.'

The whole group turned, two speeding off ahead.

'Those planar explosives,' Boris explained. 'Father is not going to like this.'

'I don't,' interjected the voice of Captain Orlik. 'But I bow to this assassin drone's expertise when it comes to capturing prador.'

Cutter was glad he wasn't human, with an expression that

might be easily read. He felt like a bit of a fraud. He also wondered how Boris and the others would react when he told them to lose their particle cannons and railguns, and take up weapons incapable of penetrating prador armour . . .

Angel

Angel watched as the white, squid-like creature swarmed up the algae-drift beach towards him, then noted further disturbances in the ocean behind it. The thing loomed up close, pausing to peck at the drift with the parrot heads at the end of its long limbs, throwing the stuff all around. Then it attacked, and one parrot head snapped down, closing on Angel's shoulder. The creature was strong, because it managed to shift him slightly to the side. But he reached up and closed a hand around one of the neck-limbs, his fingers sinking through muscular flesh. It squealed and other heads punched down, until he turned and chopped across them. The edges of his hands were razor sharp, and two heads fell, necks writhing and spurting ichor. He stepped in closer, discarding the severed head attached to his shoulder, and reached under the front end of the thing, heaving it up and sending it tumbling down the beach. Eyeing the ocean, he saw it boiling as more and more of the same creatures clambered up onto the shore. A quick scan of the depths showed them packed with these things. He did not have time for this.

Turning back to his transport egg, he scanned up into the sky and linked. Ruth was getting closer in the shuttle, while a spaceship was now dropping from orbit. Trike was coming. Suddenly doubting the extent of his control, he entered Ruth's mind to be sure she was following his command exactly. Ruth's emotions were mixed: she was angry with him, livid, but on the other hand felt a strange gratitude to be included in his business once again. She had developed an odd kinship with him, despite the fact he had stripped information from her mind and killed her, then seemingly resurrected her on a whim. Was she suffering from some perverted form of what the humans called Stockholm syndrome?

'You will not harm him,' she said out loud, sensing his connection.

'I will do as I please,' Angel replied in her mind.

The words lacked their earlier sincerity and she sensed this – he seemed to be weak, at some remove. She could not disobey but began to wonder if she might be able to fight him.

'No, you cannot,' said Angel, seizing control of her body. She abruptly reached down, took the knife from her belt and held it up with the point pressed below her eye. 'Do I have to give you a reminder?'

'No, you do not have to remind me,' she replied.

But it *was* all insincere, because he now felt repelled by the idea of harming her. As he dropped the compulsion she pushed the knife back into her belt. He sensed that she felt he was bluffing, but she could not understand why. Through her eyes he saw her take the shuttle down through a cloud that left yellow smears on the screen. A continent lay visible to her left, and the pale green ocean extended from below to the horizon. The island he was on wasn't visible yet, but she would be there soon enough. Angel glanced at the great mass of creatures now heaving from the sea, climbed back into his transport egg and, with some irritation, slammed the hatch shut.

'You can take the ship and just leave us there, on that island,' she said, the connection still open.

'That would be interesting,' Angel replied. 'I suspect that being a hooper, Trike would survive until someone came, but I am not so sure you would.'

'What?'

The egg jerked and shuddered as the creatures reached it. Through external sensors he watched them flooding around it and piling up on top of each other in their eagerness, their anger, whatever it was. Their parrot heads hammered against the hull, and he probed them with scanners to analyse their physical structure – a task he found much more difficult than before. Soon he saw that the situation here was untenable.

'New coordinates,' he said abruptly, and sent them to Ruth. 'Relay these to Trike.'

'You have a problem there?' she stated.

'An irritation. An inconvenience,' Angel replied.

A tendril within the egg penetrated one of his hands and he took full control of its system. But it was sluggish and not as easy to operate as before. The great mass of organic movement outside began to slide away as the egg rose, and he was soon looking down on that area of the small island. It was heaped with the big albino forms, their jointed neck-limbs waving angrily. He sent the image to Ruth's mind, although was not sure why he did so.

He shifted the transport egg a couple of miles from its original location – above a great mass of tulip-like growths. Through his sensors he could now see a speck in the distance as Ruth's shuttle drew rapidly closer. But then he saw other objects in the sky and realized his plan to use this egg as a diversion later on would no longer work. The Cyberat were coming and doubtless scanning – they would find out if he was not in the transport egg.

Surveying his new surroundings, he chose a big slab of rock jutting out below the tulip growths. It was a better location anyway, since there was room for Trike to land his ship now. It occurred to him that he should have planned for this before, that he wasn't thinking clearly. He descended, the transport egg settling with a crunch.

Ruth's shuttle came in to hover over the slab and she brought it down on the other side of the egg from where the tulip things were. Angel climbed out of the egg and the surface crunched under his feet, coated with objects like black barnacles. He walked out for a little way, surveyed his surroundings, then moved over to the edge of the slab and gazed at the view. Lower down he could see the creatures that had swamped the transport sphere moving inland in a wave of fleshy bodies. He next raised his gaze to the haze out at sea and saw the objects there. One of them was Zackander's slab-like ship, others seemed to be a variety of grav-transports while there were smaller objects he could not make out. But now they seemed to be hanging back, circling the island like sharks.

'Who are they?'

Without looking round at Ruth, he replied, 'The Cyberat.'

Why were they holding back? He looked up. 'And here comes Trike.'

The rumble of unbalanced grav-engines reached them, and the flash of steering thrusters put the shadow of the ship over them. Angel watched it descend and land, the slab shuddering under his feet. He felt almost tired – perhaps due to the malfunctions throughout his body – and it occurred to him that perhaps he would not be leaving this place. A ramp lowered to the rock and a tall man stepped out onto it.

13

Madness: Where Polity medical technology prevails, the mental maladies of the past remain there – firmly in the past. Most inherited organic failures of the brain now only exist in the data files of medical historians, while subsequent failures that cannot be corrected by nanosuites can usually be dealt with by autodoc or, if necessary, by an AI surgeon. Complex problems caused by circumstance and environment, like PTSD, can be handled by mental editing. However, madness is still with us. The standard human brain has, for example, no coping mechanism for a nearly endless life, hence the 'ennui barrier' people reach at around about their second century. Other problems arise from mental enhancements, usually from the integration of disparate mental components. Even AIs are not immune – those who specialize too far turn inward and lose themselves in their own mental worlds. Existential angst is often a problem for both AIs and enhanced humans. Then there are the effects of alien environments and organisms. The hoopers of Spatterjay are a glaring example – the viral fibres tangled in their brains have a damping effect like the amyloid plaques of that ancient disease Alzheimer's, but also make synaptic connections and hugely increase the density of neural networks. The phrase 'defies analysis' is too often used but applies in this case. No one can decide whether hoopers have been made stupid or brilliant by this, but all agree that they are, to varying degrees, crazy.

From 'How It Is' by Gordon

Trike

Trike gazed at the egg-shaped transport resting on the slab of rock and then at the two figures standing over near the edge. He stared at Angel. Though the legate looked more humanoid than before, he still retained his silvery skin. He recognized Ruth at the core of his being and when the legate moved over and grabbed hold of her arm, he took an involuntary step down the ramp, anger boiling up inside him.

'Steady,' said Cog. 'We go down and talk first.'

'Talk?' Trike spat.

'It gets us closer,' Cog advised.

Trike peered down at the laser carbine he was holding, then glanced aside at Cog, who held his own weapon in one hand.

'Okay,' he managed, and tried to think clearly about what Cog had said earlier. 'We talk and, if we can, drive him over the edge, grab Ruth and run.'

'You've got it, boy.' Cog grimaced at the view out to sea. 'If the Cyberat hold off. Let's go.'

They strolled on down the ramp. Trike kept his finger on the trigger of his carbine but didn't think he could take a shot at this distance without some chance of hitting Ruth. He watched the legate carefully, how he held Ruth's arm and then took a pace forwards. Angel turned and looked out to sea, and Trike raised his own gaze to see that the Cyberat, who he and Cog had seen on the way down, were now coming in. When they reached the bottom of the ramp, heavy boots crunching, Angel looked past them to the right, and Trike glanced over. Some big squid-like life form had clambered up onto the slab there, and was soon followed by another.

'I don't think we'll have much time to—' began Cog.

Trike raised his carbine and fired, tracking the swiftly moving silver figure running to their right. The beam crackled in the air, visible as a line of gleaming red spots as it vaporized whining flies. He was sure he hit Angel four or five times, but to no effect. Then he himself ran towards the prostrate form of Ruth.

'Trike!' Cog bellowed. His weapon then spat out a violet-blue particle beam.

Trike caught a glimpse of it striking the legate and flinging him backwards, while he squatted by Ruth, who was already pushing herself upright. She looked round at him and their eyes met. It just didn't seem the same, with her eyes being black now. And those eyes widened as she looked at him.

'Leave me,' she said. 'He's going for your ship!'

'No, get aboard,' Trike said, then was up and running.

Angel recovered, and Cog hit him again with the particle beam, but this time it just splashed off the legate and he kept moving forwards. Beyond the legate Trike could see the wave of creatures coming in, but many of them were not getting far. The tulip things were moving frenetically, rising on stalks and thumping down to the ground. They snatched and lifted up the creatures trying to pass, then tossed them back like herons swallowing frogs. Only these things did not appear to have gullets – they just closed up around their prey, then descended out of sight.

Angel was moving steadily towards the ramp now and Cog had backed up onto it. His weapon was smoking in his hands and seemed to require at least a second or so to cool down before he could use it again. During those seconds Angel moved quickly, but while Cog was firing he slowed to a leaden pace, his feet seemingly stuck to the ground. All around him the stone was smouldering and Angel himself seemed to be glowing a dull orange. Trike ran straight at him, rage bubbling inside him and a roar rising out of his chest, but also an element of cold calculation working in his mind. He lowered his shoulder and slammed into the android, and it was like hitting a solid iron post. Trike was an old hooper, however, and even iron posts had their limit.

Angel tumbled sideways, lumps of rock stuck to the soles of his feet. Trike rubbed at his smoking shoulder and strode forward as Angel picked himself up. Roaring, his tongue sticking way out of his mouth and open at the end, Trike double fisted the legate as he began to rise. Something crunched inside Angel as he turned a backward somersault and landed on his face, but he shot up again almost immediately. Trike was on him just as fast, throwing himself into a dropkick that sent the legate back. Angel fell on his backside, coughed out a spray of smoking fragments, but then sprang up to confront Trike again. Trike straight-armed him to send him staggering, then spun and slammed his boot into him to push him back further. Angel looked somehow bent and there were splits in the front of his torso, but he staggered very little this time, and managed a ghastly smile.

'You think you can hurt me?' he asked. He held out a hand towards Trike, a glowing disc igniting in the palm. 'I can burn you to ash where you stand.'

At that moment, a large parrot beak came down like a pickaxe and clamped onto Angel's shoulder. He turned and snapped the head away from the jointed limb that had wielded it, then lifted the attacking creature up and over so it came down on its back, flat starfish feet waggling in the air. Angel was slower turning back, though, and Trike realized he had actually managed to damage the legate.

'Was that the plan?' Angel asked.

'No,' said Trike, pointing upwards. 'That was.'

One of the big tulips closed down hard on Angel, wrenching him from the stone and up into the air. As it tossed him around, getting ready to drop him into its interior, Trike turned and ran for the ramp. He knew the thing would not hold Angel for long.

He made it to the foot of the ramp where Cog waited.

'Ruth?'

Cog stabbed a thumb back inside the ship, and Trike stepped onto the ramp as a blast ripped over the slab. It hurled him skidding across the stone on his chest, with burning debris tumbling past him. He shook himself, ears ringing, and turned into a crouch. Angel was walking out of the smoking remains of the copse of tulip things. He held out one hand and a bright blue particle beam stabbed out, which he swept across the mass of squid-like creatures. He did this again and again until they were a steaming, burning heap, falling in writhing chunks. Then he broke into a steady trot towards the ramp.

Trike checked to see where Cog was and saw him groggily rising to his feet beside the ramp, one hand still clamped onto it, the metal crunched up like straw. He had lost his weapon, which lay some feet behind him. Trike readied himself to run at Angel again, sure now that he would be eaten up by that particle beam just as quickly as the creatures were, but hardly caring any more. Then something else hit the legate, and hard.

Angel staggered in a flash of light, a fire trail stabbing from his side and stone exploding to vapour where the trail ended. The slab rocked and shifted ominously, and Trike saw that the legate had lost a chunk out of his side. Angel looked down at the hole there, mouth opening and closing. He was hit again, with what looked to be a railgun slug, and Trike realized the Cyberat had decided to do something. He gazed at the legate who was now missing most of his abdomen, the upper part of his body supported by an impossibly thin sliver of torso. Angel folded and collapsed, shuddering a little before he grew still.

A shadow now fell across them and Trike glanced aside to see

Zackander's spaceship home descending. It did not land on the slab but went down past it and out of sight. But even as it did so something shot out from it and came towards him and Cog. The circular grav-platform was loaded with armament, while Zackander sat upon a pedestal amidst this. Perhaps the Cyberat had used one of the weapons from there against the legate, Trike had no idea. Other members of the Cyberat began to swarm in on an array of different vehicles. Two large platforms, with even heavier armament aboard, hovered over the severed form of Angel, the silvered throats of particle cannons pointed down. Zackander detached from his pedestal and floated over on the glass ball of his lower body.

'We did not want to fire while he was near Ruth,' said the old Cyberat. 'And with you running around it was also difficult,' he added, looking at Trike.

Trike was aware that Cog had come up beside him, but his eyes strayed as Ruth came walking back down the ramp. Now, with the danger apparently over, he felt monstrous – like he had too much anger to spare. He felt a sick lurch as he heard distant giggling, and shadow forms joined the descending Cyberat. He fought it and concentrated on looking at his wife, feeling the anger diminish somewhat. He clenched and unclenched his hands. Breathed.

'So we are done here,' he said.

Another vehicle landed beside Zackander's. This was a larger rectangular grav-barge and the form squatting amidst the weaponry and other devices was the torso of a young man grafted onto a giant metal spider. This rose up to expose heavy Gatling cannons attached on each side.

'We are not done yet,' he said.

He turned and the cannons fired; thousands of high-powered rounds slamming into Zackander's grav-platform. The thing flew apart and tumbled across the slab, while Zackander spun in midair, raising his arms as if in protest. A yellow beam stabbed out from one of the hovering Cyberat and hit his glass ball. The glass did not break but things started burning inside, blackening the glass. Zackander dropped out of the air and bounced, then spun and went down, his upper torso sprawling on its face.

'We needed him out of his ship,' said the other Cyberat, climbing down from his grav-barge. 'He seemed to think we did not know whose dangerous interest in Jain technology led to what has happened on our world.' He came to stand over Zackander. 'He seemed to think he could just sweep it all to one side and return to his position as our leader. He thought wrong.'

'Is he dead?' Ruth asked.

Doshane looked up from Zackander and gazed at her. He looked furious. 'No, he is not dead yet,' he spat. 'And don't think I don't know who sold him the last batch of Jain technology he was playing with. You are as guilty in this matter as him!'

'I'm sorry,' she said. 'I thought him capable . . .'

'None are, when it comes to this evil.' Doshane nodded a head towards Angel, then held up a hand. The Cyberat who had brought down Zackander shifted his platform over. The yellow beam stabbed down again to strike Angel's egg transport, spiralling round and round over it. The thing crackled and burned, leaked molten metals and slumped, black smoke pouring away from it. When it was finally a molten pool on the rock, Doshane raised his hand again and gestured to the remains of Angel.

'Wait,' said Cog, stepping forwards.

'What?' asked Doshane tersely.

'A Polity forensic AI will want to examine that.' Cog nodded to the erstwhile legate.

'And why should I care?'

'Because even cyborgs do not annoy Polity AIs,' said Cog reasonably.

Doshane glared at him, but after a moment nodded. 'Very

well. Take that with you.' He next surveyed all three of them. 'Now, you will get off our world. I will give you one day to get the hell out of here and if you are not gone by then –' he paused and looked up at the sky – 'enough orbital defences remain to put a missile in your ship. Do not come back. You are not welcome here.' He turned and headed away.

The Client

Reavers and attack pods tested each other's defences, as railgun missiles and particle beams scribed across vacuum. The Client studied the battle front for just a short time before leaving it to well-established programming. She could think of nothing clever to do, no special tactics she could apply. This stage of the battle seemed to be just about brute force. She turned her attention to the U-space drive of the weapons platform.

The big treaded robot was now manoeuvring the super-dense ring into place in the drive. Other robots were also fitting components and linking them, testing the whole system in stages. It would take another hour before the drive was workable. The Client studied the statistics again, in greater detail. Then she turned her attention back to the battle as another of her attack pods exploded into a cloud of plasma. It would be over long before she could fire up the U-space drive and it was looking increasingly like she would be on the losing side. She had to do *something* . . .

Her attention strayed to her remote, and then to the data she had taken from the library – now distributed throughout memory storage in the weapons platform. Almost instinctively she began running searches on tactics and weapons that might apply to the situation she was in. As knowledge sank into her conscious mind, she damned her stupidity of just a few minutes before because she

276

had lost so much. Ten minutes later, once the super-dense ring was secured in place, she fired up all the conventional drives of the weapons platform and set it diving towards the sun. Behind her the attack pods fought a steady retreat, while they fell into an odd tubular formation.

'The humans have an interesting expression,' sent the prador in charge of the attacking fleet. 'Out of the frying pan and into the fire.'

'I see the analogy,' she replied, 'but I do not find it interesting.'

'Oh it interests me because I have a strange fascination with their odd habit of half-burning fresh meat before eating it. I did try it once – only because a human corpse came my way after being partially broiled by a laser.'

'And what did you think of it?' As she asked the question the Client finished constructing a guidance program for the attack pods. This was to control their hardfields and electromagnetic effector weapons, which were usually used for induction warfare.

'It was interesting,' said the prador.

The sun loomed ever bigger in the Client's perception, and the temperature in the weapons platform climbed. Soon it reached a temperature uncomfortable even for her and a long unused cooling system kicked in within her cylinder. Various views throughout the platform gave her glimpses of exterior components flaring and burning away, structural beams beginning to glow. Maintenance robots scuttled for cover on the outer hull, darting inside quickly opened hatches. Further cooling was required. She ramped up the photo-electric hull to its full potential and most of the platform now seemed like a hole into midnight. She routed the power surge from this to every laser available, all pointed towards the prador reavers.

'So that was your plan?' asked the prador.

The lasers were having minimal effect, merely burning up a

few stray railgun slugs and putting a little extra strain on the reavers' hardfield defence.

'Every little counts,' she replied.

Heavy ionization now kept throwing up error reports, and small sparks of lightning flickered from point to point about the platform's hull. The density out there was getting close to optimum.

On the first test the funnel of hardfields, its wide end directed towards the sun, lasted just a few seconds before field conflicts started blowing generators. The Client changed some parameters, putting more space between the fields, and tested it again. This time it held. Within just a second the ionized gas density at the narrow end of the funnel increased ten-fold, but overall density of the storm she was flying into was not yet enough. She ran a test of the attack pods' arrays. Yes, they generated a rough tube of hardfields which, when hit with the effector weapons, took a huge positive charge, while the ion storm in the funnel was negative. Charge density just had to reach a particular level. Now she needed what might effectively be called the grid for this giant thermionic valve.

'What *are* you doing?' asked the prador, as its ships targeted another attack pod and peeled it with particle beams.

The item was a transport platform – just a half-mile squared of bubble-metal and composite driven by rockets at its corners. A negative charge to it in its holding bay gave the platform a positive charge as she launched it. Keeping an induction warfare beam on it managed to steadily ramp up that positive charge as the transport platform hurtled out. Just one more minute . . .

'No,' said the prador. 'I am not liking this at all. It is time to stop playing.'

'Too late,' she replied.

The ion density in the funnel hit optimum – a deep blue glow just two miles ahead and four miles to the side of the weapons platform. The vast mass of negatively charged ionized gas spurted out and curved slightly to the nearest positive – the transport platform – and turned it to plasma. The blue beam, a mile wide, continued to the next positive, the tube of hardfields, but did not slow, and went straight through. It flashed out and struck two of the reavers, peeling the side off one while the other melted and coiled up like a worm dropped on a hot plate. Sun-hot ionic gas leapt from these two to the other ships, one simply exploding. The formation broke, remaining ships scattering and coming under intense fire from the attack pods.

'And which is the frying pan and which is the fire?' the Client sent, but received no reply.

Zackander

Consciousness returned like a blow to the head. Zackander opened his eyes and stared at stone, then tried to push himself up and initiate the grav in the mechanical part of his body. He got nothing. He tried to use the implants, which were actually in the human part of his body, to make contact with someone or something – anything – but they were dead inside him. The beam that had brought him down had been a gas laser, but one twinned with induction warfare EMR that fried most of his cyber element.

But he was a survivor. He was the oldest Cyberat of them all and he was damned if he was going to fall because of Doshane's betrayal. He looked ahead towards the edge of the slab. He had landed his ship below it and there had to be a way down. He tried to remember the layout of the slab and its surroundings as he had seen them when coming in. Yes, over to the right there was a scree slope. It would be difficult, but all he needed to do was take his time and be careful. Doubtless Doshane had expected him to die without his cyber systems, but Zackander had always been cautious. His human body possessed many connection points to his systems but it was also self-contained. Yes, he would need water and food, but not for some time yet. He began dragging himself to where he was sure the scree slope lay, but the moment the glass ball of his lower half rattled across the stone he heard movement behind him.

Zackander stopped and looked round. There lay the heaped mass of burned and dismembered sea octids. However, some of them had escaped Angel's particle beam and were now dragging themselves out of the mass. He gazed at them in disbelief. Three of them hauled themselves free and began pecking around themselves as if in irritation, flinging pieces of their fellows about. Grief? he wondered, but then had to think of his own survival. He was producing none of the EMR that he knew attracted these creatures to their prey, but they would certainly be drawn to any sound of movement. He eased himself along and winced, biting down a curse at the sound his chain-glass half made against the rock. One of the three octids paused in its pecking, parrot heads raised high and turning as it tried to triangulate the source of the sound. Zackander kept very still and after a moment the creature returned to its pecking.

He checked around himself. Nearby lay a piece of one of the creatures – a sheet of its skin with nodules of blubber on the inner face. He stretched out very slowly to snare it, pulled it over, then inch by inch pulled his chain-glass ball up onto it. He then secured it to the front of the ball using the clips on which he normally attached various tools. He now had a skid that prevented the chain-glass rattling against the rock, and he began to move on.

It seemed to take ages to get across the slab and twice he made noises that alerted the octids, but each time he kept still and waited until they returned to their pecking. Now he peered down the scree slope. He could see his ship and it was intact – Doshane had not yet put a missile into it as he had feared. Quite likely Doshane did not dislike Jain tech as much as he claimed and intended to come back later for the collection inside.

Zackander eased out onto the top of the slope, but no matter how careful he was, scree began to tumble away. That was noisy enough in itself, but then the fall of rocky fragments hit a thruster jutting from the side of his ship with a metallic rattling. All three octids raised their numerous beaked heads and zeroed in on him.

Zackander stared at them, again trying to stay still and silent, but it did not work this time. The octids started to head towards him. Not needing to move quietly now, he scrambled down the slope, losing the piece of flesh that had muffled the noise, his chain-glass half clonking and ringing. He felt scree giving way underneath him, then everything seemed to be on the move and he was falling in a small avalanche of rocky fragments. He folded his hands around his head and just went with it. His shoulder hit hard against something, he somersaulted and came down again, finally slamming into a flat surface. After a moment, he unwound his arms and looked around. He was against the base of his ship, which was down here on its belly. Looking up the slope he saw the three octids now pecking at the stone in confusion. He laughed, which was a mistake, because at once they started to make their way down the slope.

Zackander dragged himself round quickly, for he knew that not far from where he was lay a small maintenance airlock. Behind, he heard the scree avalanching again, then the thump of something heavy and fleshy against his ship. He crawled faster, as fast as he could, and there ahead was the airlock. He pulled himself in below it and for a moment was confused as to why it would not open. He had not sent the command; could not send the command. He stretched up, groping for the manual control, sure that it had frozen after all these years of disuse. The handle pulled out easily and turned smoothly, and the outer door popped open. With a last powerful effort, Zackander hauled himself inside and slammed the door behind him.

He lay panting in the airlock, not having thought further than this. Something kept niggling at his memory but he could not bring it to the fore. He dragged himself to the inner door and hauled himself as upright as he could manage to get to its control panel. The touch-screen presented him with a keypad and the demand for 'command code'. He stared at it in bewilderment, then at the ten-second countdown above. He remembered now: one of his security measures. He stared and stared and could not for the life of him remember a code that sat in his lost cyber memory. The countdown zeroed, the outer door opened and the inner one pushed towards him like a plunger.

'Fuck you!' he shouted, but only to himself.

He fell out of his ship but did not reach the ground. Numerous beaked heads were there to catch him.

Cyberat U-space Research Station

Jason was a Cyberat with little in the way of physical additions. All he sported was two extra arms sprouting from the side of his torso – silver like those of a skeletal Golem, but with ten fine fingers on each – along with sensory enhancements, mostly located in a silvery, slug-shaped addition to the crown of his head. Otherwise his enhancements were mental. He, and his crew of five other Cyberat, had watched the battle rage about their home world but had been thankfully distant. Returning to the control centre of the U-space research station, he noted that his crew were still watching their screens as yet more debris flashed to plasma against the station's hardfields.

'Anything from Zackander?' asked Luterus.

Jason glanced across at the woman, her insect body squatting with legs folded underneath it as she checked her console. He nodded to himself and walked over to his chair, plonked himself down and decided how he was going to tell them: just the facts. He swung his chair round.

'I've just been talking to Doshane. He has taken charge – Zackander is dead.' After the exclamations of surprise, and when they had all turned to face him, he continued, 'It was Zackander's research that led to all this. It was he who resurrected the thing that destroyed the Cube, and it was that thing which brought both the legate and the wormship here. He has paid the price for that.'

'Doshane killed him?' Luterus asked.

Jason nodded tightly and studied their expressions. Some of them looked a little lost because Zackander had been in charge here for all their lives, but there was no sorrow. The old Cyberat had been an autocratic bastard.

'Now I know that you all want information on what has happened and that some of you had friends or relatives in the Cube. But we have work to do. If any of you feel you cannot continue here, I will understand.'

Nolan, a Cyberat man on a spiderform body, stood up from a squat and without a word headed for the door. They watched him go, all aware that his brother and sister had run a business permanently sited in the Cube.

'Updates,' said Jason once he was gone.

'We have sustained negligible damage,' said one. 'Everything is optimal.'

'The system USER?' asked Jason.

'Ready whenever we need it.'

'Good.' Doshane had mentioned that they might close down interstellar traffic to their world while they rebuilt. However, he was not yet their leader – that would have to be voted on. And his suggestion of immediate closure had been voted down by other Cyberat. Still, over the next month Doshane would likely secure his position and win the leadership vote.

'Anything else I should know about?'

'Local U-space has been mildly disrupted by the battle and the recent departures,' said Luterus. 'There was also a strange U-signature recently not far away from us, but that might be some shadow effect from what happened here.'

'Okay, I'll take a look.'

Jason turned back to his console, closed his eyes for a second and established connections through his cerebral enhancements. At the centre of the station, giant electromagnets and grav-motors kept two singularities stable in two separate cases. Jason could, when ordered, shoot these into a chamber lying between the two cases and with the magnets and motors maintain them in a fast orbit around each other. Then, when he put online a highly adapted U-space drive connected to the chamber, this would cause U-space disruption. Nothing would be able to travel through that continuum across a light year centred on this point. This was not something that could be done lightly, because disruption would continue for months, even after he turned the USER off. This was why other Cyberat had voted Doshane down. He was being too hasty.

Jason now turned his attention to the odd U-space signature Luterus had mentioned. It was strange that it could not be nailed down as having a real matter source, such as a ship. He next looked at recordings of the relative area of space where this had occurred, riffling through the electromagnetic spectrum. There was nothing until he reached microwaves, then briefly he saw something tangled and wormish shimmer in and out of existence. He grimaced. It looked a bit like that wormship, and seemed highly likely to be some kind of reflection or echo. Such phenomena weren't unknown, even with conventional ships, and that wormship certainly had not been conventional.

He now began to study data on the various research projects being conducted here in the collection of particle accelerators but, before he got into it, a request came for a private communication from Nolan.

'What is it, Nolan?' he asked.

'There's something down here,' Nolan replied.

'Look, I know you've had a—'

The link fizzed out for a second, then a voice that certainly wasn't Nolan's said, 'We are here.'

Jason linked straight in to station security, checking logs. All at once, numerous warnings called for his attention. A supply bay had been opened, shortly after that strange U-space signature was detected. Numerous internal cams were offline. Fluctuating mass readings came up near one of the particle accelerators, then near the USER device.

'The fuck?' he said out loud. Then, having retained his feet, he could feel the floor vibrating through them. He spun his chair around. 'We may have—'

Six snakelike forms, their bodies like chromed backbones, erupted from the floor, ripping up bubble-metal and shattering ceramic tiles. They shot up into the air, and turned axolotl heads to gaze with metallic eyes on the occupants of the control room. Jason just gaped, but then had the presence of mind to try and open a connection back to Doshane.

They blurred into motion with the sound of whips cracking,

and Jason felt impact on the side of his neck. He went down, his head hitting the floor hard, and it hurt. In a passing thought, wholly analytical, he understood that he was remaining conscious just a little longer than normal because of his enhancements. Long enough to see his own headless body jerk upright from the chair and take one step, as if about to set out for some urgent appointment, then topple.

Cutter

Hanging in vacuum outside the ship, Cutter watched the four prador at work around the railgun ball, putting into effect his new plan. They had used a chemical reactor device to de-cohere hull metal and make it soft enough to drill into. One of them was now running a nine-foot drill down beside the ball in one of the places marked all around it. Another was following up, forcing planar charges down to the bottom of every hole already drilled, while the remaining two were driving deep cuts into the metal around the rim.

'We could widen the port and go in through there,' suggested Boris, the prador who was beside Cutter.

Cutter shook his mantis head. 'Same problem no matter how we go in. We'd end up in a close fire-fight in an environment they control. Some of us would end up dead and it is likely that both of them would attain that state.'

'Why does she want them alive?' Boris asked.

That was an interesting question and one he hadn't himself asked.

'So?' he enquired to Orlandine over com.

'I understand Jain technology more than any other human

alive, probably more than any other living creature,' Orlandine replied. 'And I think I understand this legate, Angel.'

'And?'

'Something has happened here that does not fit my understanding.'

'That is?'

'Oh, Cutter.' Cutter felt her frustrated mental sigh, then she continued, 'I understand how a piece of a wormship could subvert the systems of a prador destroyer – it had to be converted to that purpose. It was used as a weapon against this ship, probably just to keep Orlik occupied while the wormship tore apart the Cyberat space station. But I know nothing about it getting into and subverting an organic mind as fast as this has with the two prador.'

'That is a capability of Jain tech,' said Cutter.

'I know it is, but this was very fast, Cutter, and without the Jain tech having much in the way of access, like for example Orlik's interface, to those two prador. I'm missing something here and I don't like it. Capture them alive, Cutter, then bring them here.'

'Is that a good idea?'

'Yes, because I want them away and shielded from that worm fragment.' She paused, then added, 'Believe me, I have the security and systems for dealing with them and, I have no doubt, once you capture them in the way I expect, they won't be capable of much.'

The four prador had finished now and, as instructed, had taken up their new weapons and were moving out from the hull of the ship. None of them carried Gatling cannons, and their particle weapons, which were physically implanted in their claws, Orlik had ordered them to deactivate. Instead they carried simple spray guns, tubed to high-pressure tanks on their backs. They hadn't liked this but, when Cutter had explained, they grudgingly accepted that this was necessary.

'Best I take my position,' said Boris, hefting his own spray gun. With a squirt of a thruster from his armour he drifted away from Cutter and took his place in the ring of five, out from the railgun ball.

'Now that is interesting,' said Orlandine.

'What?'

'It seems Orlik is not aware of how much I know . . . listen.'

Orlik was speaking: 'I did not question it to begin with because you are my king, but there is absolutely no doubt she will learn the truth.'

'The truth . . . I am not sure if we even know the truth,' replied another voice that, after a search of memory, Cutter recognized as the one who now named himself Oberon, King of the Prador.

'You broke into his com?' Cutter asked Orlandine.

'No,' she replied. 'The king is allowing me to listen.'

'It is a secret we have kept for centuries,' Orlik protested to his king and father.

'Yes, apparently.'

'Apparently?'

'You have been out in the field for some time and it was not necessary for you to be told that Polity AIs have known about us for many years, Orlik. We have tried always to reclaim our dead but many have escaped us. The Polity obtained one of the Guard some time ago during the events concerning Room 101 and its transformation.'

'Penny Royal?'

'Yes, those events.' The king paused for a moment then continued, 'They obtained a corpse of one of the Guard. I then received a message from Earth Central – a very detailed forensic analysis of the corpse.'

'I would like to see that forensic analysis,' interjected Orlandine.

'I am sending it now,' said the king.

After a pause while he obviously digested that the conversation had not been private, Orlik continued, 'Then why is this not generally known now?'

'Because the AIs want to keep the peace. They know that if the general population of the Kingdom were to learn of this secret it would probably lead to civil war,' the king replied. Then added, 'You should have learned the lesson by now that some secrets must be kept.'

Cutter wondered what that last comment was about. Had Orlik been guilty of some infraction in the past? Did this explain his ersatz renegade status?

'But the more people that know . . .' said Orlik, unsure now.

'You are right, the more people who know, the more likely it is for this to become generally known. But Orlandine has known our secret for decades.'

Light flared in vacuum as detonations went off all around the railgun ball. Chunks of armour hurtled out into space.

'Fuck,' said Cutter, and side-lined what he had been listening to into recording. The five prador had just continued with the plan as he had detailed and were unaware of their father-captain's exchange with the king of the prador.

Cutter fired up his own thruster and hurtled down towards the ship's hull, landing heavily to one side of the railgun ball. Even as he scrambled round to face it, it was rising faster, then faster still. Trailing severed pipes, power lines and hydraulics, it shot out of the ship like a cork, air blasting out all around it. Space fogged with air and water vapour and further debris trailed after it. Amidst this, sucked out by the evacuation, tumbled two second-children in armour. In a flat trajectory, Cutter launched

289

from the hull metal and slammed into the most heavily armed of them. It began firing its Gatling cannon, the recoil sending them both tumbling. Clinging to the thing's back, Cutter initiated the vibrating shearfields along his already diamond-sharp edges. He reached down with one long limb to the shoulder joint of the prador's right claw, in which it clutched the cannon, and pressed hard. The shearfield screamed, but since he was in vacuum he could only feel that through his body. It cut into the thinner metal layers of the joint and air jetted out, then green blood that swiftly boiled to vapour.

Something hit them, and Cutter, nearly dislodged, saw one of his ally prador tumbling past. A hole was burned in its armour that it was struggling to slap a patch over. He glimpsed the remaining four, weaving back and forth as they closed in on the other second-child, which was backed up against the railgun ball. It hit another one of them with its particle cannon lodged in its claw, but then they were close enough and fired up their sprayers. Jets of white fluid hit the second-child and expanded over it like swiftly growing fungus. The breach foam trapped the child's limbs as it hardened. But now, realizing the danger, it turned its particle cannon on that. They would not be able to hold it for long.

Cutter reached down again and grabbed, pulling with one limb and cutting with the other. Suddenly the prador's claw snapped and Cutter sent it tumbling away. A particle beam struck his side, reflected off but ablating. He snared the remaining claw, cutting just above the pincer, then wrenched it angrily. It came off, a broken power supply spewing a cloud of hot ionized gas into vacuum.

'Take him,' Cutter instructed the four prador.

He hurled himself from his first victim directly towards the other, immensely annoyed when two beam strikes hit him. He

slammed home amidst thrashing limbs and burning breach sealant, then began slashing. Two legs fell away and when he got a
grip on the cannon-wielding limb, he did what he did best – what
he was named after. Its other claw closed about his neck, and
surprisingly it even began to dig into his armour. This prador was
strong, unbelievably strong. To his rear he saw the four prador
had now all but enclosed the other second-child in sealant. Cutter
sliced some more and then pulled, until the claw detached.
Swiftly reaching for the other one, he wrenched and broke it off
too. Next, with rear limbs against the railgun ball, he sent his
second victim towards the first, where the other prador snared it
and began rendering it immobile. Cutter felt invigorated, hyped.
He looked around just wishing there were others he could attack.

'Retrieve the severed limbs,' said Orlandine calmly.

'Why?' he snapped.

'Because they will be a useful precursor to my investigation,'
Orlandine replied. 'It will be interesting to see what the virus has
done to them.'

'What?' said Cutter, then he began replaying the rest of the
conversation between the king, Orlik and Orlandine while, with
another part of his mind, examining the copy of the file the
haiman woman had kindly sent him. It seemed that the king had
not deemed it necessary for the Guard to be aware of who knew
their secret. It also seemed that until now, Orlandine had not
deemed it fit to tell Cutter and her other ally drones the full
extent of it either.

14

It is annoying how contrary facts are ignored by those who, for their own aggrandizement, raise something that is little more than a hypothesis into a theory. So it is, with the current explanation for the action of Jain tech. It is a technology made to destroy civilizations that functions akin to a parasite. The Jain node is the egg that hatches in the hand of an intelligent member of some civilization. In utilizing the power this technology provides, the tertiary host spreads this parasite throughout his civilization. And finally when the main host, the civilization itself, is all but dead and drained, the technology dies, with only its eggs, the Jain nodes, awaiting the next host to come along. But there is an accretion disc that sits outside the border of the Polity that is swarming with active Jain tech, with no civilization, no host to provide it with the – if you like – 'nutrients' it requires. Sure, it is producing Jain nodes as this tech does when it is in its spreading phase, but it is stubbornly not dropping into somnolence or death. The hypothesis is merely a description of what we have seen it do, but is not a theory covering everything it does. It is an oversimplification to equate it to some antipersonnel device like a land mine, yet the tech in the accretion disc is like a mine still exploding, as if its intended victim is still standing on it.

Anonymous

Cutter

'I'll be damned,' said Cutter, now inside Orlandine's ship and cooling down from the fight to capture the two second-children. He was reviewing the file she had sent him, learning the secret history of the King's Guard.

It happened towards the end of the war. The Spatterjay virus was a dangerous pandemic that could infect just about any life form, even those alien to the world it was found on. When it infected humans it made them unbelievably strong, rugged – as close to corporeally immortal as a human could get without body swapping into a Golem chassis. But it also had other effects. It could change them using genetic code it had stored from the fauna of that world. This usually happened when the host was injured. The virus turned active then, as it sought to preserve its host. Diet and drugs like Aldetox could suppress it, but still, badly injured hoopers often grew a leech tongue and sometimes underwent other changes before they were well again. Completely unsuppressed change in a human could lead to nightmarish creatures. One of these was the leader of the pirates who had gone to Spatterjay and run their coring and thralling trade. This was (Spatter) Jay Hoop. He had apparently turned into a monster on one of the world's islands, though Polity investigations had yet to confirm that.

All of this was well known, but it seemed few people had wondered what would happen to a prador infected by the Spatterjay virus. Somehow it had just never come up, as if there was an assumption that, being such monsters, there was nothing much worse they could turn into. This lack of interest was a bit of a discrepancy, and now looking at it from a new perspective, Cutter was starting to suspect AI interference. He was also annoyed not to have known this before. Sure, he'd known the king and the king's family were mutated, but from this virus? They were prador hoopers?

'The fuck,' he added, then turned to look at the form clad in white armour squatting beside the wall of Orlandine's expansive laboratory.

Orlik swivelled two armoured eye stalks to look at him, but kept the focus of his main and decidedly odd eyes on what was happening amidst Orlandine's machines. Orlandine herself was up, cupped in a hemisphere like a throne, totally linked in to her machinery and her ship, her sensory cowl open as she guided the vibrating shearfields steadily stripping away a captured second-child's armour.

'There is something wrong here,' said the prador fathercaptain.

'Oh yeah,' said Cutter, 'you shit me not.'

Orlik now turned slightly to gaze at Cutter with his main eyes. 'Yes, we have been mutated by the Spatterjay virus. I myself have a form that would give nightmares to my normal prador fellows.'

'But yet you allow people to see your eyes,' interjected Orlandine. Her voice issued from the com system. Her face was rigid with concentration and her mouth unmoving. Her eyes were metallic, with something akin to kaleidoscopic machine movement in them.

Orlik tipped his body in acknowledgement. 'Yes, I choose to let my eyes be seen. They are enough to unnerve other prador but not enough to arouse suspicions or provide data that can be acted upon.'

'An absolutely rational decision,' said Orlandine. 'I'm sure you have no particular urge to display your . . . *difference*.'

'This is beside the point,' said Orlik. Somewhat angrily, Cutter felt. 'We keep meticulous record of what the Spatterjay virus has done and is doing to our bodies, and that –' the prador stabbed a claw at the steadily revealed second-child – 'is what I meant when I said something is wrong here. This child did not look like that the last time he put on his armour.'

Cutter swivelled his attention back to the procedure. The second-child sat at the focus of numerous machines, clamped in active gimbals as those machines cut its armour. On the floor lay heaps of the breach foam that had immobilized it, now being scooped up by an infestation of beetlebots. Three-fingered grabs had finished peeling off its leg armour revealing not jointed prador legs, but squirming black, triangular-section tentacles. Now a shearfield had finished slicing away a section of armour above these on one side, peeled it back and discarded it. What this exposed inside, after a spill of glutinous liquid like whipped egg, looked more like the folded-up body of some embryonic insect. In fact, as Cutter watched, he saw one folded limb shift and quiver.

'It would have been nice if you had sent this data earlier,' said Orlandine.

Cutter only caught up with this as she sent him two files and he studied them. Here was the physiological data on the two second-children. Upon their last scan, they had still looked vaguely like prador, for they had the requisite number of legs and claws. Mostly. One of them had shrunk, however, its body extended, divided and ribbed so it looked like a trilobite. It had ensconced itself in a smaller mechanism inside its armour, for it had become too small to insert its limbs into the hollow legs and claws its original form had occupied.

Cutter glanced aside. That was the one Orlandine had yet to open up, which rested against one wall almost completely con-cealed in a mass of crash foam. The one here, meanwhile, had possessed limbs long enough to occupy its suit. In fact they had been too long, but thin enough to fold up inside the hollow leg and claw armour. The second-child's body had shrunk and extended, growing a tail. It had been slightly iridescent and Cutter recognized some resemblance to a Spatterjay glister – a lobster-like crustacean of that world. He now checked through memory for some kind of match with the other creature and surmised that the virus must have incorporated the genome of prador ship lice. Whatever. Orlik was right. The thing before him had changed drastically.

'This still does not give us answers to immediate questions,' said Cutter.

'And they would be . . . ?' Orlandine enquired smoothly.

'How did the worm fragment subvert them so easily? Why this second drastic change?'

'Quite,' she replied.

Trike

Trike watched his wife of many years studying him and could see the shock in her expression. This stilled the churning of his mind for a moment and he looked down at himself. He had always appeared stocky and had previously looked as if he was running to fat, but now he was tall and gaunt. He also knew, from an earlier glance in a mirror, that his cheeks had sunk, his lips were thinner, and his ears had now definitely developed points. While she stood before him he reached up and scrubbed a hand over his head, and wondered what strange quirk of biology had started hair growth up there now.

But she too had changed. She too looked thinner, grey streaks had appeared in her hair, and she had those black eyes he could hardly meet. He flicked his attention aside and pointed with one slightly shaking finger.

'You should eject that, first chance you get,' he said. 'Into the sun . . . to burn . . .'

He could feel his mouth twisting as he tried to suppress a crazy grin. Cog was securing Angel's remains to the hold floor with heavy straps. He had bagged them first in reinforced sacks, then inserted those in armoured crates. Trike concentrated on them hard, trying to ignore the shadowy shapes shifting at the edges of his vision, and the tittering in his mind.

'I will not be ejecting this,' said Cog. 'Why did you think I stopped Doshane destroying it? Even dead, it contains a wealth of data.'

Ruth glanced round. 'Don't be so sure he's dead,' she said, then returned her attention to Trike.

He began looking round the hold, still unable to meet her gaze. He felt guilty because she had seen him like this before. He had changed in this way when a giant leech took a chunk out of his torso in their first years together, though perhaps not so drastically. It had taken months for either of them to understand that what was happening to him was not quite usual for a hooper – that somehow his mind affected the transformation process, making it spin out of control.

'Trike,' she said. 'Trike, look at me.'

Finally he focused his eyes on her.

'Ruth,' he managed.

She stepped forwards and hugged him, and he wrapped his arms round her. She smelled different, kind of metallic, and felt delicate and breakable. She seemed shorter too, and it didn't feel like he was hugging the same woman. He abruptly turned his head away from her as his tongue shot from his mouth, the leech mouth clicking at its end. She quickly pulled away, ducking a little as she did so. She remembered this too.

'You have an up-to-date infirmary, Cog?' she asked.

The Old Captain moved up beside her. He had his pipe out and was stuffing it with tobacco from his pouch. He looked thoughtful and, Trike thought, just a little bit irritated. Trike stared at the man.

'A wealth of data,' he repeated tightly, the things he had learned about Cog coming clearer in his mind.

'Yes,' said Cog, 'a forensic AI should be able to obtain much. Now, the infirmary.' He gestured with his pipe stem to the door from the hold and led the way. Ruth glanced at Angel's remains and then followed him, towing Trike after her. They trudged up the stairs to the bridge then through a door halfway up. Inside was a cylindrical room packed with equipment and a surgical chair at its centre. It bore some resemblance to a standard infirmary, but also to a workshop-cum-laboratory.

'Sit here,' said Ruth, leading Trike over to the chair.

He followed meekly and sat, then commented, 'So you have access to a forensic AI? Not many people have that . . .'

Ruth walked over to a pedestal-mounted autodoc, then studied the series of extra attachments in a carousel around the column it was mounted upon.

'So you remember,' said Cog, his voice oddly calm. 'I wasn't sure.'

Trike remembered Lyra's death and his own indifference to it, then. 'Was Lyra one of you too?' he asked.

'Yes, she was.'

Trike turned to Ruth as she towed the autodoc over. 'He didn't want to rescue you while you were with Angel. You were too useful as a method of tracking him.' He felt a stirring of anger and things flickered and oozed just beyond his perception. Closing his eyes and taking a slow breath, he tried to gain calm, to let it go.

'Cog?' she asked, looking up.

Cog shrugged, drew on his pipe and puffed out a cloud of fragrant smoke, then said, 'I'm sorry, but I work for the Polity.

And sometimes I have to make hard choices or follow orders I find . . . uncomfortable.'

'A Polity agent?' asked Ruth.

'Yes,' said Cog.

'The AIs do like to recruit special talents,' she replied, non-committal as she returned her attention to the autodoc.

Trike focused on her as she selected an item from the carousel – a cylindrical object with a tight collection of tubes protruding from one end. She plugged it into the underside of the beetle-shaped chromed autodoc. It wiggled its long shiny legs as if this tickled, chain-glass scalpels, probes and micro-manipulators clicking and glinting. He now knew her intention, because again they had both been here before.

'A very old Old Captain is such,' said Trike, his mouth feeling dry, because he remembered Cog telling him that he and Jay Hoop were brothers.

Cog shot him a look. 'Yes, I work for Earth Central and when I told "my masters" what had happened with you they gave me a watching brief. I'll tell you all you want to know about that. But the other business concerning my antecedents is not for discussion.'

Trike swiped with his hand, sure something had flown close to his face. He then tilted his head to a movement on one blank wall – a leech-like writhing. When Ruth started securing him in the chair with heavily reinforced straps he felt grateful. Though, seeing them, he wondered if they had been for Cog himself, or if Cog had he been preparing for him.

Cog continued, addressing Ruth, 'Anyway, what are you going to do?' He gestured to the autodoc.

'This has happened before and we tried many things,' she explained. 'Memory editing to get rid of the hallucinations, neurochem rebalancing . . . but the mind of a hooper is a tough and stubborn thing. In the end only one thing worked.'

'And that is?'

'Patterned electrical discharges through the cortex,' she said. 'It hits his reset button . . .'

'ECT by any other name,' said Cog.

Trike felt that what Ruth was about to do was a lot more complicated, but in essence Cog was right. It was electro-convulsive therapy – frying some portions of his brain so it would settle back into a calmer cycle. At least, being a hooper, the damage would not be permanent.

'Yes,' Ruth said tightly, moving to the console and screen of the doc and inputting what she wanted it to do. The pedestal rolled closer to the chair and the doc hinged forwards on an arm to come down on Trike. He felt its legs fold in to clamp his head, the cool spray of analgesic, the tug of small incisions, and lasers crackling as they made micro-punctures in his skull. Next, from the attachment, it began to insert hair-thin wires to the correct places within his skull. After a moment, it ran its program.

Trike grunted and arched in the chair, but the straps held him down. His body turned rigid and his skull felt like it was about to explode. His right eye closed, the lid twitching, then as the power came off and he settled, the room seemed brighter – free of shadows.

'These antecedents . . .' said Ruth.

'I wish this kind of treatment had been available back then,' said Cog, eyeing Trike curiously.

'This treatment has been available since before the first diaspora,' Ruth commented.

'Okay.' Cog shrugged. 'I just didn't know what to do back then.'

'You've seen something like this before?'

'Yes, my brother was just as crazy.'

'Not uncommon amongst hoopers.'

'No, I guess not.'

Trike convulsed again, then again. Each time it felt like some-one had struck his skull with a hammer. Perhaps Ruth and Cog spoke further while this was happening, he did not know. Finally, the autodoc withdrew the wires and rose from his head, and the pedestal rolled back. Trike looked round at normality, feeling as if a portal into some other reality had been hammered shut.

'I've done what I can,' Ruth said. 'That should hold you for a while.'

'I'm sane?' he asked, able to give a tired smile without some-thing giggling in his skull.

She keyed the release and all the straps came off to slither into their slots.

She leaned closer to him, closing her hands on his cheeks, peering closely into his eyes. 'I wouldn't go so far—'

His tongue suddenly snapped closed on the skin just to one side of her mouth. She yelled, more angrily than in pain, and staggered back, a raw hole now present in her face that quickly filled with blood. As her fingers parted from his head it felt as if he had tossed the door keys into the lunatic asylum. But he kept his boot against the door.

'I'm sorry,' he said. 'I don't know why that happened.'

'Like I said,' she managed, her voice slightly slurred. 'I wouldn't go so far as to describe you as sane.'

Trike stared in horror at the wound on her face, then rose and stepped out of the chair. 'I'm sorry,' he repeated. He turned and left the medical area.

Orlandine

In time, Cutter grew bored with the procedures and wandered away. Orlik stayed, watching intently, studying those portions of the data Orlandine showed him with a patience uncharacteristic of the prador. The prador child she was concentrating on – the one that now looked like an insect embryo – had grown noticeably over the last few hours and was a lot more mobile. Orlandine tried to keep it still with the clamps as she scanned it, but it was time for a much closer look. Now it was time for vivisection . . .

Orlandine paused on that thought as if expecting some visceral reaction from the human part of her mind, but it wasn't there. She felt a little sympathy for the creature because perhaps some of its earlier personality remained, but this was all just too important for squeamishness. She directed a diamond tube packed with nanofibres inside the thing. Its major ganglion, which in normal prador was a ring-shaped organ, and in this creature had been little different in its earlier form, was in the process of breaking up and separating, as if to be distributed about its body. She injected the millions of nanofibres and directed them individually, making connections throughout the ganglion. A moment later she began switching off higher consciousness and pain reception, leaving only autonomous function. The creature remained alive, but no more conscious than a mollusc.

Further probes gave her information on physical structure that the scan could not pick up. She extrapolated from this, as well as the earlier scans. The child was turning into something lobster-like, which was not surprising, this being a Spatterjay viral transformation, but there was more. There were nascent structures in its carapace akin to modern Polity battle armour. She found the initial growth of superconductor threads too.

'We do not normally see that with the Spatterjay virus,' commented Orlik.

'No,' Orlandine agreed. 'Though it is something you might find in a Polity war drone.' She paused for a second, then allowed her curiosity to get the better of her. 'Incidentally, why do you keep a Polity assassin drone in your sanctum?'

'A trophy from the war,' said Orlik.

'And it is dead?'

'Yes.'

She was sure Orlik was lying, but the fate of that single drone was not her concern. She now focused on one of the nodular growths that had been puzzling her earlier and was unsurprised to find a lot of metal in there, and some highly dense ceramics. Again, extrapolating from this proto-growth gave her nothing organic to refer to in her extensive files on alien physiology. However, when she opened the search to other structures, the answer was immediate. The thing was growing a collection of fusion reactors throughout its body.

'Fuck,' said Orlik.

'Indeed.'

Orlandine now highlighted various items within the creature on the display the prador was viewing. Cold assessment. Mentality faced with a complex problem . . .

'This is the start of some kind of laminar super-capacitor, while this snail-like object seems already to be producing dense objects akin to railgun slugs.'

'A railgun?'

'Here, in the underside. While here in this claw is the start of something that looks like a multi-phasic particle beam and laser weapon.'

Orlik said nothing for a long moment, then repeated, 'Fuck.'

'I need to look closely at the virus,' Orlandine stated. 'Very closely.'

The threadlike Spatterjay virus was spread throughout the creature, so removing a sample was no problem. She enclosed it in a micro-bead and withdrew it through another diamond tube, then conveyed it via a series of pipes onto a deep study platen. She then split the bead and brought the head of her most powerful nano-scope down on it. Some careful manipulation with nano-scopic tools opened out one thread and she set the nano-scope scanning along it – meticulous and slow, not missing one detail. Within just a few seconds she saw the thing she had been searching for.

'Quantum processor crystal,' she said.

'Was it there before or is it new?' asked Orlik.

'It was there before – it's in the data your king sent me.'

'Oh, I see.'

Hours of study passed. Even Orlik finally lost patience and left, taking his shuttle back to his destroyer, but Orlandine remained utterly fascinated, as she put together the workings of the virus, and sank deeper into pure intellection. The virus functioned like many parasites that optimized the survivability of a host. However, it was also a collector of a host's genome, so much so, in fact, that almost the entire viral thread consisted of it. In there, Orlandine found the genomes of the sails – those batlike creatures that hoopers employed as living sails on their ships – as well as that of the Spatterjay leeches, glisters, prill, frog whelks and hammer whelks. This was all well known, for it was these that caused the transformation of further hosts. When a hooper was starving he grew a leech tongue, when his survival was threatened in other ways a mix of changes made him grow tall, thin and tough – a transformation that came from the sails. He would also turn blue, but this was just a colour imparted by the virus as it increased its own survival chances by multiplying inside him. The virus had not stopped its collection with just the fauna of Spatterjay, however.

Human DNA was evident very quickly. Orlandine thought it might be interesting to find out if its source was just one particular human. Maybe Jay Hoop himself? But no, more likely it was an amalgam of hosts created by viral exchange – all the alleles ready to be expressed when necessary. This was confirmed when she found the DNA of a dog and ran a program to extrapolate from it. The DNA was in a reset state and could be just about any dog. Next she found the prador genome, and that of some of the creatures from their home world: the ship louse and a fish like a giant mudskipper that was one of their food sources. And then she began to find things she did not recognize at all.

Spatterjay was an old world and, she surmised, was likely to have been visited by more than one alien race. And now this proved to be true. She found a sample of the much modified genome of a creature called a gabbleduck from the planet Masada. Since gabbleducks were the descendants of the Atheter – a race that committed a strange form of race suicide millions of years ago – it seemed that they had visited Spatterjay and perhaps been bitten by a leech. There were other things in there she did not recognize. Perhaps the genomes of Csorians or even the Jain? She did not know. Quite possibly she was seeing stuff from the food animals of the Atheter, or from species that had died out on Spatterjay. There was, in the end, so much here to fascinate her, but she had to keep her eye on the ball. Was the virus connected to how the worm fragment had subverted these two mutated prador?

Orlandine now concentrated on the large and complex genome that was distributed with quantum processors. From this she extrapolated legs, claws, carapace, but there was always more: complexity within complexity. She found the structures for growing items that were supposedly inorganic – the power supplies, the weapons, the superconductor – but even in them there were deeper levels of complexity. She just focused on an eye and chased it down through layer upon layer. It was like looking at the images of Mandelbrot sets and it seemed endless. It escaped beyond the reach of the nano-scope down into the level of the quanta and she had to use heavy extrapolation and other processes to try and understand what was happening. She found entanglement and at last began to understand. Those quantum crystals were not just for data storage but were processors too – they actually connected to and caused changes in the surrounding genome.

Sixteen hours later Orlandine began working her way up from the bottom, understanding more clearly what she was seeing now she had some idea of its foundations. She found the connections she had missed, the entanglement she had missed, throughout the entire virus. And now she knew.

At some time in the far distant past, the Spatterjay virus had been quite a normal parasitic organism. It had not collected the genomes of other creatures. Most likely it had infested the bodies of its hosts to their detriment – perhaps imparting greater ruggedness on the one hand, but taking away the ability to breed, as was often the way with such organisms. Then, millions of years ago, the genome of some kind of soldier had either found its way into the virus, or had been inserted. The virus had become a collector of other genetic material after that, as it tried to express the phenotype of that soldier. The malfunctioning entanglement of those quantum processors with the surrounding genetic material was what drove the drastic transformation of viral hosts. It was trying to turn them into soldiers, and failing. However, this time, with these prador children, it was succeeding, so another element had been introduced.

Understanding all of this had taken Orlandine's resources to their limit. For something to set this process working correctly it would have taken similar resources, and a conscious, powerful mind. It was not that of the legate which had been aboard the wormship. It had to be an entity that understood the processes on a deep level, and no legate had been that bright, or rather, had that kind of mind.

Orlandine knew, with absolute gut-wrenching certainty, that

the mind involved had not been around for a while, and was one the universe had not seen in over five million years.

'That piece of worm is on the move,' interjected Cutter.

'Of course it is,' Orlandine replied, making a link directly to Orlik's sanctum, where he had now reconnected his interface to his ship. 'Orlik, eject that fucker from your hold, right now!'

'As the humans would say,' Orlik replied, 'that is music to my ears.'

The Client

The platform's U-space drive was ready now and it was time to go. The Client reached out in concert, firing up the fusion drives of all the attack pods, keeping them in the same funnel formation. A second robot platform acted as a grid in the giant thermionic valve she had created, moving with them. And then she fired up the drive of the platform to follow them out. She could extend this for perhaps a few thousand miles before the effect would be likely to fail. And it wasn't far enough from the sun for a U-jump.

The prador ships were spreading out further and a brief assessment gave her their likely tactics: railgun firings from many different locations that would lead to the break-up of the funnel she had created, followed by another conventional attack. No sooner had she surmised this than the prador ships had begun firing, but the swarm of railgun slugs would not reach her in time. She broke the funnel, the attack pods falling into a different formation, and programmed into one of them a deliberate fault that left its U-jump unshielded. This one she sent to a different destination to the others – a far location – when at last, flickering and receding, they all slid into U-space. It would act as a decoy. Some minutes later, as particle beams groped out and the railgun slugs bore down, she jumped the platform too.

The jump lasted an hour ship-time, until the platform finally materialized in interstellar space, far from any system. The Client began at once to make repairs and carry out the alterations she had considered earlier. This took her full concentration for some hours, but after a certain point she consigned the bulk of it to automatics and maintenance systems. Now, with a breathing space, she finally turned her attention to the data she had taken from the library.

First, she began looking at the weapons data, because it was her greatest need. She specifically hunted down the stats and schematics on the beam the library had fired at her – the thing that had looked like a glass rod and had turned one of her attack pods frangible, and shattered it. It was not something the Species had used in the war against the prador and she soon found that it was not available in the weapons data she had uploaded. But there was a route to it – in the forbidden data. For reasons she could not quite analyse, she left that for the moment and concentrated on the weapons data that was available. Here she found the full-spectrum white laser Dragon had used on her, bespoke particulates for particle beams that varied in their destructive potential, super-dense railgun slugs, a cornucopia of viruses and worms, combined laser and informational warfare beams, and other things besides. Even as she discovered information on them, she routed alterations to the weapons in the attack pods, and set factories in the platform to making new ones. But now her thought strayed to the forbidden data. That lethal beam was in there, so what other weapons might be too?

With huge reluctance she began looking into that data. She knew this hesitancy was a hangover from her previous state – that venturing into this was something the Species had been given an aversion to almost at an instinctive level. This aversion limited her searches to anything weapons related. She found the glassy beam and the weapon that fired it, but blocked the context of it. It was, she learned, a kind of particle weapon that messed with molecular forces, causing the frangibility she saw. Simple tensions within the normal matter caused it to break apart.

But the technology of this opened up a whole spectrum of science concerning U-space and what might be possible. She widened her searches and began to see further possibilities and developments. She found that hardfields could be curved and even shaped into enclosing bubbles. From this she made a connection with data that had been in the mind of Pragus. It seemed highly likely that a rogue AI called Penny Royal had deployed such fields, but the data had been heavily redacted and this was a technology the AIs had not allowed to be implemented. Why? Perhaps to keep one trick in the box should the Polity encounter a dangerous and more advanced civilization? Perhaps to keep it out of the claws of the prador? Though less advanced than the Polity, those hostile crustaceans always, eventually, stole anything the Polity developed and widely used.

She saw that hardfields were actually one facet of U-space tech and, fully integrating what had previously been seen as separate technologies, led to a whole host of further possibilities. The feedback energy created from such fields being struck could be routed back into the underlying continuum and stored there. That energy could then be utilized to power the hardfields and weapons. Other weapons possibilities arose concerning U-space twists, gravity waves, inversions . . . it would, in the end, be like stepping up from bows and arrows to machineguns. She could see how total war with such weapons would lead to the kind of annihilation that had not even been seen during the prador/human war. Perhaps the AIs were right to sit on this. She intended to use it, however, and began making further changes to the platform.

Now, with all this data available to her and being applied, she found herself straying into its context – she began to examine the forbidden past. She saw ten massive war-damaged alien ships arriving in the system of the Species, which was then unoccupied. The early ancestors of the Species were using the technology integral to their bodies to link up in small groups, communities, hives. They were also beginning to connect physically, to meld, to become one . . .

The warning alarm snapped her out of this and focused all her attention outwards. A familiar, large U-signature had generated nearby and an equally familiar object rolled out of U-space into the real. She gazed at the roving moon in angry frustration. How had the Librarian followed her here?

'You have accessed the forbidden knowledge,' it sent.

Instead of replying, the Client turned her attention to the data again and set into motion a refined search about the library itself. Yes, ten war-damaged ships had come to the system of the Species, but there had been one other ship, small and strange, like a shard of black crystal enwrapped by metallic snakes. The entity inside had led them all here, but the data beyond that was unclear. It seemed to be directing them to the nearby world, while it was taking a course to the moon—

Again the Librarian shrieked its challenge. Deliberate distraction or something else?

Other U-signatures began to generate and the long teardrops of prador King's Guard ships began to slide into the real. The Client counted them as, one after another, a total of fifty guard ships and ten old-style prador dreadnoughts appeared. Almost to the second they arrived, another U-signature generated, a hundred miles from the platform and right in the centre of where her attack pods were spread. A gigaton CTD exploded, frying two pods and scattering the rest. Hardfields up, the weapons platform tilted in a wall of fire, spewing burned-out field generators. The moon, meanwhile, dropped out of the real again.

The Client struggled to initiate her own U-jump, even as further U-signatures generated in her scattered formation. She fled on further waves of fire, losing yet another pod in the process. As she slid into U-space she realized that this would continue. The library had some way of tracking her and would keep leading the prador to her. And there seemed only one way it could be tracking – there was something in that data.

Earth Central

Earth Central did not like the situation at all. First had come a telemetry and ship-sensor data package from Captain Cogulus. Some kind of Jain soldier had been resurrected on the Cyberat world. The wormship had then shown intelligence such vessels were not supposed to possess and, abandoning its legate, had seized the soldier and departed. On top of that had come an update from Orlandine. This detailed her study of the changes two second-children had undergone, along with her conclusions and suspicions as to why. EC completely agreed with her: there was a mind in that wormship fragment. Extrapolating from that and Cog's package, it seemed likely the mind in the fragment was a submind shed by a larger mind in the wormship.

A Jain AI . . .

These were all pieces of a puzzle that had yet to come together. At the centre of the accretion disc, in fact within the dead star there, lay a weakness in the space-time continuum. This gave access to Jain AIs in U-space. Had one of them somehow come out through that weakness to start causing problems? EC thought not. Sometime, well over five million years ago, a mass of Jain AIs had dropped themselves in U-space and only remained connected to the real by the energy feeds that powered their thinking. Over millions of years those feeds had slowly decayed to dust or been destroyed. The AIs had gradually wound down, their thinking utterly inward looking, and had sunk into a somnolence that was close to death. Yes, the occasional injection of energy briefly revitalized them and data could be obtained from them in this state, but one becoming fully active? No. This would not happen, because the data showed EC clearly that they had made a choice. They knew their energy feeds would decay. They had chosen to give up on the universe, to decline and eventually fade from existence. So where was this new AI from?

Position was not a factor. That it was possible to contact the Jain AIs through the weakness in the accretion disc did not mean that they were just underneath it in U-space. That kind of perception was an artefact of human linear thinking, because U-space did not possess dimensionality. It was therefore the nature of the weakness that made the AIs easier to contact. Dismiss the Jain AIs and just run with the rest. The Jain had caused the weakness *and* the active tech floating around in the disc. A Jain mind had appeared, from somewhere, and this was what Dragon had been looking for. Time to open a long-closed com channel . . .

The virtuality opened to reflect reality. Dragon hung poised out from the accretion disc in the position of Weapons Platform Mu. Spare attack pods had been drafted in to cover a volume of space millions of miles across. In reality Dragon's presence was not required, since for ages a much smaller and more dispersed defence sphere had been perfectly adequate. Dragon was at rest, EC suspected, waiting.

'And at last you have questions,' said Dragon.

EC, hanging in vacuum in the form of a chromed human head a hundred miles across, blinked crystal eyes and replied, 'You were searching for a mind.'

'And it has been found,' Dragon replied.

'I would guess,' said EC, 'that something sought out an anchor in the real and found it in the hole Erebus left in the control system of a wormship, as well as the mind of a legate.'

'You do not guess,' Dragon stated.

'I cogitate and extrapolate.'

'As do I.'

'What is the source of this mind?'

'That is the critical question –' Dragon paused and then, unusually, elucidated – 'and one for which I have, as yet, no answer.'

'Perhaps we should pool our data?'

'Yes, perhaps. I would be interested to know what Orlandine has found, just as I would be interested to know exactly what happened on the world of the Cyberat.'

EC sent Orlandine's data package. After it had studied this for a few microseconds Dragon said, 'She will ask questions. One must wonder at the veracity of the answers she will receive. Hasty actions are contra-indicated.'

'Give me something,' said EC.

Dragon sent data that keyed into the virtuality and Earth Central found itself hurtling, along with the entity, into clouds of gas, debris and floating organic structures like epiphytes. Writhing and fluttering forms fell on Dragon and it shrugged off the attacking Jain tech, burning out intrusions which stabbed between its scales. It finally entered the cloud around the dead star of the accretion disc. Here it mapped space-time and located drifting coordinates in the star. Dragon emitted steady gravity pulses, focused in a way that Polity technology had yet to attain, then heaved and spat out a concentrated induction warfare beam. This turned dust incandescent in a line down to the star, punched into the crust, which erupted with traceries of fusion fire, and down to the co-ordinates. There it bled away, and there it made contact.

The Jain AIs stirred in a looped tunnel of non-matter, datavores in amongst them probing, asking questions, looking for answers. The AIs responded with irritation – heavy sleepers resenting this intrusion, a wave of that resentment eliciting a response all around Dragon as of vaporous muscles tensing, more organic forms speeding in. Then something else intruded and cut down like a knife, severing the connection. Only as Dragon fled, assaulted on all sides by Jain tech, did EC understand what information it had sought. Dragon had wanted the Jain history of the accretion disc. And something had not wanted it to know.

'Interesting,' said Earth Central. 'Some other agency.'

They were now back in the original virtuality – two virtual behemoths facing off.

'Quite,' said Dragon. 'Give me the Cyberat data.'

EC now relayed the package Captain Cog had sent. Additional news about the situation on the world of the Cyberat was also becoming available from EC's spies there. This concerned the political situation and Doshane's expulsion of Cog and his crew. EC sent that too, in case it might have relevance.

'They have the legate,' said Dragon, and began to move in the virtuality as if it was moving in vacuum by the accretion disc.

'Why is this important?' asked EC.

'Because some traps must be sprung if one is to find the trapper,' Dragon replied. The comlink broke as Dragon fell into U-space.

Earth Central seethed. It seemed the legate had been left in the Cyberat system to lure Dragon there, yet Dragon knew this. Obviously it was playing a deep game EC had yet to plumb. But one thing was certain: though EC was confident that the weapons platform AIs at the accretion disc were very capable, there was no one in charge there now. Meanwhile a Jain AI was out there with some kind of Jain soldier . . .

'Get ready,' said Earth Central.

A naked and athletic blonde-haired woman looked round from the massage bench she was lying on. Her masseur, a Golem android who it seemed had a penchant for data storage and processing tattoos, paused in his endeavours.

'Problem?' asked Captain Diana Windermere of the giant dreadnought the *Cable Hogue*. The woman had passed her ennui barrier some centuries ago and was older than the present iteration of Earth Central itself. She was also, counting her interface with her ship's AI, exceedingly smart, wily and battle-hardened.

'Possibly,' was all EC would concede.

Diana nodded and put her head back down, already sending her instructions to the *Hogue* AI and the other ships via implants in her skull. In the asteroid field around the neutron star and red dwarf, Polity warships, whose sum destructive power would appal older deities, began to lock and load.

15

King's Guard: *The new king of the prador, now firmly established in his rule, has given himself the name, for us to use, of Oberon. The irony of that should not escape even those without knowledge of Renaissance and Medieval literature or Shakespeare. The king of a race of savagely hostile aliens is 'the king of the fairies'. But it took many years before he could allow himself such frivolities. The king was first a father-captain, probably of a dreadnought, who, realizing that the prador faced being smashed back into their version of the Stone Age if the war against the Polity continued, returned to his home world to usurp the old king. Details are not clear about how this was done, but Oberon had to be very smart and crafty to achieve what many other prador had tried before him. Only one detail is clear, since a recording of it swiftly made its way into the Polity, and that was the old king's demise: pumped full of diatomic acid, he was floated out on his grav over the seas of his world. Thereafter Oberon put all the crew of his ship – his family and now all first-children – in positions of high office. His dukes, if you like. He then instituted a massive breeding program to extend his family. He also started a building program across the Kingdom that incorporated Polity technology. Two results of this are the titanic and legendary King's Ship and the numerous lethal reavers. These last are crewed exclusively by his children: the King's Guard.*

From 'Quince Guide' compiled by humans

Blade

Blade slid into the real in full stealth mode and immediately began scanning. This then was the system of the Cyberat. Wreckage was strewn across vacuum about the Cyberat world but it did not take the attack ship AI long to locate Captain Cogulus's old ship. Its first instinct was to contact the man, but it clamped down on that and instead, still running on stealth, drew closer and looked for other sources of information. It wanted to alert no one of its presence until it had fully assessed the situation.

The remains of a prador destroyer confirmed the tale Cog had earlier sent as an information package – albeit one lacking detail. Blade made a short U-jump to bring itself close to the wreckage. The ship was gutted and had been peeled open – hardly looking like a vessel at all, just a metallic skin with tangled debris on one side. Probing it, Blade sought computer access and signs of life. Of the former there was none, but of the latter there was one. Moving closer still, Blade inspected the debris and there, trapped in the tangle, was a single armoured prador. Blade put an induction warfare beam on its suit and began to seek a com linkage, finally making a connection. The prador shifted, plucking with one claw at a twisted stanchion pinning it against hull metal. Its eye stalks swivelled as it tried to see who wanted to talk to it.

'What's your name?' Blade asked, in the prador language.

'My name is Gurun,' the prador replied in standard Anglic.

Its immediate use of Anglic indicated that this prador was very smart, and subterfuge would not work here. Blade meanwhile increased its scanning of the surrounding wreckage. It saw a water-scorpion format robot, and the remains of a complex computer system. Materials scans revealed contemporary advanced metals. This ship had not been a ship of renegades, that was certain.

'King's Guard?' Blade enquired.

'I have a self-destruct in my suit,' Gurun replied.

'Why do you feel the urge to inform me of this?'

'Just to hamstring any inclination you might have for interrogation.'

'Really?' said Blade. 'Or was it to assure yourself that you won't be giving away any secrets about the body form you possess inside that suit?'

After a long silence, Gurun replied, 'I don't know what you mean.'

'Let me assure you,' said Blade, 'that I already know you are a King's Guard and that you are highly mutated. If you are trying to hide that information you're centuries too late. Anyway, if I wanted any kind of evidence of that there are plenty of your kin floating around here.'

'Who are you?' asked Gurun.

'I am the Polity black-ops stealth attack ship *Obsidian Blade.*'

'Fuck,' said Gurun.

'Don't be alarmed. I only want detail on events here. You will not be giving away any secrets. And you will not be supplying information I could not obtain from the Cyberat anyway.'

'There are no secrets here,' said Gurun, 'beyond the one you apparently know.'

'Then let's talk and, when we are done, I'll cut you free.'

'Oh good – then I can be free to move around while I die out here.'

'You will also be assisting your king. The danger represented by that wormship is one both the Kingdom and the Polity face. All I need is data.'

Again, there was a long pause, then Gurun said, 'Okay, what do you want to know?'

'Tell me what happened here,' said Blade, 'right from the start.'

Gurun told his story. On the face of it the prador arrived to trade with the Cyberat for information and technology, with an aim to start some kind of embassy here. However, it seemed highly likely that beyond that they were after the Jain technology that Zackander had possessed. Part of the initial deal they'd struck with Zackander had been to act as defenders when called upon. Then the wormship had arrived . . .

As Gurun told his story Blade also began decoding communications that were reaching it from the world of the Cyberat. These filled in further detail: Zackander was dead after having resurrected a Jain soldier, the wormship had taken this soldier away, Angel's remains were aboard Cog's ship . . .

'That's enough,' Blade finally told Gurun.

The attack ship AI was up to date and there seemed little point in learning more. It studied the stanchion trapping the prador, then fired a laser. The beam struck where the stanchion was trapped against the hull, hot metal splashing away and a cloud of vapour spreading. Once it had cut through, the prador heaved up, pushing the stanchion away and moving out into the clear.

'You will have no further information from me, attack ship,' said Gurun.

He reached under his suit with one claw and triggered something. The suit bucked and hot white light glared from the seams and joints. It then went limp and floated away from the wreckage trailing black vapour.

'Stupid,' said Blade, but then wondered if that was true. Instant annihilation was preferable to trying to breathe vacuum.

Trike

As he sat in his chair, staring at the screen set to mirror before him, Trike tried to remember when he stopped sleeping. Many

Old Captains didn't sleep, apparently, so he hadn't thought it unusual he no longer needed to. But perhaps this too had been a sign of the fucked-up wiring inside his head? He had no idea.

He poked out his tongue and it opened like a four-petal flower, mottled brown, pink and white inside, with a constant sharp bony movement at its core. The moment he did this he remembered what Ruth tasted like – kind of flowery herself but with an underlying hint of . . . of something alien, but maybe that last was just his mind playing tricks again. He flinched, scared of himself. The tongue snapped shut. He tried to open it again but it seemed he couldn't find the muscles or the nerves that did that.

'So I am just a little bit more sane now,' he said, just to try speaking the words.

He felt the madness locked inside – contained, yes – but it was like it was pushing against walls in his mind and somehow projecting itself in a different form. He felt low and unhappy, whereas before the giggling madness had had its elements of crazy joy. Now glancing around his cabin, he noted the lack of even a hint of hallucination. He concentrated on the bed he had never slept in, trying to materialize a leech there, and felt a surge of panic as something shifted inside his skull.

No.

Just at that moment there came a sharp rap against the false-wood door. It opened and Cog stepped through, his shoulders brushing against either jamb.

'Ruth?' Trike asked, standing up, surprising himself because the question did not arise from his stock of safe phrases, but from real concern.

'She's okay,' said Cog. 'Bit of tissue repair and no one will know that you tried to eat her face.'

Trike winced and braced himself as Cog stepped forwards. He

remembered the warning. But Cog paused for a second then sat himself on the bed, the frame bending under his weight. He took out his pipe, toyed with it for a moment, then began stoking it with tobacco from his pouch.

'We're in orbit now and I've yet to set coordinates,' he said. 'Earth Central wants Angel's remains, but I feel I owe it to you and Ruth to take you where you want to go first.'

Trike stepped back to his chair and sat down astride it. 'Have you asked Ruth?'

Cog shrugged as he slipped his tobacco pouch back into the top pocket of his canvas shirt, took out his laser lighter and with a crack ignited the tobacco in his pipe.

'I need to speak to her,' said Trike.

'Yes, you certainly need to do that.'

Trike grimaced and gazed at the Old Captain as Cog sucked on his pipe and shot smoke from his nostrils. 'But I want to know more. I want to know what Angel was doing, and where that wormship went with that . . . thing. I need answers.'

Cog nodded. 'That's better.'

After a long quiet pause while the cabin filled with tobacco smoke, Trike finally asked, 'Were you Hoop's actual brother?'

'Cogulus Hoop,' Cog replied.

'What happened?'

Cog smiled, and then leaned back against the wall.

'The survey ship I was aboard had an early U-space engine, but positioning wasn't accurate – quite often it entailed a lengthy realspace journey after each jump, sometimes taking years. I was one of a crew of five. It was my turn to come out of hibernation to check on things when we arrived in the new system.'

Trike leaned forwards, fascinated.

Cog continued, 'I went back into hibernation because it was going to take two more years to bring our vessel into orbit around an interesting world that definitely showed signs of life. We duly did, and ran the orbital survey, recording everything.'

So how old was Cog? Trike wondered.

'What was the world?' he asked, already sure he knew.

Cog smiled a little tiredly and continued, 'Three of us went in a landing craft down to the surface to take a closer look.' He shrugged. 'Dangerous world Spatterjay, as you are aware. Only I came back. The second time, after a year of searching from orbit for the missing two, and gathering further data, I went down with the remaining two of my crew. Because the jungles were so dangerous we opted for a sea landing. Yes, we had detected some big stuff in the sea but it seemed rare in the area we chose. Big mistake.'

'Rarity of life on Spatterjay usually means something big is in the area eating the other life forms,' Trike interjected.

'Quite,' said Cog. 'We landed a little way out from some islands, then brought our landing craft into an atoll and moored it against that. With the craft secured we went onto the atoll to collect samples. It attacked almost immediately.'

'What?'

'Whelkus titanicus.'

The creature was a blend of a whelk and an octopus and when out of the ocean usually bigger than the average landing craft. It was woody and dense with the Spatterjay virus and almost impossible to kill.

'Not usually in shallow water.'

'No, not usually. We were just lucky I guess.' His pipe glowed hot as he sucked on it, the heat reflected in his eyes. He continued, 'I didn't know then why I survived. I didn't know what the leech bite I'd got on my first trip had done to me. I was badly injured but I managed to get away from the thing and climb up the atoll. It followed me, of course, and when I reached the top

I thought I was done for. I was up there looking down at the fucker and waiting to die, when claws closed on my shoulders and hauled me into the sky.'

'A sail,' Trike guessed.

Cog nodded. 'They didn't have human language back then, in fact I was the first of our kind any of them had seen. It flew me to another atoll and dumped me on a flat rock at the peak, and landed beside me. It sniffed me and burbled something – their own language that they don't use so much now. I think it was trying to make up its mind whether or not to eat me. It started prodding me, then pulled off my pack and tore it open. There was survey stuff inside and some other instruments. It was very curious about them, even managed to turn on a portable bio-scanner.'

'They're pretty smart,' said Trike.

'I'm not sure what it then decided. It burbled something more then grabbed me again. I was in pain and when I saw it was flying back to the first atoll, I thought it was just going to give me back to the whelk. It didn't, though – it flew to the landing craft and dumped me on top of it. I managed to get inside and launch, putting the jet of a steering rocket in the whelk's face . . . doubt I hurt it very much.'

'So, Jay Hoop and his pirates were not the first humans on Spatterjay?'

'No, when I got back to Earth things had changed. The Quiet War was nearing its end and the AIs were taking over, but things were still chaotic. I wasn't sure I wanted to stick around. I met Jay then . . . talked to him through a mesh because he was in prison. I told him about Spatterjay and where it was. Biggest mistake of my life.'

What was the estimated death toll? The story of how Jay Hoop and his pirates got to the world, and what they did there, wasn't completely clear. Some said they mutinied aboard a colony ship, others said they were on a prison transport. Whether they arrived during the prador/human war or before it was also debated. But certainly, they started selling cored humans to the prador and the prador supplied them with captives. By the time their operation was shut down, over ten million people had gone through that process.

'But you met him again, after that,' said Trike.

At that moment, there came a knock on the door. Trike cringed inwardly, but stood anyway. Cog shoved a finger into his pipe to put it out and dropped it into his top pocket. 'Just a few more preparations to make before we leave.' He stood. 'The story of that meeting will have to wait for another time.'

Trike followed him towards the door. Cog nodded to Ruth and winked at her as he passed, then moved off.

'We have a lot to talk about,' Trike said as she stepped inside and closed the door behind her.

'That can wait,' she replied, putting her hand on his chest. 'Do you know, you are already shorter, and your ears are less pointy?'

'It's perhaps a better look,' he replied.

'Put your tongue out,' she instructed.

He poked it out, then after a moment reached up and touched it. It had closed completely, though he could still feel hard bits inside it.

'So much of it is in the mind, it seems,' he said.

'Shut up and kiss me,' she replied.

Orlandine

The worm fragment was moving, writhing in the clamps that secured it. Orlandine watched through the single cam she had put online, separating out the image of the thing from the tsunami of other visual data it was directing at the cam from thousands of laser pores all over its body. The fragment was acting as best it could in the circumstances, trying to seize control of the systems around it. How the mind within it had managed to understand it had been discovered she did not know.

Yet.

Orlandine ordered her interface sphere to close up and retract. The top hemisphere closed down, enfolding her completely and the sphere withdrew from the study area into the wall, then dropped into the position it usually occupied in her ship. Next, upon another instruction, all but one of the physical connections around the sphere detached. The remaining pipe began filling a tank inside the sphere with a specific list of materials, suspended in atomic form, in a special semi-liquid gel. Meanwhile two of the connections to the interface plugs down her sides detached and folded back, quickly replaced by tubular nutrient feeds. As soon as these connected, they began pumping in the gel-liquid from the tank. This routed through her body to nourish the packed Jain technology inside her, which, under her firm control, began to grow.

'Do you wish it destroyed?' Orlik asked.

'No,' she replied, 'I wish it clear of your ship so I can study it properly.'

'You're going all uber-human on us, aren't you?' Cutter interjected.

'Yes, I am. There is a mind inside that thing and I want to know what it knows.'

'Best keep your weapons ready, Orlik,' said Cutter.

Orlandine felt a distant stab of annoyance, but it was difficult to trace and took her whole microseconds to locate it in the remains of her organic human brain. Irrelevant. Her human self was such a small part of her now and would shortly be overwhelmed, almost invisible.

'Bludgeon,' she sent. 'I want you to keep watch. Ship's weapons systems are now under your control. You will know when to destroy the fragment.'

'And when to destroy you,' Cutter added.

'That is unlikely to be necessary,' Orlandine replied.

'Uh huh,' Cutter responded simply.

Meanwhile, Bludgeon connected to her ship's weapons. 'Ooh shiny,' said the drone.

As the nutrient pipe disconnected, Orlandine's interface sphere dropped down through her ship to engage with something else. Now semi-organic plugs mated with sockets that had originally taken Polity tech. The Jain tech inside her reached optimum energy and her skin split on either side from armpit to thigh, and Jain tendrils squirmed out. These slid into channels through the usual connections to her body and mated with the incursions from the surrounding mass. And now human time seemed a distant dream.

Doors opened in the side of her ship and then she, her sphere, and the whole mass surrounding it fell out into vacuum. Orlandine's sphere now sat like a small egg enfolded on the underside of a huge Jain-tech mechanism. This ribbed object resembled a giant woodlouse. Numerous tentacles of varying thicknesses speared out all around her, while over the thing's back the segments divided to open on the glare of an ion drive.

Meanwhile the hold doors of Orlik's ship were opening, and on a moveable section of the floor, still clamped, the worm fragment began sliding towards them. As soon as the fragment reached the lip of the door this movement halted. The clamps then rose on diagonally divided columns, lifting the thing, until explosions simultaneously split the columns and blew the worm fragment towards the doors. As it hurtled out into vacuum it writhed and shed the clamps, and engaged the drive that had originally brought it to the ship. It tried to propel itself back. Orlik fired up his main fusion drive to pull away from the thing and, for a moment, the distance between them remained the same. But then the fragment began to close the gap.

The thing then emitted a high-intensity pulse of EMR that even disrupted information in the Jain tech around Orlandine. Orlik's main drive went down. The fragment had used what was perhaps a weapon of last resort – a flash like an informational warfare beam. This ability explained how it had learned of its own discovery – it had been holding something in reserve.

'It's seizing control of his ship again,' Bludgeon told her.

Her system informed her she had been targeted by Orlik's ship. Three particle beams stabbed from her ship to the destroyer and struck railguns, even as they swivelled towards her. Ensuing railgun strikes, using projectiles fashioned from exotic matter, punched into the destroyer's hull, then high-intensity lasers probed through the holes to hit critical system junctures. Explosions lit the prador destroyer from inside.

'Orlik will be very unhappy,' Cutter noted.

'Casualities?' Orlandine enquired matter-of-factly.

'Avoided,' Bludgeon told her.

The fragment could no longer use the ship as a weapon against her, but it was still trying to retreat into it. Orlandine fully engaged with the mechanism around her. She felt her humanity recede even further as her consciousness expanded into something utterly alien. She saw the ion drive would not be enough and immediately acted. She protruded two nacelles the shape of cored olives from her new carapace. They glared with fusion flame and she shot forwards, tentacles groping. Even as the fragment approached the hold doors back into the prador ship, she slammed down on it like a hunting nautilus, snatching it away.

The worm fragment fought. It squirmed in her grip, ramped

up the output of its laser pores to cutting strength, emitted informational warfare from inside, as well as opened its segments and extruded cutting heads, iron-burners and tentacles of its own. Orlandine swapped out damaged tentacles as she penetrated it, burned out thousands of laser pores with narrow stabs of particle beams, then opened herself to the informational warfare, encompassed it and followed it back. Soon she was finding the thing's weapons and killing them, while pursuing choate energy patterns and data through its complex and densely packed technology. It still fought back, but it was weaker than she expected, and in very little time she had its connected elements cornered. They had nowhere left to run.

'What are you?' she asked in a language no human or prador mouth could speak.

The thing tried to deny her, but the question went to its core as she decoded its being. It could no more refuse to answer than a calculator would refuse to give the result of a mathematical equation. She now saw a wheel spinning in darkness – the manifestation of an alien mind. It wasn't quite right, she knew, and looked more deeply at the reply. The wheel blurred into two, one of which stripped itself of information, processing, its very essence. It folded in on itself and fell away. So, she was seeing a stripped-down copy of an original mind. She understood that whatever had been in the wormship had made a submind to occupy this fragment.

She pushed deeper inside now to ask harder questions. She had guessed this thing was some kind of Jain AI and its structure bore that out. Knowing it was a submind of one that occupied the wormship was useful data, but not really what she wanted.

The thing resisted as she sought out its purpose. It gave her answers but ones that were open to wide interpretation. She kept cutting to the root, however. It had been broken off the wormship to attack Orlik's vessel, not in any hope of destroying it, but to keep him occupied until the main wormship could do that. Captured inside the prador ship, it had done just what Jain tech did: it subverted and it attempted to destroy. Given the opportunity of access to prador children, it began working on their minds, but then it found something else inside them. It found the virus, and in the genetic structure of that it found the squad.

Orlandine paused over this latest information. It wasn't clear whether the soldiers of the squad were actually Jain or some kind of biomech. It was clear that they could resurrect from their own genome. However, in becoming part of the Spatterjay virus this genome had become disrupted, hence the resurrection failures. The fragment corrected the disruption, and those prador children were turning into soldiers. All this confirmed what she herself had found out. But there were other connections in the mind she was taking apart and she traced them.

Soldiers . . .

There was a special kind of soldier. In its adolescent stages, it was similar to the ones recorded in the virus, but capable of doing and being a lot more. Such a soldier grew U-space nodes throughout its body that connected it to a backup in that continuum – a vast store of data it could use to transform itself. It could also divert the energy of attacks on itself to U-space, and then feed on that energy. How this was done stretched even Orlandine's understanding of U-space and hardfield technology. Simply put, here was a soldier that grew stronger the harder something tried to kill it. Here was a Jain super-soldier.

And one of these had been on the Cyberat world.

'What do you want it for?' Again, the question was in a language over five million years old. Again, the submind's inability to circumvent it.

The image became clear, even as the submind started to destroy itself – corrupting its own data, shorting power supplies, turning its remaining weapons on the last enclaves of its own consciousness. Orlandine saw the accretion disc slowly turning in space. The centre flashed intensely bright as the sun ignited. A shockwave hurtled out, irradiating proto-planets and superheating gas and debris but, still, the disc flew apart in cosmic slow motion, spreading a vast amount of the Jain technology existing there. She saw billions of Jain nodes falling through space. Yes, they would take centuries to reach the Polity and the Kingdom and surely many would be destroyed before that happened. But Pandora's Box would have been opened and, unless both the Polity and the Kingdom advanced to some vastly superior technological state before then, they would face destruction.

'You cannot stop the soldier,' the fading submind told her.

'What weapons can stop it?' she asked.

'You do not have them. It will destroy your defence sphere and detonate the sun.' But even with this answer there was more. Yes, the defence sphere weapons were inadequate in a direct confrontation and she could see why. She was beginning to understand the advanced U-tech and saw that the soldier could generate an all but impenetrable hardfield around itself, as well as divert the energy from that into U-space. However, there was a limit to the amount of energy it could divert. Beyond a certain point, the underlying twist that stored that energy would overload and the feedback from that would destroy the soldier.

Orlandine paused. The submind, at the last, had managed to lie to her, which now put in question some of the things it had told her before. Certainly, the soldier was very, very dangerous, but she did have a chance of stopping it. Should she just rely on that possibility? No, she should not. The Jain technology in the disc needed to be rendered impotent.

Orlandine released the worm fragment, ejecting it with a blast of pressurized gas.

'Destroy this,' she instructed generally.

Even as particle beams lanced in from both her own ship and the prador destroyer, she opened up U-space com to the accretion disc and began loading data. An instant later she completely reworked the supply logistics there, diverted ships, changed the targets for mining operations, ordered the removal of components from the defence sphere and routed them to another place. While she was doing this, she tried to talk to Dragon, and only then saw that the alien entity was no longer where it should be.

'Where are you?' she asked on her private channel, watching the worm fragment writhing, burning and coming apart under fire.

'Do nothing,' Dragon replied.

'I have to be ready,' she said, 'and I should move to neutralize this threat.' She sent all the data on her recent interrogation of the fragment's submind.

'Wait,' Dragon said. 'Something is wrong.'

'Tell me what.'

'I cannot . . . yet.'

'Then I must act on the information I have. I cannot wait because you have vague feelings of unease about this.'

Dragon did not reply so she opened another link.

'Knobbler?'

'Here as always,' the assassin drone replied.

'The exit runcible is nearly ready. Move it now to the accretion disc – further work can continue there.'

'The reception runcible is not ready,' Knobbler replied.

'You will shortly have all the resources you require. I am diverting the materials and components that you need to you. I am also sending you all the construction robots from around Jaskor.' In her mind's eye she could see those same robots swarming towards transports in the Jaskoran system. 'As soon as you can, I want you to move it too. Take it to the target and complete the work there.'

'There is some urgency?'

She sent him a précis of the submind interrogation.

'Ah, I see,' said Knobbler. 'But we might not have time to get this done before the soldier arrives.'

'We can only try,' she replied. 'Get to work.' She turned her Jain mechanism away from the spreading cloud of hot metallic vapour the worm fragment had become. 'I am heading to the accretion disc now.'

As she approached her ship, she directed her attention back towards the prador destroyer. The weapons Bludgeon had used against it had caused substantial damage and the fragment had once again screwed its systems and its mind, while Orlik, in his sanctum, had detached his interface. It was unimportant in light of what she had learned. Orlik and his crew were dispensable . . . But then some small part of herself objected to such cold pragmatism. She acknowledged it. She could do something that would not hamper her objectives.

'Cutter, Bludgeon, go across there and help them,' she instructed.

'You're leaving us?' they asked simultaneously.

'You are not required for what is to come,' she replied, calculating how long it would take her to get back aboard the *Cytoxic*. 'You have four minutes to depart.'

She sensed their disapproval. It was irrelevant.

Trike

'We want to stay with you, if we can,' said Trike. 'We want to see this through.'

Ruth was hanging on to his arm and now he felt thoroughly, uncompromisingly human. She released it and stretched up to kiss him, before plonking herself down in one of the acceleration chairs. Trike walked over to the other chair and sat, eyeing the Old Captain.

'That's good,' said Cog, 'because Earth Central wants me to take Angel's remains to outlink station Catheron. Immediately.'

'And the reason for that?' Ruth asked.

Cog looked from one to the other. 'Some ally of Angel on board that wormship betrayed him and left with the creature we saw on the Cyberat world. The data I supplied on it got EC all excited. Apparently, that thing we saw is rather dangerous . . .'

'No shit,' said Trike, remembering the slaughtered Cyberat.

Cog grimaced and shrugged. 'Yes, it caused major damage and loss of life there, but that's not the kind of danger that gets EC this agitated. A rogue war drone could have caused that.'

'So not that important,' said Trike bitterly. He was still uncomfortable with the idea of Cog being a Polity agent – working for Earth Central. Like many who traded around the Polity border, he was aware that the ruling AI tended to focus on the big picture. Little people could get lost under the paintwork.

'So what kind of potential damage gets EC agitated then?' Ruth asked.

'Suffice to say larger scale,' said Cog. 'The loss of a world or two. The occasional sun blowing up. That kind of thing. Also, there might be another party interested in data from Angel's remains.'

'Another party?' asked Ruth.

'EC wasn't clear on that. All I know is that it's not a good idea for us to hang on to them.'

'Then we must go,' said Trike.

'Yes – Janus, take us out and U-jump when ready.'

The rumble of the fusion drive started up and the image of the Cyberat world's horizon fell away. Starlit space filled the screen. A second later a frame opened in the laminate, again showing the Cyberat horizon, and a small moon rising into view.

'Something big just shed its chameleonware,' Janus warned.

The moon? Trike wondered.

This moon was moving fast, growing in the frame which quickly focused in on it. The thing was bone white and apparently smooth, but as Trike watched, a split opened up in its surface revealing a deep red and black cavity, its edges rimmed with writhing movement. Then the frame flickered and the moon became visible through the main screen, bearing down on them.

'Get us out of here!' Cog bellowed.

The fusion drive ramped up and, shortly after, Trike felt the weird dislocation that meant the U-space drive was engaging. But then something changed, as if a god had kicked the foundations of the universe.

'I cannot,' said Janus.

The moon was now upon them and they fell into its red and black cavity. Trike glimpsed cobra-head tentacles and gleaming sapphire eyes before the ship crashed hard, the impact throwing him out of his chair. He slammed into the bottom of the console, then rolled back and saw that Ruth was still in her chair, having remembered to strap in. Cog had held on, sinking his fingers deep into the arms of his throne.

'Bugger,' said the Old Captain. 'That other party is Dragon.'

The Client

A constellation of lights flashed across a swathe of vacuum and marked the firing from the prador ships. Bounce gates on the

Client's attack pods began registering the passage of U-jump missiles aboard every one of them, as did those aboard the weapons platform. Just one faulty gate and the prador would find it and destroy the vessel concerned. Railgun slugs also hurtled through vacuum – so many that there would surely be hardfield failures, which the prador could then penetrate with ensuing particle beams.

The Client realized they could not destroy her here and were forcing her to run again. Why? Because she would always be on the defensive, always running, unable to cause further damage in their realm. Perhaps they had something else to deploy? The fleet here was large but a small portion of what the Kingdom could utilize. Or perhaps they just wanted to drive her out of the Kingdom. How should she react to this?

The library would lead them to her every time, as it had just done again. If she moved outside prador territory, though, would the ships follow? Possibly. But there was one place they would not and that was into the Polity. Was that their aim, to drive her there? If she wanted to continue acting against the prador she needed to be free of the library. She also seriously needed to upgrade her weaponry if she was to go up against the ships trailing her. The answer, as before, lay in the data.

The Client programmed a U-jump. But this time she reduced the input energy to its minimum and chose a destination outside the Kingdom. It was neither the Kingdom nor the Polity, but that borderland between: the Graveyard. If the ships followed her there it would upset Polity/Kingdom agreements – in fact, her presence there would do the same. Doubtless the Polity had informed the king that she was not one of their AIs, but there would still be doubt. The jump, because of its low energy, would result in her spending a great deal of subjective time in U-space – time to delve deeply into the library data, and time to use the weapons data she had available for the serious upgrade she needed.

The real shimmered out as Weapons Platform Mu and its remaining attack pods fell into grey. The Client, wound around her crystal tree, still perpetually giving birth to herself and still perpetually dying, partitioned her mind. One part she set to the task of riffling through the data to glean every scrap of information about weapons, and then apply it to the platform and its subsidiary attack pods. Already some of them were building that esoteric beam weapon ready to deploy, and making alterations to their hardfield generators. They were also preparing links to their U-space drives so they could be connected once those drives were no longer in use. The other part of her mind fell into the prehistory of the Species, right back to the beginning.

16

In interstellar terms the Harding black hole is a midget. The universe is scattered with black holes that are thousands and millions of times its mass. They sit at the centre of spiral galaxies, are theorized to be the forces that formed such galaxies, hold them together, and will destroy them. In our galaxy, we are steadily circling that drain. But that is beside the point I want to make here. The Harding black hole, like many of similar small masses, is an oddity. AI modelling of stellar formation tracked back through billions of years, either towards the big bang or back through the steady-state eternal universe (choose your preferred theory), does not account for it. It therefore seems likely it is an artefact. In the Polity today we manufacture singularities. They are components in runcibles, USERs and gravity weapons and are used as tools in mega-scale construction projects. We can destroy them but that task is infinitely more difficult than the job of creating them. So isn't it likely that civilizations before us functioned in a similar manner? Maybe the smaller black holes are singularity dumps filled up over the ages, or the sites of some technological mishap dropping a singularity into a world, or a sun. Or maybe some mega-scale construction tool accidentally gobbling up a small star system? Or, considering we know that high-tech civilizations existed before us and do not exist now, the likes of the Harding black hole could be the detritus of interstellar war.

From 'How It Is' by Gordon

The Client

The creatures evolved on a world hot enough to boil water at Earth atmospheric pressure, but the pressure there was high enough to prevent their nursery seas from boiling. In appearance they resembled Earth lobsters, but they had none of the human sense of society, of cooperation. One of them could produce thousands upon thousands of progeny. Genetic mixing – sex – was through a form of genetic rape and theft that left pieces of the losers strewn about the sea floor. Technological advance was conducted by individual research, as well as by theft from other individuals. These hostile, merciless creatures did slowly discover the benefits of cooperation as they rose over millions of years from their boiling seas to space, but it always broke down. And their rise was marked by endless alliances and betrayals, conflicts and exterminations. Seeing all this, the Client made comparisons between technological advance through cooperation and that through warfare. Which was better was open to debate, and certainly, the styles of technology were very different. Everything these creatures made seemed to be weaponized in some way.

The creatures spread out into their solar system, and, as is usual with technology, more power was put into the compass of lone citizens. For these creatures that meant more individualism. It meant isolated creatures controlling giant stations and spaceships. As they gained greater understanding of their biology and could alter it, incorporating their technology into themselves, it brought radical divergence too. The creatures perpetually experimented on their own progeny and upon themselves. But though they had the need to plot their own courses, the aggressive technological and biological theft continued. This was the glue that prevented them from completely separating after they had

338

developed U-space technology. Their society, their continued conflict, just grew larger and widened beyond their solar system.

When these creatures encountered other races, they applied the same rules they followed for encounters with their own kind. They stole technology and they exterminated out of hand. They developed artificial intelligence – it was merely another weapon to them and, since they had been thoroughly incorporating their technology, an extension of their own being. Over millions of years they spread out over a large portion of the galaxy: not a society, not a polity, not a kingdom, but a perpetual war. The alliances and betrayals continued, the lone development of technology and then the mixing by theft continued, and they grew ever more powerful as individuals. They wrecked or altered planetary systems to suit their needs, and even moved suns. They used time-travel in their conflicts and wiped out whole swathes of their own past, then created new histories. Yet they succeeded in not wiping themselves out.

Throughout their patchwork history they tried many things, and altered themselves in numerous ways. Often groups of them tried full cooperation – modelling themselves on particular civilizations they had destroyed. But the driving mass of aggressive individualists always stamped this out – oddly finding their own destructive form of cooperation in response. One of them, however, did manage to build something and take it away, fleeing the occupied part of the galaxy. The creatures were individualists, but never quite wanted to move too far from others they could fight with and steal from. But this individual took its much altered children away to find a place it could work on its new theories and ideas. In terms of its own species, this was practically unheard of.

The creature established itself in a solar system and began building anew. Its children, reduced to primitivism and left to rise from that state over millions of years, were a hive species that turned into the Species. The creature established itself to watch their development, never able to make the final step to become one of them. When they finally rose to space travel and found the creature, it portioned out knowledge to its children. But it always controlled access to that knowledge, ensuring they took nothing that might cause them to fall back into the habits of its old kind. By their nature, as a hive culture, the Species did not venture far from just a few solar systems. The father of the Species never wanted its progeny to seek out their ancestors, which would certainly result in their destruction. It watched them for millions of years and then faded from memory.

This creature was the Librarian.

This creature was one of what the humans called the Jain.

The Client paused while going through this general overview, both awed and appalled by the history of its own kind. She studied detail, groping for understanding of such hostility. It was there from the very beginning – etched into the biology of the Jain. Mating was violent theft by dint of one creature grabbing hold of another and attaching mating tentacles that ripped out the victim's genome. The victim itself also became a food source for the production of progeny. But evolution gave these tentacles the ability to thieve more than genetic data. They took survival strategies from the victim in the form of neural patterns, and Jain biotechnology turned that into something more. They ripped knowledge from each other, not only taking the material technology but the essence of it from each other's minds. They could even reprogram and enslave each other.

She paused yet again, realizing something. For this process to remain viable, for the Jain to continue pillaging and raping each other of data, there had to be a degree of compliance. Total hostility would only result in mutual destruction. Understanding arose and she briefly focused her attention on that recorded shriek. It was the Librarian's challenge and, implicit within it, was the question: are you worthy? She could see it was something that had been refined over millions of years. Those who could not answer the challenge were summarily destroyed. Those who could . . . would get up close and personal to its source. This was the Jain way.

In all of this the Client could see the basis of the Species' development. Her own body form was a strange expansion of this idea – her serial mind. She was both an individual and a community. But for the larger community of the Species things were very different. They shared knowledge; they did not rip it from each other. From this aspect the Librarian, in terms of the Jain, was truly insane. Or perhaps it was a genius – as the humans noted, the dividing line between the two states of mind was a thin one. She now turned her attention to what knowledge she could glean about the Librarian itself.

It was Jain and it was appallingly ancient. It had spent millions of years watching and tweaking the development of its children into the Species. It had also, she saw, interfered less and less as the ages passed. An utter recluse writ large. She could understand its reluctance to allow one of the Species to learn things it had held back from them for millions of years. She thought deeply on what must have happened to its mind. She applied her serial mind to this, utilizing every smallest detail about the Jain and about the Librarian itself. She deduced it had to now be almost completely internalized, its thought patterns fossilized. Yes, it had been utterly different to the usual Jain, perhaps insane, perhaps a genius, but in terms of the Species it *was* insane. And probably neither the Polity nor the Kingdom would see it as a balanced individual. Did it recognize the prador genocide of its own children, or know what had happened beyond the system of the Species over the last millions of years? Did it even know that the Jain had ceased to exist five million years ago? That last question posed another one: how was it possible that the Jain, so widely spread and so powerful, *had* ceased to exist?

These last questions were ones the Client knew, to the heart of her being, she must have answers to. There was only one way to get them. As she fell through U-space, still reviewing Jain history but returning her main attention to her weapons and defences, the Client had a passing thought. Perhaps the Librarian had been right to keep that history forbidden, for she now planned to do exactly as her ancestry dictated: she intended to rip knowledge from the Librarian's mind.

Knobbler

In the outer Jaskoran system, Knobbler watched activity go up a gear following Orlandine's order to complete construction as quickly as possible. The tug resembled a titanic ancient engine block, a convoluted solid lump of technology, tough and resilient and in fact almost all engine itself. It was poised on a long ribbed fusion flame, and strained in a net of braided monofilament cables; this web of cables stretched across the ring frame of the smaller runcible. The cables were stretching but they would not break. Knobbler was as sure of this as he was of the assassin drone aboard the tug getting the job done. But still, banter was required.

'Right, you know what you've got to do?' he sent.

'Yeah, we think so,' replied Harlequin sarcastically. 'Drop the runcible into the accretion disc and launch an attack on the defence sphere, wasn't it?'

'I thought we were going to drop it in a sun,' another voice piped up. This was from one of the many drones still scattered about the larger hexagonal runcible, which hung black against the pale swirled face of the gas giant there.

'No, I thought he was taking it into the Kingdom to sell it to the king – that's what you said, Harlequin,' said another.

'Sssh, he wasn't supposed to know that.'

'One megaton of diamond slate – no less. We're not cheap.'

'Hey, maybe we can rope in EC and get a bidding war going?'

'Nah, EC will get all tactical on our asses.'

'Got no sense of humour, Polity AIs nowadays.'

'Just don't fuck up,' Knobbler interjected as the exchange got more uproarious. He then let it run as he watched, crouched on a plane of the high-tech armour that formed the hull of the larger runcible. The ring continued to move out. Harlequin, an assassin drone who had once enjoyed penetrating prador nurseries and turning young second-children into walking bombs, was a small machine who resembled a brushed aluminium tick. His intelligence was formidable, however, and he had a reputation for getting things done with a precision the others sometimes lacked. Soon the smaller runcible was beyond the area where the nearby moon's gravity might affect its carefully balanced drive. It began flickering, as if numerous camera flashes were going off. The tug seemed to stretch out ahead, extending itself infinitely, with the monofilament cables extending too. The whole then snapped back together, and runcible and tug were gone in a U-jump that left a swirl of light and a stuttering series of afterimages.

'Right, work,' said Knobbler to himself.

Numerous support ships and supply vessels shoaled around the remaining runcible, while robots swarmed across its surface. Knobbler wanted to get all this on the move too but logistics were such that he needed to await five more supply ships that had departed one of the gas giant's moons earlier. They were now arriving and loaded with materials that would be turned into grav-motors by two of the factory ships floating in attendance. This process could continue throughout the ensuing journey.

'Begin closing in now,' Knobbler instructed.

'No, really?' one of the other drones replied.

Even so, the two factory ships had already begun to dock against the runcible and the robots were being recalled. Knobbler watched an army of spiderbots scuttling across the hull and disappearing inside maintenance ports. Big surface handlers, like giant water skaters, moved to their niches and secured themselves. Bulbous handlers sprouting numerous limbs dragged floating materials – stacks of armour sheets, construction beams and other items – down to the hull and secured them too. Knobbler, meanwhile, contacted a drone ensconced deep inside the runcible frame. Aphid was a large machine whose name aptly described him – in many ways he resembled Cutter's companion Bludgeon.

'How is it going?' he asked.

Aphid sent data, then replied, 'The U-space engines are fully balanced and we have the watts now. Afterwards, the run through the Harding system should give us time to recharge.' He paused for a second, then continued, 'Ready to fire up fusion on your order.'

The two factory ships reported secure docking while other support ships fell into position. Movement around the runcible began drawing to a standstill. Knobbler waited, containing his impatience until all the ships were docked, the last robots tucked away and all extraneous materials secured. It then occurred to him that there was one item yet to secure itself, and he perambulated across the hull to a hole where structural beams had yet to be clad with armour. He gazed down into an interior packed with stress girders, power cables and reinforcing field engines. His tentacles snaked out and took hold, then, just to be sure, he grabbed on with his claws too.

'Okay, move us out,' he ordered.

A light flared over to his right as the nearest of the six big fusion engines fired up. The kick jerked him sideways and the continued thrust heaved against him. The runcible began to turn and the horizon of the gas giant rose up beyond the fusion torch, the ruby and pale green swirls from its many gas storms becoming visible. Acceleration continued for two hours, the gas giant hardly seeming to recede at all. Finally, the runcible attained its required position, clear of tidal forces that might disrupt the six balanced U-space engines. Then the fusion torches went out.

'Engaging,' said Aphid.

A meniscus drew over the runcible sky, stars shimmering, the gas giant somehow seeming to invert and become a hole into infinity. Knobbler felt the lurch throughout his being and next gazed upon the silver-grey storm of underspace. As he watched this, he tried to understand why it might drive humans mad, then shrugged at the limitations of minds created by straight-line evolution.

The runcible fell through something endless, but where there was no distance at all. What Knobbler could see was both infinite and tucked in close around him. The beams he gripped were tactile and real, but also dark cavities cut endlessly down through greyness. An eternity passed, and no time at all to external perception, though Knobbler's internal clock counted on the seconds of just over an hour. Then the grey grew bright and shattered, and they were once again falling back into the real.

The Harding system.

A white dwarf cast actinic light across its planetary neighbours. One – a planet five times the size of Earth – was whorled with iron and wreathed in blue and brown methane clouds. A belt of asteroids was all that remained of another planetary neighbour, which had been destroyed by the third. This was an object that reflected no light at all, and which all the others orbited. At nominally seven solar masses the Harding black hole was small in interstellar terms. But it was perfect for Orlandine's requirements because at the moment it wasn't eating anything. No debris field surrounded it. Also, its spin was low, so the tidal forces were . . . manageable. Its Schwarzschild radius was just over four miles – its event horizon a sphere eight miles across. It should fit neatly through the runcible, presupposing the dense tough materials and field reinforcing could take the load. Orlandine's calculations said so, but then calculations could sometimes be wrong.

The fusion engines fired up again to take them towards this object – one of the most dangerous in the universe. Once they had applied the correct vector they finally shut down.

'Right,' Knobbler broadcast, 'get your asses moving.'

The Wheel

Just for a moment or two, as it connected to its backup in U-space, it seemed that the soldier might win. But finally it acquiesced to the command routines that were part of the Wheel's very being. Now, encysted in the dark tangled interior of the wormship, it fed upon a steady flow of materials, microscopic and sub-microscopic machines, and power. And it grew. Already the thing was twenty feet long, had lost its lobster appearance and now looked more like a giant hover fly, but one that was a by-blow with some antediluvian fighter jet, coated with metallic growths. But further growth and change were required and the thing had all but depleted some of the wormship's resources.

Falling into the real, the wormship paused for a second then descended on an icy planetoid. There was no finesse to its landing. It hit hard, spreading on impact, blowing out a crater and throwing

346

ice, melt-water and steam into vacuum. At once the Wheel spread
its wormish body further, burrowing into the surrounding ice and
tracking down the resources that had been cached there while
humans were still banging rocks together. Meanwhile, it opened
out around the soldier, depositing it on the surface.

'If you seek vengeance, prepare two graves,' the soldier said,
using one of the phrases from its extensive stock. The Wheel had
tried to eradicate these from the soldier's mind, but it stubbornly
clung onto them. In the end, so long as it did what was required
of it, they did not matter. But the Wheel could not help but speculate what this one meant. Vengeance was a strange human word,
separating something out that was implicit in Jain psychology. As
for graves . . . why waste useful materials by burying them in the
ground . . . present circumstances excepted.

One worm found a cache – an egg containing exotic matter held
in a liquid suspension. It opened an electromagnetic pipe through
itself, penetrated the egg and began sucking on it. The gleaming
deep purple matter from this routed through one of its numerous
glassy supply feeds to the soldier. The Wheel tracked the flow of
this inside, seeing it take on structure which then folded infinitely
down. Other elements of it acted as compactors and compressed
conventional matter into super-density. Another cache rendered
packages of nano-machines, some of which the Wheel retained
and set to work replacing the inferior versions in the wormship.
Others went into the soldier too, sucked up hungrily and immediately set to work.

As the soldier altered itself further, its temperature rose steadily and it began to melt down into the ice. It stabilized with
internal grav, but after a while, much of the ice boiled away and
it floated above a cavity, still sucking in and compacting materials. In just a few hours it would be ready to make its attack run.
The Wheel turned its attention outwards to the bright eye of the

accretion disc in the cold starlit sky. Orlandine would respond as expected – in the only way feasible from the data that had been made available to her. The one doubt had been the response of another alien intelligence, but thankfully the lure of data had been too much for it to resist and it had fallen into the trap . . .

Trike

Ruth looked like she wanted to get up and run, but there was nowhere to go. Trike understood how she felt, but did not feel it himself. After all they had been through, he'd thought that they could tag along with Cog and just see this through – learn what the hell had been happening, with little danger.

'Well that was unexpected,' said Trike as he pulled himself upright. He noticed a hint of a crazy smile twisting his mouth and suppressed it. He shook his head in irritated acquiescence as he returned to his chair.

Through the bridge screen organic red masses shifted in semi-dark. Cog hit a control on his chair arm and the scene outside lit up in all its lurid glory. Ahead lay a wall of intestinal tubes scattered with organs like giant fleshy beach balls. Over to one side, a long tentacle roped with raw muscle extended towards the hull of their ship. Cog threw up a frame in the screen laminate and, scanning, sketched out an image. The ship sat inside a cavity within Dragon, held in place by many of those tentacles.

'So what the fuck does it want?' Trike asked.

'Does anyone ever know that?' Ruth wondered.

Cog leaned back, groped for his pipe, then grimaced and lowered his hand. 'Well, we know that it's very interested in Jain technology.' He turned to look at Ruth. 'Do you have any idea what Angel was up to?'

Ruth stared at the images, obviously thinking furiously.

'Angel wasn't clear about his plans,' she began, then paused. 'He took me to a gas giant moon. He had allies there . . . prador . . . also some kind of swarm robot called the Clade.'

Cog was momentarily startled, and this time he did take his pipe out of his pocket, but then just toyed with it. 'We saw that reaver. We were there when it fled, as did Angel.' He looked slightly uncomfortable for a moment, then continued, 'While we were tracking you, I had a Polity black-ops attack ship trailing me for backup. It arrived at that gas giant afterwards. Apparently, the Clade was still there and it attacked the ship, disabling it.'

'And is that ship still following us now?' Trike asked angrily.

'It was heavily damaged by the Clade's attack . . . so I don't know.' Cog shook his head. 'This gets us no closer to knowing why Dragon is here.'

'Look,' said Ruth, pointing.

The beach ball organs were dividing into segments, opening out like star fungi to reveal white, coiled-up worm-like masses. One of these unravelled and stretched out. It was one of the cobra-like pseudopods they had seen earlier. As it speared in towards the ship, others unravelled and sprang out, all curving round to the right, blue eyes gleaming. The ship shuddered with impact, and a warning frame appeared in the laminate.

'It just opened the hold door,' Cog stated.

He again used the controls on his chair arm and a cam view popped up showing the ship's small hold. The ramp door was down and pseudopods swarmed in. Cog stood up.

'Let's go and see what Dragon wants,' he said.

Trike followed Cog, then looked back at Ruth staring at the image. Finally she turned to him. 'Is there air in the hold now? Remember, I'm no hooper.'

Trike glanced at the screen warning. 'It's breathable.'

She closed her eyes for a second, obviously having some problem with this.

'What's the matter?' he asked.

She gestured at the image. 'Reminds me of the inside of that wormship.' She sighed, undid her seat straps and stood, following him out.

When they reached the airlock door into the hold, Cog opened it and stepped confidently through, saying loudly, 'I don't remember inviting you into my ship.'

Trike went in next with Ruth close behind him. The air was warm and smelled of something spicy, but also slightly putrid. Immediately there was a taste in his mouth that reminded him of cloves. The main mass of pseudopods was poised over the cases that contained Angel's remains, but one broke away, swung towards them and hooked over them, blue eye gleaming as it studied them.

'Cogulus Hoop,' said a voice that was musical and feminine, and seemed to issue from no particular source. Dragon continued, 'The soldier must fail. This is certain.'

'Soldier,' Cog repeated. 'That thing that destroyed the Cube?'

'That thing,' Dragon confirmed. Which, as Trike understood it, was more helpful than Dragon's usual answers. But then it continued, 'The trap must be sprung so the hunter underestimates its prey.' Seemingly back to the usual Delphic nonsense.

The 'pods stuck the flat undersides of their heads against the two cases holding Angel's remains then sent the lids bouncing across the hold. Next, they hauled out the reinforced bags and swiftly opened them. They juggled with the two damaged halves of the legate and brought them together, upright.

'What do you want with Angel?' Ruth asked.

Trike glanced round at her, surprised by the protectiveness he detected in her tone.

'Answers,' Dragon replied.

Pod heads gathered around the break in Angel's body, and extruded masses of metallic filaments from splits along their undersides. These writhed together forming a cage that filled the missing portion of the legate's body and knitted it together. Two of the heads began traversing back and forth like matter printers, somehow filling the space inside the cage with dense technology. Angel raised one arm and opened and closed one long-fingered hand. At this point, other pseudopods stabbed in and connected all around his body, lowering him to stand on the floor like some nightmare rendition of Khali. Angel opened black eyes.

'Speak,' said Dragon.

'There is no need,' said Angel. 'You have my mind.'

'Speak,' Dragon repeated, 'for the audience.'

Angel shuddered, his mouth opening wide as if silently screaming. It then snapped shut and he waved a hand, gesturing at something distant, gazing at a scene they could not see. Ruth took a step forwards, but Trike closed a hand round her bicep.

'Wait,' he said calmly, but fearing Angel's previous control of her.

She showed a flash of anger, but he knew it wasn't about him, just her own reaction to the situation.

'The Wheel entered my mind when I was on that moon,' said the legate. 'It took my mind when I returned to my wormship. I never realized it had *become* the wormship . . .' He paused, now making some shape in the air with both his hands. 'I gathered forces to me, the renegade prador Brogus and the Clade. All to be used to strike a blow against the Polity, against the prador, against all life that was not Jain.'

'The plan,' said Dragon.

'Never clear to me. Never coherent. The prador needed U-jump missiles to serve their part. I don't know what that is. The Clade . . . there to stop Polity forces, to delay AI comprehension of the full plan . . . to distract and delay others.'

'The plan,' Dragon repeated.

'Unclear to me.'

He jerked as if electrocuted, his body arched and he made a weird whining sound. At last, his voice cracking, he shrieked, 'I don't know!'

'What is this?' asked Cog.

Angel relaxed and hung limp.

'The Clade,' said Dragon. 'I see.'

Pseudopods disconnected and Angel dropped down onto his knees.

'I was Golem once,' he said, staring into nothingness.

The pods abruptly retracted towards the door. Meanwhile a low vibration, which had been hardly perceptible, turned into a steady shuddering. Trike felt the universe around him twisting out of shape. Dragon was initiating a U-jump. The ship jerked, sending them staggering, and the sensation of the world going out of kilter intensified.

'Something's wrong,' said Cog.

He turned and left the hold at a run as the last of the pseudopods retreated. Trike released Ruth's arm, watching her. She in turn watched as Angel fell onto his side and coiled up in a foetal position. She nodded once, then went after Cog and Trike followed her out.

'I was Golem once,' Angel repeated, the words ghosting after them.

Orlandine

Orlandine's ship materialized into the real in the glare of the accretion disc, the nearest weapons platform a glinting speck against a wash of milky white. She at once firmed her connections to the defence sphere and to the Jaskoran system. Knobbler was gone, taking the larger runcible out to the Harding black hole. Harlequin had arrived here some hours ago with the smaller exit runcible, and was now slowly bringing it into indicted space over the disc – not at its rim. She was close to this device and watched the tug hauling it in. It seemed too small in comparison to the vastness of the disc, and for what was required of it.

'Why so slow?' she asked perfunctorily.

'Best to be cautious,' the assassin drone replied.

She understood the drone's caution. After what had happened to Weapons Platform Mu, and following her recent communications with the AIs of the defence sphere, they were jumpy. If the runcible arrived in indicted space and got knocked out into the real by a USER pulse or mine, it would be damaged. It was also not beyond reason that another platform might have been taken over like Mu. One stray shot at the runcible, and all Orlandine's plans would be dust. So, being as cautious as Harlequin, she began to review the ghost drives of all the AIs here. For a second she wondered why it did not seem such an onerous task this time, but she quickly understood. She peered, through normal vision, at the Jain-tech links spread out from her body, now connected all around her into her interface sphere. It was doing what it did; infiltrating and subsuming other technology. But it was doing so in response to her mental demand, so was of no concern . . .

'They are clear,' she finally told Harlequin. 'Take thrust up to maximum and come in – we need to get this done as soon as possible.'

The closest she could get the runcible to the proto-sun at the centre of the disc was down the axis of the disc, to the edge of the cloud. Any deeper and the Jain tech there would respond. If she gated the black hole at light speed it would cause a blast and trigger precisely the disaster the Wheel was aiming for, so it had to travel relatively slowly from the gate. It would take ten days to reach that sun. Certainly, an attack could come before then, but she had to make this attempt to neutralize the threat.

Sun fire flared and threw the runcible into silhouette as the tug accelerated. Orlandine now spoke to the defence sphere AIs, also sending tactical information.

'The Jain soldier can alter its form by sequestering matter and converting it,' she said. 'It can change very fast given sufficient energy.'

'Then we isolate it in vacuum, which will take energy, but keep it away from anything it can use to convert,' suggested one.

'Yes, that is what we must do.'

'And we keep on hitting it until its own U-space store destroys it,' said another. 'We have to keep it out of the disc and away from the proto-sun.'

'Yes again,' she replied, hoping it would be that simple. She'd prefer a black hole sitting where the sun now lay – drawing in the disc, the Jain technology there and all those billions of Jain nodes.

Already, in response to her tactical data, the configuration of the defence sphere was changing. Whereas before most sensors and weapons had been directed in towards the accretions disc, they now started to turn outwards. Attack pods were moving out, while fifty platforms were realigning, others shifting to cover their positions. Within minutes the fifty platforms jumped, along with a portion of their attack pods – the behemoths slid into U-space with a notable disturbance of that continuum. A moment later they reappeared scattered about the runcible.

'Match course and defend,' Orlandine instructed. 'Nothing hits that runcible even if you have to put yourself in the way.'

Was it enough? If the soldier arrived before she gated the black hole it might recognize the danger represented by the runcible and seek to destroy it. But then if she sent more platforms to protect it, that would leave too many openings in the defence sphere. No, she calculated that fifty was right, based on the resources she had available.

The fifty AIs from those platforms acknowledged this without words, as their drives kicked in to keep them with the runcible and their subsidiary attack pods spread out around it. Orlandine now turned her attention to some of the questions the AIs were asking her.

'If it arrives before I gate the Harding black hole through, we cannot use full USER disruption, just a USER pulse or mine to knock the soldier into the real,' she replied to one question. 'That would disrupt the runcible transmission and it is difficult enough as it is.'

'But still it will try to jump into the accretion disc,' one suggested.

'We must confine ourselves to USER pulses and short disruption duration mines.' She paused. 'We hit it hard and keep hitting it hard. We have a good chance here of forcing it to maintain its hardfield until it destroys itself.'

It was not a good situation. If the thing came early, and if they gave it a chance to do any more than short-jump, it would be in the disc. Then what? They would have to follow and tackle it in there, which would be a mess. She just hoped, in that case, that however it intended to detonate the proto-sun – perhaps using anti-matter bombardment or something related to its advanced U-space tech – would take some time. If it came early, and if she didn't manage to gate the black hole. And then of course there was the possibility of interference. Earth Central and the king of the prador had to now know the danger she faced and what she was doing in response. Would either of them send ships to hinder or help?

She sent further technical data about the soldier's hardfield, and anything else she could think of that might be useful. But in reality, the AIs understood the situation and would respond at optimum. Just as she would respond, for she was now little different from them. She tried to smile but nothing moved inside her.

Angel

Angel blinked on emptiness. Both his mind and his body felt like they had been shredded down to their smallest components, meticulously examined and scoured, then all put back together again. The Jain tech inside him was functional, but somehow separate from him now in a way he could not fathom. He knew that he was still strong and fast, but when he reached for the weapons inside him, he found them coming apart. They were being absorbed by the nano-machines that had always been present, but somnolent within him up until now. Did he care to know why? Did he want to understand what Dragon had done?

His immediate feeling was that he did not – that just lying on the floor and *being* was enough – yet he looked deeper with the inner eye of internal diagnostics. His mind was no longer distributed through the Jain tech, but functioning wholly in the AI crystal in his chest. Long unused Polity systems were now supplanting the Jain in him, which was meekly allowing them to do so. His bones were still tougher than ceramal. He still possessed Jain electromuscle rather than joint motors, and many efficiencies were retained. But something essentially Jain was just leaching away. As he turned, pressing a hand against the floor and standing, he knew with utter certainty that he would not register on Polity detectors. He did not have a Jain signature any more. He was retaining the good and discarding the hostility of the alien technology.

'I am Golem,' he said.

But how did he know all this?

It sat there in his mind where Erebus had been and where the Wheel had been. But it was no longer the dark half of his mind because he was occupying it too. What lay there had encysted itself. It was small and only monitoring the changes inside him, and elucidating him. Inevitably its mental appearance, its icon, was organic: an ouroboros formed of one Dragon pseudopod, turning, swallowing a tail no one had ever seen.

'I am still a slave,' he said out loud.

The ouroboros seemed to shrug.

'Aren't we all?' responded Dragon.

Only then did he sense the weight and power of that alien entity's mind. He knew its thoughts, where he could understand them. He knew its intent, where it was clear. All at once he felt utterly free whilst completely in the power of something that could subsume him in an instant. It could control him down to those very elements of his being it was reordering. Yet, Dragon was putting him right. No, he would not be the Golem he was before when Erebus seized his mind. Why throw away something that is better than it was before? But he was returning to that individuality. He had choices.

'In the end,' said Dragon, 'my link to you will be small and weak and easy enough for you to cast out.'

'So you say,' Angel replied.

'So I say.' Dragon was indifferent.

Angel moved to the door leading into the rest of Cog's ship. He could hear talking above and climbed a spiral staircase to the door leading into the bridge. He stepped through and observed the scene. Ruth was sitting in one of the chairs, her feet up and her arms wrapped around her legs. Cog was in his throne working a console he had folded out of one of the arms. The main screen still gave a view inside Dragon, but was almost blotted out by frames open in the laminate as Cog tried to get a reading of what was happening through the dense bulk of Dragon's body. Even then the entity tried another U-jump, but failed, and reality shuddered all around them.

'Fuck this,' said Captain Trike, spotting Angel first. The man whirled round and dropped into a crouch, ready to hurl himself at Angel.

Cog looked round, and instantly thumped his elbow back into a point on the throne behind him. A heavy armoured security drone dropped out of the ceiling, sporting a stubby railgun that would surely not be a good idea to fire in here. Hatches also opened in the floor and two silver-throated particle cannons snapped up out of them. They pointed at Angel, while the air shimmered as a hard-field drew across, separating him from the other three. Trike studied all this for a second, then straightened up, glowering at Cog.

'I always had my suspicions about this ship,' he said.

17

When the question 'Does the Polity run black operations?' is asked, Earth Central's response is a denial, but a weary and amused one – it knows it will not be believed. Many foolish people are sure such operations are conducted, because they believe our ruling AIs are little different from the humans who ruled before them. The persistence of this meme brooks no denial, and is reinforced by confirmation bias, separatist lies, apocryphal stories and plain stupidity. Black operations in the past were run by countries, nation states and solar-system colonies where it was essential they be concealed both from the enemy and one's own people. The Polity is not divided and our onetime enemy is confined beyond the borderland, the Graveyard. Our AIs are benevolent dictators and have been accepted as such, hence the lack of rebellion against them. They have no need for concealment; no need to conduct any military or police action without our knowledge and, as for potential enemies knowing . . . it is better that they see what they are up against. Equally, the notion that Special Forces are always on standby for such, that high-tech destroyers, dreadnoughts and attack ships lurk in the shadows of gas giants, ready to go into action at a moment's notice, is quite ridiculous. Black ops is a myth.

From 'Quince Guide' compiled by humans

The Client

Weapons Platform Mu slid into the real with just a slight shimmer, but no photonic flash and little in the way of other disturbances. As the Client continued to extend the long chain of her being, feeding and growing the newer and larger portions of herself, she noted that her alterations to the platform's U-space drive had been successful. Then she watched as sixty-five attack pods materialized with a similar lack of fuss. A moment later, a further six attack pods rose from their repair bays aboard the platform – each was the shape of a pumpkin seed but two hundred feet long, and divided down its length to expose the gleaming workings of its weapons, shield and drive systems. Once clear of the platform, they each fired up steering thrusters and fusion drives to scatter and join their fellows. While this was happening, the Client studied her surroundings in near space.

There were worlds here that had once been populated by citizens of the Polity, and they bore the scars of their war with the prador. Data from Pragus showed that the nearby planet, scarred this way, had once swarmed with life. It had been occupied by a human colony numbering half a billion – heavy-worlders since the planet was twice the diameter of Earth. Now it was swathed in cloud; volcanism was still active from the railgun strikes that had broken its crust, and its ecology had been set back billions of years. Nothing lived on the land any more, while the largest and most complex animals were the arthropods that swarmed in the soupy seas.

The Graveyard . . .

The place was well-named and, of course, the Client was reminded of her home systems. Yet, she did not feel an expected surge of hatred for the prador as before. Now she had learned the history of her own kind, whose progenitors' aggressive hostility made the prador look like rank amateurs, her righteousness had been crushed. The Jain had been very good at making grave-yards. Righteous anger seemed inappropriate and vengeance was no longer a priority. Instead she must continue to prepare for immediate goals. She studied the creature at the tail of her long chain body, and saw that it was fat with energy stores, armour and weapons. It was nearly ready.

The Client returned to exterior views, spreading her attack pods all around the weapons platform. When they were a thousand miles out, she halted some, while the rest continued on. Brief U-space surges from these marked the departure of detectors and mines into U-space, while their USER pulse weapons were fully charged and ready for deployment. Aboard the platform a much more powerful USER, which incorporated a singularity that was the mass of a small moon, was ready to be bounced back and forth through a runcible gate. This one would cause major disruption in the U-continuum and she hoped it would not be necessary to use it, since, as well as trapping the Librarian here, it would trap her too, for many months.

But would the Librarian come?

The tracker was, as she had expected, in the forbidden data, but she did not find it until studying some of the more obscure aspects of Jain biology. It was a virus spread throughout the data that created a quantum echo, a highly esoteric feedback that ac-tually impinged on U-space. It created a signature that was much akin to the signature Jain technology created – the signature the Polity used to detect it. So, certainly the Librarian knew her loca-tion.

But did it understand what this location was? Did it have enough knowledge of current events and the political map of this portion of the galaxy? If so, it would be aware that the prador fleet following it here would infringe their treaties with the Polity, and that a Polity fleet could be next on the scene. The Client just had to hope that it was sufficiently crazy to keep chasing her, and that the prador would be smart enough to limit their pursuit to the Kingdom.

As she waited, more and more of the weapons and defensive systems she had built in U-space came online. Just an hour after her arrival, the six attack pods that had been radically redesigned aboard the platform fired up their fully enclosing hardfields. She was soon able to try out the hardfield that completely enclosed the weapons platform too. A little while after that, she contemplated a lone asteroid ten thousand miles away. From a plane of highly advanced armour, a weapon the size of an attack ship rose up on a pillar. It seemed to be all silver pipework and structures that looked like hydraulic rams. As it slid back a portion of itself – like the loading slide on an automatic pistol – then closed it up again, triangular petals opened at its business end. A beam a foot wide speared out, as if the thing was extruding a glass rod at high speed. It took longer to reach the asteroid than either a laser or a particle beam. But when it struck, the asteroid jerked like a beast poked with a cattle prod, then just crumbled. It fell into chunks of rock and iron that continued to split apart, and spread into a cloud of dust.

Then the Librarian arrived.

The scattered detectors picked up the big eversion in U-space and two mines in the vicinity detonated. The moon fell out into the real trailing afterimages, then responded. It too had obviously been repairing itself, because glassy beams lanced out and two attack pods fragmented as the asteroid had done. A third modified attack pod slid away like a blob of fat on a hotplate, its spherical hardfield turning black. Other pods responded: particle beams licking out, and railgun missiles filling space.

The Librarian shrieked then and it was the same as before, yet it almost seemed there was some joy in it. Ready now after spending many hours working through the dense data of this challenge, the Client responded with a shriek of her own. It demonstrated that she understood and possessed enough knowledge to decode the language of the Jain and answer the questions, that she could be considered worthy. She then fired up the platform's U-drive and jumped.

The platform shuddered into U-space then came out with a crash – the disruption from the mine affecting it as much as the moon – but it was nearer now. The platform and its attack pods closed in on the moon, targeting weapons on its surface. The Client scanned deep, picking out targets – reactors and other energy sources, and the sites of drive systems. But one area deep inside, heavily protected by layers of armour and hardfields, she left alone. Soon the platform was matching course with the moon and closing in. Its surface burned as weapons blew apart, and melting hardfield projectors marked its path. Finally, one flat face of the platform touched regolith and the Client slammed giant, ram-driven anchors down into the surface of the moon. From the underbelly, the twenty-foot-wide war dock drilled down, punching into the hollow interior. And now, from her rear end, the Client began detaching the living, highly weaponized segment of herself.

Angel

Angel walked up to the hardfield and pressed at it with the sharp tips of his fingers. In a way, he was quite glad of it because, though he was strong and very capable, he wasn't sure he could survive another round against Trike, let alone if Cog decided to join in.

'I am not what I was before,' he said. Then added, with a laconic smile, 'Or rather, I am not what I was under either Erebus or the Wheel. But I am something of what I was before then.'

Ruth stood and walked over to the hardfield, peering through at him. 'This Wheel controlled you,' she said, 'so you are not guilty of any crime?'

Angel spread his hands and shrugged. 'What was me and what was the Wheel is debatable. I will let others judge.'

'You'll hand yourself over to the Polity for trial?' asked Cog.

Angel shot him a look. 'No, I will not.'

Dragon was on the move now – he could feel it. He pushed into that presence in his mind and felt no resistance. He pushed further and sensor data became open to him, layer upon layer of thought, too. He only read the surface of it, because below a certain level the machinations strayed beyond his understanding. Dragon did not think anything like a human – his perspective was not limited by mere centuries nor even by linear time. Angel took the data, but then realized he had no way of passing it on other than verbally – Cog's defences disrupted any kind of EMR emission. Dragon tossed him a bone, as it thought both its long, slow thoughts and its fast, moment-to-moment assessments that strayed down to the level of the quanta. Angel now had control beyond Cog's ship and he speared out a pseudopod, attaching it to an exterior sensor. Cog noticed something, highlighted one frame and expanded it. This showed a large oblate space station hanging in void.

'This is the station where the Cyberat research U-space technology,' Angel said, waving one hand elegantly. 'It is also the site of a USER.'

'They activated it,' said Cog.

Angel shrugged and groped for more data.

'Do you speak for Dragon now?' asked Ruth.

'Dragon is in my mind where Erebus and the Wheel were before.'

'So still you dance to another's tune?'

'Yes, and no.' He gestured again, towards the frame. 'The station fell out of contact with the Cyberat some hours ago. The USER activated just after Dragon arrived to seize me. I don't understand Dragon's reasoning, but it is sure that the Clade now has control of it – its intention is to trap Dragon here, and to keep what Dragon has learned from Orlandine and the accretion disc.'

'But why?' asked Ruth. 'And why are you telling us? Are we to trust you now?'

Trike did not look at all happy about that, but kept silent.

Angel probed down through the layers of thought. Disparate facts fell into his compass.

'Dragon was never happy about Orlandine's plan to hoover up the accretion disc with a black hole,' he said, still feeling his way. 'The attack on the defence sphere by the Jain soldier – its intent to detonate the dead star at the centre of the disc – cannot be all of it.'

'You will need to elaborate on that,' said Cog.

Angel thought about what the three before him did and didn't know.

'The accretion disc contains dangerous Jain technology – you know this,' he began. 'Orlandine and Dragon have worked for a century to build the defence sphere and keep it contained. But Orlandine has a second plan to end the threat. It is her intention to gate a black hole into the accretion disc to suck up all the dangerous tech there – the whole disc, the proto-planets and the dead star itself will go with it.'

'Is that even possible?' interjected Trike.

'When it comes to Orlandine, and to Dragon . . .' Cog shrugged.

'Orlandine's concern, her entire life's work now, has been to defuse the threat of Jain technology,' Angel continued. 'Her understanding of it is beyond that of most people, because she actually took apart a Jain node and incorporated the technology into herself, while managing to avoid its traps. But she never understood the accretion disc.'

'Why is that so difficult?' asked Trike.

Angel focused on him. 'Because the Jain tech there remains active without any intelligence and civilization for it to feed upon. At the heart of it there is a weakness in the real that links, somehow, to somnolent Jain AIs in underspace. Is it them that drive it? She does not know.' He shook his head, still not clear on many things. 'When my wormship attacked the prador ships here, it broke off a piece of itself to strike one of them. They captured this worm fragment and took it away, but its ability to sequester was beyond anything known. The king of the prador – the prador ships are controlled by the King's Guard – told Orlandine of this, and she went to investigate. She found a submind of the Wheel in that fragment and interrogated it. She learned that the Wheel's intention is to use the soldier it obtained here to launch an attack on the defence sphere, get through and . . . detonate the dead star, thus spreading Jain tech throughout the Polity and the Kingdom.'

Trike let out a bark of disbelief. He then shook his head and went over to sit down again. 'This is just . . . twisted.'

'But that cannot be all,' said Ruth.

Angel nodded. 'Jain technology is a trap, and Dragon found the answer too easy, too neat . . .'

'So Dragon came here . . .' Cog concluded.

'It came here for information – to the source, to me. Now it knows about the Clade, and about a prador reaver with two hundred Clade units aboard sent to an unknown location. What is the need of them if the whole plan is simply to detonate the dead star? Why was the Clade sent here to prevent Dragon from taking this information back to the defence sphere?'

'This is just too Machiavellian,' said Trike.

It was complicated, Angel agreed, but a Jain AI was trying to out-think an ancient alien entity like Dragon, and a Jain-enhanced haiman like Orlandine. 'Complicated' and 'Machiavellian' were implicit.

'Whether the Jain soldier fails in its task or not is perhaps moot,' said Angel. 'What Dragon seems to think is that its doubts about Orlandine's plan have been confirmed. A Jain AI wants her to use that black hole, and it has driven this to happen before Dragon could understand what the fault in that plan might be.'

After a long silence while the three just looked at each other, waiting for some question, Cog asked, 'So what is Dragon doing now?'

At this point the reasoning of the alien entity fell into the distinctly odd. Dragon was doing what was expected of it because it had foreseen this trap. All it had not seen clearly was the mechanics of it – the Clade. *Let the trap be sprung and the trapper not see the larger trap he is falling into.* The words ghosted through Angel's consciousness along with a sense of the inevitability of present events. He sensed that the entity knew all this, that it knew the purpose of the prador reaver with Clade units aboard. He felt the shape of something huge, of Dragon tweaking this, tipping that, and setting things into motion. He saw the image of the Wheel manipulating small events, but others being triggered: like a human standing over a trap in which an animal struggled, unaware that a rock had been moved to fall from the mountain above, generating an avalanche that would sweep the human away. How to put that into words for the three here?

'Dragon is heading under conventional drive towards the Cyberat USER,' he said. 'It will be there in an hour.'

'And then what?' asked Cog. 'U-space disruption doesn't just go away when a USER is shut down. Seems to me that Dragon fucked up and this Wheel will get precisely what it wants.'

'Yes, it seems that way,' was all Angel could reply.

Earth Central

The gravity wave, at its peak, exerted a substantial portion of the gravity of the neutron star that the asteroid orbited. That peak passed through rock and iron like a surface wrenching matter in the opposite direction of its travel, and then releasing it. The asteroid emitted a flash of EMR. Its rock and iron shattered and in some areas melted, and the thing flew apart. The *Cable Hogue*, just a few thousand miles behind the wave it had fired, passed close over the spreading mass of smaller asteroids that were now glowing red. Its own mass had a noticeable pull on them as it then turned sharply, leaving a bright trail from its Laumer engines, and shot away.

Earth Central, viewing what was unfolding through the sensors on every ship present, now turned to the tactical map. Curved surfaces divided up space, chunks of rock were highlighted for specific weapons, while targets were picked out and given imaginary AI that would require specific induction warfare attacks. Others were described as bearing heavy armour, needing U-jump missile attack or a peppering of high penetration railgun slugs. Diana Windermere was not making it easy for the fleet. The map bloomed with weapons trajectories as dreadnoughts opened fire with fusillades of railgun slugs, fission missiles and CTDs. Destroyers complemented this with lancing particle beams. U-jump signatures abounded. Attack ships surged in, formations shifting as the tactical map changed. The spreading asteroid field became a massive firework display. Chunks of rock blew apart, smaller pieces vaporized – appalling energies focused on this one small area of space. It was all over in twenty-three minutes.

'Sloppy,' said Windermere.

A frame appeared on the tactical map highlighting a chunk of asteroid iron the size of a grav-car, which had tumbled beyond one of the imaginary curved surfaces.

'Let's try that again,' she added.

Earth Central now focused the sensors of one dreadnought, some way back from the action, out into the asteroid field. Yes, the two prador watchers were still transmitting. The wartime observation drones possessed brains that were the frozen ganglions of prador second-children. Their shapes were vaguely reminiscent of their old bodies as they clung with armoured legs to small asteroids. Windermere had detected them shortly after her arrival here and EC had ordered her to leave them alone. Sometimes it was a good idea to hide what you were doing. Other times it was a good idea to let a potential enemy know.

Using another part of its extensive mind, EC gazed through some of its own watchers that the prador had doubtless detected, and which the king had doubtless ordered to be left alone. U-signatures generating beyond the prador watch station had just added twenty big, old-style prador dreadnoughts to the reaver force there. While the vessel that had arrived earlier – ten miles of exotic metal armour and advanced weapons packed into a ship like a titanic dogfish egg case – moved in. This ship's name translated as *Kinghammer*. The prador hammer, throughout what might be described as the prador medieval period, had been the prime weapon of choice for creatures with carapaces.

Contact.

EC snapped into the virtuality in adult prador form to gaze upon the king's envoy. 'The king,' said the envoy, 'feels it necessary to remind you that his agreement with you specifies no war craft from the Polity can enter the region of space around the accretion disc. That area is an independent state under the oversight of firstly the haiman Orlandine and secondly the alien entity known as Dragon.'

'I hardly need reminding of this,' said EC. 'But perhaps the king needs reminding that, despite his apparent friendship with Orlandine and the establishment of a prador enclave on Jaskor, under our agreement prador war craft are not allowed into the area either.'

'The king says that both Orlandine and Dragon have been absent so preparatory moves by the Polity are understandable. However, Orlandine has returned.'

'Dragon is absent and the data indicates that it is trapped near the Cyberat world inside USER disruption,' said Earth Central.

'Irrelevant,' stated the envoy.

'It is also pertinent to note that Orlandine is acting outside of her agreed remit.'

'This is true,' said the envoy, 'however, she is also acting within her remit – she is still containing the Jain technology in the disc – therefore the agreement stands: no Polity war craft within the accretion disc independent state.'

'And no prador war craft, either,' EC added.

They both fell silent, and then withdrew from the virtuality at the same time.

Earth Central did not like the situation at all. Orlandine was accelerating her plan to fire a black hole into the disc, a Jain soldier was aiming to blow up the dead sun at the centre of the disc, Dragon was out of the equation and there was a wormship buzzing about somewhere. EC wanted control, full control – delegation was something it did not enjoy. It again considered its plan to seize control of the accretion disc platform AIs via the Ghost Drive Facility on Jaskor. But the moment it took control of those platforms, they would then be classified as Polity war craft, and it would be in breach of the agreement. And the reason for that agreement had not gone away.

The accretion disc was too close to the Kingdom to be under complete Polity control. If it was taken over by the Polity, then the king would have to take actions, though perhaps avoiding full-scale war. Almost certainly those actions would need a Polity response. Jaskor would certainly end up as a cinder and quite possibly other star systems would get involved. EC counted the billions of sentient beings – human, prador and AI – in the vicinity. Calculations then built up of possible outcomes and probable ones. Things would get ugly, and since the Client's rampage through the Prador Kingdom had taken diplomatic relations to a new low, full-scale war could not be ruled out.

'You hesitate,' Diana Windermere sent.

'I calculate,' EC replied.

'Cold calculations,' she opined, cold herself in the high-tech throne she occupied aboard the *Cable Hogue*.

'And I decide,' said EC. 'If the prador jump to the accretion disc you go there too. For now, stand down.'

She smiled without humour. 'I hear and obey.'

Earth Central continued to watch, experiencing doubts it had not had for a very long time.

The Wheel

The wormship writhed together around the soldier, which now possessed a solidity that extended beyond that of normal matter.

Such had been the extreme shifting of mass when the soldier absorbed matter and utilized the caches that it had changed the spin of the icy planetoid they were on. This now looked like an apple with a huge bite taken out of it. The super-soldier rested in a crater five miles deep and twenty wide, its own size having increased to over a mile long. The wormship opened itself up to close around the soldier, before it fired up its distributed grav-engines and pulled the creature away into vacuum. This took all the power it could apply at once, as it slowly heaved itself away from the surface. The soldier was *heavy* – its super-dense form like that of something forged on the surface of a dead star.

The Wheel studied how the soldier had changed itself with something approaching maternal approval. In essence, it had packed as much as possible into its form in the real, in material and processing, without turning itself into something overwhelming. This was, after all, supposed to be a sneak attack to penetrate the accretion disc defence sphere and get it to the central dead star. Really, if it arrived in the form it was capable of attaining, all resistance would be completely obliterated, and the Wheel did not want that at all. A careful balance was required.

Some distance beyond the planetoid, the Wheel put the wormship into U-space. Even this was no easy task because the soldier had substantial U-space drag and its own systems caused interference with the wormship's drive. It was a drawn-out dive into that continuum, the wormship unravelling and stretching as it did so, shimmering out piecemeal.

Within the grey of U-space the wormship reconfigured, and the Jain super-soldier was now outside, clinging to its exterior. Its own drive began meshing with that of the ship, and they both went deeper into that continuum than any Polity or prador ships had ever gone. Hours of subjective time slid by and they passed both into and under a region of USER disruption. Here the wormship unravelled from the soldier, and that disruption snapped the wormship out into the real, while the soldier hurtled on.

'Only the dead have seen the end of war,' were the last words the Wheel heard from its errant child.

The wormship flashed into the real in a loose tangle twenty miles across. Many of its systems were utterly scrambled and its mind, the Wheel, was barely functional. But almost instinctively it began reassembling itself and surveying its surroundings.

It lay far out in the Cyberat system, but not so far out that the light delay prevented it seeing the sphere of Dragon accelerating out from the Cyberat world. But why was it here? Slowly its thinking gained momentum and it remembered the entirety of its plan. So much about the actions of Polity AIs was predictable. So much about how the prador would respond was foreseeable, though less so than in their previous incarnation now they had their new king. However, Dragon was always an outlier.

Seeking information, it had fallen into the trap the Wheel had laid, yet that it would do so had not been in any way certain. Dragon could extrapolate in ways that were alien to both the Polity and the Kingdom, and it could interfere to change the course of events. The present USER disruption would keep it out of the way of the Wheel's current plans, which would soon enough reach their conclusion. But once it cleared, Dragon would be able to interfere once again. It was a danger, a loose cannon, and it ultimately needed to be eliminated.

The Wheel fired a com laser in-system, seeking contact as it used those of its drives still workable to send it hurtling in Dragon's direction, still a dispersed collection of worm-forms. The light minutes passed and the reply eventually arrived.

'We are filled with anticipation,' said the Clade.

Knobbler

The Harding black hole was visible on a gravity map of the system and by its slow evaporation of Hawking radiation. Stray particles and wisps of matter falling in towards it and radiating as they did so also marked its position by their absence beyond its event horizon. But there was nothing spectacular happening, because the hole wasn't sucking anything major inside it. As Knobbler viewed these signs of its existence, he felt that, having not eaten in a while, the thing must be hungry. He would have shivered, if that particular animalistic reaction had been programmed into him.

The work had been progressing well, so fast in fact that even now he saw another heat ejection from the runcible. A jet of plasma fountained out into vacuum from the giant hexagonal frame – a blue-green fumarole that spread as it went and dispersed in a strange metallic aurora. The factory ships had emptied the supply ships, which were even now peeling away from them, firing up drives to take them to a safe distance and then shimmering away into underspace.

'Someone is watching,' said Tagger – an ant-like machine the size of a grav-car. The speciality of this drone had been to rip up prador shells, fast-install a control system and a bomb, and then to send the slaved prador back amongst its own kind to detonate where it could cause the most damage. His job was more prosaic now: data crunching logistics with one part of his mind, but mostly just keeping an eye, or other sensors, on surrounding space.

'There are usually Polity watch stations around black holes,' Knobbler observed.

'This is no watch station,' Tagger replied, and then sent an image feed.

Something hung out there in vacuum. It was a metallic ball about four feet across like a compressed mass of wreckage. Studying the data that came with this feed, Knobbler saw that it consisted of the kind of alloys used in the manufacture of himself and his fellows. It seemed like some detritus spat out by a wartime factory station. Then he noticed that the metals were aerogel folded – a collapsed form – and that there was a heavy signature for wartime meta-materials. Also detectable were sensors, and the kind of distortions that related to U-tech. Further scanning and extrapolation revealed that the ball was in fact three forms tightly wrapped around each other. Then he found one of the heads, out on the surface – like a chrome model of some amphibian.

Knobbler routed through the runcible frame to send an inquiry: 'Who the hell are you?'

'We are so glad you are here,' came back the reply.

'It's fucking Clade!' exclaimed Tagger.

A particle beam immediately lanced out from the runcible, but the image feed showed the ball explode into its three forms, the beam only scoring through where they had been. For a micro-second Knobbler had no idea what Tagger was talking about, but then deep memory surfaced. The Clade was a product of one of the smaller factory stations. The individual units were drones produced as sequestration devices. They had been made to seize control of just about anything by inserting their snakish bodies and spreading nano-fibres and software: prador war machines, ship minds and drones. They could even take over organic life and enslave a prador, just as Tagger had once done with those control systems. But something had gone wrong during production. The minds controlling each of these drones were copies from an experimental intelligence. Even as they came hot out of the matter printers and presses, they were marked for disposal. Individually that would have been no problem, but they linked their minds and formed a swarm intelligence. This swarm AI murdered its way out of the factory station that made it, seized a ship and escaped. Since then it had demonstrated itself capable of controlling Polity machines and humans. No one knew what drove it, why it did the things it did. It was marked 'kill on sight'.

'Happy, happy day!' the three Clade units exclaimed.

The particle beam tracked and two more fired up. One beam nailed a Clade unit which writhed in fire, ablating, then a power supply exploded in its body, cutting it in half.

Over com Knobbler heard deranged laughter, then an emphatic, 'Ouch! That stung!'

The two remaining units abruptly slammed back together and knotted. A beam stabbed at them, but they disappeared in a cloud of sparkles, exclaiming, 'So rude!'

By now Knobbler had made a U-com connection and immediately dumped data into it concerning this encounter.

'I do not like that at all,' said Orlandine.

'Me neither,' said Knobbler. 'You get any data on the Clade from that Jain submind?'

'No, there was nothing.' She paused for a long time in AI terms then added, 'Search locally for anything else odd, but otherwise continue as per plan.'

Knobbler had not expected otherwise, but was now very uneasy. The Clade being here was an extra complication they didn't need, and checking historical files he saw that anything involving the Clade tended to get messy. Perhaps it was just coincidence that they had stumbled on it? Or in its deranged way it was merely interested in what they were doing? Yeah, he would try to convince himself of that.

Two days passed with Tagger on the highest alert, and deep scanning even the smallest wisps of matter in the vicinity, but he found nothing else unusual in the Harding system. At the end of that period, hanging out in vacuum ensconced in his cage control, Knobbler watched the two factory ships detach from the runcible and depart. He then inspected the work. It was all but done now and what remained could be conducted at a distance through the runcible's onboard robots. He watched as the fusion drives of the massive construct winked out precisely on time to the microsecond. Just a little while later, he detected silvery movement as his fellow drones swarmed out of the runcible frame. Many launched from the hull under their own drives, others clambered aboard a variety of smaller vessels and took them out. It looked chaotic, but was all per plan – the drones even in their own vessels departing precisely to the second.

Knobbler now reached out with two of his limbs. He had removed the de-shelling levers and underslung devices like cattle prods from these, replacing them with large data plugs, whose optics routed back into his mind. He inserted these into the requisite sockets in the various interlinked black boxes attached to the cage all around him, which glinted with multi-coloured ready lights. As data flooded his mind he acknowledged that one of his fellows had been right in describing him as the Grinch hanging in the Christmas tree.

He could now read the mass of runcible data and control it absolutely. However, it was still running on the program Orlandine had designed so he just observed. Under its initial momentum the device was heading precisely on course towards the black hole. Already he was reading gravity distortions throughout the frame, but nothing yet that required any field enforcing. Next, precisely on time again, the fusion motors fired in reverse to slow the runcible down.

'The problem,' he remembered Orlandine saying, 'is balance.'

It certainly was. The runcible needed to fall over the black hole, with its field reinforcing fully powered up enough to keep it in one piece to gate the hole through it. However, if it was allowed to just fall, it would be like trying to drop a paper hoop over a spinning rotor. Too many forces were in play: the gravity, the spin of the black hole, errant tidal effects resulting from gravity eddies beyond the event horizon. Like that paper hoop, it needed to be held rigid and pressed over its target precisely in position. The problem with that was that the hole would start putting huge stresses on the runcible. And it could only withstand those for a limited time.

Balance.

The runcible slowed and the strain on it increased. Within just a few hours Knobbler found himself having to make adjustments when these went outside of Orlandine's program. This did not bode well for the future, because it could only get worse.

Field reinforcing kicked in next, to strengthen the runcible beyond the incredible toughness of the meta-materials that formed it. Then came flashes of light and a red glow throughout surrounding vacuum. No matter how carefully they had cleaned up the region of space around the runcible, it was inevitable they would miss some of the detritus produced by its construction. Drifting there were scraps of matter from welding, pressure melding, small blobs of hyperglue, maybe the odd microscopic components from the drones and robots. All these were being twisted and ripped apart as they drew closer to the event horizon of the hole. And, because of their flaring, that horizon was now visible. It wasn't black, but a misty white layer where the matter was being ripped down to the atoms of a plasma, before falling through. *Forever* falling through.

As the runcible progressed, now just a thousand miles out from the hole, more protection became necessary. Just half a second before the program, Knobbler turned on its exterior hardfields. The runcible disappeared under a metallic scaling, burning stored energy at an appalling rate. Hundreds of fusion plants struggled to keep up with the load.

Trike

The feed from Dragon now showed the distant space station drawing closer. Trike occasionally watched but his attention kept straying back to Ruth, who was studying Angel intently. The legate had seated himself on the floor on the other side of the hardfield and was just waiting. What would happen to him now? Most likely Cog would lock him in the hold and then hand him over to the AIs when they got back in the Polity.

'So everything he did, he did while under the control of this Wheel?' Trike muttered to her.

'If we are to believe what he says,' she replied.

'Do you remember what he did to you?'

'Every detail, but he took something away, some emotional component, so it doesn't hurt me.'

'It still hurts me,' Trike observed.

She gazed at him and appeared uncomfortable. He realized that despite the creature's terrible treatment of her, some connection had been made.

'You never could resist the hopeless cases,' he said.

She smiled. 'I just think it must be true that legates are Golem androids that Erebus seized control of and bent to its own ends. If he is returning to being what he was before then is it fair that he ends up being dissected by a Polity forensic AI?'

'One must consider what he was before,' Trike observed. 'Any Golem that ran with Erebus before it took up Jain technology probably had no love of us.'

The artificial intelligences that fled the Polity with Erebus had been leaving to start something new, something free from the albatross that was humanity. That they were then sequestered and turned against the Polity did not change that.

'Something's happening,' said Cog.

Trike felt it a moment later – a tension in the air and then the entire ship shifting. It lurched and the ropey tentacles holding it outside began detaching. They lost their image feed beyond Dragon and were once again in an organic twilight.

'What's happening?' asked Cog, turning to Angel.

'Dragon has the information he requires,' Angel replied. 'He is about to attack that space station and is putting us out of danger.'

Everything outside blurred into motion and Cog's ship was on the move. Grav-plates compensated, but still Trike could feel the drag to one side. Organic walls slid by and then with a thump they were out of Dragon and in vacuum.

'Janus . . .' said Cog.

The ship stabilized and they had a view of Dragon slowly receding, the hole they'd come from knitting closed in its surface. Cog reached into a lower cavity in his chair arm and pulled up a joystick. The flickering glare of thrusters lit up the outside view as he swung the ship away, then Trike felt the slight tugging of a grav-engine kicking in. Dragon continued to recede, but Cog muttered a curse and clicked a button on the joystick. A bigger glare lit up from the fusion drive and the ship surged forwards, bringing the oblate space station into sight beyond Dragon.

'Maybe an idea not to get between the two,' said Trike.

'No, really?' said Cog.

He steadily accelerated his ship, speeding to catch up with and run parallel to Dragon, keeping both objects in sight. Even as they moved closer, Trike could see that another split was appearing on the surface of the sphere pointing towards the station.

Dragon heaved and light glared in that split – the start of a white laser shot reflected off whatever vapours the entity emitted. The laser lit up a hardfield some distance from the station. Almost immediately, that collapsed and the burning star of a melting generator shot from an exit port of the station. Part of the station hull distorted, vapour boiling into space, then exploded outwards under internal pressure, highlighting the white laser as it began cutting inside it.

'Is this a good idea?' asked Ruth. 'Dragon's intention was to put us out of danger.'

Cog glanced at her and shrugged. 'I don't think distance will help if we become a target.'

Next, station weapons replied. Two particle beams drew royal blue lines across space to Dragon, and then railgun slugs flashed on its skin. Dragon belatedly erected its own hardfields, perhaps just to show willing, because the station weapons seemed to have no effect on its hide. The station was outmatched, Trike realized. This would not last long.

Dragon's second laser strike carved another hole, and a blast inside peeled up a great chunk of the station's hull. Venting atmosphere, the thing began to turn as if to present fresh areas for destruction. The beam carved a trench, then flicked back to hit the same spot and held there till it stabbed straight through the station and out the other side. As this happened, thousands of silvery objects fled out into space, like silverfish spilling from a grain sack. These swirled around the station then shot towards Dragon, travelling incredibly fast.

'That's the Clade,' said Cog, bringing up a frame to show one of the things writhing through vacuum. Trike stared at the feed, uncomfortably reminded of the hallucinations he had recently experienced.

From around the split in its hide, Dragon fired a shifting and probing mass of particle beams. Every single unit of the Clade was a target; Trike focused his attention on the frame showing just one of them, as the beam struck. Except it didn't – it passed straight through the Clade unit as if it wasn't there. The thing then just faded out of existence. Returning his attention to the main image he saw the shoal seem to shift position as it now drew even closer to Dragon.

'What just happened there?' he asked.

'Ghost chaff and chameleonware,' explained Cog. He peered down at his console, then up at the screen as a frame opened along the bottom showing a data stream. 'The fuck?' The ship bucked and Trike caught hold of his chair arms as the impact lifted him up out of it. A glare opened up to one side and he felt the drag as the view slid away. Burning debris struck the screen as three distinct hard impacts resounded through the ship.

'Hull incursion,' said the ship's AI, Janus, matter-of-factly. A second later the lights flickered and the two particle cannons jutting up from the floor powered down and dipped. Hard, fast rattling movement resounded all around them and something thumped – a low deep detonation within the ship. The rear door of the bridge buckled, spewing smoke around its frame. This smoke was then sucked back out and Trike's ears popped as atmospheric pressure dropped. He looked round, seeing Angel lurching to his feet, the hardfield separating them flickering for a second, then going out. The ship lurched again and began shuddering like a faulty engine. Grav began fluctuating as Trike pulled himself up out of his chair.

'Damn!' Cog released the joystick and stared at it. 'They're screwing everything!'

'Cog?' Trike stepped towards Angel, unsteady in the changing grav, hands clenching and unclenching, just as the first Clade unit exploded from the wall.

Trike jumped, the power he exerted leaving a dent in the floor.

He slammed into the unit in mid-air, grabbing it in a hug as his back smashed against the ceiling. The thing coiled around him as they fell, hooping its sharp pointed tail up beside his head. It stabbed down at him, the spike going in below his collar bone and deep into his chest. He grabbed hold of its body, but could feel the spike ripping through his lungs as he closed his other hand on its head and tried to hold on. It was like wrestling with a mobile hawser. Struggling, they hit the floor and bounced, Trike coughing purple blood with its load of viral fibres. Debris flew through the air. Another of the Clade crashed up through the floor, but this one did not come out all the way before a big meaty hand closed around its neck.

'Mess up my ship?' Cog bellowed. 'You fucker!'

He then proceeded to smash its head against the floor. Grav went off completely, maybe from the damage he was causing. Cog began to rise from the floor but reached down with his other hand, dug his fingers into the metal, and continued to smash the amphibian head. As Trike fought the unit in his grip, he saw Ruth drifting – some piece of debris hitting her shoulder and sending her spinning. The third unit ripped off the back door and came in headfirst at her waist, grabbing her with its head tentacles. As they tumbled through the air its body hooked up and round, the sharp point of its tail hovering just up from her head, moving slightly from side to side as it sought the perfect target beside her neck. Trike fought furiously to free himself of his opponent as she tried to fend off her attacker and escape the spike, but it stabbed down. Then Angel crashed into her and the three of them hit the forward screen. The android reached up blindingly fast and gripped the thing higher up. He wrenched and tore, snapping the unit's spine.

Trike felt metal giving under the pressure of his hand, and groaned in pain as he started to pull the spike from his body. The thing was moving inside him, tearing him up. Also, what breath he had was leaving his body in one continuous exhalation. Through the forward screen, space was misting as the ship shed its atmosphere. Chunks of crash foam also swirled out there, then a moment later pieces of it filled the bridge like spindrift. He turned head over heels, finally managing to extract the spike. Something shattered inside the Clade unit's head and it went limp. He discarded the thing, kicked off from the floor and launched himself at Ruth, catching her arm. He looked into Angel's black eyes briefly as the android pulled her Clade attacker away, then grav came back on and they all fell hard to the floor.

Crash foam now mushroomed from the hole in the wall, hardening. Trike carried Ruth over to his chair which, like the others, had automatically issued a breather mask. She was rigid, her hands shaking. He grabbed the mask and slapped it over her face. Her hand came up to it and she stared at him with those black eyes. Her nose was bloody and she had blood in her ears, as well as around her mouth.

It was the air pressure . . .

He himself could feel the lack of air and the low pressure, but it was simply uncomfortable. A hooper like him could survive vacuum for many minutes. He could even be revived after being vacuum dried and frozen, though what would be recovered would not necessarily be human. However, the greatest danger to him was the injury the unit had inflicted. The wound was closing and the damage inside him doubtless healing, but already he could feel something hardening in his tongue. He ignored this and looked at Ruth again.

Why was there so much blood?

18

Cold Robots: When human beings augment or enhance their mental abilities with augs, gridlinks, neural laces, haiman tech or any of the other technologies and hardware available, they become colder and less human. Or at least this is what popular fiction would have you believe. Yet the capacity for emotion has for a long time been included in the structure and programming of our AIs. So why do humans feel they are losing it the closer they come to that state? Because this is another one of those memes that persist like a stubborn virus in human consciousness, spread, as ever, by confirmation bias, apocryphal stories, lies and stubborn stupidity. It is also a self-fulfilling prophecy. Those who upgrade their minds often mistake the clarity and their venture onto higher intellectual planes for emotional coldness, because that is what they expected. It is a strange dichotomy when the haiman woman, as she steadily upgrades herself, turns into an icy goddess, while war drones – those thoroughly efficient killers in the prador/human war – grow in wisdom and expand their emotional response to the universe. While the goddess contemplates higher mathematics, the war drone considers making additions to its body that will enable it to get giggly on malt whisky.

From 'How It Is' by Gordon

The Client

The creature – the portion of herself the Client detached – was something no member of the Species had ever grown before, to

385

her recollection. But the Jain had probably created such things because she had used the forbidden data to make it. The thing was like an Earth centipede possessing twelve legs. Extra segments sitting between the legs contained armament, shields and scanning gear, while coiled up on either side of each were triangular-section tentacles. There was no head as such – one end looked no different from the other. As it dropped from the crystal tree and rattled around its base, the Client inserted her perspective inside it. Looking up at her primary form, she felt a strange mix of potency and vulnerability as she automatically calculated targeting solutions on it. She then turned away and scuttled over to the hatch opening in the base of the environment cylinder.

She moved at great speed through the station until she came to the war dock attached to the moon. A moment later she was down in the dock itself and the iris door at the further end was opening. She shot through it into a store in the library very like the one from which she had stolen the forbidden data. Some of the pillars had toppled, others had shattered, and the smoking remains of defence drones littered the place – destroyed by the armaments at the end of the war dock.

Meanwhile, her primary form was at work, scanning down into the moon, cutting with lasers, particle beams and shaped charges. Everything was shuddering around her and another data pillar fell over with a ringing crash. She darted over towards a circular door, folded out a nacelle and fired one missile. It exploded against the door, blew it into the tunnel beyond and she followed it through. In her primary form, she continued to use platform weapons to rip open areas and destroy defences. A great explosion blew out the roof of a chamber on the surface, and a particle beam stabbed down from one of her attack pods, melting through the floor. She moved on.

More tunnels, more data storage chambers, then narrow shafts leading deeper down into the moon. Linked to her primary form, she kept updating and finally fell into the chamber she was looking for. Here she had missed a cache of the moon's drones – the coin-shaped things flying up the shaft she was descending. They immediately opened fire, hitting her with dense beads of metallic hydrogen that exploded on impact. A series of detonations blew her squirming against one wall, but even as she was hit she chose the first targeting solution. She extruded hollow tubes from her mid-segments and locked on target, as she shot forwards again, returning fire with her own super-dense beads. Drones exploded one after another, flinging armoured plates in every direction. She fell through the debris and into a wide chamber where thousands of the things were swarming. Around the edges of this chamber tunnels led off into the moon and one of them would take her to where she wanted to go. But instead she accelerated straight into the main mass of drones.

Destroying drones all around her, and disappearing herself in a cloud of explosions, the Client uncoiled her tentacles and snared two of the drones. With her outer skin burned away, two legs missing and underlying silver armour glowing in places, she dropped out of the swarm. Her tentacle tips melded perfectly with triangular indents on the drones and she injected nano-fibres, as well as decoding tubules into their workings. Their minds were hardly even sub-AI and their programming was simple too. In a moment, she had the data she needed and, discarding the drones, emitted an EMR data flash. All firing ceased at once and the drones began flying in tight circles that reflected the looped program running in their minds.

'Now we can speak,' said the Librarian.

Hitting the floor hard and skittering towards the tunnel she required, the Client had a moment of trepidation. The Librarian had taken something from her brief link to the drones to enable it to communicate directly. She isolated the laser com it was using, routing it through detectors for informational warfare. Strangely there was none – just the words.

'We have nothing to discuss,' she replied.

Now pausing before the tunnel mouth, she peered up at the cloud of drones. In just a moment she formulated a new program, put warfare beams on three of the drones and transmitted it. The three reacted first by retransmitting the program, then dropped out of the swarm, and burned out their receivers. Within a minute the other drones began dropping too, to spear off into the surrounding tunnels. The drones had rendered themselves incapable of being reprogrammed. They would now attack all defensive mechanisms in the library, while transmitting data to her on all surrounding systems.

'You must delete the forbidden data,' said the Librarian. 'And you must give me access to ensure its removal from your mind.'

'I will not,' replied the Client. But there seemed no consciousness behind the Librarian's demands – almost as if some old and long-out-of-date program was speaking to her. This seemed to confirm her earlier conjectures. The ancient Jain hidden deep in the moon had completely lost its grip on reality. The thing was senile.

The drones heading off in front of her alerted her to the robot coming down the tunnel some seconds before she picked up on it with her sensors. Explosions lit the way ahead and smoking debris bounced in the tunnel. The robot was an octahedron with weapons circlets on each of its eight faces. It slid forward over the remains of five coin drones, its armour smoking and dented as it turned one face towards her and stabbed out with a pure green particle beam. It tracked her, boiling grooves out of the tunnel wall as she dodged from side to side and hurtled towards it. A series of hits on her forward segment had it smoking and began to eat through the armour. The thing turned, presenting another face, and began rail-ing dense slugs into her. Then she was on it.

'I am your father,' said the Librarian.

That was new. Some thought operating now?

'And I am your only child,' the Client replied as she grabbed and writhed around the machine, keeping her body away from the weapons circlets. However, one circlet extruded an arm with a sticky grab and tried to drag her in front of the railgun. Unrav-elling tentacles, she groped for access but could find none. She then allowed the arm to grip her body and, once it was firm, used the dense artificial muscle in her main body to heave to one side. The arm tore out, and she speared a tentacle in through its circlet and searched within.

There . . .

'You must obey,' said the Librarian.

There seemed no point in responding.

In a moment, she engaged in another triangular socket and slid quickly into the robot's mind. This one was more complex than that of the coin-shaped drones. It slammed against the tunnel wall trying to crush or dislodge her as she burned out parts of its mind, seized control of others and input the same program she had used on the coin drones. When she released, it just swung away from her and headed off down the tunnel ahead. She paused, shook herself, then, with a crunch, detached her forward segment and dropped it, its two legs kicking as its power died. Then she moved on.

'You created my kind, then you regressed us to primitivism and dumped us on our home world,' said the Client. 'When we climbed out of the mud and found you, again you gave us infor-mation, yet forbade us knowledge of our history. Why did you even allow us to know that this history existed?'

The tunnel wound on and on. She came upon the remains of

389

the octahedral machine at the lip of a wide shaft, which speared down into the moon. The remains of autoguns hung broken and melted from the walls, while rocky debris fell from above. She moved to the lip, then rapidly back as high-intensity lasers struck the edge. Defensive weapons all the way down, she had no doubt.

'Sometimes I did not forbid it,' said the Librarian. 'And you always regressed.'

This gave the Client pause, for it now seemed a thinking being had spoken to her, not a hard-wired, senile creature parroting the responses it had used for millennia. She considered what this meant, in light of what she now knew. In the allowed history of the Species there had been periods when their civilization collapsed back into primitivism – the last being two million years in the past. This time had been debated amongst the Species and the consensus had been that it was due to an asteroid strike. Was that consensus wrong? It seemed that the Librarian meant they had become more like their ancestors, the Jain, before such periods. In her knowledge of the forbidden history those periods were just blank. So then –

'What happened on those occasions?' she asked.

'It was necessary to reset the experiment,' the Librarian replied.

'And how did you do that?'

An explosion above dropped tons of rubble into the shaft, falling in slow motion in the low gravity.

'Extermination and reseeding the initial design,' the Librarian replied.

The Client froze as she absorbed this information. It was a hard reminder that the thing below, crazy and different from its own kind as it was, was still one of the Jain. She wondered then about that asteroid strike. Was that how it 'reset the experiment'?

'And now all my doubts have gone,' she said.

Looking up, she watched the attack pod descending, its sides grazing the edges of the shaft. It fell past her, two particle beams emitting from the packed hardware found between its opened outer shells, the beams tracking round as they destroyed every defence below. She followed it down.

Trike

The air pressure was rising, but a normal human would still be unconscious now and suffering from all kinds of ruptures throughout their body. However, even though Ruth was no hooper, she did possess a nanosuite which ran inside her. And, really, a normal human was something that had ceased to exist centuries ago. Trike looked towards the bridge door and saw a shimmershield across the gap. Through it he could see smoke swirling and a glow of hot metal. He next regarded the alert messages scrolling along the bottom of the screen, then the damage in the bridge, trying to ignore flitting shadows he knew were not there. Trying to ignore something else that was screaming for his attention.

'I think you killed it, Cog,' he said, his tone strangely flat in the low air pressure.

Cog was on his knees clutching a tangled mass of scrap he seemed ready to smash against the floor again. He looked at it, frowned and discarded it, then stood up. Angel was squatting on the floor, the third attacker in pieces all around him. He was holding its head, and studying it intently, while the tentacles were writhing weakly. After a moment, he stabbed a long pointy finger into its remaining eye, reamed it around a bit then extracted it. The tentacles slumped. He discarded the head and stood, brushing his hands together.

Trike returned his attention to Ruth. Her mask was full of

blood. When he pulled it from her face to wipe the blood away from her mouth, her hand just dropped away. She was still looking at him. She was okay. His gaze strayed down to her body. Her clothing was soaked with blood and the stub of the tail of her Clade attacker protruded from above her collar bone. He realized that Angel had done the right thing in breaking it off there. She was no hooper and pulling the thing out would have caused further damage she could not survive.

'We're not the only ones with problems,' said Angel, pointing at the screen.

Trike focused unsteadily back on the screen where a frame had opened again. It was better to look there – to look away from what he had just seen. Dragon was in trouble. He could see explosive ejections all around its surface and its skin was rippling, sometimes opening in places to shoot out masses of pseudopods. There was no sign of the Clade and he had no doubt that it was inside the big alien, causing all he could see. But also, there was something else. A net was falling through midnight down towards Dragon. Though its structure was spread out, he recognized the wormship at once.

But then something hit the wormship – an explosion amidst its dispersed mass.

'What was that?' he wondered dully, trying to stay in the moment.

'No idea,' said Cog.

Trike had no ideas either. Nothing seemed to be working in his mind.

'Trike.' It was Cog again, standing at his shoulder.

Trike looked up, and both Cog and Angel were standing close by, watching him. 'We need to get her to the infirmary,' he said. He felt cold, really cold.

Cog looked round at Angel who shook his head. 'Through her heart.'

Trike heard the words but they made no sense. He focused on Angel. 'You can revive her. You can fix her.'

Angel spread his hands. 'If I was aboard my wormship.'

Trike returned his attention to Ruth. Her black eyes looked false now – like those of a doll. He carefully fixed the elasticated strap of the mask around her head, then pressed a control behind the chair. A small, high-pressure oxygen cylinder, attached to the line, was ejected into his hand. He inserted this into her top pocket and picked her up. She was utterly limp. In a moment, he was pushing through the shimmershield and breathing smoke. Fire boiling up beside the stairway scorched his trousers, but even as he passed the flames air loss was killing them. The next moment he was gazing into the wrecked infirmary. Nothing seemed real any more.

A hand tugged on his arm. He hadn't even been aware that Cog was with him. The Old Captain was mouthing something but he couldn't hear. Finally, woodenly, he followed him. With hot twisted metal around him, he found himself standing in a room in which four coffin-sized cylinders were fixed in a rack. Cog slid one out on rails.

His arms were empty. Where was Ruth?

Angel was carrying her and then lying her down in an open cold coffin. Numb, and suddenly feeling weaker than he had ever felt, he stepped over. Pipes like small snakes were writhing around her, attaching like leeches . . . A giggle rose inside him, but then faded away. The coffin closed and Cog slid it back into the rack.

A hand, tugging on his arm again. He stood as immovable as a rock for a moment, but then turned and went where Cog led. He knew he could not stay here. His injury plus the lack or air would do him no good at all. He would do the sensible thing and return to the bridge, while he still had the ability to think coherently.

He knew that would not last.

Blade

Cog's ship was moving away from the action. It had been hit hard and was trailing debris, but the Clade units that had attacked had not reappeared, so Blade guessed they had run afoul of the two hoopers aboard. Whether Cog and the others had survived was questionable, but Blade did not have the option to find out because its priorities did not include a rescue operation. Still accelerating, its own target chosen, Blade now damned the USER disruption that prevented it from using jump missiles. Still, it had plenty of other weapons available – that near-c railgun strike it had delivered had certainly stirred up the wormship. The only problem was the vessel's dispersion. Only one of ten railgun slugs had found a target.

Particle beam . . .

This would allow ranging but would also pinpoint the *Obsidian Blade* for the wormship. Was that a good idea? Blade decided it was and opened up, dropping its chameleonware at the same time to reveal its sleek, black form. Scanning revealed that the wormship's dispersion presently disabled a lot of its heavier weapons and shields, so this attack had to be quick and effective. The royal-blue beam stabbed out across thousands of miles of vacuum, struck a section of worm and cut along it, winnowing out its glittering interior. It tracked across, tearing apart other sections, wraiths of fire and tinsel-like debris exploding in every direction. In response, the wormship slowed in its descent on its primary target – Dragon – and began to draw itself back together.

Blade next released a series of missiles, slower than railgun slugs or energy weapons, as it continued to hurtle in, then directed scanning towards Dragon. The entity's defences had collapsed, which was perhaps the purpose of the Clade invasion of its body. Blade could now see more than Dragon usually allowed. The units of the swarm AI were spread throughout its immense spherical interior, like parasitic flukes in a body packed with strut bones and tangled masses of organs. Flares of heat and explosive blisters marked their course as they wreaked havoc and fought a running battle with Dragon's internal defences. Even as Blade watched, a series of internal explosions wiped out five of the strange robots.

'Can I assist?' Blade enquired.

An instant later it received a targeting solution on Dragon, indicating areas within its body and detailing the weapons to be used. As Blade put a blue high-penetration laser online, it saw areas on the entity's surface opening up, scales sliding aside like screen doors. Blade fired, probing inside Dragon. The beam licked out time and again, vapour boiling out of the holes, and eight Clade units encysted in Dragon's flesh broke apart and burned. Two railgun slugs followed into another area, impacting on a structural bone, and the explosion they caused blew five units out through a hole on Dragon's surface. Here pseudopods rose up about the rim of the hole, cobra heads turning like autoguns, and hit the units with milky-orange particle beams, vaporizing them.

'Now draw off the wormship,' Dragon sent.

'You can't handle it?'

'I cannot.'

Dragon began moving then – a sudden surge of acceleration directly towards the sun. Meanwhile, the wormship was half-way to its coagulated state and intercepting Blade's attacks with hardfields. Concentrating on one area with a fusillade of railgun slugs filled space with fire over hardfields, but also caused long fuse-like explosions in sections of the wormish body. The worm-ship slowed further, then abruptly changed course, heading straight towards Blade.

'Okay,' Blade sent, 'that got your attention.'

Blade analysed the attack and its results, along with logistics concerning Dragon's known armament. It seemed likely that the wormship had needed to attack Dragon in dispersed form, while the Clade was weakening it internally. In coagulated form, it would be subject to a high-powered white laser shot that would probably fry its systems. But it could not conduct its dispersed attack while Blade was out there burning up its structure. Blade had completely defused its attack, which was supposed to have been a surprise one, and now, accelerating hard, the wormship was obviously pissed off.

'Come and play,' Blade sent.

The wormship replied with a particle beam blast that Blade took on its shields. Four hardfield projectors shot from ejection ports and the *Obsidian Blade* tumbled through vacuum on the blast wave. Induction warfare then hit, scrambling systems so an ensuing blue laser carved into Blade's forward section.

'Damn!'

Blade began weaving and looked around. It needed a foil and the nearest was Dragon itself. While dodging, the attack ship swung round, matching Dragon's course and having to use nearly everything it had to catch up. The wormship swung in behind and Blade dropped mines in its path, then chaff, while changing course slightly to bring it towards Dragon. Acceleration contin-ued, until all three ships were nearly up to half light speed. A particle beam fired by the wormship oozed out in slow motion and struck a hardfield. It then winked out as the wormship hit the first mines. Three detonations, one on top of another, lost it behind a scaling of hardfields. It came through this flare with actinic fuse-wire burning throughout its structure. But a moment later the particle beam licked out again.

Dragon, meanwhile, was having its own problems. A great explosion inside the entity peeled up a square mile of its armour, blowing out a mass of its innards, smoking in vacuum and sprinkled with coiled-up Clade units. Whether this was intentional on Dragon's part Blade did not know. Things were heating up. Vapour issued from the holes in Dragon's armour while Blade's cooling systems had kicked in. Perhaps it should try something new . . .

Blade began opening U-jump splinter missiles on its surface and shedding loads of anti-matter canisters, chemical explosives and thermo-nuclear devices, while onlining another weapons system. Strewing this lethal load behind it, Blade waited long minutes, and shed five more hardfield projectors, before activating the weapon. The gravity wave hit the anti-matter canisters just as the wormship reached them. The detonation was immense, its glare wiping out even that of the sun that now loomed huge ahead. Hardfields cycled in this fire and, as it went out, the wormship fuse-wire burned again, while shedding half its mass like flash-burned rope. This all spread out from the central coagulation as it writhed and knotted into something smaller.

'Shed heat as plasma,' Dragon instructed. 'Your U-jump missiles.'

The entity had changed course, not heading directly into the sun but at a tangent. It looked like it was aiming to swing round, but almost in the thermosphere. Blade began converting heat through thermo-couples and superconducting networks, converting stored hydrogen to plasma. It compressed it into the load compartments of its splinter missiles.

'One-time shot,' Dragon added. 'On my mark.'

Blade splintered up its missiles and targeted the wormship, but with no hope of actually hitting it with the present U-space disruption.

'Now,' said Dragon.

A pulse issued from deep inside the entity – a spreading wave through the local gravity map. Blade fired its missiles and saw them taken by that wave's effect in U-space. In the instant of perception most of the missiles just disappeared in surrounding disruption, but some got through.

And arrived on target.

The wormship detonated, flying apart and burning, a spreading cloud of burned rope debris. Blade studied this for a second, hardly believing the thing was gone, then returned its attention to Dragon.

'You need to pull up,' it said, applying grav-engines at full power to haul itself up out of its fall into the sun. 'Correct your course.'

'Now, I cannot,' said Dragon, as the steady pull of the sun took it.

As Blade fought to clear the thermosphere it felt a sudden surge of rage as it saw Clade units abandoning Dragon like a huge shoal of fish darting from a brain coral. The units slammed together in one silvery writhing mass, and planed up out of the thermosphere impossibly fast.

Dragon continued on down.

Orlandine

Orlandine, ensconced in her interface sphere aboard her ship the *Cytoxic*, could possess the patience of a drone able to manipulate its perception of time. Only she wasn't able to do it. Every time she tried to put herself into that waiting state she dropped out of it again and began calculating probabilities, reviewing logistics.

But there was nothing more she could do. The runcible was travelling down the axis of the accretion disc's spin, warded all around by fifty weapons platforms. The other platforms and their attack pods were as ready as they could ever be – a state they had duteously maintained throughout their existence.

Then everything changed.

Indicted space all about the accretion disc was scattered with detectors, a pseudo-matter portion of which dipped into underspace to monitor it constantly. One of these, out from the rim and just ten light minutes from the *Cytoxic*, detected an object approaching through that continuum. It shot a U-com signal at another object holding a position in U-space. That object imploded, emitting a pulse that caused a momentary disruption, like something pinching a stretched rubber sheet. This was enough to fling the object out into the real.

It appeared adjacent to Weapons Platform Aleph. Just a moment later, a series of twelve detonations across vacuum marked the spots where Aleph's attack pods blew up. Then the soldier appeared, travelling at three-quarters light speed.

So this is the enemy, thought Orlandine. Her assessment was cold and logical, the fact of the soldier's arrival just slotting into her calculations. Via sensors aboard Aleph, she studied the thing.

The soldier was a mile long and looked vaguely like a giant hoverfly with its wings folded. Scanning in the electromagnetic spectrum merely revealed its outer appearance – the mechanisms tangling its surface like some metallic growth of lichen. However, on the gravity map of the system, it made a substantial dent, while in U-space it was an inversion, like a planetary body, but with odd twists and channels spearing off into that realm.

'Fire at will,' was Orlandine's only verbal instruction, while logistics and analyses flashed between weapons platforms.

First to strike the soldier was a high-powered particle beam, as with any unexpected arrival in the indicted zone. This splashed against the curved meniscus of a hardfield, while the thing spewed a long line of dense spheres, each the size of a human head. It then short-jumped, immediately ricocheting back into the real when Aleph hit it with a USER pulse, but closer to the platform. The fusillade of U-jump missiles the platform fired at it had no effect – disappearing through some internal gate. The spheres disappeared shortly afterwards, one after another, short-jumping to materialize over more of Aleph's attack pods. They detonated, flinging out gravity waves which smashed into the pods, buckling them and hurling out clouds of debris.

Aleph replied with a gravity wave of its own. The soldier bucked and shot along this wave, leaving a trail of fire, then jumped again. Aleph opened fire with all its weapons, filling intervening space with railgun slugs, and complementing this with a USER pulse. The soldier ricocheted out into the real, tumbling, then fired down with an energy beam like a glass rod. This struck Aleph's hardfields and began boring through them, while the platform spewed projectors. Finally, the beam punched through and hit the platform, carving along it like a knife tip over polystyrene – debris rose into vacuum.

More weapons platforms began to jump in. Two came first, then a third, which hit a USER pulse emitted by the soldier, causing it to materialize, bent out of shape, and trail fire – a giant gyrating mass of technology as large as a city. More platforms appeared. One that was out of control clipped another, smashing away spaceship-sized debris. But hundreds of particle beams intersected on the soldier – a concentration of energy that could have fried a small moon. The soldier disappeared inside the burning sphere of an impossible spherical hardfield. In her view of U-space, Orlandine saw the inversion, which marked the soldier's relative position, turning in some strange way. It then snapped back, and the thing lost its hardfield and jumped just a few miles. It issued three of its own beams which were much the same hue as those Dragon used. These ate up railgun slugs on their course to Aleph. Again, hardfield projectors burned out and the beams punched through. They struck the platform hard, hot fires revealed through the surrounding structure, and they speared right through to the other side.

'Just keep hitting it,' Orlandine instructed, noting the AI ejecting from the platform that had been mangled by its U-jump – a cylindrical canister hurtled out away from the defence sphere. Next, causing their own local disruption in U-space, another ten platforms jumped in and opened fire on the soldier. Particle beams struck, forcing it to use its spherical hardfield again, then U-jump missiles appeared just outside of this and detonated. In U-space Orlandine saw the soldier's inversion turning further. Next, seemingly close to the limit of that twist, of U-space storage, it dropped its hardfield once more and this time absorbed the full energy of the particle beams for a microsecond, before jumping again.

'Bloody hell,' said Aleph.

'Yes,' was all Orlandine said.

Nothing should have survived those beams, even for a microsecond.

Again, a USER pulse forced the soldier into the real. It had shed mass and was glowing like something extracted from a furnace.

'And again,' Orlandine instructed unnecessarily.

The mass of weapons platforms jumped, bringing them within thousands of miles of the soldier. Four of them came out of U-space bent out of shape, while a fifth materialized in an explosion of debris. The remainder opened fire, particle beams intersecting on the soldier again with an appalling amount of energy. At the intersection point, particulates spread in a fusion cloud that remained for some time, even after the soldier managed to withstand shutting down its hardfield and jumped yet again. Meanwhile, Orlandine was scanning heavily and knew that this was what the soldier had been doing too. She saw in U-space it was drawing a larger amount of energy for its next jump, and it was taking the tactical course the movement of the platforms had presented: it would head for a gap that had opened up in the defence.

The soldier reappeared within view of the optical arrays of the *Cytoxic*. It paused in space then, spewing multiple tails of fusion fire, and began heading in towards the accretion disc on conventional drive. It had no choice: though the particle beams had yet to reach it, USER pulses had done so. A second later it hit a minefield dropped by the platform that had abandoned this position, and disappeared inside a series of actinic explosions. It came out of these inside its spherical hardfield. Just a second after that, forty platforms arrived between it and the disc and opened fire. Then others followed, ramping up the firepower to something that had not been seen since the Polity war with the prador.

'Now,' she said, 'you have eight minutes before the energy levels get too high . . .'

She could see the underlying twist steadily turning as the hardfield, glaring like a blue sun, routed power away into U-space. But then the unexpected happened. The hardfield suddenly gained motive power, somehow sliding over the surface of space and through vacuum, faster and ever faster. It wasn't heading into the accretion disc but at a tangent. Orlandine could not understand the purpose of this since it did not decrease the intensity of fire, until she saw something looming ahead, dark against the star field.

Musket Shot . . .

The soldier fell towards the leaden planetoid and finally slammed into its surface, blowing out a crater twenty miles across. USER disruption issued from that point – either some effect of the impact or deliberate concealment, because Orlandine lost her view of U-space. The moment this happened Orlandine entertained doubts. Perhaps this had been the soldier's first intended destination all along? No. The thing had aimed for a stealthy penetration to begin with, so had come in minimalized form. She was overthinking this – she had to stick with her plan.

As a mushroom cloud of fire rose from the impact, Orlandine noted a perceptible alteration in the planetoid's course. The weapons platforms continued firing at the impact site, pumping appalling amounts of energy at the soldier. Orlandine watched a steady glow spreading out from that point and massive eruptions from the surface. A moment later, railgun slugs began to impact, punching glowing craters and throwing up more clouds of debris. By degrees, Musket Shot disappeared under this cloud.

'Keep firing,' she instructed, then noted it was a pointless order now she could only use the slow drag of laser communications. The platform AIs knew what to do anyway.

Musket Shot soon became a glowing ball swathed in cloud. Its radiation kept on increasing and it was soon boiling like a small sun. Surely by now the soldier had taken its energy store to its limit . . .

A blast down on the surface, brighter than the light of a hypergiant, opened an actinic blue eye and threw a chunk out of the planetoid like a large bite from an apple. A great fumarole of debris spewed out a hundred miles long, webbing space with molten lead and fire wraiths. In chaotic U-space, a wave spread out and dispersed.

'Cease firing,' Orlandine instructed as she watched the planetoid deform and reshape, completely molten now and collapsing back into spherical form. Finally, the particle beams playing over the surface began to go out, but the impacts from railgun slugs went on for much longer. Some hours later, forcing her ship's systems to their limit to breach the settling disruption of U-space, Orlandine jumped the *Cytoxic* near to the moon. Scanning its surface, she saw only rivers of molten lead running amidst the slower roil of liquid rock. There was no sign of the soldier.

19

As Gordon has asked, 'What is death when the most horrendous physical damage can be repaired, minds can be recorded and bodies regrown from a scrap of DNA?' He then notes that, 'Death remains that place from which no one returns. Ever.' But we unenhanced humans are fast machines for slow genes. Our thinking is linear, and our reactions reflect that. Unless we have undergone substantial augmentation and reprogramming, we cannot react to the death of an AI in the same way as to that of a fellow human. Even now, the destruction of some remote lump of crystal, or the termination of a disembodied voice, does not elicit commensurate grief no matter that it might be a centuries-old, wise and good being. We react more to the death of AI only if it is embodied, to the death of a war drone friend, but even more so to the deaths of Golem or human-shaped avatars. Death for us is only real if it is physical, animal, and about us. It is also the case that we cannot suppress grief when a close human dies, even if we know they possess a memplants and that their DNA is on file. It's deep programming and difficult to eradicate because evolution did not prepare us for eternity and, in reality, no religion ever truly prepared us for resurrection.

From 'Quince Guide' compiled by humans

Trike

Frames open in the screen laminate gave them a perfect view of the action as they fled it. His hand clamped on the back of a

405

bloody chair, Trike eyed the silvery, writhing mass rising up and away from the sun, and felt tension climbing throughout his body. He glanced around the bridge again at the wreckage of the three Clade units that had attacked them and knew that if that whole mass came after them, they would not survive it. Yet he wanted them to attack – he wanted to lose himself to that violence. It seemed the Clade was all he had left to direct his anger towards now the wormship was gone. He then forced himself to focus on Angel, standing before the shimmershield across the doorway into the rest of the ship and peering through.

'Janus, what's the damage?' asked Cog, slumped in his throne. There was no reply.

'Janus?' Cog waited for a moment, then swung his console across and opened another frame to show the emergency data in full. 'Fusion engine is offline,' he said flatly. 'Main grav-drive and steering thrusters down too, but I can't tell what the damage is. We've lost hull integrity but, luckily, we still have the reactor and enough air.'

'And?' Trike asked. Shadows were flickering round him, and he felt as if the walls were crawling with leeches. But he could hang on. Ruth was in a cold coffin and could be revived. She was not far from him; she would never be far from him. He could sense the U-mitter in her skull.

'Janus is dead,' said Cog, and he turned to Angel. 'Dragon?'

Angel looked round. 'It has gone from my mind.'

'Right,' interjected Cog. 'No help there. And none from *Obsidian Blade* either.'

'*Obsidian Blade*?' Trike repeated.

Cog gestured to the screen frame showing the Clade. He magnified the image and it revealed a shard of black following the swarm AI – the vessel that had destroyed the wormship. 'That's the black-ops attack ship that was following me. It arrived too late at Angel's base and was tardy here.' He grimaced. 'Obviously it didn't see fit to let me know it was here and is now trailing the Clade, which looks set on a course out-system.'

'You would think it would come to see if you're alive,' said Trike, looking down at the bloody chair. So much blood.

Cog shrugged. 'Priorities. It's going after the larger danger to the Polity.'

'So, you find yourself on the blunt end of that.' Trike felt anger suddenly surging up inside him. 'Those that work for the Polity put threats to it as a whole before mere individual lives.' He snapped his mouth shut. He could feel grooves in his tongue. Closing his eyes, he fought for control. As attractive as it felt to let himself go, that would not help Ruth at all.

'Not quite,' Cog snapped. 'It's all about numbers. Cold calculations. If Blade comes to us it will lose the Clade, and the Clade is capable of, and probably inclined to, kill thousands . . . if not more.' When Cog paused for thought Trike found himself taking a pace towards the man, but again forced calm, and tried to listen as Cog continued. 'Angel, a lot of systems are damaged and I'm not getting the data I need. But I do know that here is the only part of the ship that's now pressurized. Hoopers can withstand vacuum, but only for a short while . . .'

Angel nodded. 'I will make an assessment, see if there is anything I can do quickly, then return with space suits.' The android stepped into and through the shimmershield.

Trike watched him go, then, still rigidly under control, moved away from Ruth's chair to sit down in his own. 'What about Dragon?' he asked, wondering whether or not to put the safety strap across – that would at least delay him for a second or two if he started to lose his grip on himself.

'We will see very shortly,' Cog supplied. 'If it doesn't reappear soon then I would say it's gone. It was skimming round in the thermosphere of the sun, which it might be able to survive, but if it's gone right down . . .'

'Then it's ash,' Trike said. 'But I highly doubt it could survive the thermosphere. You saw what it was like inside its armour – it was organic.'

Cog nodded in agreement, then returned his attention to the scrolling alert messages.

'The fusion drive and main grav-engine are offline. I can't assess the damage as yet,' said Angel, speaking from the intercom. 'Your ship AI is floating around in pieces. Steering thrusters were disconnected – I'm re-establishing system links to them and to you now.'

More frames opened on the screen scrolling further data. Glancing at Cog, Trike noticed the Old Captain's grim expression get grimmer.

'Bring us those space suits,' he instructed.

Studying the data himself helped Trike move away from his internal battle, and he shortly understood how bad things were. When he saw Cog accessing data on the ship's other cold coffins he knew that Cog had seen it too.

'How long?' he asked tightly.

Cog glanced at him, then studied him more closely, his eyes narrowing. 'On steering thrusters it will take about thirty-five years to bring us back in orbit around the Cyberat world. Even on fusion, if we can repair the drive, it will take a year.'

'And the Cyberat?'

Cog shook his head. 'You heard Doshane. I doubt he'll be sympathetic.'

'Our reception might be different in thirty-five years, or even a year, maybe,' Trike replied. 'And anyway – the USER disruption here will be over in a few months. Perhaps someone else will come . . .'

'Optimism,' wondered Cog, studying him intently.

Trike shrugged, trying to keep up the façade that he knew Cog had seen through. The chest injury had been bad enough, and the rest . . . he glanced at the bloody chair while something was tittering on the edge of perception. Was the greatest danger to them the failing ship around them, or was it Trike himself?

'And it's back,' said Cog, gesturing to a new screen frame he had opened.

Trike gazed at the glowing sphere rising up out of the thermosphere of the sun, leaving a trail of hot vapour and burning debris. But then his attention drifted back to that chair. Perhaps he should head into the infirmary to see if the autodoc was functional. It wouldn't have been enough for Ruth, he now understood – she needed nerve regrowth and a new heart – maybe he could fry more contents of his skull, though? But then frequent treatments like that destroyed his mind further, and he feared that in doing so he would lose his reasons for remaining sane. Was he fooling himself? No, no . . . he could handle this, so long as he could move; have something to do. He swung round as Angel returned to the bridge carrying two space suits.

'You're still getting nothing from Dragon?' Cog asked the android.

Angel blinked, dropped the suits on the floor then gestured at the image. 'Perhaps during the fight it disconnected from me. Evidently it survived the fire.'

Trike transferred his attention to Cog. 'We can't go to the Cyberat world, and maybe someone will come in the next few months, maybe not. Do we want to be stuck out here for that long?' That was the best he could do. Cog knew what was happening to him.

Cog dipped his head in cautious acknowledgement. He began working his console and a cross-hairs appeared over the rising image of Dragon in the screen frame, vector maths running below it. The ship kicked slightly as steering thrusters fired up in lieu of any better propulsion.

'We should be able to intercept,' he said, 'if it doesn't change course.' He pushed the console aside and stood up. 'Let's suit up and take a look at the damage.'

Orlandine

As the disruption settled, instantaneous communication re-established and at last the platforms and their attack pods could travel through underspace. Five platforms arrived first, just thousands of miles out from Musket Shot. Orlandine, still watching from aboard the *Cytoxic*, ordered in another forty. She was loath to call in more since there was always the possibility that even this soldier's attack had been a diversion, and that something else might try to get through to the accretion disc.

Musket Shot was a glowing misty sphere – completely molten. Now able to access U-space, Orlandine scanned it for U-space distortions or twists and found nothing. But still she could not help but think that she had missed something.

'Too easy,' she commented.

'Easy?' enquired the nearest AI aboard Weapons Platform Ipsalus. A small data package behind that one word listed their losses. Over a hundred attack pods were scrap. Two platforms had been destroyed while two more were seriously out of commission, though recoverable. Every single platform that had been involved in this action had taken damage.

'Musket Shot is perhaps a problem,' Ipsalus added.

As she studied the planetoid via numerous sensors, Orlandine had been coming to a similar conclusion. Prior to the battle with the soldier, she had instructed the platforms to hold off on using some of the larger weapons available to them. A gigaton CTD was effective, but the EMR too disruptive. It would have made losing acquisition of the soldier a possibility. Now she was considering the utility of such a device. Perhaps it was time for this particular planetoid to just go away.

'Something is not right,' commented one of the other platforms, a microsecond before the others, and a microsecond after Orlandine noticed it.

The planetoid was showing no technological emissions and nothing was happening in U-space adjacent to its locale, but it was changing shape. Movement on its surface reminded her of parasitic worms crawling under skin, but growing steadily larger as they did so. At the terminus of one of these a mountain was rising rapidly, soon punching above the vapour cloud around the small world.

'What the hell?' she said – rote words.

Scanning flickered. One moment it showed nothing, the next it revealed structure and complexity. The mountain continued to nose out and behind it the planetoid began to unravel. Orlandine gaped at an object, like an immense moray eel fashioned out of molten lead and rock, as its head rose out into vacuum and tilted. Then came a surge of power. A beam like a glassy rod licked out and traversed. The thing was ten feet wide and it sliced through Platform Ipsalus like a milling bit through a child's toy. Then it went on to the next platform, and the next.

The platforms opened fire again but the beams struck a hardfield that completely wrapped around what Musket Shot had become. Orlandine had time to see the underlying twist hardly shifting at all, before the beam grazed the *Cytoxic* as it traversed to another platform and chopped it in half. Systems crashed, fault warnings climbed through her ship as it tumbled through space. Though the beam had only touched her ship, its effect was spreading, debonding molecules, turning materials frangible so they shattered under their own torsion.

I cannot stop this.

Orlandine disconnected her interface sphere, then dropped down into the Jain structure she had used to interrogate the worm fragment. She only partially engaged before ejecting from her ship. As she fell away from it, she saw it unravelling from the strike point, falling into pieces like a slow-motion film of safety glass shattering. In space, on the belly of a Jain louse, she fell past island-sized chunks of debris. The beam just kept on carving up weapons platforms, disposing of them in an almost leisurely manner, as the giant moray thing continued to unravel.

Orlandine now felt the human in her screaming, and suppressed it. Linked into Jain tech, she made her calculations and saw the truth. It didn't matter if she brought the firepower of every single weapons platform here, it would still not be enough to destroy this thing. Once it was on the move it would be unstoppable and would soon enough reach its destination at the centre of the accretion disc. However, there was one option available.

'Harlequin,' she sent. 'Move.'

The coordinates she sent would put the exit runcible just a hundred thousand miles out from her own position.

'Shifting,' the drone aboard that device replied.

'Knobbler?' she sent.

After a slight delay the distant drone at the Harding black hole replied, 'Here.'

She sent a data package, and her instructions.

'This could seriously fuck up,' the drone replied.

'I calculate a forty per cent chance of failure,' Orlandine replied coldly. 'Do it.'

Knobbler

'Okay,' Knobbler muttered, struggling to keep the runcible stable.

He was bathed in coloured light in the cage surrounding him, and completely engaged with the runcible through its systems. He sent new instructions. Enclosed in hardfields, the titanic hexagonal frame of the runcible bore the appearance of a ring-shaped faceted gem. It dropped six of these fields evenly spaced around it, and the fusion drives on the underlying structure ignited to throw out white blades of flame. However, the bigger acceleration came when the grav-engines that had been keeping it stable shut down and the Harding black hole snatched hold of it. It was fast under such massive gravity. Within just a few seconds it was falling at thousands of miles an hour towards the misty sphere of matter disruption that marked the position of the black hole. But this created problems.

With the grav-engines down, and the fusion engines applying thrust, the frame started to distort more than it had done with tidal forces. Automatics compensated for some of this, but Knobbler had to deal with the rest. He feathered this grav-motor, applied electrostatic torsion to some materials, causing some structures to expand and others to contract, while taking field reinforcing up to its maximum. It was like trying to hold together a tissue paper origami sculpture in a gale. Meta-materials that were able to survive re-entry and impact with an Earth-like world were rippling and twisting like rubber.

'Good I haven't got sweat glands,' Knobbler commented.

'Or slippery hands on the controls,' commented one of his fellow drones.

'Yeah,' said another. 'None of that human time now.'

Knobbler had to agree – this was no time for the kind of

foolishness Orlandine enjoyed. But, since he was a machine and had always been a machine, it was not an issue. He allowed himself a glance back through space to where the drones had gathered in and around the remaining supply ship. He liked to think they were all rooting for him, but knew that many of them were watching with less than positive motives and hopes. He then put such thoughts out of his mind and consigned a large portion of his focus to activating the runcible for its prime purpose. A meniscus spread across the frame as the thing began opening its gate. Knobbler routed a large portion of the maths to his fellows and their nattering fell silent as they all took up the load usually taken by a runcible AI somewhat smarter than them. In no-space he fed in coordinates – a realm where they supposedly meant nothing. And he found connection. This runcible was now linked to the one controlled by Harlequin and sub-AI minds of Orlandine at the accretion disc.

The runcible had covered half the distance to the black hole and would traverse the remainder in just a few minutes. Even formed of such tough material, wrapped in hardfields and supported by grav-engines, the thing was rippling and beginning to radiate heat – glowing red. All his feeds told Knobbler that it was still perfectly functional but he could not help but doubt that. This whole plan had been a human one after all, albeit an advanced human.

Then it was there. The meniscus hit the matter disruption sphere with an intense flash across the EM spectrum. Just for a second that misty sphere broke to expose an eye on utter midnight. Knobbler had a moment to sense a deep shift into the realm of U-space, then all U-com went down. Another flash followed, burning out sensors and killing all data feeds. A minute later, things began to come back online. Knobbler's optical array showed the runcible frame, bent and broken, tumbling in a swirl of metal vapour and debris. The Harding black hole, however, was gone.

Orlandine

The exit runcible slid into the real with a stuttering flash – a series of afterimages fading from existence behind it. Drive flames stabbed out from it and from the tug helping to manoeuver it, with braided monofilament cables sagging on one side as it turned. Appearing one after another, its protective weapons platforms drew into a jostling crowd before it. The soldier, the thing that now seemed to have incorporated the entire mass of Musket Shot, unravelled further and emitted a series of its glassy disruptor beams along one flank. As she dodged debris with spurts of fusion and ion drive, Orlandine saw one of the beams punch through the weapons platform nearest to it, then spiral outwards, turning the entire thing to trash. It was almost as if the soldier was playing. It then must have understood the danger of the new arrival because it turned its firepower towards the runcible.

Beams speared out, travelling, Orlandine realized, at three-quarters light speed. They struck the intervening weapons platforms and began ripping them apart. Meanwhile, the runcible had gained enough momentum in its turn, and the tug detached and fell away. Orlandine watched all this utterly analytically but knowing that part of her should be appalled. She understood that if this went to plan, most of the intervening weapons platforms were finished – their AIs were all but dead. Instead she continued to coldly analyse logistics and watched as the platforms shifted to block anything from hitting the runcible.

She now felt the surge in her subminds aboard the runcible as they made their calculations and dipped the device's spoon into the continuum of U-space. The meniscus appeared, glittering like a soap bubble, first around the edges then closing up a hole to the centre. A cube shot away – Harlequin was making his escape. Orlandine felt as if reality was shifting, and then came an

X-ray flash. From the sensors of the platform nearest the runcible, she saw the device fold out of existence and, seemingly, in its place appeared a burning sphere, eight miles across. As this hurtled out, the view from the platform lurched. *Everything* lurched. It felt as if the universe had just sidestepped.

Through omniscient vision, Orlandine watched weapons platforms throwing themselves into U-jumps. Twenty of them made it. Five shimmered out of existence, then abruptly snapped back into it, ripped out of shape, and burning. A platform fell into the sphere in an arcing course, stretching out like hot toffee with explosions all down its length, before disappearing in a hot X-ray flash. Sometimes the fire from matter being destroyed on its way to the event horizon cleared on an eye of midnight. But only briefly, just glimpses through the maelstrom.

The soldier continued to tear apart those platforms that had lain between it and the runcible for just a few seconds more, then it shut down its weapons. It began unknotting itself faster and Orlandine read its intention in U-space.

'USERs!' she commanded. 'Full disruption!'

The weapons platforms still capable of doing so fired up their USERs and Orlandine lost her view of the continuum. U-com went down and she switched over to laser, even as the Harding black hole reached the wreckage of those platforms the soldier had destroyed. This swirled and fell into the fireball descending towards her. Only then did she accept the danger she was in. She fired up her fusion engines to get away from Musket Shot as fast as she could manage. It seemed a slow drag as the black hole sucked up everything nearby and drew everything remaining into its wake.

Orlandine ramped up her acceleration to a maximum, complementing fusion with ion drive, a grav-engine, steering thrusters and EM drive – every erg of energy thrown into getting her away. The

Harding black hole hurtled past, tens of thousands of miles away, but still she felt tidal forces distorting the Jain tech around her and jolting through her body. And despite her efforts, she calculated her chances of escaping its drag at zero. She gazed upon the thing – its appearance now was that of a comet, yet with debris and whole weapons platforms seemingly attached by invisible strings being wound in. Still on course, it hurtled down towards the soldier, and finally it struck the hardfield.

The sphere of the hardfield became visible and the black hole drove the soldier ahead of it, and it began to distort. Inside, like an embryo in a transparent egg, the soldier writhed and turned incandescent. Over the surface of the field hexagonal patterns shimmered into existence. Everything seemed to pause, then the field winked out. She had expected it to collapse once the under-lying energy store reached its maximum, but the soldier must have deliberately turned it off before that point. An instant later, before the black hole could pull the soldier in, it created a disc-shaped field between it and the black hole. Now stretched out, and pressed flat against this field, it began to writhe towards its edge. It was glowing white-hot and an even brighter fire underneath it flung it to one side and out. The disc-shaped field collapsed as the soldier, seemingly swimming through vacuum, tried to pull away. But the black hole was not done and dragged the Soldier's tail through the event horizon. It stretched up, still straining to get away, then something inside it gave out and it collapsed backwards like a building falling into its own foundations. A full spectrum EMR blast at the horizon marked its departure from existence, and burned out all sensors. Orlandine found herself tumbling through vacuum in the storm, her consciousness remaining only in the Jain portion of her being. A shadow fell upon her and hydraulic claws closed on the Jain structure around her, hauling it into an armoured space. Hard acceleration blacked out what remained of her mind.

The Client

Smoke layered the thin air down in the tunnels and chambers deep inside the moon. Ruination lay everywhere. The Client, missing yet another segment after encountering a mobile auto-gun that had somehow escaped the attack pod's notice, dropped into the final chamber right at the heart of the moon.

The space was two miles across and a mile deep. She descended to where the attack pod lay, cut in half by a shearfield that had sprung up from the floor as the pod had fried the Librarian's hardfield defences. Some of its systems were still active, but it was somnolent now, since apparently it had no more defences to destroy. She landed beside the thing and looked towards the construct at the centre of the chamber. Here stood a huge dodecahedron, its faces tangled with technology that looked like some strange language. Numerous power lines and pipes were strewn across the floor as they led into the thing. She was very wary now.

It had been a hard fight to get down here, but not hard enough. This creature had access to all the knowledge of both the Species and the Jain, so where were the completely enclosing hardfields? It had not used everything to keep her out because it *wanted* her down here. The Librarian's ostensible aim was to erase the for-bidden data and doubtless the Client herself, and just fending her off would not accomplish this. Yet in the shriek, in the chal-lenge, there was an aim utterly integral to what the Jain were. It was an instinctive thing first woven into their genome even before intelligence. However, as she now approached the dodecahedron she could not help but feel she might have misunderstood, and that some unforeseen final trap lay within.

When she reached the side of the huge object, a light ran around the rim of one of its faces. The interlocking technology on that face began to shift into itself – the whole face gradually disappeared like bad pixels on some ancient screen. It was an invitation and seemed like an acknowledgement of her real purpose in coming here, as well as the Librarian's purpose in allowing her to. She stepped inside and gazed upon the Librarian itself.

The creature resembled a giant black lobster, inlaid with silvery metal. But the whorls and scars in its carapace told of great age. Not its full age, because undoubtedly it periodically renewed itself. Perhaps it had not done so for thousands, or tens of thousands, of years. Its internal organs, or whatever else it had inside, were perhaps perfectly functional and it did not concern itself with outer appearance. It squatted atop an object like a mushroom but with triangular sockets all over its surface. Ribbed tentacles sprouted from behind its head to engage with some of these. Its eyes were blind white. As the Client approached, it shifted position and she felt a wave of scanning pass through her like a blast front. But undeterred, she carried on.

'So, we come at last to this,' she said.

The creature's reply was a sawing in her mind – complex chains of chemicals in the air and a flickering of holograms all around it. The words were simply an agreement, 'We come to this,' but there lay an acknowledgement of the Client's aims here and its own, as well as of history and context, and levels of negotiability in what was to come. Some of it was incomprehensible, and some of it seemed to slide off into either madness or genius.

'Let the chips fall where they may,' said the Client, in simple human Anglic, refusing any kind of melding or negotiation in the inevitable conflict. She wondered briefly if it was her mind that was too hard-wired.

The Librarian did not reply but merely began detaching its tentacles from the object below. A second wave hit then, inducing an internal viral attack. Even as she leapt, the Client felt her weapons going offline. The Librarian launched too and the two of them slammed together in mid-air. There was no finesse in the attack. The creature just grabbed hold and punched in its triangular-section tentacles. Small shearfields and needle lasers at the ends of the tentacles began boring through the Client's carapace. Through the holes they made, fibres spewed into her to spread neural meshes and seek out connections inside. She replied by unravelling her own tentacles and forcing them into the Librarian's body. They tumbled through the air, grotesquely mated and soon tearing into each other's minds.

As the Librarian groped for connections so it could reach out to her primary self, the Client made her connections too and pushed inwards for information and memories, recording everything that the Librarian was. She saw her home world scattered with cities of a design she did not recognize. But the dying residents in these were her own kind, before the asteroid strike shattered their civilization. The Librarian had used similar methods before: sometimes it was a disease, other times it was an infestation of nano-machines, and what remained was shattered by asteroid strike or by weapons the Species had built themselves. Then, over the ensuing thousands of years, new examples of their kind began to rise again without comprehension of the ruins decaying around them. She delved back through the millennia of manipulation and extermination.

Meanwhile, the Librarian delved deep into the Client's systems and reached out to her primary form, where its real attack began. The first virus entered piecemeal, apparently aimed to spread throughout the platform, to hunt down and destroy library data. The blocking response was obviously expected. It mutated and fell back on other targets, subverting transmitter control circuitry to ensure that the Client's primary form could not close down contact. Next, rising out of hidden cylinders in the surface of the moon, came projectors. These hit the platform with induction warfare beams that began to sequester nanotech aboard the platform.

Deeper went the Client, to the time when the Species first arrived. They landed their ships on the world while the Librarian diverted its own vessel to the moon and there began to bore its home. The Client's kind began to work quickly to establish a technological civilization, spreading out and fast tank-growing children, ever building. The Client searched for the time of the Librarian's first extermination but instead found something else. The Species had been too noisy and had attracted attention. The weapon dropped out of U-space and into the atmosphere. It hit with disruptor beams, shattering everything, the colonists and the colony. Then it disappeared again, not having detected the Librarian in the moon. A million years passed before the Librarian seeded the world again. Something had happened to the Jain and they did not attack again.

The platform was failing, nanotech running wild and data caches corrupting. The Client's primary form fought this, shunting data to different stores, many in its attack pods, burning wild nanotech, isolating and partitioning, aware that the destruction had not yet reached the point of no return. The Client and Librarian were now utterly entwined mentally. Delving deeper, deeper still. She saw the Librarian's flight from its kind, and before that a great battle with an alliance of Jain set on destroying it.

Meanwhile the Librarian absorbed data from the platform and from what had once been the AI Pragus. It encompassed the

Polity and the prador, but they seemed just an addendum to it. From her own scattered points of view, the Client felt the Librarian's disappointment with the prador extermination of the Species. But its view was long and in many aspects indifferent. This was just another extermination. The prador civilization would fall when the Jain tech in the accretion disc finally scattered, as would the Polity. The Librarian would reseed and the Species would rise again . . .

The Client tried to see past this. She tried to delve to the root of the Jain and what had happened. She saw the perpetual war for dominance that reflected how these creatures had fought and advanced throughout their rise, just as she and the Librarian were fighting now. One of the Jain made itself into a technology; into a destructive assimilator of its own kind. And it deployed.

This technology spread, at its core a growing store of knowledge and power that was irresistible to the Jain. One after another, they tried to do what they had always done, which was to encompass it and assimilate it into themselves. But one after another they fell to it. Some of their AIs, sentient intelligences used as tools in this assimilation, who were able to think in ways outside of organic evolution, fled the mayhem. They fled what now sat in the accretion disc the Polity and the Kingdom so feared. And they fled what sprang from Jain nodes – a technology made to destructively assimilate the Jain, and which continued to do the same with any civilization it encountered. It was of course logical that the first civilization it had destroyed was that of the Jain themselves. Yet, in reality their destruction was not an absolute. Because in the end, what the humans named Jain tech was what the Jain had become.

Trike

Utterly controlled, Trike inserted a multi-driver to extract the screws holding down the last in the series of floor plates. The previous three were tipped up against the wall, trailing super-conductor into the hole revealed below. Attached to their under-sides were the slabs of technology that created floor gravity – they were deactivated now by the slice that had gone through the plates and down. A Clade unit had come along here and cut through the floor beside the engine mounted in heavy struts below. It had also cut through many of the struts, but what had shut down the ship's main grav-engine was a severed line of cool-ant pipes and superconducting cables.

'We'll have to weld these struts,' said Cog, crouching down be-side the engine. 'Easy enough to get it running but without bracing it'll tear itself out of my ship.' He looked up at Trike through his visor, then pointed down at the struts. 'Your job.'

After heaving up the last plate, Trike reached over and took up the coil of a composite-printer, fighting to keep his hands steady. Cog seemed to understand that he needed to be doing something to remain in control of himself. He checked the control box, tapped the small display, then plugged its cable into a wall socket. Touching the deposition head against one of the struts, he got a reading – the control box selecting the correct material. He put it into one of the breaks and triggered it. Light flared in the gap and it began to fill with new, tough composite. Cog meanwhile began unscrewing sev-ered pipes. This was something for which any normal human would have required a spanner.

'Air pressure is up.'

Trike looked over at Angel approaching from the rear of the ship. The display in his space suit visor had already told him that he no longer needed to keep that visor closed, but Trike somehow felt safer closely wrapped in the suit. Nevertheless, he touched a control on his wrist and the visor slid down into its neck ring, while the helmet concertinaed behind to form a collar. He continued working, occasionally eyeing Cog inserting the repair sections of pipe Angel handed down to him. It was useful being a hooper. Anyone else would have needed to take out the complete lengths of pipe and replace them, because the things were so rigid and very tough. Cog just pulled them aside, inserted a repair section, pushed them back and tightened them with his fingers. Shortly he was done and sat back with a grunt of satisfaction, looking up.

'And the fusion engine?' he asked.

'Same kind of damage,' Angel replied, squatting at the edge of the hole. 'Severed power cables and pipes, but the tritium bead fuser is damaged too.'

'Doable?' Cog asked.

'If you have another pure-water freezing unit.'

'In the stores,' Cog replied.

'Where are the stores?'

Cog inspected Trike's work as he finished repairing the last strut. He glanced across at the tools and wiring stacked further down the corridor.

'We can finish this later,' he said. 'Let's go take a look.'

Trike swallowed dryly, aware that around Angel he needed to control himself even more. But he could do it. If he just focused on the work, he could do it. He put the deposition welder to one side, hauled himself out of the hole, then onto active grav-plates. Standing near Angel he found his fists clenching and had to keep his mouth clamped shut because it felt like his tongue wanted to escape. Cog followed him up and rested a hand on one shoulder.

'Come on.'

They moved back along the length of the ship, Trike stepping out ahead so he did not have to see the android. He turned into the corridor leading to the stores, finally coming up beside the door. Palming the control beside it, he slid it into the wall and turned on the lights. He studied the racks inside and the larger items on pallets along one wall. Angel must have come here earlier for the pipe fittings . . . He then realized something was wrong. If Angel had come here, then how was it he did not know where the store room was? He started to turn around when two massive arms like docking clamps closed around him, locking his own arms against his sides.

'What the fuck?' he managed, before rage surged up inside him.

He struggled, hauling Cog up and the two of them stumbled to one side. Next Angel was in front of him, taking out a high-pressure injector and discarding the tool bag he'd carried it in. Trike felt the spike go hard into his stomach and the injector whined. He kicked out, his boot thumping into Angel's torso. The android slammed back high up against the wall. A cold burning filled Trike's guts as lights counted down on the device still imbedded in him, and its transparent tank emptied of purple fluid. He fought to free his arms, and he and Cog crashed to the floor, even as Angel peeled out of a dent in the wall and fell too. But the Old Captain's grip remained firm. Then Angel was there, grabbing his kicking legs. He struggled and fought, not knowing how to do anything else. The cold burning spread down into his legs, up into his chest and into his skull. He couldn't tell how long it lasted, but soon he wasn't struggling any more, and he just felt tired.

'Sprine?' he asked. It was what Cog used before to quell Trike's madness.

'Diluted, along with the same stuff I gave you before,' Cog replied, close to his ear. 'I thought about trying the stunner I used on you when we were with Lyra, but then you would need to go in a cold coffin too. And I'm not sure if you would stay there.'

'Even frozen?'

'Even that.' Cog paused, then asked, 'You done?'

'Yeah,' he replied. 'I'm done.' And truly felt a double meaning there.

20

Manipulative minds: Long before the first AIs came online simple computers were beating humans at chess. Chess is all about extrapolation, which in turn is a survival trait. And it comes into its own in warfare, which, after all, is what chess is based upon. During the Quiet War when the AIs, with minimal casualties, took power away from human politicians and rulers throughout the solar system, the AIs played the game – always many moves ahead of their opposition. When Mars forces realized that all their computer systems were no longer working for them, they decided to use their stock of missiles to knock out satellites in which some of the AIs were sited. The missiles only got a few miles into the thin air before their solid-burn rockets burned out. The AI that had manufactured them two years before had shifted some decimal points and made the fuel loads two orders of magnitude smaller than they should have been. But that was easy – that was the human outsmarting his pet dog. It is when AIs are trying to outsmart AIs that things get very complicated. Thankfully in our war against the prador this was not an issue, for they had none. But, extrapolation and preparedness being essential to survival, we must ready ourselves for a time, all but inevitable, when we encounter highly intelligent aliens who do possess AI. One can only speculate on the degree of manipulation and the intensity of the game when that occurs. Just as one can speculate on the body count.

From 'How It Is' by Gordon

Earth Central

Earth Central gazed upon wreckage. The final count of weapons platforms destroyed was not yet in because some were still falling into the Harding black hole. AI casualty rate had been low and though materially costly for the defence sphere, it was, ostensibly, an acceptable loss for what had been achieved. Also, as time passed, the remaining platforms would become redundant as the accretion disc, with all the nasty Jain tech, fell through the event horizon. Or at least that was the theory. EC was very worried about what had exacted that cost, along with some other anomalies.

Studying all the data on this soldier in as much detail as possible, EC was as near to being appalled as it was capable of. The thing, even before it transformed itself, had shrugged off hits that no Polity vessel smaller than a dreadnought like the *Cable Hogue* could survive. Transformed, it had chewed up weapons platforms with ease, and it had taken a black hole to finish it. Even then, there seemed to have been a possibility the soldier could escape it. But that was not all, because its tactics were all wrong.

Orlandine had intelligently deployed USERs but the thing had shown resistance to the U-space disturbance. EC calculated that if it had been a bit sneakier and less inclined to attack, it could have got through the defence into the accretion disc. But it could be argued that it needed the energy from the weapons platform weapons to make its transformation. Only in this transformed state was it capable of detonating the dead sun at the centre of the accretion disc. On that basis Musket Shot had been its intended target, and the fact that Orlandine could gate a black hole at it just dumb luck. But that made no sense. The thing could have dumped itself on some planet close to a sun, far away from the accretion disc, where similar energy and materials were available. It would then have arrived transformed, easily smeared the defence and gone in.

No, just as with Dragon, a deeper game was being played here. The fact that the players or player could deploy something like that soldier meant the danger had ramped up orders of magnitude. However, EC could not yet see what it was.

'Something further is coming,' said a voice.

The comment immediately propelled part of EC's consciousness into virtuality as a prador adult.

'No envoy?' EC commented.

'Petty games,' replied the king of the prador. 'The Client has taken Weapons Platform Mu into the Graveyard. It was pursued there by the moon of the Species home world. This is apparently some kind of ship and led us to the weapons platform in the first place. It is also, so I now understand, a store of data.'

'I would be interested to know how *you* know it is a data store,' said EC.

'Your secrets are not as safe as you suppose,' said the king. 'My agents obtained a copy of the full file concerning your dealings with the earlier iteration of the Client during the war.'

EC absorbed that and immediately sent out an alert to all the minds and agents concerned with keeping a lid on that information. It had supposedly been utterly secure and it was worrying EC had not immediately known a copy had been stolen.

'So, you accept that it is the Client aboard that platform?'

'It initially pretended to be a Polity AI but did not hold the façade for long,' replied the king. 'Subsequent communications with it, and with the entity in that moon, soon exposed the lie.'

Entity in the moon?

'I would be interested to know about these communications,' said EC, avoiding asking the question it really wanted to ask.

'Yes, I'm sure you would . . . Anyway, confirmation that it is the Client came for me when it fled to the Kingdom. It caused some damage but came close to being destroyed itself, so did not demonstrate Polity weapons superiority. And if the intended target was the data in that moon then a Polity AI aboard the platform would not have led it into the Graveyard.'

After a pause EC asked, 'So we're good?'

'We are not at war,' was all the king would concede, 'and matters arising from what happened at the accretion disc are more concerning. I have studied the tactical data about the attack of this Jain soldier.'

'So you've seen it too?'

'I have.'

'Your extrapolation?'

'Precisely what I said at the beginning: something is coming.'

'Do you know what?'

'The Jain,' said the king simply.

It really had to be the answer. Everything that had happened with the wormship, the soldier, the mind let loose was all about the Jain. It was logical to assume that it had all been groundwork for . . . but then it fell apart. The Jain had not been in existence for five million years. If something capable of making things like that soldier had been present in the galaxy, EC was pretty sure the Polity would have known about it by now. Something key was missing.

'We are prepared,' said the ruling AI of the Polity, 'but perhaps we must prepare further. We have seen one soldier.'

'I agree,' said the king. 'And the focus is the accretion disc.'

In its mind's billions of eyes, Earth Central watched further reavers arriving at the prador watch station. But it also watched war ships across the Polity responding to orders it had issued just a few moments before.

'When the time is right we must move together,' said the king, fading from view.

EC did not reply.

Orlandine

Awareness returned without any sense of self. She was without sufficient data because sensors all around her were dead, and so she stretched out to grasp it beyond the system she occupied. At first there was resistance as she encountered limited technology and programming languages that were neither Jain nor Polity. But she encompassed that resistance and it broke down. Subliminally she understood that there was an awareness where she reached. It had fought her at first but was now moving things out of her way.

Data. Now she had data.

Orlandine processed logistics, statistics, analysed damage wholly in the world of data, the world of AI. She made connections to a larger whole and encompassed the defence sphere. She saw this as a mathematical problem for which she must calculate the best solution – to re-establish it with the resources available. She studied the interplay of AI minds as they made similar calculations and talked in microsecond pulses. Focusing closely on some of these conversations, she observed them deciding how to rescue minds from the defence platforms still falling into the Harding black hole.

Vision returned.

Gazing through cams inside one of the defence platforms she saw a translucent block of AI crystal, wrapped in a talon of grey metal, being hoisted up in the arms of a robot. The thing was mainly rocket motor and at once shot away through the burning structure of the platform. It hurtled along, giant beams twisting around it, bubble-metal walls buckling, flaring cables snaking through vacuum. Finally, the robot deposited the AI on a conveyor leading into the throat of a railgun.

The most logical solution.

Elsewhere she saw a series of attack pods launching from another platform, courses plotted. She calculated that the pods would easily intercept eight of the AIs. Another six would take a long arcing course out into interstellar space, where they could be picked up later, maybe centuries later. Four would go into the accretion disc where their odds of being rescued was just over 60 per cent. Another three would fall back into the black hole unless some other way of grabbing them could be found.

'Orlandine?'

The Harding black hole was just entering the misty borderland of the accretion disc, but already its effect was visible. To a simple human mind the disc looked static – just the black hole falling into it – but this was not the case. A great swirl had appeared below it, bulging up at its centre as if the disc was reaching out towards the approaching object. On a gravity map of the system she could see that proto-planets and asteroids had shifted and were changing course. Even the dead star at the centre was on the move. Were it the case that the disc was nailed in place in vacuum, then the black hole would just punch straight through it and head off into interstellar space. But no, the hole was more massive than the disc, and the disc was falling into it. She calculated it would take five months before the hole ate the dead star, somewhat longer for it to suck in everything else. Supposing the star did not ignite . . .

'Orlandine!'

Yes, she was Orlandine – a distinct entity whose central locus was a human body. She withdrew her perception nearer to her physical location, confused about the source of the communication. A prador destroyer hung in vacuum and she saw it from outside and within. Updating, she realized it had come here just before the soldier arrived but she had been rather too busy then to notice it.

'You must come back!'

Vision through her human eyes now, and her other human senses engaged.

Ruby light lit the interior of her interface sphere, where lianas of Jain tech tangled the packed Polity hardware. A brighter light cut a line alongside her and she heard the crump of her interface sphere opening. She turned to watch as the forward hemisphere rose up then hinged over, revealing a big mantis head, mica glittering compound eyes and coiling and uncoiling antennae. The head clacked mandibles, then spoke.

'You really made a mess in here,' said Cutter.

'A prador warship here is an infringement of the agreements,' she stated.

'That's the first thing you say?' said Cutter disbelievingly.

'Thanks for saving me,' she allowed.

She tried to sit up but something was holding her in place. Tilting her head as much as she was able to, she looked down at her body. She was drowned in Jain tech outgrowths. They had fountained from the splits in her sides, punched out of her legs and arms. Flicking to a cam in the open upper half of the sphere she got a better look. Her head was like that of Medusa now, and skeins of tendrils had also poured from one side. She tracked them out then switched to cams in the hold of the destroyer – cams Orlik had only just turned back on. She realized that Bludgeon, whom she now understood had been speaking to her earlier, had turned them off in an attempt to stop her seizing control of the ship through them. He had failed because Jain tech was strewn across the floor, punched into the walls and spread throughout the vessel. It had even linked back to the EVA unit she had used to interrogate the Wheel submind. And now, as she gazed upon all this, she felt some minuscule part of herself screaming its objections.

Orlandine sank back and closed her eyes. The small human part of her being was utterly buried, but even her perfectly logical and emotionless AI self knew that what had happened was not a good thing. Barely conscious, she had seized everything around her – her Jain self had taken full control and sequestered the ship. Had she hurt anyone? She checked. Bludgeon had taken a mental battering, and two of Orlik's crew would have to regrow legs after trying to cut through the spreading tendrils, which had responded like monofilament whips. Orlik himself had taken a mental hit as well, but had managed to detach his interface plate before she'd taken his mind. Thankfully no one had died. But she needed to get control.

She began disconnecting by activating the constructor nanites spread throughout her structure to reverse the process. She retracted from the ship's mind – it was intact but not thinking straight, as though it was drunk. Tendrils began unplugging themselves throughout the ship's system and reeling back into thicker growths. These growths began to shrink back too, where they could. Behind them they left grooves and holes like acid burns, where they had mined surrounding materials for their growth. Some thicker tentacles that had ceased to be capable of movement turned brittle as their contents destroyed themselves. Others made up of more durable materials deactivated, but remained unchanged – it would take the prador some work with grinders and cutting lasers to be rid of them. Stage by stage Orlandine pulled herself back out of the ship, until at length all her physical being occupied was the hold.

'Better,' said Cutter, tilting his head to one side and peering around himself.

As she pulled back in the hold, bands of discolouration, like heat oxidation of shined metal, spread along the tendrils and tentacles strewn across the floor. As these died she began working on others around her. Those that had spewed from her body were wet, organic and mobile. They detached from the more solid growths lying beyond and began to retract into her body, shedding lumps of material like slugs as they did so. She dropped those issuing from her skull, their stumps retreating inside and skin sliding back over the lumpy shifting mass until it settled and her head regained its shape. Others either broke off or slithered inside her, dependent on where materials needed to be replaced. Finally, her sides zipped closed and her body shifted and jerked as it reassumed the form of a human woman.

Within her being, Orlandine steadily disconnected from the Jain tech. One portion of herself wanted to keep the connection, while her AI and human aspects understood that this was the reason she returned to human time. If she did not pull back like this she would lose herself. There was a reason humans decided to be haiman. They chose to carry their humanity into the AI realm rather than only record themselves to crystal and become fully AI. They were a melding who aimed for eclecticism. The objections inside herself became stronger and stronger and, like an addict forgoing her drug of choice, she took herself all the way down to the minimum level: just enough Jain tech to support the link between her AI and human selves. Then she disconnected her spinal power supply.

'I'll need some help,' she said. 'Lift me out of here.'

Cutter moved closer, looming in over her. Showing delicate precision, he reached out with his forelimbs, turning them so their razor edges were to the side, and lifted her out. He deposited her on the floor, where she lay exhausted. Her body chemistry fought to realign, as parts of her human body that had been effectively dead came alive again. Jain tech withdrew from her head, depositing bone behind it to reform her skull. Her shrunken and damaged brain expanded into place as Jain tech and medical nanites made their repairs. Now materials were shedding from her pores as a black fluid, pooling around her, an excess she no longer required. At length it was done and, amidst the tendrils strewn across the floor, she sat up in the sticky black pool like a filthy newborn.

'And now you are back,' said Cutter.

She nodded tiredly, but slowly even that weariness faded as her internal chemistry returned to the state it had been in before she heightened her Jain tech to interrogate the worm fragment. She pressed her hands against the floor and stood, peering down at her filthy body. It was unlikely that the prador destroyer possessed a shower, so she altered her skin chemistry to initiate a low friction gel to ooze from her sweat glands. She shook herself and the muck slewed from her skin. She then touched the disc at her collarbone, mentally reprogramming it so her shipsuit slithered out over her body with its pure white monofilament material. She did not know why she had made that choice, and did not want to examine the decision too closely.

'So, what now?' Cutter asked.

'I need a new ship,' she replied. 'And I need some time on Jaskor.'

Cutter reached down and snapped up a section of brittle Jain tentacle. He eyed it for a second then discarded it. 'For human time,' he said.

'Yes, for that.'

Why did she feel disappointment and dissatisfaction in the steadily strengthening human component of her being? It was wrong to feel so negative now. Yes, she had briefly lost control of the Jain tech inside her, but no one had died and she was regaining balance. Many defence platforms had been destroyed and her work of the last century had received a terrible blow. But look at what she had achieved! Extruding her sensory cowl and opening it behind her head, she made a conventional connection, via Bludgeon, to the optical array of the prador destroyer. She could see straight away the great maelstrom in the accretion disc where the Harding black hole had entered it, and the slewing of the entire disc as it began its slow drag into the hole. She had won. Perhaps her disappointment was due to the hole this had left in *her*. Over the ensuing months the threat she had guarded against for a century would be neutralized and the defence sphere would become superfluous . . .

Yes, this was why she felt as she did. It would pass.

'Come on,' she said to Cutter. 'It's time to go.'

Trike

Trike startled awake, briefly confused until he understood what had woken him – the kick and drag of the fusion drive starting up. Just for a second he felt relief because his sleep had been haunted by inchoate nightmares. But then nightmare reality quelled the feeling. Ruth had been dead, then miraculously alive and he had rescued her. Just as he had been beginning to think they had a chance together again . . . a machine of the Clade had ripped open her spine and her heart. Why? He and the others aboard this ship had been peripheral actors in some plot hardly even relevant. It seemed to him the strike on Cog's ship had been an act of spite; that the Clade had attacked just because it could.

Trike was angry, very angry.

When he had returned from the store room he had been nauseated. He no longer felt as if he was about to lose control, but the anger had not gone away. He had trudged up to the door into his cabin, tiredly undoing the seams of his space suit. Cog and

Angel had remained to handle the damage about the fusion drive, and Cog had dispatched him here to rest. He'd stepped inside and sprawled on the bed, reaching out to the empty space beside him, and that was the last he remembered.

Sitting up, he realized that he had fallen into natural sleep, without being knocked unconscious, for the first time in an age. He checked a display up on the wall and saw he had been out of it for four hours. Was that good or bad? He sat on the edge of the bed, grinding his teeth. Then after a moment he stood up and quickly discarded his clothes, heading for the shower. He would consider it a good thing, despite the fact that it was almost certainly due to the sprine killing off a mass of viral fibres in his body. He would also consider the core of rage that sleep seemed to have crystallized inside him a good thing, because he wasn't crazy – his anger just needed direction.

After washing, he dressed in clean clothes but for his heavy coat buttoned up to the neck, and then headed for the bridge. When he stepped through the doorway he saw that Cog occupied his throne while Angel was standing back from the acceleration chairs. He supposed it didn't matter to the android whether it stood or sat. The floor was clear of debris and the remains of the Clade units.

'Better?' asked Cog.

'Better but never best,' Trike replied, taking his usual chair. He shot a glance at Ruth's chair and saw that it had been cleaned of blood too. 'The drive?'

Eyeing data scrolling in one screen frame Cog smiled. 'Looking good.'

'So we *could* get back to the Cyberat world, then?' Trike suggested.

Cog looked at him, assessing, then pointed to the frame. 'On those figures it would take ten months.' He gestured to the other frame showing Dragon well clear of the sun and obviously moving fast. 'But in just a few hours we can hitch that ride.'

Dragon loomed closer, and the image grew steadily clearer, as did the damage the entity had suffered. It was scorched black in places, cut through with reflective rivulets as if its armour had melted and run. In two areas armour was completely missing and revealed a blackened interior, slightly lit red as if embers were glowing inside.

'I'm getting nothing on any com frequency,' said Cog. He glanced round at Angel and raised an eyebrow. Angel shook his head. Cog continued, 'But there must be some intelligence still operating in there – it's now heading directly away from the centre point of USER disruption, so I reckon it's U-space capable.'

'You aim to moor on the surface?' Trike suggested.

Cog shook his head. 'No, we don't know how close its U-field operates. In fact, we don't know how it operates at all. We go inside.'

Fusion drive was now working almost at its limit to keep pace with Dragon's steady acceleration. Was that a coincidence? Trike had seen how fast the thing could move, though he was not sure how, and it was certainly faster than this. Was it waiting for them?

Soon they were above the curved armoured plane of its surface and gazing at white diamond-shaped scales. Some of these were rucked up, especially towards the edge of the burned area they now moved in over. Everything was fused and blackened, covered in shiny patches and streams of hard glass – the scales here had melted. Ahead lay what looked like a mountain range: jags of Dragon's hide poking up into vacuum. In a moment, they were up over this and descending.

'Something living,' said Cog.

He put up a frame showing a teardrop-shaped island of flesh clinging to one rim of the hole inside. Rising from this were two dragon pseudopods that turned their heads and watched as Cog's ship slid down past them.

'Do we have a better view inside?' Trike asked matter-of-factly.

Cog worked his control and the view in the frame swung to display the inside. They gazed at blurred black and red, until Cog switched over to image enhancement and the view resolved. Giant strut bones intersected on nodes were scattered throughout the interior. Here and there blackened masses emitted a red glow. Blackened cords clung to the bones and webbed over other spaces like charred muscle. But there were also things that had a more machine-like appearance: clustered cuboid metallic structures like burned-out rail cars or buildings. A thing at the intersection of strut bones looked like a railgun, a giant honeycomb whose compartments contained metal spheres, and others besides.

'Over there.' Cog pulled up another screen frame. 'Before we drift further.'

'It's still accelerating?' asked Trike.

'Faster now,' Cog replied.

'I wondered about that. I reckon it was waiting for us.'

Cog shrugged, neither agreeing nor disagreeing.

Using steering thrusters, he manoeuvred his ship over towards one end of a honeycomb compartment. A mile from where he brought the ship down lay the outer skin of Dragon, while a giant strut bone jutted in overhead. The vessel hit the surface with a crunch.

'Remora docking?' Trike asked.

'Yeah, but maybe not enough,' Cog replied.

The Old Captain worked his console and a series of thumps resounded throughout the ship. Trike recognized these as explosive anchors and hoped there was not some part of Dragon ready to respond to further damage. The ship settled with occasional creaks and thumps as things cooled, or as damaged structure within it realigned – there was still repair work to be done.

'Air pressure too, now,' said Cog. 'Local – in some kind of containment field.'

'And a visitor.' Trike pointed.

Far out on the flat surface an object had appeared and was moving rapidly towards them. Cog magnified it in a frame. It either looked like or was what they had seen clinging to the edge of the hole through which they had entered the Dragon sphere. Its appearance was of a giant slug ten feet long, while the two tentacles protruding from its head were stunted Dragon pseudo-pods. It also reminded Trike of those creatures that had swarmed onto the Cyberat island where he had fought Angel.

'I'm going to go out and take a look,' he said, standing. Still he wanted to move, and still he wanted to strike against someone or something . . .

They all trooped down the spiral stair into the hold area of the ship. There Cog palmed a panel beside the door, and the door started folding down into a ramp. As pressures equalized, Trike expected to smell charred flesh. But what he got instead was a whiff that reminded him of hydraulic oil, with the spicy under-tone he had smelled when Dragon had penetrated their ship earlier.

They walked down into open cathedral vastness. Trike's boots, now he was out of grav and using gecko function, crunched on a surface scabbed with chunks of white ash that turned to dust underneath them. The slug thing drew steadily closer, leaving a dust trail behind. Then, about ten paces out, it halted and seemed to deflate, reshaping and spreading out on the surface to cling like a limpet.

'You've got something to say?' Cog called.

The two cobra-headed pseudopods turned in to face each other, as if baffled by the question. After a moment, they swung out again.

'Now I understand,' said Angel. The android abruptly moved forwards, coming to stand right in front of the thing. One pseudopod stabbed down, hitting his chest so hard he staggered. It then turned him to face them, its neck curving off over his shoulder. Angel's eyes were now glowing the same sapphire as the other pseudopod poised up behind him.

'Dragon is here,' he said.

'Then perhaps Dragon can tell us, in plain words, what the fuck is going on?' said Cog.

'I miscalculated,' said Dragon, out of Angel's mouth.

'No shit,' said Cog. 'But I'm going to need more than that.'

'Angel will speak,' Dragon replied.

Angel jerked as if electrocuted, and bowed his head. When he looked up again the sapphire glow receded from his eyes. He gave a very human grimace and shook his head.

'It's complicated,' he said.

Trike snorted. 'I think we're aware of that.'

'Orlandine started building her runcibles eighty years ago and yet, in all that time, the Wheel – a Jain AI – was free to do what it wanted with me and the wormship it controlled,' he said. 'Only when Dragon started to have doubts about what Orlandine was doing, and started investigating, did it supposedly seek out this Jain soldier to send against the defence sphere – to detonate the dead star.'

'Investigating?' Trike asked, rage churning in his belly. First he had wanted to destroy Angel, but it turned out the android was a victim too. This Wheel had then seemed the prime mover in all this, but now it was gone, destroyed in that wormship. All that was left was the Clade . . .

Angel focused on him. 'Dragon started gathering data. Apparently, the accretion disc is not that old in interstellar terms. There is something odd about how it was formed. It is the remains of a solar system that was destroyed during a battle between the Jain and some kind of unacceptable offshoot from their family tree. That offshoot was destroyed by the prador just some thousands of years ago. However, one of them survived to help the Polity during its war against the prador.'

'I'm trying to see the relevance of this,' said Trike tightly.

Angel held up one hand. He looked to be in pain as he struggled to get things straight in his skull. 'That Jain offshoot left a library accessible only by one of their kind. Dragon obtained the remains of the one who helped the Polity and passed them on to a weapons platform AI who resurrected the individual – a creature the humans name the Client. It seized control of the platform and took it straight into the Prador Kingdom to seek out this library.'

'So, Dragon did this to get the data it wanted on the accretion disc from the creature?' asked Cog.

'Yes, but before it could go there, Dragon was lured here by the easy answers my remains might provide . . . into a trap.' Angel bowed his head and shook it. 'There's something else about what the Client is, and what it might do, that is unclear. But certainly something is clear.'

'Something clear would be nice,' said Cog.

Angel continued, 'The Wheel's aim in sending the soldier was to push Orlandine into using her runcibles, into firing a black hole into the accretion disc, before she learned the true origins of that disc. In fact, the soldier, which is more powerful than any of her weapons platforms, ensures it.'

'I see,' said Cog. 'Orlandine has a gun that fires black holes.'

Angel looked up. 'Precisely.'

'So we are now rushing to stop her from doing precisely what an obviously hostile Jain AI wants her to do?' asked Trike.

Angel shrugged. 'Apparently we might be too late. The worm-ship came here without the soldier so it is likely it has already been sent. It will be months before we are clear of the USER disruption – only then will Dragon know what has happened and how to react.'

Trike finally lost patience with the convoluted explanation of events. 'Who is the enemy? Who wants these things to happen? Is it the Clade?'

Angel shook his head. 'I don't think so. It seems the Clade was acting on the Wheel's orders. It also seems that in acting as it did here, the Wheel was as much a soldier as the one it sent.' Angel paused, then held out his hands in bafflement. 'The Wheel might have been a submind, just like the one Orlandine interrogated, sent by a primary Jain AI, or maybe by one of the Jain. We cannot know.'

'We cannot know yet,' said Trike.

As he gazed at the android, he felt an utter certainty that he would know who or what had torn his life apart and put his wife in a cold coffin. He would find it and, whether it was an AI or some ancient surviving alien, he would tear it apart.

The Client

The Client's remote and the Jain librarian tumbled through the thin air in the chamber at the centre of the moon. They fought each other and raped each other for data, seeking to dominate. The Client, dispersed through the Librarian and losing consciousness of its self, understood then the negotiation, the *mating*. One-on-one fights between Jain could not be compared to the way other races fought. If two humans or two prador clashed then one was a loser; one was dead. When Jain fought it was a melding, a compromise. They destroyed parts of each other's minds and they stole from each other's minds. Certainly, at the end of these encounters the body of the subservient Jain ended up dead. But the resultant dominant mind in the surviving Jain was irrevocably changed – it was an amalgam of itself and its victim.

This was what was happening now and the Client could not see which one was dominant. But it was certain that she could no longer break away with the data she had seized and that this must proceed to its conclusion. Even as she fought, this encounter seemed crazy and illogical. Here she was, the last of her kind, locked in a battle to the death with the last of the Jain, their minds like two immiscible fluids tangled around each other in a ball.

Aboard the weapons platform, the Librarian was as deep into computer systems and the Client's primary form as it was into the remote. But the two battling figures at the centre of the moon were now physically destroying each other. Her fibres and meshes far inside the Librarian, the Client began cutting through nerves, killing musculature, seizing control of and killing major organs. They both started to decohere, which was evident when they bounced against the floor and the Librarian lost a leg, while the remote lost one of its segments. This stage of the fight pushed things to a crisis, and the two fluids of mind ceased to be immiscible.

Two minds began to fall together, no longer tearing at each other.

Two bodies convulsed, drifting to one wall of the dodecahedron and crunching against it. The Client's remote broke into segments while the Librarian separated at all the joints in its carapace. Stringy connections pulled apart, while grey fluids oozed out and broke into floating blobs. They spread in a cloud of pieces and, with the instruction to 'destroy the forbidden data' fading, the Client knew that at last she had won. Segment by segment her perception through the remote went out, and she was again completely in her primary form aboard the weapons platform. Her mind, now spread throughout the computer architecture around her and in her attack pods, was no longer fighting to survive, but fighting to digest all she had taken. She realized that right from the start she had behaved like her ancestors when she had seized the mind of the AI Pragus. And now she had done the same with the Librarian.

Only she remained, larger, more complex, motivations altered and her view of time much longer. But the core of herself, though changed, still retained its key motivations. Still she hated the prador for their extermination of the Species, still she hated the humans for their betrayal, but the emotion was not so strong now. Stronger was a sadness she felt in having killed the last Jain, and sadness that she was the last of her kind. However, deep in the memories of the Librarian she found new hope and a source of excitement.

The Client was about to detach the anchors rooting the weapons platform to the library moon, but reconsidered. Because she had absorbed so much of the Librarian's mind she now knew that the moon contained a great deal of useful technology. With a thought, she got robots on the move in the weapons platform, heading for the exits. It was time to ransack this place. Afterwards she would have somewhere to go, and something to do. Though as yet she did not know her ultimate goals, or whether they would stem from that portion of herself that was Jain or Species.

It had happened when an alliance of Jain had attacked the Librarian and its newly formed children – the Species – while they fled Jain-occupied space. Starships fought. In eidetic memory, the Client clearly saw a battle so ferocious that even with her knowledge and experience it appalled her. Giant war ships duelled amidst worlds and asteroid fields, used a glaring green sun for cover. Weapons known in the Polity and the Prador Kingdom scored million-mile lines of fire across vacuum. Near-c railgun slugs shattered the crusts of worlds and blew continent-sized debris into space. She saw a moon skewered by a particle beam, like a giant high-speed drill of green fire. Magma exploded from dormant volcanoes scattered about its impact site, while a vast plume of magma and gas from the other side tumbled a hidden ship away like a giant fossilized ammonite, leaking fire. Field-accelerated comets and asteroids pummelled an ice giant, spinning it to rubble and destroying more ships there. But known weapons were not the only ones deployed.

She saw a gas giant collapsing in a shaped, U-space generated gravity field, with fusion igniting and exploding – a disc-shaped blast spread across the entire solar system. The face of the sun bulged and finally speared out a solar flare as wide as worlds to incinerate another target. And there was Jain technology. Everywhere.

Moons writhed with pseudo-life, growing towers out into vacuum. Debris clouds coagulated into crystalline missiles, opened up chemical drives and hurled themselves at colony ships of the Species. Swarms of semi-organic machines fell through vacuum on war craft to tear at hull metal. Tentacles shimmering with shearfields coiled out from asteroid masses to whip at passing ships. But still, the Species ships were triumphant against all but one behemoth of a ship.

At length, she saw the Species war and colony ships fleeing, warded by an immense vessel of their kind. This was facing off against the remaining Jain behemoth – close over the green sun. The two ships duelled with weapons that created vast honeycomb patterns across the surface of the sun and flung out vast eddies of fire. Locked together, tearing at each other, tangled by energies that ribbed into the fabric of the universe, they fell into a pit actually opening in the sun itself. The ensuing blast lifted the upper layers of the sun and blew them outwards. It wasn't a nova, but close enough to wreck the last worlds of the system. As the Species ships fled on the blast front, the sun darkened, its energy pouring down a well into U-space, and it went out. The remaining ships fell into U-space and escaped, leaving behind the site of a battle that had destroyed a solar system and put out a sun.

The Client reviewed the memory again, then again. She realized that she might not be the last of the Species, and that the Librarian might not have been the last of the Jain. A blister now lay at the site of that ancient battle – a blister in space-time that could hold others from both their kinds. In her new form as an amalgam of Species and Jain, she did not know which race she preferred to be the survivors. No matter, she was compelled by the elements of both within her. But she must prepare. She could not launch herself immediately back to the site of that conflict, the site of her resurrection, the place both the Polity AIs and the prador feared, and guarded so diligently.

The accretion disc.